THEIR DOUBLE BABY GIFT

BY

LOUISA HEATON

SAVING BABY AMY

BY

ANNIE CLAYDON

MILLS
BOON

Louisa Heaton lives on Hayling Island, Hampshire, with her husband, four children and a small zoo. She has worked in various roles in the health industry—most recently four years as a Community First Responder, answering 999 calls. When not writing Louisa enjoys other creative pursuits, including reading, quilting and patchwork—usually instead of the things she *ought* to be doing!

Cursed with a poor sense of direction and a propensity to read, **Annie Claydon** spent much of her childhood lost in books. A degree in English Literature followed by a career in computing didn't lead directly to her perfect job—writing romance for Mills & Boon—but she has no regrets in taking the scenic route. She lives in London: a city where getting lost can be a joy.

THEIR
DOUBLE BABY GIFT

BY
LOUISA HEATON

This is a work of fiction. Names, characters, places, locations and
incidents are purely fictional and bear no relationship to any real
life individuals, living or dead, or to any actual places, business
establishments, locations, events or incidents. Any resemblance is
entirely coincidental.

Published in Great Britain 2017
By Mills & Boon, an imprint of HarperCollins*Publishers*
1 London Bridge Street, London, SE1 9GF

© 2017 Louisa Heaton

ISBN: 978-0-263-92658-3

Our policy is to use papers that are natural, renewable and recyclable
products and made from wood grown in sustainable forests. The logging
and manufacturing processes conform to the legal environmental
regulations of the country of origin.

Printed and bound in Spain
by CPI, Barcelona

Dear Reader,

When I had my babies I went to a variety of baby classes. One of them was a Music and Movement class, where I naively thought that I'd get to sit on the floor holding my baby and helping her move to music—kind of like baby yoga.

Only it wasn't a class where I could sit on my butt and pretend my baby was enjoying herself. It was a singing and dancing class, and the leader announced at the first one that we would *'all go round the circle, take it in turns to dance into the centre, and introduce yourself and your baby!'*

I'm sure you can imagine my horror.

So I had to include something similar in Brooke and Matt's story. It was hilarious revisiting all those old feelings and memories and the cringe-worthy stuff you put yourself through in an effort to be a good parent.

Brooke and Matt are trying to be excellent parents. They want to do what's best for their babies, no matter how strong their urge to stay indoors and hibernate away from the rest of the world. They learn, as we all do, that some days you just have to push through.

I hope you enjoy reading their story as much as I enjoyed writing it.

Love,

Louisa xxx

For Becca xxx

Books by Louisa Heaton

Mills & Boon Medical Romance

The Baby That Changed Her Life
His Perfect Bride?
A Father This Christmas?
One Life-Changing Night
Seven Nights with Her Ex
Christmas with the Single Dad
Reunited by Their Pregnancy Surprise

Visit the Author Profile page
at millsandboon.co.uk for more titles.

CHAPTER ONE

SHE WAS RUNNING LATE. *Very* late. And as she stared at the clock on the car dashboard it seemed to be whizzing through minutes, as if a mischievous imp was maniacally pressing down hard on the fast-forward button.

Why was this happening *today?* Today of all days? Her first day back after maternity leave. Her first day as a single working mother, back in the A&E department she loved. A department that would now be all the quieter because Jen wasn't in it.

Dr Brooke Bailey had *so* wanted this day to start well. Because if it did—if she got through it—then that would be all the proof she needed that her decision to do this on her own was a good one.

It had seemed doable in the early months of her pregnancy, when bravado and optimism had got her through the days. She didn't need a man. She didn't need anyone. Only herself—which was just as well, seeing as there wasn't a whole lot of people she could turn to now. Millions of other single mothers held down a job and coped, didn't they? Why should it be any more difficult for *her*?

Only back then, with her rose-tinted spectacles on, she hadn't predicted that she'd be awake the night before going back to work, doing hourly feeds because Morgan wouldn't settle. She hadn't expected that the very second she'd decided to strap Morgan into the car for her commute to work Morgan would have an almighty nappy explosion and would need to be taken back inside the house to be bathed and have everything changed.

Nor had she forecast that she would get caught in an endless traffic jam, tapping her fingers impatiently on the wheel as she glanced at the London Grace Hospital—so temptingly close, but unattainable—as she sat bumper to bumper between a four-wheel drive and a large white delivery van, listening to people sounding their horns. She was wincing with each one, hoping that the noise wouldn't wake her daughter, who was finally—thankfully—asleep.

Beside her on the passenger seat her mobile phone trilled with a message, and as the traffic wasn't moving she decided to check her hands-free device.

It was Kelly.

Where are you? X

She couldn't respond. Not behind the wheel. Even if she *was* stuck in traffic. She'd seen enough evidence of what happened to people when they drove and texted. The cars might move at any moment. She could be texting and have someone rear-end her and give her whiplash as well as a late mark for her first day.

Not only had she to find a space and park the car, she also had to get Morgan to the hospital crèche.

An event she'd been worrying about for weeks.

It had seemed such a simple thing when she'd first planned it—*I'll just put the baby in the crèche.* But what if her baby didn't like it? What if she screamed the place down? What if she clung to her mother and refused to let go?

She'd never left Morgan alone with a *friend*, let alone in a crèche for ten hours a day. Eric had seen to it that she'd lost touch with most of her friends. Had isolated her until no one was left. So that when she had walked away, when she had broken free, she'd felt so ashamed about what she'd allowed to happen she'd felt she couldn't call anyone.

It had just been her and Morgan. And that had been enough. Till now.

Snakes of anticipation coiled in her stomach at the thought of leaving her daughter, and she was just contemplating sounding her own horn when the traffic finally began to move and she could make the turning into the hospital car park. Free, she zoomed up to the barrier, wound down her window to let in the mixed aroma of exhaust fumes and recent rain, swiped her card over the scanner and watched the barrier slowly rise.

For the first time ever she could take advantage of the parent and child spaces on the ground floor near the lift, and she pulled into an empty space. 'Thank you, thank you, thank you…' she muttered to any car park god there might be, and got out of the car, opening up the boot to assemble the buggy.

She got Morgan into it in record time, and without tears, and headed on over to the lift.

As the lift slowly took her up to the floor she needed she contemplated what it would be like to work a shift without Jen.

Jen had been a recent friend. But an amazing one. An unexpected treasure Brooke had located when she'd first started working at the London Grace. At the time she had still been with Eric, but she'd been having serious doubts, starting to be sure that she would have to walk away from him, but struggling with her conscience about the best way to do it with her pride still intact.

Her mood had been low and pensive as she'd stood in the staff room one day, dunking a tea bag over and over. In had walked a woman with a bright streak of pink in her short blonde hair—a shade of pink that had matched the stethoscope draped around her neck.

She'd taken one look at Brooke, walked right up to her, put her arm around Brooke's shoulder and said, *'Whoever he is, dump him. No man should make you look like that!'*

It had been the beginning of a beautiful friendship, and when Brooke had dumped Eric, and then found out a few weeks later that she was pregnant and Eric wanted nothing to do with her or the baby, Jen had been the one who had picked her up, dusted her down and taken her to a show where there'd been masses of gyrating male strippers and lots and lots of hot, writhing, perfectly muscled flesh.

Brooke smiled as she recalled that night. Jen had been an absolute diamond. Rough-cut, maybe, but still one of a kind. And when Jen had discovered that she too was pregnant, and that they had due dates within days of each other that had just solidified their friendship all the more.

Jen's husband Matt had been in the army medical corps, and hardly ever at home, so she and Jen had grown their babies together, comparing bump sizes and ankle swellings and seeing who could hold their pee the longest before having to wobble off to the bathroom.

But I don't have Jen to pick me up any more. No one to pick me up if the day turns out to be the biggest mistake of my entire life.

As the lift pinged open and Brooke began striding down the long corridor that would take her to the hospital crèche she tried not to go over that phone call once again. When Kelly had called to let her know that Jen had died during the birth—complications from eclampsia.

At the time she herself had just delivered Morgan. Had been home for just three days and struggling to get her daughter to latch on. Frustration had been building and the sound of the phone had been a welcome distraction. A few moments to gather herself and calm down. Contact from the outside world.

And then...

She swallowed back tears. She could not cry today. It was stressful enough without going over Jen's death all the time. Life moved on. You couldn't stop its inexorable march. Jen was dead. Brooke was alone. *Again*. She was back at work. Late. She needed to get a move on or she'd have a cranky boss to deal with too.

She buzzed at the door and a staff member let her in.

'I've brought Morgan Bailey. It's her first day...' She tried to sound braver and more together than she really felt.

The crèche nurse wore a bright tabard decorated in a multitude of teddy bears, with a name badge that said *'Daisy'*. Like the flower, she seemed bright and sunny, as if her face had a permanent smile upon it.

Behind her, Brooke could see children playing in a small ball pit, others daubing painted handprints onto a long strip of what looked like wallpaper, others at a table drawing, another group listening to a story. Beyond was another door, labelled *'Baby Room'*, and as she looked the door opened and a tall man with a military demeanour stepped out.

But she had no time to concentrate on him—despite the fact that some tired, exhausted part of her sex-starved brain still worked and had registered how attractive he was. The bossier part of her brain—the exhausted, sleep-deprived, worried-about-being-late part—overrode all other messages.

She unbuckled Morgan from the buggy and lifted her out. 'She's been up most of the night, I'm afraid, so she might be a little grumpy. There are bottles in the bag...' she unhooked the baby bag from the handles of the buggy and handed it over '...with expressed milk. I've labelled them with her name, so you can give her the right ones. There's a teddy in the bag, that's her favourite—Mr Cuddles. She likes to sleep with it. You usually have to wind her twice before she'll go to sleep, and if you sing her *"Baa-Baa Black Sheep"* she'll cry, so please don't do that. And...and...'

She couldn't help it. The tears that had been stinging the backs of her eyes now readily began to fall. The moment of having to hand her daughter over was too much. Her little girl had been the one to keep her together these past few months. She was all she had, and now...

Morgan, sensing her mother's distress, began to cry, and now Brooke was feeling worse about leaving her baby. She stood there clutching her daughter, hiccupping her way through her own tears, as if giving her up to the crèche meant certain death.

I can't do this! I don't need to work, do I? I could wait a little longer, take some more time off. I—

Daisy reached forward to take the crying Morgan. 'We'll be fine—don't worry. Have you got the crèche app on your phone?'

The hospital crèche had developed its own app, so that parents could click in at any time during the day

and receive updates about their child—whether they'd
slept, when they'd eaten or had a bottle, what the child
was playing with. There was even an option to access
the crèche's webcam.

Grateful for the fact that Daisy was ignoring Brooke's
embarrassing tears, she tried to breathe. Sucking in a
breath and dragging a tissue from her pocket to wipe
her nose, Brooke nodded. 'Yes.'

Daisy was still smiling and bobbing up and down as
she gently swayed Morgan, trying to soothe her. 'You
go off to work, then, Mummy. Don't worry about us.'

Morgan looked sickeningly distressed to be in
a stranger's arms, which was disconcerting for her
mother. 'I've never left her before. You'll call me if
there's any problem?'

'Of course we will.'

'Anything at all?'

Daisy nodded, but as Brooke opened her mouth to
ask another question she felt a firm hand upon her arm.
The man she'd seen before looked down at her with intense blue eyes and said, 'It's best to just walk away.
Don't look back.'

Brooke looked up at him hopefully, gratefully, with
her ugly crying face still at full throttle, dabbing at her
tears and trying to hold on to his words of wisdom. Had
he done this, then? Did he know what he was talking
about? He'd just come out of the Baby Room, so perhaps he'd just dropped off his own child?

'Really?'

'Really. Come on.'

He had a stern, no-nonsense tone to his voice. A
voice that was used to issuing commands and having
them obeyed without question. It was clear he expected
the same from her. He gently draped his hands over

hers, forcing her fingers to release the death grip she'd had on the buggy since letting go of her daughter, then took the buggy from her and parked it in the buggy bay. With a guiding hand in the small of her back, he purposefully escorted her to the exit.

Brooke was desperate to turn around and make sure Morgan was okay. She could still hear her baby wailing. Her daughter *needed* her. But the man blocked her view and ushered her out through the door and into the corridor like an expert collie dog herding a reluctant sheep.

'But I need to—'

He held up his hand for silence. 'No. You don't.'

Brooke stepped away and looked him up and down, irritated that he thought he knew what she needed. Sniffing desperately and wiping her nose with the tissue, she wondered just who this man was, anyway. She'd never seen him before at the hospital. But, then again, she'd never had reason to come to the crèche before and the hospital was a big place. He might work anywhere. He might be a new employee.

Wiping away the last of her tears, she stared up at him. He was a good head taller than she. With very short dark blond hair, longer on top. Piercing blue eyes. Trim. Oozing strength and quiet, confident dominance. That was something that usually rubbed her up the wrong way. Eric had been overbearing. Had tried to control her. It was the kind of thing to send up the warning flags.

'Look, I appreciate that you're trying to help me, but—'

'If they sense weakness it makes them more upset.'

She wiped her nose again for good measure, sure it was now probably as red as strawberry jelly. 'The babies?'

He gave one curt nod.

'She's five months old. The only thing she senses is hunger, tiredness and whether she's wet or not.'

'You'd be surprised.' He began to walk away.

Narrowing her eyes, Brooke followed after him. He was going in her direction anyway. She needed the lift again, to go down a couple of floors to A&E.

She pulled her mobile from her pocket to check the time.

Damn it!

The man got into the lift ahead of her. 'Which floor?'

'Ground level.' She noticed he'd pressed the 'G' button, but no other. Frowning, she realised that he must work on her floor. He might work anywhere, though— A&E, the Medical Assessment Unit, Nuclear Medicine, Radiology...

He was looking at her. Looking her up and down. And, sickeningly, she noticed his gaze appeared to be centred on her chest. *Men!* Feeling her cheeks heat, she stared back at him, trying to make him lift his gaze a good few inches upwards, towards her face.

'Is there a problem?'

'You...er...might want to get out of those clothes.'

'Excuse me?' He had some front! He'd only just met her!

What is it with men? They do you one tiny favour and suddenly expect you to drop your—

'You've got milk on your blouse, something questionable on your skirt, and you appear to be...' he smiled and looked away, as if he was preserving her modesty '...leaking.'

Leaking? Brooke looked down at herself and instantly felt her cheeks flame with heat. She was indeed in a state. Her boobs *had* leaked milk—no doubt due to Morgan's cries—she had a smear of what might possibly be poo at the top of her thigh from the earlier explosion, and there was indeed a smelly, sour milk stain, crusting away on her shoulder.

'Oh, God...'

She reached into her handbag for wipes, but she didn't have any. They were all in the nappy bag that she'd left with Daisy down in the crèche. She couldn't work looking like this! She'd have to put some scrubs on. Making her even more late!

The lift doors pinged open and both she and the military man stepped out and turned left towards A&E. Frowning, Brooke looked at him once again, noting his proud bearing, his *march* rather than stride, and the fact that they were both most definitely heading towards the same department.

'Do you work in A&E?' she asked, curious.

Had she embarrassed herself in front of a new work colleague? Staff did come and go frequently. It was a pressured environment—stressful. Some people couldn't hack it. But Brooke could. She loved it there.

'I do.'

'I work there, too.'

He stopped in his tracks immediately and looked at her, this time with a single raised eyebrow. 'This is your first day back after maternity leave?'

How did he know that? Unless her friends had mentioned it to him... 'Yes.'

His eyes widened. '*You're* Dr Bailey?'

She nodded, surprised that he knew her name. 'Yes. Who are *you*?'

He didn't answer right away, and it took him a moment before he held out his hand. 'Major Matt Galloway. Jen's husband.'

She was unaware that her mouth had dropped open. But she numbly reached forward and shook his hand anyway.

She'd meant to call. She'd *meant* to. Only... Life had got in the way and she'd been struggling to cope herself. Life was harder and busier than she'd suspected it would be with a baby, and she was doing everything alone. Jen's death three days after she'd given birth to Morgan had made her postnatal blues a lot worse and she'd been grieving herself.

Trying to get herself together just to get dressed and out of the house had seemed an insurmountable task—and then there was the fact that she'd never met Jen's husband. She'd thought it might be awkward if she just turned up at their house on the other side of London. So she'd put it off and put it off, and when finally she'd thought that she really ought to go and offer her condolences and help so much time had passed she'd just felt that it wouldn't be right.

It had made her feel incredibly guilty, and now the last person she'd expected to run into at work was Jen's widower.

Had he just dropped off Lily?

She hadn't even been able to make it to Jen's funeral on time. She'd misjudged how long it would take her to get ready and out of the house, and when she'd got there the funeral had already started. She'd slipped into the back of the church and huddled in a pew at the back. Then—naturally—Morgan had begun crying and, not wishing to disturb the service, she'd crept back out. The only thing that would settle her daughter was being pushed in her pram, so she'd gone for a walk.

Returning to the church long after the service had

finished she had stood looking down at Jen's grave, tears dripping down her cheeks. Feeling *so* alone.

She'd thought maybe that Jen would have forgiven her for being late. It was the kind of person she'd been.

But Matt…? She had no idea how he'd feel. All she knew from Jen was that he was a stickler for rules and regulations.

'Erm…hello.' She managed a smile, aware now that he had seen her at her worst. 'I didn't expect to see you here.'

'I work here.'

He did?

'I've taken up Jen's post. I needed to be working after—' He stopped talking suddenly, his eyes darkening, and looked away.

'I'm so sorry for your loss. I did make it to the funeral. And I tried to stay, but…'

'But your baby started to cry and you took her outside.'

'You noticed?'

He nodded, looking at her strangely. 'I heard.'

'I tried to make it back, but by the time she'd settled you'd all gone.'

'That's okay. I imagine you had your hands full.'

'Well, I'm sure you did, too. How *are* things with the baby? It's Lily, isn't it?'

'Yes. They're difficult. She's teething. Not sleeping very well.'

Morgan had just started teething too, so Brooke knew the misery of that. 'It gets easier, they say. Let's hang on to that.'

He continued to look at her carefully. 'We should show our faces, seeing as we're both late.'

She nodded. 'Yes—yes, you're right. Don't want to anger the boss on the first day.'

'You haven't angered me.'

Brooke blinked. '*You're* my boss?'

'I'm Clinical Lead, yes.'

'Right…'

She wasn't sure what to say to that. The department had obviously gone through some changes she didn't know about. Why hadn't Kelly let her know? She'd mentioned they'd got some new eye candy in charge, but hadn't mentioned who he was. Why not?

'Well, I'm sorry I'm late.'

'Why don't you get changed and meet me in my office in ten minutes? There are a few new protocols you need to be aware of, and then I'll assign you your duties.'

'Sure.' She nodded and smiled as he marched off towards his office.

Her new boss.

Jen's *husband*.

She looked upwards, as if to heaven, and muttered, 'You had to throw me one last curveball, huh?'

She shook her head in disbelief and pictured Jen grinning down at her.

Her first patient was a guy in his forties. When she called his name in the waiting room he stood up, one hand supporting the other. His triage card said '*Query fracture left wrist*'.

Matt had assigned her to Minors. She'd gone to the changing room, got into a pair of dark blue scrubs. When she'd gone to put her own clothes into her locker she'd done a double-take, noticing that Jen's locker was just as she'd left it. No one had cleared it out yet. Seeing it there, with her friend's name still on it, plastered with pictures of Hollywood heartthrobs, had made her heart miss a beat. In a way she was glad that no one had rushed to empty it. It meant that Jen had been valued. Loved.

Brooke had scooped her long brown hair up into a messy bun and set off to see Matt.

He'd looked every inch an army officer, seated behind his desk with his straight back in his neat office, everything perfectly positioned and aligned. He'd clasped his hands on the desk in front of him and run her through the new burns protocols and triage assessments.

Sitting there, looking at him, she'd wondered if the reason he held himself so formally in check was because he might fall apart if he relaxed. He seemed very stiff and distant now he was working—nothing like his relaxed, friendly, affable wife, who'd thought nothing of draping her arms around the shoulders of friends, who'd positively warmed everyone with her wide smile and closeness.

And then he'd said, 'When you've dealt with each of your patients I'd like you to run your results past me before you discharge anyone.'

Run her results past him?

'Why?'

'Because I've asked you to.'

'You don't trust my judgement? I've been a doctor for many years. I know what I'm doing.'

'But I've never worked with you before, and though I'm sure you have a stellar reputation, Dr Bailey, I'd like to make sure that my department is operating at its optimum level.'

So…the sympathetic father persona had disappeared

the second he'd clocked on. He was all business, and Brooke had felt slighted that she wasn't being trusted to treat a patient by herself, but would have to check in with Matt.

'Fine— Major.'

She escorted her first patient through to a vacant cubicle and got him to sit down whilst she pulled out a new file. 'So, do you want to tell me what happened?'

'Nothing happened. That's why I can't understand why my wrist hurts so much!'

Brooke frowned. 'Why don't you start at the beginning? When did the pain start?'

'I went to bed last night and my wrist was fine, but in the night I got woken suddenly by this intense pain in it—like lightning, it was. I sat up immediately and rubbed at it, and took some painkillers, but it was ages before I could get back to sleep. When I woke up it still hurt, and I noticed this bruising to the side of it.'

Brooke peered at his wrist. There was some bruising to it—like a dark cloud. Not much, though. 'Have you had a fall recently?'

'Not really. I was crouched down loading the washing machine the other day and I lost my balance slightly, put out my hands to stop myself from falling, but that's all. It wasn't a *fall*, as such.'

She examined his wrist and checked his range of motion. He could bend it and move it around without causing any extra pain. But he said he felt a constant burning sensation in the centre. She touched his fingers, asked if he could feel the sensation, if he had any numbness or tingling. He reported some tingling in his ring and little fingers. Capillary refill was good, and there didn't seem to be any occlusion of the blood vessels.

'I think, Mr Goodman, that you may have carpal

tunnel syndrome. The pain waking you in the night is a classic symptom. But I'm going to send you for an X-ray just in case you've got a small fracture in one of the wrist bones, because carpal tunnel wouldn't cause this bruising.'

'Oh, right. Okay…'

'Do you need any more painkillers whilst you wait?'

'No, I can cope.'

She scribbled her findings onto his notes and then filled out a small slip of paper. 'Right, would you like to come with me?'

Brooke walked him to the main corridor and pointed out a red line on the floor.

'Follow that. It'll take you to a new waiting area in Radiology. Hand in the form, they'll take an X-ray or two, and then come back to the main waiting room. I'll call you in when we've got the result.'

'Thank you, Doctor.' Mr Goodman headed off.

Brooke headed over to the doctors' station to transfer her notes to the computer. Her friend Kelly was there too.

'Welcome back! Finally got here, then?'

'Yeah… Hey, why didn't you tell me that our new boss was Jen's husband?'

Kelly smiled. 'Because I knew how guilty you felt about not calling in on him, and I thought that if you knew he was going to be your boss then you would just fret for weeks about starting work and today was going to be hard enough for you! How is Morgan? Did she settle into the crèche okay?'

'She screamed her head off, which caused me to get upset, and that allowed our kind new Major to take great pleasure in letting me know I'd sprung a leak.' She patted her chest and raised an eyebrow at her friend.

Kelly laughed. 'Pads are in now, though, right?'

Brooke smiled. 'Pads are most definitely in. They might be the most unsexy thing a woman ever has to wear, but they don't half make your boobs look good.'

She pushed out her chest to emphasise their impressive size to her friend, unaware that at that moment Matt had come up right behind her.

He cleared his throat and Brooke instantly hunched over and spun in her chair to smile at him, cheeks flaming. 'Hi.'

There was a ghost of a smile on his face. 'How's everything going, Dr Bailey?'

'Erm...yeah...good, I think.'

She could hear Kelly sniggering behind her and made a mental note to kick her under the table later. How many more times would she get to embarrass herself in front of him? So far she'd cried, leaked milk everywhere, worn poo-stained clothes and thrust her breasts out on show like an amateur glamour model. What must he think of her?

'How are things with you?' she asked awkwardly, trying to fill the silence.

He smiled, and she briefly wondered why he didn't do that more often. It transformed his face completely. He was a good-looking guy, but holding that stern, stoic I-am-not-amused pose did nothing for him. But *smiling*? *Genuinely* smiling? He could compete with the best of those heartthrobs stuck on Jen's locker.

'I'm good, thank you.'

'That's great.' She smiled back, wondering what to say, what to do.

Why was this so awkward? She didn't normally have difficulty getting on with colleagues or superiors. Why was talking to him so different?

In her scrubs pocket, her phone trilled. Not wanting to check her phone with him standing there, she continued to grin at him, waiting for him to say or do something.

'Kelly, I'd like a quick word, if I may, when you're free?'

Kelly nodded. 'I'll be five minutes.'

'I'll be in my office.' And Matt turned on a dime and headed off.

Brooke let out a breath she hadn't been aware she was holding. Then she turned to Kelly. 'Wow. Way to go, Brooke. How come he calls you by your first name but calls *me* Dr Bailey?'

Kelly grinned. 'Probably because of my stellar good looks and beauty and because he wants to get in my pants.'

Brooke gaped. *'What?'*

Her friend laughed. 'I'm kidding! We've been working together for weeks now—he knows me more than you. This is your first day. He's just being polite. He hasn't met you properly over a packet of chocolate biscuits and a good mug of tea in the staff room yet.'

'And he has you?'

In her mind she could still see him striding away. Tall. Straight-backed. Determined. A man on a mission. He didn't seem the type to bond over a chocolate biscuit. Not with normal civilians, anyway. She wondered what he was like with his patients. Warm and fuzzy?

I don't think so.

'Absolutely. You don't know the man until you've shared your deep and darkest secrets over a good brew.'

She sighed. 'He doesn't seem the type to do that. He seems quite standoffish to me. At least on duty, anyway.'

'It's hard for him.'

Brooke looked at her friend sharply. 'It's hard for us all.'

'He's stepped into his wife's shoes. Taken her post. And he *knows* that we all knew her, that we all lost her, and most of all I think he's frightened of *you*.'

'Me? Why?'

'You were her best friend. Everyone here knows how close you two got. And when Jen *did* get a call from him, from the deepest darkest jungle that Costa Rica could offer, and got to tell him about her day... she talked about *you*.'

'She did?'

'Of course she did. Jen loved you very much. She loved us all, but you the most. And he knows that of all the people in the world, you had a special place in his wife's heart. Apart from him, you were the one who comforted her, who gave her a soft place to fall when he could not. Who looked after her as she carried his child.' Kelly smiled. 'You're different to the rest of us mere mortals. He doesn't know how to be with you yet.'

'He doesn't have to be afraid of me. We both loved her.' All the sweet things Kelly had said had caused a lump to appear in her throat.

'He'll call you, Brooke. When he's ready.'

'He's keeping me at a distance on purpose?'

Kelly nodded, then grinned. 'Perhaps he needs to.'

Brooke gave her friend a questioning look. She was being ridiculous! She was no threat to anyone. Never had been, never would be. Men didn't need to worry about her. They never had. Not her father, not Eric, not anyone.

Major Matt Galloway was the least likely man she would want to get too close to. He was abrupt and controlling and...and...

And she'd sworn never to have another man control her ever again. Not after the way Eric had become. That had been bad.

'Do you need to wear make-up?'

'Why have you put on perfume?'

'I really don't think you should wear that *dress.'*

'Cover up more.'

'Were you flirting with that guy?'

She shuddered just thinking about him.

No. Brooke was never going to get involved with another man again. They were too much trouble. Look at Eric! Look at her father! Every man there had ever been in her life had let her down. Walked away when she needed them the most.

It had made her self-sufficient. Taught her that she could stand on her own two feet. Getting pregnant with Morgan and becoming a single mother had taught her that she could do anything, but most of all it had shown her that she didn't need anyone else.

And most definitely—most importantly—she knew that she did not need, or want, the approval or attention of her new boss Major Matt Galloway.

'Well, he has nothing to fear from me. My heart most definitely has a *"Do Not Enter"* sign.'

CHAPTER TWO

'DO YOU BELIEVE in broken hearts, Doc?'

Major Matt Galloway peered at his patient. She was seventy-nine, with fluffy white hair, and sat huddled in her wheelchair, as if life had beaten her down gradually, day after day. Pale, with dark circles under her eyes, she looked as if she needed a damned long sleep.

Yes, he *did* believe you could have a broken heart. Physically, there were lots of ways a heart could fail. But literally...? He saw people give up on life after the death of a loved one—die within days, hours or even minutes of a husband, wife or child. He'd thought it might happen to him once, but his body had stubbornly refused to give up. His logical mind had overpowered his heart and told it to suck it up, because he had a job to do. He had to be a *father*. And his principles had refused to let him leave someone behind who needed him.

'I do,' he said, but he was not keen to discuss his personal feelings with this patient. At work, he liked to remain professional. 'It says here on your chart that you have non-specific chest pain. Your ECG was normal, as was your BP. Why don't you tell me what you're feeling and when it started?'

His patient rubbed at her chest. 'I lost my Alfred three weeks ago. Cancer. After the funeral my chest began to hurt—up here.' She rubbed at a spot just above her sternum. 'It won't go away.'

'And if you had to rate the pain between zero and ten, ten being the worst pain you've ever felt, what would you score it at?'

'A good seven.'

'Does it hurt more when you breathe in? When you take deep breaths?'

'Sometimes. And when I twist in my chair, reach for something, sometimes it can be like someone is stabbing me with a hot pick.'

It sounded skeletal or muscular to Matt. But they'd taken bloods and he wanted to see what they said before he made a diagnosis. 'I'd like to examine you, if I may?'

She smiled at him good-naturedly. 'Normally I wouldn't mind if a good-looking man wanted to see more of me, but would you mind if you got a lady doctor to do it?'

He smiled back, not offended at all. 'I'll just get someone. Give me two minutes.'

He closed the curtain of the cubicle behind him and went looking for a spare doctor. They all looked incredibly busy, hurrying here and there. The only person he could see who was apparently doing nothing, standing by the triage board, checking her mobile phone, was Dr Bailey.

He'd known today was the day. That she would be returning after maternity leave. He'd known that today they would finally get to meet and his stomach had been a jumbled mess in anticipation. He'd heard so much about her—and not just from Jen. Apparently Dr Bailey was a wonderfully warm doctor—kind, caring, well-liked and respected in the department. But Jen had also said that Bailey was the loneliest person she had ever met. It was why she had befriended her. She'd said that this doctor gave so much of herself to others, including her patients, but always seemed somehow to be so alone. Afraid to reach out and depend on others.

He'd not known how to interpret that. Matt had never been alone. Raised in a large family of brothers, he had left them to study medicine, then enlisted. He'd had an army family. A whole platoon! And he'd had Jen, and then the news that there would be a little one coming along.

He'd never been alone until now. Oh, his brothers were always on the phone, and he sometimes heard from old comrades-in-arms, but Jen's death had isolated him. It was as if her death had quarantined him from others. As if he was contagious. There'd been plenty of visitors to bring him food, and to offer to help with Lily, but something was different. He felt tainted. As if people were afraid to get too close to him in case something happened to them too. Or maybe it was a vibe that *he* was giving off, making people feel that they *couldn't* get too close?

Jen had adored Dr Bailey. Loved her. He'd lost count of the amount of times his wife had laughed down the phone saying, 'Oh, you'll never guess what Brooke said today…'

He'd not expected the leaking, poo-stained, crying woman he'd met this morning to be *the* Dr Brooke Bailey. Nor for her to have awoken in him a protective streak when he'd heard her crying at the crèche. He'd empathised with her pain. Remembered how it had felt for *him* to leave Lily with a relative stranger.

The sound of her heartbroken sobs had tugged at his heartstrings and made his gut lurch. And that had been before he'd even known who she actually was! And that brief moment when she'd leaned against him, *into* him, enveloping him in her perfume as he'd guided her out through the crèche door, had made him yearn to wrap his arms around her.

And then he'd remembered she was a *stranger*. Someone he didn't even know. Whom he'd probably never meet again.

Until he'd found out who she was.

Now he would have to work with her, keeping her at a safe distance while knowing that the two of them shared a bond—their love for a woman now gone.

He knew Brooke Bailey had been the most important person in his wife's life—after him and Lily—and he'd been keen to meet this woman whom he'd felt sure would be intelligent, warm and sociable, just like his wife. A *together* person. Someone with whom he could also build a bond. No, he'd definitely not expected the woman he'd met this morning. Emotionally wrought and no doubt sleep-deprived too, if Lily's current behaviour was anything to go by.

'Dr Bailey?'

He saw her guiltily drop her mobile phone back into her scrubs pocket and look up, her cheeks colouring with a most beautiful shade of rose.

'Major! Sorry, I was just checking everything was okay at the crèche.'

He could understand that. The first few days he had left his daughter there he had done the same thing. Lily was the most precious thing in the world to him, and to hand her over to strangers had been difficult. It was easier for him now. He'd been doing it for over a month. Not so Dr Bailey. He had to make allowances.

'And is it?'

She nodded, seeming surprised that he had even asked.

'A patient has requested a female doctor for an examination. Are you free?'

'Yes. I was just looking for you, actually. You wanted me to report in before I discharged my patients.'

He could hear the reluctant tone in her voice but he dismissed it. It wasn't a personal thing he'd done, just because she'd been away from work for a while. He'd asked it of all his staff. He needed to know how the people who were on his team worked.

'Okay. I'll take a look at your findings once we've dealt with Mrs Merchant.'

He led her over to his patient's cubicle and, once inside, explained her symptoms and the results of her tests so far. Then he stepped back. 'I'll step outside.' And closed the curtain behind him, listening as Dr Bailey conducted her examination. He heard her ask to listen to the patient's chest, heard her check the range of movement and finally warning Mrs Merchant that she was about to press on the front of her chest...

'Ow! That hurts!' His patient cried out.

'Here?'

'Yes! Dear Lordy—what do you think is causing *that*?'

Dr Bailey let Mrs Merchant fasten her clothing again and invited Matt back in.

Matt nodded to let her know he'd heard what had happened and to deliver the diagnosis. 'I think you may have costochondritis.'

'What's that when it's at home?'

'It's an inflammation of the cartilage that joins your ribs to your breastbone. It's a very painful condition.'

'I know it is. I can feel it!'

'We'll just check your bloods first, but I think we

can safely say we need to get you on some anti-inflammatories. I'll be back in a moment.'

They left Mrs Merchant and headed over to the doctors' station. Dr Bailey handed him her notes from the guy with carpal tunnel syndrome. He'd also got a non-displaced break in his scaphoid, the small bone at the base of his thumb, and she'd given him a splint to wear and prescribed painkillers in case it got worse. Simple enough. Direct, effective, and she hadn't wasted resources on tests that he hadn't needed. Exactly what he'd wanted to see.

'That's excellent. You can discharge him.' He handed back the file, expecting her to walk away from him and get on with her work, but she lingered, as if wanting to ask him something. 'Anything else?'

'Yes...' She looked around her, lowering her voice. 'Jen's locker.'

He straightened, felt his chin lifting. He was defensive because he hadn't got around to sorting it out yet. He'd felt that by doing so he would finally be wiping away the existence of his wife here. Seeing it still there each morning was reassuring. He could almost pretend that she was about to walk in through the door at any moment.

'Yes?'

'If you need someone to help sort it...when you feel ready... I'd like to offer to help.'

Jen's locker.

It was one last tiny island of his wife. Coming back home to the house from Costa Rica had been bad enough. There had been a whole houseful of her possessions to sort through. At first he'd not wanted to get rid of anything, thinking that Lily would want to know all about her mother when she got older. But seeing his wife's clothes draped over radiators and the shower rail in the bathroom had got too much, and he'd conducted a vast cleaning frenzy, taking bags of her stuff to local charity shops but keeping small things like jewellery, the odd knick-knack that Jen had loved, just in case Lily wanted them when she grew up.

Items that were precious—her wedding ring, her engagement ring, a clay pot she'd once tried to make at a pottery class. The pot had gone drastically wrong, and looked as if a four-year-old had tried to make it, but it didn't matter that it was ugly and misshapen. His wife's hands had made it—her fingers had deftly tried to mould the clay—and he'd been unable to throw it out. He knew that one day Lily would hold it in her hands and imagine her mother's fingers in the same places.

There were still photos of Jen at the house. He'd not made a clean sweep and erased her completely. She was still there. Her paint choices on the walls. Her silly magnets on the fridge. Her perfume in the bathroom.

Getting rid of her things had been painful, and when he'd come to work at the London Grace he'd forgotten that she would have a locker here. That was going to be very difficult. Touching the things she'd used and worn every day. Things that were as familiar to her as they would be new to him.

He knew he had to do it. At some point. It had been there too long already and everyone else had been too polite to mention it. Not that Dr Bailey was being impolite. Just concerned. And he understood that. She was right. It was maudlin to think that keeping a dead woman's locker undisturbed somehow kept her alive.

'Yes. I'll...get round to it later today.'

Her mouth dropped open. 'Oh! I didn't mean to force you to do it straight away. I—'

'It's fine. I should have done it a long time ago.'

'I'll help, if you need it.'

'I should be fine doing it myself. Thank you, Dr Bailey.'

He hadn't meant to be so dismissive of her. She was only offering to help him do a task he'd been shirking for too long now. But the tone in his voice had risen because she'd reminded him that he was afraid to tackle it on his own. Worried about what he might find in there. Something uniquely personal, perhaps. Some keepsake that would strike another blow to his heart when it was already so weakened.

She nodded, blushing at his tone, and though he liked the way the soft rosy colour in her cheeks somehow made her eyes sparkle that little bit more, he felt guilty as she walked away with that look of hurt in her eyes.

Had he meant to be so acerbic? Could he not have reined that in? After all, he'd become a master at doing that lately. Putting a tight leash on his emotions. It was easier, after all, to pretend that things didn't hurt. When you were on your own it was easier, anyway.

He briefly wondered who was there for Dr Bailey. Surely she wasn't as alone as his wife had made out? For a start, there had to be a father to her baby. Where was he? Jen had mentioned he was some low-life who had adhered to the adage *Treat them mean, keep them keen*. Though, thank the Lord, Dr Bailey had had enough self-respect to walk away from someone like that!

Matt sucked in a breath. Was he ready to do this? Was he prepared? There could be anything in that locker. Jen had been like a magpie at home, storing away anything that caught her eye, that she thought was cute. He might open the door and have tons of things fall out. She'd never been one for neatly folding stuff and putting it away properly.

Hopefully it wouldn't take too long.

He didn't know how long he'd been standing there, staring at the locker. It was just a bit of metal. Adorned with all the Hollywood heartthrobs that she'd liked to swoon over and gently tease him about. But it was her name on the door that seemed to be stopping him—*Dr Jennifer Galloway*.

It was like the entry to a forbidden land. A doorway to a world he wasn't ready to face. He kept trying to tell himself that he was being stupid. It was just a locker—it probably just held some clothes, or a pair of shoes and a hairbrush or something, but for some reason his brain and his heart were telling him that this was something he wasn't ready for—getting rid of the last vestiges of his wife at work.

'Can I help?'

He almost jumped at her voice. Turned to see Brooke standing in the doorway, watching him. And, though he'd been abrupt with her the last time they'd spoken, she appeared to be speaking to him with all the gentle patience of a mother to a child. No retribution. No blame. No hurt. Just a genuine desire to help him out.

Matt nodded and beckoned her in. 'I don't know what's stopping me.'

'What stops any of us but the fear of getting hurt?'

He gazed back at the locker. 'I'm a soldier.'

'You're a husband.' She leaned against the lockers and he glanced over at her. 'Being a soldier doesn't stop you from being human. From feeling.'

'I guess both of us have been confronted by things we didn't want to do today.'

She nodded. 'Have you a key?'

He pulled it from his pocket. So small. So insignificant. All he had to do was insert it into the lock.

A heavy sigh escaped him and he closed his eyes, trying to build up the courage to do what had to be done. But he just couldn't bring himself to do it. What if he opened her locker and it held her scent? Flowers and a summer's day? It would hit him like an avalanche, burying him and smothering him, away from all that was light. He wasn't ready. But he wanted to do it. Wanted to get it over with. Maybe if he just…

Fingers enveloped his and he opened his eyes to see Dr Bailey taking the key and inserting it into the lock. She turned it, and they both heard the clank of the metal lever.

Blue eyes peered into his soul. 'Open it.'

He didn't want to think about what he'd felt when her hand had wrapped around his. Didn't want to analyse the fact that his heart had begun to gallop, his pulse had soared and his mouth had gone as dry as centuries-old dust.

Instead, he stared at the locker. Hoping. Praying. And with an unsteady hand he reached forward to pull it open.

A pair of wind-up false teeth was the first thing that caught his eye and it made him laugh. *Relief!* He picked it up, turning it in his hands, looking at Dr Bailey in question.

'She used it sometimes with children.'

She smiled as she took it from him and he could see plainly on her face that she was reliving a memory. A memory of his wife that he didn't have.

He reached into the locker and pulled out a change of clothes—a tie-dye tee shirt and a pair of jeans. Beyond them were a couple of books that were extremely late going back to the library, a couple of pens, some soft-soled flat shoes and a notebook that said *Trust Me, I'm A Doctor*. And there, at the back, where only she would see it when she opened her locker for each shift to get ready, a picture of them both on their wedding day.

Gently, he released it from the tape holding it in place and looked at it.

'Your wedding day. How long ago did you get married?'

He glanced at Dr Bailey. 'Five short years ago.'

'You both look very happy.'

'We were.' It hurt to look at the picture, but not as much as it once had. He'd learned to accept it. Absorb it. Grief wasn't something you got over. Like an obstacle. It was something that you accepted, knowing it would stay with you for the rest of your days.

'I wish I'd known her for longer. You're lucky that way.'

He gazed intently at her and nodded, before putting the picture with the rest of the things. 'It's no use either of us living in the past. We've both got difficult futures ahead.'

'Being single parents, you mean? I think it's easier now than it was twenty years ago. At least it's accepted.'

He nodded. 'Who do you have helping you?'

She shook her head. 'No one. Not really.'

'There must be someone. Family?'

'I'm an only child. My mother died when I was very little and my dad... Well, he's never been the reliable sort. We talk on the phone. When he remembers.'

He could tell there was something she wasn't saying. Whatever it was, it was obviously hurtful.

'Any friends?'

'Jen was my friend. The only person who got close. So it's pretty much me and Morgan right now.'

'It's difficult, isn't it? Being alone.'

And then he realised he'd let his guard drop and he stiffened slightly, busying himself with Jen's things, laying them in the box he'd brought from his office, neatly and in order.

He was surprised. He'd thought there'd be more. All this time he'd spent fearing this job, and now that he'd done it he realised there had been nothing to worry about. He let out a breath and then he closed his wife's locker reverently, slid her name tag from the front of it and slowly started to remove her Hollywood heroes.

What to do with *them*? Throw them into the bin?

'I'll take them.'

Dr Bailey closed her hand around his and, surprised again by how her brief touch made him feel, he released the pictures and stared hard at her as she opened her own locker and put them inside. It had been the weirdest thing. Not lightning, not fireworks. More a gentle warmth. And he'd felt...*soothed.* As if a balm had been applied to his soul.

'Thank you. For doing this with me.'

She turned to face him and smiled. 'It was my pleasure.'

No, he thought. *It was mine.*

By the end of the day Matt had already decided that Dr Brooke Bailey was a very good member of his team. She worked at a steady pace, and she didn't order extraneous tests that would upset the department's budget. She got on well with everyone, seemed very popular, and though she might chat a little too much with her patients, rather than discharge them quickly, he didn't think he had too much to complain about.

Before she'd come back he'd heard from everyone that she was a good doctor, but Matt lived by the axiom that he'd make up his own mind about people. He took them as *he* found them, and so far he liked what he'd found in Dr Bailey. Now the drama of the morning crèche drop-off was long gone he could see the woman and the professional that his wife had become friends with.

As he headed towards the lift, so that he could get his daughter from the crèche, he saw that she was standing waiting for it to arrive, too. They'd spoken on numerous occasions throughout the day since emptying Jen's locker, and already he could sense that a tentative friendship was beginning.

'Enjoy your first day?'

She smiled at him. 'I did! Even though I was fretting about Morgan for most of it, it was nice to use my brain again and interact with adults. I think the most taxing thought I've had over the last few months has been whenever I've had to change a nappy, seen the contents and wondered, *What colour is that?*'

He smiled, having gone through the poo initiation tests that all babies presented to their parents. A sticky black tar to start, which looked like something that ought to be in a horror movie, oozing from a monster, then a khaki green that would hide any soldier in a jungle, and now they were into a kind of peanut butter effect. It had been an interesting journey, and one quite different from the Bristol Stool Chart that all doctors knew so well.

The lift doors pinged open and they both got inside.

'At least I didn't have to examine any grown-up's stools today.'

Matt smiled to himself. Life as an A&E doctor did have that unknown element to it. You never knew what kind of case was going to walk through those doors, from something as simple as a splinter in the finger right through to a dramatic cardiac arrest. That was why he liked it. There was so much variety.

It had been the same in the army. One minute he might be dealing with a gunshot wound, the next dealing with an ingrowing toenail.

But he liked the adrenaline of working in A&E. The cases that needed to be worked on fast and efficiently, with each member of the team knowing their job, all of them working as a finely tuned machine to save someone's life. There was nothing quite like it.

'All jobs have their perks. Who knows? Perhaps tomorrow you might get your chance?'

She laughed, and the sound did strange things to his insides.

'I hope not!'

He glanced at her briefly, curious as to why this woman, above all others, somehow seemed to make him feel...*what?* Uneasy? No, that was wrong. It wasn't a *bad* feeling as such, it was...an awareness. Like the feeling you might get before a static storm. The air pregnant with expectation, holding a heat to it, a humidity.

Was it because of her connection to Jen? Was it simply because he'd been waiting for her return to work so that he could meet this woman his wife had loved?

That's it. It's because I know she was special to Jen.

He'd wanted to see just what it was about the enigmatic Dr Bailey that had made her so appealing to his wife. He could see that she liked to laugh, liked to enjoy herself and to make close connections with her patients. She liked others to feel listened to and cared for. But there was also a quiet assuredness about her. A silent strength that she didn't seem aware she had. It was her solitude, perhaps, that did that. That shielded her from her own possibilities.

'I'm sorry you caught me using my phone today. I don't normally. Not at work. In fact I don't normally carry my phone with me. But with it being Morgan's first day...'

He waved away her concerns with a swift movement of his hand, staring at the lift display, watching as they ascended to the floor they needed. 'It's fine. We all worry about our children—especially when we're new parents.'

She nodded. 'Thank you. I appreciate that. I really do.'

She was looking up at him, trying to convey her sincerity in her eyes. But it was hard for him to stand there, that close to her, and maintain eye contact, so he looked away. She had very pretty eyes. Bright and friendly. Welcoming. Open. Innocent.

He cleared his throat. 'It's not a problem.'

Was the lift much smaller today? There seemed to be less air. The walls seemed to be pressing them towards each other.

To his relief, the doors pinged open again and he walked behind her towards the crèche, feeling somewhat awkward. He wasn't sure what had caused it, or why thirty seconds in a lift with Dr Bailey had changed things when a whole ten hours with her in the same department had not.

So he walked slightly behind her, allowing her to go first and press the buzzer for the crèche.

Daisy let them in, beaming her ever-present smile at both of them, all white gleaming teeth and bright eyes, showing no signs of fatigue after spending an entire day with thirty-odd children under the age of five.

Matt wasn't sure he'd look as calm and collected as Daisy did if *he'd* spent that long with that many children. He loved kids, he really did, but he was finding it hard looking after even one baby on his own. There was no one to share the workload or the worries with and he missed that.

In the army there'd always been someone to talk to—colleagues, friends and, on the occasions when he had come home, there'd always been Jen. Now his home was conspicuously quiet.

'Lily's been an absolute treasure today! She did a handprint painting for you!'

Daisy unpegged a messy picture that was hanging from a string above their heads, like washing on a line. He looked at it, barely able to ascertain his daughter's handprint in the smudge of red, purple and brown. But her name *'Lily Galloway'* had been written in pencil at the bottom.

'Her first work of art...' He wasn't sure whether to act pleased or show that to him it was just a mash-up of paint on a page.

'Watch out, Michelangelo.'

Dr Bailey smiled at him, mildly amused.

'There's one for you, too, Dr Bailey.' Daisy unpegged another picture, this one in yellow and orange, and passed it over.

They both stood there awkwardly, trying to work out whether the pictures were upside down or not.

'I'll get Lily for you.'

'Thanks.' He collected Lily's buggy from the bay and folded his daughter's painting into the basket underneath.

Daisy came out of the Baby Room, carrying his daughter, who looked as if she'd just woken up, her blonde hair all mussed up and wafting around her head like a furry halo.

'Hello, Lily!' He reached out for her and, as always, was happy to see her reach for him, too. 'Hello, my darling, how are you today?' He kissed her on the cheek, inhaling that sweet baby scent and enjoying the soft squishiness of her little body against his.

Lily laid her head against his chest.

'Wow! She looks just like her mum. She's beautiful.'

He looked at Dr Bailey over his daughter's head, hearing the wistfulness in his colleague's voice. 'Thank you.'

'I mean it. She really does.'

Matt knew she was being sincere, but there was something else there, too. Loss. Grief. It reminded him that he wasn't the only one who had lost someone special. She had too. Her best friend.

As Daisy brought out Dr Bailey's daughter, he was struck by the similarity between the two. Morgan also had a thick head of brown hair that was slightly curling and wispy around her shoulders, and they both had the same eyes. Morgan peered at him, as if uncertain of this tall stranger who stood next to her mother.

He stooped over to put Lily into her buggy and then stood up again. 'Well, I'll see you in the morning. Goodnight, Dr Bailey.'

'Goodnight, Major.'

She smiled back and it so disarmed him, hitting him

like a sucker punch to the gut, that he turned quickly and hurried away.

Five months.

It had been only five months since his wife had died. The wife he had loved and adored and had expected to be with right into old age. And yet he was already noticing another woman.

It's just loneliness. That's what it is. Missing someone to talk to, that's all. I don't have to read anything else into it.

He kept his head down as he headed back to his car. Trying to remain focused on his daughter's chubby little legs in white tights, the cute pink trainers his mother had bought for her. He tried to think about what his daughter had done that day, the painting she had done, the way she'd reached for him earlier. He was all Lily had now. She'd never known the love of a mother. Nor would she. He would have to provide everything for her. Be both parents, if he could. Provide the dreams for both of them.

Briefly, he cast his mind back in time to the day he and Jen had discussed moving to New Zealand. How amazing it would be. What a brilliant life it would provide for their future children. Jen had been in the back garden, swinging in the hammock, six months pregnant and eating an ice cream.

'*I'd really like to go back there, Matt. My gap year there was the most amazing time in the world. The people were great—really friendly—and there'd be no problem with either of us getting work out there. There's a great little suburb in North Shore City, Auckland, that's perfect for kids. We should do it. Really consider it, I mean.*'

At the time, he'd been busy planting some fruit trees in the back garden and Jen had been supervising.

'Move that one to the left a bit. Bit more. Bit more. That's it!'

He'd been home on a week's leave before he'd had to ship out to Costa Rica, and it had been one of the last times he'd seen her alive. He'd only been meant to be out there for ten weeks. He'd thought—they'd *both* thought—he would be home in time for the birth. But after he'd left, Jen had begun having problems with her blood pressure and they'd had to induce her early.

It had still been too late. Jen had had a massive fit from which she hadn't recovered. They'd put her on life support until he could get back from South America and then, holding his baby daughter in his arms, he had watched through a veil of tears as they had switched off the machines.

Just five months ago.

He'd had to adapt quickly, and he'd been thankful he had Lily to look after. His daughter had saved him from falling into a deep depression. She'd anchored him in the present when he'd been in danger of drowning in the past. He'd not had time to dwell on his loss the way he would have if she hadn't been around.

So, instead of never getting out of bed and living in the depths of despair under his duvet, he'd got out of bed. Got dressed. Taken his daughter out in her pram and walked. Sometimes for miles. Strangers had stopped him to admire his daughter, keeping his spirits lifted. They'd had no idea of the tragedy that had recently befallen him. They'd just seen a father out with his child. A beautiful baby girl. They'd wanted to admire her and cup her rosy cheeks and tell him how gorgeous she was, and each comment, each person, had unwittingly given him a reason to keep going.

'You're doing a good job.'

'Lily's okay.'

'She's thriving with just you.'

Jen would not have wanted him to wallow. That wasn't who she had been. She'd been a grab-hold-of-life person. A person who'd squeezed enjoyment into every second—as much as she could. And she'd told him once that when she died she didn't want a funeral full of people in black clothes, sobbing quietly into tissues. She'd wanted a celebration of her life.

Only that celebration had come too soon.

And now he was noticing another woman.

Guilt was a horrible sensation. He'd never really suffered from it before. Not like this. And, logically, he knew he shouldn't really feel guilty. Jen would have been *happy* that he was getting to know her new best friend. And it wasn't as if he were cheating on his wife. No. He might no longer be married, but he was determined that Dr Bailey was just going to be his friend, the way she had been Jen's.

He stopped for moment and looked down at his wedding band. He hadn't removed it. It had never felt right. Its presence had somehow given him an extra layer of…protection.

But from what?

He decided he would wait to get home and then think about it some more. Right now he had to concentrate on his daughter. She was what was important.

But as he drove them home, as he sat waiting at traffic lights, humming to the music playing on the radio, his mind kept teasing him with glimpses of the beautiful and enigmatic Dr Brooke Bailey.

CHAPTER THREE

OVER THE NEXT week Brooke settled into a nice routine. She only had to work day shifts whilst Morgan was so little, and so each day she would drop her daughter off at the crèche, work ten hours, pick Morgan up, go home, get something to eat and then attempt to shoehorn Morgan into a night-time routine of bath, bottle, story and sleep.

It didn't always work.

Morgan seemed determined not to stick to anything as pre-planned as that. She was her own woman. Already! Sometimes she just wanted her mum to hold her and never put her down. Sometimes she wanted to be rocked. Other times she wanted to lie under her baby gym and bat at her toys, babbling away until the early hours of the morning. None of which helped Brooke get much sleep.

Morgan had no set sleep pattern that she could decipher, which meant that neither did her mother, and Brooke was beginning to notice on her drive into work that she was getting less and less accepting of delays and idiots on the road. Her temper was quick, her fuse almost non-existent. Thankfully at work her love for her job was somehow able to put her bad mood to one side. At least until the commute home again.

Then back at home her love for her daughter and her desire to spend quality time with her, after having left her at the crèche all day, ensured that she forgot about doing things for herself and instead concentrated on just being with Morgan, no matter how it happened. If it meant reading baby board books over and over again—fine. If it meant rocking her daughter in her arms all night—excellent. No problem.

She would do what her daughter needed because she was all Morgan had in this world. Morgan's dad, Eric, was not interested in her—thankfully—and Morgan's grandfather, Brooke's dad, was worse than useless and could not be depended upon. He'd met Morgan only once. In the hospital. He had not seen her since.

Brooke was used to such desertions. It didn't hurt her any more. Or at least she could pretend that it didn't. She just had to hope that when Morgan got older she didn't feel that she'd missed out on a grandfather. Or a dad.

Walking into work today, Brooke was mightily pleased with herself for not having to get changed into scrubs. She could wear her own clothes, having made it through breakfast without getting any baby food on her garments. It was a landmark day! Hopefully, she thought, the first of many.

So she was humming a little tune to herself as she picked up her next chart and headed to the waiting room to call in her next patient.

'Charlie Alcott?'

A young man stood up and made his way over to her.

'Hello, Charlie, I'm Dr Bailey. Follow me and I'll take you through.'

She led the way, still hearing a happy tune in her head, still feeling as if her whole body was smiling. It was good to be back at work and she was in her groove.

As much as she adored and loved her daughter, she was happy to claim back her own body and use her brain to help people.

She closed the curtain behind Charlie and asked him to take a seat. 'So, what can I do for you today?'

'I think I've got Addison's disease.'

She frowned. Okay... This sounded more as if it ought to be something a GP dealt with, but who knew? You got all sorts of people coming into A&E, thinking it meant *Anything and Everything* rather than *Accident and Emergency.*

'Why do you think that?'

'I don't handle stress very well and I keep passing out. I looked online and a few websites mentioned Addison's, and as that can sometimes be fatal I thought I ought to come in and be checked immediately.'

Addison's disease was actually quite a rare condition of the adrenal glands that produced cortisol, the stress hormone, and aldosterone. It could affect anyone, but mainly affected women between the ages of thirty and fifty. Charlie was obviously male, and it said on his chart that he'd just turned twenty.

'You say you keep passing out?'

'Yeah. If I stand up too quick I get that head rush thing and dizziness and I have to sit back down again.'

She nodded. 'Okay. Well, first of all I usually advise people not to try and diagnose themselves over the internet. The online world is full of dramatic diseases and bad luck tales, and it doesn't have that real world advantage of examining a patient in person. Because everyone is different, Charlie—you know that, right?'

He nodded.

'Getting that head rush on standing might just mean

you have low blood pressure, so let's check that first of all.'

She grabbed the BP cuff that was standard issue in each cubicle and wrapped it around Charlie's arm.

'Right—stay nice and still for me.' She inflated it and took his reading. It seemed normal. So was his heart-rate. 'I'm going to ask you to stand up and I'm going to check your BP and heart-rate again, okay?'

'Okay.'

'And stand.' When he stood, she inflated the cuff and watched him carefully. He grimaced slightly and went a little pale. 'Stay standing for me, if you can, I know it feels weird, but I'm here to catch you—don't worry.'

Charlie stood through it and she noticed on the machine that her patient's BP lowered only slightly, but his heart-rate soared.

She guided him back down into the chair. 'Do you experience any other symptoms?'

He thought for a moment. 'I've always been like this, I think. Sometimes I get palpitations. Like I can feel my heart missing a beat? And sometimes I feel sick and shaky when it happens.'

Brooke nodded, writing down his experiences. She was beginning to suspect something—but it wasn't Addison's and it wasn't something that usually showed in men. However, the one rule she could remember her first ever professor stating at university was: *Keep an open mind. There will always be someone who breaks the mould.*

She'd definitely begun to suspect that this was the situation here, but Charlie would need further tests to prove her theory of PoTS—postural tachycardia syndrome.

It was caused by an abnormal increase in heart-rate

whenever the affected person stood up after sitting or lying down, and it mostly showed in Charlie's symptoms. His heart-rate had increased by just over thirty beats when he'd stood up, but that wasn't enough for a diagnosis. He needed an ECG and a tilt table test to confirm it properly. And they couldn't do that here in A&E.

'Okay, Charlie, I'm going to take some bloods from you to check your kidney, liver and thyroid function. And I want to check your blood count, calcium and glucose levels. I'm also going to perform an ECG, which will take a tracing of your heart.'

'There's something wrong with my *heart*?'

'From my initial investigation it seems unlikely, but we need to run some further tests to rule out other conditions. I think you have something called postural tachycardia syndrome, and I'm going to write to your GP and recommend that he refers you for a tilt test, which we can't do here. The ECG and the blood results will be through by then, to help with a diagnosis.'

'Is it dangerous?'

'Well, postural tachycardia syndrome isn't fatal, but sufferers are at risk of hurting themselves by falling or passing out. Whilst you're waiting for your appointment to come through be very careful getting up. Do it gradually, and if you feel faint try to sit or lie down and raise your legs. Drink plenty of fluids, keep active, but pace yourself. Don't overdo it and try to avoid long periods of standing. What do you do for a job?'

'I work in a call centre.'

'Okay—good. Try and stay away from too much caffeine, if you can. I'm going to write to your doctor now and see if we can get this sorted for you.'

'Thanks.'

He looked a little more relieved now that he'd talked

over his worries. She was sure that he would be okay, but if he did have PoTS then they would need to rule out any other underlying conditions, such as diabetes or lupus, as soon as possible.

She drew some blood and stuck a small round plaster in the crook of his elbow, and then went to find Matt to report in.

It had niggled at first, when she'd found she had to report in to Matt. Initially she'd thought he was doubting her abilities. But she'd found out that he'd checked everyone's work and approved their tests during the first week he'd started in the department. Apparently she'd missed his starting speech to the staff about wanting to ensure an *'efficient and highly capable department'*, but she could appreciate that.

Now her first week was nearly over and this would be the last day she checked in with him after each case.

I think I'll miss it.

The thought made her feel slightly perturbed.

After her initial annoyance, she'd grown to enjoy discussing her cases with Major Matt Galloway. He was always pleased to see her, always listened intently, and always gave great suggestions for further treatment if she found herself torn between the right way forward. He always told her she was doing a great job and when she'd made a great catch.

Was it the feedback? Was it getting approval? She'd never had that before, from anyone who mattered, and receiving it felt strange. Oddly unsettling, but immensely gratifying. She'd miss not going to him for advice. Miss checking in with him all day long.

He was a nice guy, and she could see why Jen had married him.

She'd struggled at first to match the severe, law-abiding soldier husband to her fun-loving, spontaneous friend. The couple seemed chalk and cheese. But as the days had passed Matt had become more familiar to her, and she to him. His guard had come down somewhat and he'd smiled more, laughed more.

He'd even stood chatting to her one day in the staff room, over a mug of tea and a chocolate biscuit, and it had been just as Kelly had said. He was different when you got to know him and saw past his rules and regulations and the army officer bearing that he used as a shield.

He still wasn't calling her Brooke, though. It was always Dr Bailey and she, in turn, always called him Major. It had become a game. A tennis match. He would serve and she would volley.

She found him labelling a vial of blood and waited for him to finish before presenting her case, running through Charlie's symptoms, her diagnosis and referral.

'I agree, Dr Bailey. I imagine he'll also need an echo-cardiogram at some point, but we'll leave that to his specialist. That's excellent. I think I can happily sign you off now.'

He looked up at her and smiled and it totally disarmed her.

'Sign me off?'

'You don't need to check in with me any more. I feel totally assured that your practice as a doctor is just the type I need in this department. I trust you completely. You should be happy about that.'

'I am. It's just…' She floundered for words. Her brain had gone blank.

Why was she having such a hard time with this? She'd only been doing it for a week, and she hadn't liked it at the beginning, but that had been before she'd realised just how much she would get out of it. She didn't want to let that go. Realising how needy that made her feel, she frowned, angry at herself.

I am not a needy person!

She had promised herself, when she'd made the decision to carry on with her pregnancy and be a single mother, that she would do so with determination, authority and a belief in herself that she could do anything alone. Wasn't that what she had always done anyway? She was used to standing alone. Surviving without someone else's input. So why should a week of running to Matt have made her feel this way?

Brooke didn't like it. And all of those emotions must be running across her face, because suddenly Matt was standing up and had laid a concerned hand upon her upper arm.

'Are you okay?'

She snapped her head up, determined and bright. 'Of course. Why wouldn't I be?'

He looked at her carefully. As if he were assessing her. As he would a patient.

'I don't know.'

'I know I'm capable. I trust my own practice, I know what I'm doing and even though I've been away for seven months or so it doesn't mean that I lack any confidence in my own abilities!'

She was flustered. She could hear it in her own voice. That and a small note of hysteria. What the *hell* was happening to her? Was it still the effect of all those hormones that she'd had to suffer after she'd had her baby? The bloody things could linger for an age...torturing women with doubts and uncertainties.

You're not being a good enough mother...you don't know what you're doing!

And Matt…? Matt had been drip-feeding lovely words of encouragement into her empty soul and like a dry sponge she had sucked up every droplet of its goodness. Unaware that she had needed it so badly. It was like when she'd been at school, finishing her work before everyone else and taking it up to teacher to be marked and receiving words of praise and a gold star sticker. It had made her beam inside.

Matt frowned and made her sit in his chair. Then he knelt down in front of her, those eyes of his diving into her soul and having a good old rummage around.

Afraid of what he might see if she let him in, she pulled back.

'Go back to your patient. Discharge him.'

He glanced at his wristwatch. He was one of the few people she knew who still wore one.

'It's nearly eleven. We're owed a break. Find me and we'll go for a coffee. In the cafeteria,' he added, which was a special treat, instead of them hunkering down in the staff room.

The cafeteria at the London Grace had an excellent range of refreshments—including home-made cakes that were made on site and were full of calorie-laden deliciousness.

'Oh, I don't think we need to—'

He put his hands on both arms of the swivel chair. 'I insist.'

His voice had softened and that drop in tone went straight to her heart. He was not going to let her get away from this. Perhaps he knew something. That she needed this break?

Brooke stood up abruptly, breaking the prison of his arms, and went to discharge Charlie. She forced herself to focus, giving Charlie the best advice she could to keep himself safe until he got to see a specialist. Then she found herself walking back through the department as if on numb autopilot.

How had things changed so quickly? One moment she'd been humming tunes, sure of herself, and yet suddenly she was feeling lost at sea. Cast away on an ocean with no sign of land.

I'm exhausted!

Tiredness. That had to be it. She'd been so determined to come back to work and blaze a trail, making sure that everyone had missed her, needed her back with them. But Morgan's lack of any need for sleep had caused *her* to lose too many hours too, and she'd been running on optimistic adrenaline.

When had she last cooked herself a proper meal? She'd been going home and just grabbing whatever was in the fridge—usually a sandwich, or something on toast. Something quick that she could eat cold if Morgan demanded her attention.

It was impossible to work the way she'd been doing on hardly any sleep and without enough proper, nutritious food. Add to that the fact that she was breastfeeding, and she was totally drained. Seeing Matt throughout the day had kept her tank topped up. Had allowed her to keep going from one patient to the next because she'd known she would get to see him again. She'd become dependent upon him like...

Brooke swallowed hard and raised her chin. Perhaps she was like someone that she knew. And the idea of that sickened her—because she'd thought she was nothing like *him*.

Across the department, Matt caught her eye and beckoned with a tilt of his head. Pulled towards him like a magnet, she walked over to him and they headed out of the department to the cafeteria. Matt guided her to a table and told her to sit down, then went over to the self-service counter and came back with two cups of strong-smelling coffee, a bowl of fruit salad and a large apple turnover.

'Thanks.'

'They're both for you.'

'Both?'

'You look like you need it. When did you last eat?'

She searched her brain for any memory of a meal and vaguely remembered grabbing a yoghurt when she'd got home last night. 'A while ago.'

'You're breastfeeding, Dr Bailey. Keep going at this rate and you'll either make yourself unwell or run out of milk. Which would you prefer?'

She felt her cheeks colour at him asking her such a personal question, but then she remembered that first day when she'd leaked milk all over her new blouse. 'Neither.'

'I thought not. You've had that running-on-empty look for a while.'

Embarrassed that she hadn't been giving her all in looking after herself, or as a doctor, realising she really ought to know better, she shook her head. She'd kept herself going on fluids. 'I keep trying to be everything to everyone. My patients. Morgan. I guess I forget about myself sometimes.'

'Sometimes?' He poured milk and put two sugars into her coffee. 'For energy.' He smiled. 'It's hard trying to be both parents—I know how you feel.'

Of course he did. But *he* wasn't the one falling apart in the hospital cafeteria, was he? She pulled the cling film off the top of the fruit salad and forked a strawberry into her mouth. It tasted great, bursting with juice, flavour and sweetness. She hardly had to chew at all, and the next thing she knew she was spearing a piece of melon.

'I bet you make yourself a three-course meal every night, huh, Major?'

He smiled back at her and pinched a piece of kiwi fruit. 'Restaurant standard. I even do *petit fours* with my coffee afterwards.'

She looked at him with raised eyebrows, totally impressed, and then when he started to laugh realised he was joking. She took back the piece of kiwi fruit and popped it into her mouth. 'You don't need it, apparently.'

Matt smiled warmly at her, then glanced down and stirred his own coffee. 'Jen mentioned that you were on your own... You can tell me to mind my own business, but do you want to tell me what happened?'

She broke a piece of pastry off the turnover and ate it before speaking. 'Eric was...' She paused to think of the right expression. 'A learning experience.'

He nodded. 'What did he do for a living?'

'He was an actor—in more ways than one. We met at an after-show party. He'd just finished a run at the theatre, playing the part of the Bard, and I'd won VIP tickets to go backstage and meet the cast and crew. Theatre isn't really my thing—not unless it's got scalpels in it and an anaesthetist—but I went anyway and I met Eric. He was charming, handsome...a bit insecure but he hid it well. At first.'

'What happened?'

'He asked me out, I said yes, and we started dating. I thought he was great. Really nice, listened well, asked a lot of questions, seemed interested in me... But really he was gathering information...to make the best attack possible.'

Matt's brows furrowed. 'How do you mean?'

'It was nothing physical. It was mental. He started going out on his own, saying he was with friends when I suspected otherwise. And because I had no proof he made me feel like a crazy woman for even considering it. But then the comments started—questions that made me second-guess myself. Was I really going to wear that dress when it didn't suit me? Was I really not going to take any of the blame for the fact that he'd lost out on an audition? Was I really going to go out with friends from work when I should be spending time with him? He slowly and methodically tried to close me off from everyone I knew, and when he realised I wasn't going to put up with it he turned toxic. Getting hold of me at work to call me horrible names—that sort of thing. So I broke it off. Something I should have done earlier, but he'd made me doubt myself for a while—made me think that *I* was the one being unreasonable, that I didn't have the strength to leave him. He was wrong.'

'How did he react to you ending it?'

'Well, let's just say he has an amazing capability with swear words and derogatory terms.'

'I see.' Matt looked down at his coffee and took a small sip.

'He'd tried to make out he was a gentleman, but he couldn't carry off that role. Not full-time, anyway. I was glad to be out of it.'

'And when did you discover you were pregnant?'

'A couple of months afterwards. Usual thing—working so hard I wasn't paying attention to the calendar. It was only when I was educating a young girl about her own cycle that I realised the date and I just *knew*.' She munched on a piece of apple. 'Jen told me to forget him, and took me out on the town to show me that there was still fun in life.'

He smiled at the image. 'I can imagine her doing that.'

'She was great. She lifted my spirits. And when she discovered she was pregnant, too…' She laughed as she recalled it. 'She came over to me, bumped her belly against mine and said, *"The race is on!"*'

Matt carefully sipped at his coffee.

'I told Eric about the baby. He might not have deserved it, but I thought he still had the right to know. Just because he was an awful boyfriend, it didn't mean he would be an awful father.'

'Is he?'

'A rubbish father? Yes!' She laughed again, wondering why she was laughing about it. Because was it truly funny? That Morgan didn't have a dad?

She'd never wanted the children she had to want for anything. She'd dreamed of having the perfect family. Two parents for her children. Children loved and adored from both sides. Enveloped in love and acceptance no matter what.

The smile died on her face. 'He didn't want to know. Said it was my *"mess"* to clear up. That he was with someone else now—as if I might want him back. I soon put him right on that score.'

'I'm glad you did.'

'I was so scared. About doing it alone. I wasn't sure whether I could continue on with the pregnancy.'

She felt awful about that now. Even admitting it was hard.

'I didn't know if I'd know what to do. I can't remember my own mother, what she was like and so I told myself it wasn't the right time to have a baby. I wasn't in a good situation, being on my own, and I had a demanding job, with long hours away. I didn't think I'd be able to do it—not without family to help. But...' She smiled again, lost in the past. 'I couldn't bear the idea of just ending the pregnancy. Jen convinced me I could do it alone. Told me that she would be there for me and that we'd raise our babies together.'

She tried to ignore the lump in her throat as she spoke. Jen had been unable to keep that promise, and Brooke had been so low when that call had come and she'd realised she would be on her own.

'You really have no family?'

She shook her head, determined not to let herself cry. 'As I said before, I have a father. Not that you'd know it.'

'He's not local?'

'Oh, he's local. He lives in Wandsworth. But he's not *present*. All my life my father has had an issue with alcohol—always looking for his next drink, thinking of nothing and no one else.'

'Addiction is hard.'

'You're telling me.'

She thought of how addicted *she* had become to seeing Matt after each patient. She hadn't been knocking back vodka at every opportunity, but she had become very quickly addicted to that uplifting note in her day. To that brief conversation in which she had been made to feel lifted. Better. Her cares gone away. Strangely soothed...her edges softened.

Just like an addict.

'The last time he saw Morgan she was hours old. Then he went out and got drunk to toast her arrival. Wet the baby's head.'

Matt reached across the table to lay his hand over

hers. Then his features changed suddenly and he withdrew it again.

She was surprised, then reassured. The warmth and weight of his hand had been a reassuring presence that she'd needed. Needed. There was that word again. How quickly addiction could establish itself...

But why was she addicted to *him*? This was Jen's husband. He belonged to her dead friend. Was that it? Because he represented that friendship and the affection that she had lost? Was she trying to find it in him? Surely it had nothing to do with his dirty blond hair, his clear blue eyes and stubbled jaw. It couldn't have anything to do with the fact that he oozed masculinity from every pore whilst at the same time being kind, empathetic and respectful?

A gentleman.

Matt was everything Eric wasn't.

He cleared his throat. 'I was working on a patient who'd dislocated his knee when they told me that the General wanted to see me.'

She focused on his voice. The look in his eyes. Faraway and sad.

'I didn't think it was anything to worry about. I popped the knee into place and strapped up the leg before I headed over to his office. He told me to sit down, and the look on his face changed to one of such discomfort I honestly wondered if he was about to ask me to examine him privately.'

The ghost of a smile made its presence felt in the corners of her mouth as she imagined it.

'He told me that there'd been a telephone call from the Maternity Suite at the London Grace, and just for a brief second my heart soared at the thought that I'd become a father. That my wife had gone into labour early and already had Lily. But the General looked so sorry for me that I can remember my heart thudding in my chest as I waited for him to tell me that they were both okay.'

Matt stiffened in the cafeteria chair.

'He said that Lily was in the NICU. That it had been an emergency delivery and that Jen had not recovered from complications surrounding the birth. They'd put her on life support and I was to fly back to England immediately.'

He shook his head, as if he still couldn't believe the memory even now. After all this time.

'My brain couldn't compute that. All I could think of was the guy I'd just strapped up and sent on his way. The fact that I had other patients awaiting my attention, you know? It was as if to protect itself my brain had switched off from what the General had said.'

'It happens.'

'I got on the plane home in a daze. Looking at all of these people around me, busy with their lives—couples, families... And yet there I was, travelling back to switch off a machine that would end my own.'

Brooke saw his eyes darken as he recalled this painful memory, empathising with his grief, having felt the loss of Jen, too. Strange how grief could rip some people asunder but unite others. It was a powerful force. It did strange things. Caused people to behave oddly. Out of character.

'I can't imagine the strength you must have needed to find inside.'

He looked at her. 'None of us know the strengths we have until we're tested.'

He was absolutely right. Brooke felt that she'd spent her life digging deep for unknown lodes of strength.

'And none of us know the battles that others have faced or still face.' He leant forward again. 'There are lots of soldiers who come back home and look whole, but are broken inside.'

'You must know a lot of people like that?'

Matt nodded. 'Unfortunately. But we're here to talk about *you*. I don't want you pushing yourself to exhaustion, Dr Bailey. I value you as a doctor too much to lose you.'

He valued her.

As a *doctor*.

He hadn't said he valued her as a friend.

But she'd take it anyway. It had been a long time since anyone had valued her at all, and he was right. Perhaps she *had* been pushing the envelope a bit too much. If she didn't start looking after herself better then she wouldn't be able to help her patients or Morgan at all.

'Message received loud and clear, Major.'

He stood up and eased his way out from behind the table. 'I'm ordering you to stay here until you've consumed everything on both plates, and then at one o'clock you can meet me for lunch.'

'Lunch?'

'So I can make sure you refuel properly.' Matt smiled at her and gave her a mock salute before he marched away.

Brooke watched him go, a surprised smile on her face. Normally she didn't like men telling her what to do, and after Eric she had been determined never to let it happen again.

But there was something different about Matt. He wasn't overbearing. It hadn't been a demand, the way Eric would have delivered it. He hadn't said it to her as if she were stupid and he were trying to demean her.

He *cared*. Genuinely. About *her* welfare. And she wasn't used to someone doing that for her.

She'd always had to care for herself. Even when she was little…sitting at home, waiting for her dad to come back for hours, starving hungry. And when he had made it back the most he'd been able to manage to make for her had been something out of a can on toast.

With hindsight, it was probably the safest thing for him to have been in charge of. And although she'd yearned every day for him to ask her about her day at school he never had. And although she would get her paintings and her ten-out-of-ten spelling tests out of her bag to show him, her hard work had barely received a glance.

Her dad had physically been there, but it had been as if there was an invisible force field around him that she hadn't been able to penetrate. The fug of alcohol fumes had been a barrier she hadn't been able to break through. He hadn't connected to her at all.

She knew he'd turned to alcohol to get through the death of his wife—her mother. But by doing so he had caused Brooke to lose her father too. She'd been so young, just five years old, when it happened and all she had left were photographs of what they should have been. A happy, united family staring at the camera lens.

Coping on her own had become something so natural to her it was always a surprise when someone else looked out for her, no matter how small the occasion was.

Brooke sat there and ate the rest of her fruit salad and pastry, washing them down with the coffee and looking around at the other people in the cafeteria. Families. Mothers *and* fathers. Little toddlers being asked to sit still, to eat up, not to play with their food.

She smiled. It was all so normal for them.

Why had *she* not achieved that? Where had she gone wrong? Eric had been a mistake, but not Morgan. She adored her daughter, and would not be without her, but it didn't stop Brooke from feeling alone.

Had *she* caused it? Losing Jen just after the birth of her own daughter had made Brooke hibernate in the house. Not going out much...not being with people. Not letting anyone in. It had been easier to retreat into herself because that was familiar country. She knew the landscape. There were no surprises if she relied on just herself.

But wasn't life about overcoming obstacles? Facing the challenges set before you? Fighting to be with those who would love you?

I need to let people in. Open up the borders.
Before I'm deserted altogether.

CHAPTER FOUR

MATT WAS STILL busy with a patient when Brooke had finished, ready for lunch. She sat at the doctors' desk and watched him carefully as he taught a young girl to use a pair of crutches. The girl, no more than eight years old, had a plaster cast around her foot and appeared to be struggling with her co-ordination. Matt kept adjusting the height of the crutches and knelt on the floor in front of his patient, smiling, encouraging her to move forward.

'Standing on your good leg, bring both crutches forward. That's it. Then swing your body forward, landing on your good leg. Excellent! Well done!'

She watched him stand and shake hands with the girl's father, and then he stooped one last time to say something to the little girl, who smiled shyly and nodded her head.

A warm smile appeared on Brooke's face as she watched, and she was still smiling when Matt came over to the desk to finish writing his notes.

'She looked sweet.'

Matt nodded, watching the father and daughter head out of the department, the little girl steady and determined on her new walking aids. 'She fell off a trampoline.'

Brooke raised an eyebrow. 'We ought to ban those things. I'm sure we could cut down a good quarter of our workload if we did.'

'I agree.' He glanced at her and grinned. 'Though I'm sure our own daughters will want to spend time on trampolines at some point.'

'Yes, well, not if I can help it. I'll be keeping Morgan well away from anything like that.'

'Me too. But we can't wrap them in cotton wool. I know Jen would have *loved* the idea of Lily on a trampoline. And secondary schools often have trampolining in a physical education class. Are you going to ask for her to be withdrawn from those?'

She nodded firmly. 'Yes.'

'And what if all her friends start asking her why? What if she starts to feel embarrassed for being left out? You'll still be okay with that?'

She shifted in her chair. 'Yes.'

'Dr Bailey... I don't believe a single word.' He turned to face her, looking as if he was daring her to say otherwise.

'We all have to do things that sometimes go against the grain. I'm sure I can find other activities to occupy her and make up for the fact that I'm not risking her neck or her back or her ankles.'

'And what do *you* do that goes against the grain?'

She stopped to think. Unsure. 'How do you mean?'

'What do you do with Morgan that's different to anyone else?'

She opened her mouth as she struggled to find an answer, then closed it again when she realised, sharply that she didn't do *anything* with Morgan apart from feed, clothe and change her. They didn't really go out anywhere, except to the local park. But Morgan was too small to do anything. She hadn't even taken her to the local swimming pool for a splash-around, and Morgan *loved* being in water. Perhaps she wasn't the kind of radical, unique mother she'd thought she was.

'You know, there's something I need to tell you,' he said. He looked awkward. Uncomfortable. Whatever could it be?

'Such as?'

'Jen signed Lily up to this class months in advance, because it was oversubscribed. You know what things are like in London… Apparently it's very popular—great for babies' development…that kind of thing… and she kind of signed you and Morgan up to it, too.' He glanced quickly at her to see the effect of his revelation. 'I wasn't going to go, but…' He sighed. 'Perhaps we both ought to give it a try. Seeing as Jen wanted us to do it.'

She blinked. Remembered some vague conversation months back that she and Jen had had about baby development classes. They'd laughed about it. Chuckling about how silly they sounded, how pretentious. How it was more about the parents wanting to show off and have their offspring with a busier social calendar than they had themselves.

'A class?'

'Music Melody. I'm going to go—and you should too. It starts this Saturday morning at St David's Church Hall.'

Music Melody? A baby development class? In a draughty church hall? With a bunch of yummy mummies she wouldn't know, listening to babies banging away randomly on some clanging tin xylophones? It sounded like her worst nightmare.

'I…er…don't think so.' She laughed, as if it were the most ridiculous suggestion she'd ever heard.

'When did you last go out with Morgan to do something fun?'

'We have plenty of fun at home.'

He smiled. '*You* do, maybe. But what about Morgan? This kind of thing will get us out of our comfort zone and stop us from staying cooped up inside. Come on. I'm sure Morgan would love it.'

'But what about *me*?' she pleaded.

Going to a parent-and-baby group didn't sound like her idea of fun *at all*. She'd never been one for parties, or meeting up with friends outside of school. She never usually went to work bashes—not unless Jen had dragged her there.

Jen.

Jen had booked it for *them*! For *both* of them! She'd promised to be there for her, had said they would do things together. She'd *meant* it. Not knowing that she would never get the chance to fulfil that promise.

But Brooke could.

She sighed as she looked back at him, saw the twinkle of humour in his eyes and felt herself giving in. Perhaps it might be okay… And if it gave her a headache then she could take some painkillers afterwards.

'Fine. But why do you want me to go so badly?'

He let out a big sigh. 'Because I want to honour Jen's promise to you.'

She swallowed. 'Her promise?'

'To not let you do this alone. She told me about that.'

Oh. She felt oddly perturbed that he should want to do that. Honour an obligation made by his wife. He didn't have to. She'd managed all these months alone, and she and Morgan were doing okay. But it was sweet of him. Gentlemanly.

'You don't have to.'

'It's the right thing.'

'But we hardly know each other. I'm still a stranger…'

'As all the other parents will be. But I want to do right by my daughter and expose her to as much fun and joy as I can.'

She grimaced. 'Those places are germ factories. We'll probably all come down with bugs. Is *that* doing right by our children?'

'Building up their immune system! We put them in a crèche all day. It's the same thing.'

She supposed he was right. 'Okay.'

'Good. I've already told them you're coming.'

She stood up, grabbing her bag so they could go and get some lunch. 'How did you know I'd agree?'

He leant against the desk, his tall, lean frame effortlessly sexy. Even more so because he seemed totally unaware of it.

'Because you wouldn't let a good friend go to one of those terrible places alone.' He stepped away again. 'I'll probably be the only guy there. I'll get *the looks*.'

'Looks?'

'You know the ones… *Why has he come and not the mum? Where's his wife? Is he single?* You being there will protect me from all that.'

'You don't strike me as the type to need protection, Major. Don't you know how to kill people with just your thumbs?'

He smiled. 'Yes…but I think that's frowned upon at parent-and-baby groups, Dr Bailey.'

Brooke stared at him as he grabbed his jacket,

checked his pocket for his wallet and wondered just what the hell she was letting herself in for...

As the days passed Brooke grew more and more nervous about meeting Matt at the Music Melody class. Sitting with him at work for lunch was one thing—but socialising with him *outside* of work? What did *that* mean?

He knew it was just friendship, right? He knew it could never go any further than that? Yes, she'd socialised with Jen out of hours—but Jen had been a girl. She and Matt were the opposite sex to each other, and it was a fine line for them to walk.

She was already having difficulties with that smile of his. Not only did it totally transform his face, but every time he sent it her way she found herself wanting more and more of it. She enjoyed making him smile. She adored the camaraderie that was building between them. And he had a wicked sense of humour when he let it out. He made her laugh. Brightened her day.

But was that *all* that was developing? She couldn't allow anything else to occur between them. That way madness lay. Just the thought of it right now was turning her insides into all kinds of jumble. She could even feel her mouth going dry. And to think she'd once complained about him keeping his distance by calling her Dr Bailey and not Brooke...

Right now she was *ecstatic* that he was calling her Dr Bailey.

You stay over there, Major—that's right. Imagine I've got a minefield around me.

Brooke looked down at her next chart and frowned. Two patients on one chart? She quickly scanned the notes that the triage nurse had added: *Glued together.*

Smiling at the silliness of some people, she headed to the waiting room. 'Rachel and Jake?'

A young teenage couple stood up, their hands locked together, and following behind them, looking less amused, two sets of parents.

Brooke raised her eyebrows at the teens and sent a look of sympathy towards the parents. 'Follow me.'

She took them to a cubicle and got them to sit on the small bed.

'You've glued yourselves together?'

They raised their clasped hands, looking quite pleased with themselves. 'We had to.'

'You *had* to?'

Rachel turned to look at her father and sneered. '*They* kept trying to split us up. Said Jake wasn't good enough for me—but they're wrong! We love each other and want to be together for ever, so we decided to prove it.'

'By gluing your hands together?'

Rachel nodded. 'That's right.'

'You couldn't just wait until you were old enough to get married?'

One of the parents bristled slightly. 'Don't give them ideas. As if *this* isn't bad enough! I've had to take time off work for this—and they're missing school. All because they're so childish they can't see what they're doing!'

Fair enough. She could understand the parents' point of view. 'Can I have a look at your hands?'

She examined Rachel and Jake's hands. They were stuck tight—glued around their palms and fingers. She'd have to be careful not to damage the skin in removing the glue.

She'd heard of other people coming across this in A&E, but this was a first for her. Rachel and Jake probably thought they were being unique and different, proving their devotion to each other, but all they had done was alienate everyone and give their parents even more reason to try and keep the two of them apart.

'Okay, I'll need to check which solution to use on this. Sit tight for a moment. I'll be back in a few minutes.'

She headed back to the doctors' desk and shared with Kelly the details of the case she'd got.

'Oh, I had a couple do that once.'

'Really? What? Here?'

'No, when I worked up in Birmingham. But they didn't glue their *hands*.'

She raised an eyebrow at her and Brooke grimaced.

'*Eurgh!* People do mad things when they think they're in love.'

'It's certainly an emotion that ought to come with a health warning.'

Brooke mused. 'Do you think anyone would pay attention to it, though?'

'I don't know. It would have to be a really clever TV advert. *'Warning! Falling in love can result in sleepless nights, stomach ache and heart pain. Use with caution.'*'

Brooke smiled. 'Let's not forget the terrible grief at its end. Look at what Major Galloway has had to go through.'

'Matt? He's survived it. He's in one piece, anyway.'

Was he? Or was he just very good at hiding his wounds? Brooke hadn't known Jen long. Less than a year. But they had become such great friends, so quickly, that she'd given her entire heart to their friendship. When she'd lost Jen it had hurt her terribly. And she still mourned the mother she'd never really known, too. Was she destined to always have a piece missing in her heart?

Was anyone totally whole?

Don't all of us have chipped, broken edges?

'I'm thinking of using warm, soapy water first.'

'On Matt?' Kelly raised an eyebrow. 'Could be interesting…'

Brooke smiled at her friend. 'On the two lovebirds in Cubicle Six.'

'Oh, right… Yeah, lots of soap and warm water. Slowly ease their hands apart—no tugging, no ripping. That should do it.'

Brooke stood up to get herself a basin, but then turned to ask Kelly one last question. 'How would *you* prove that you loved somebody?'

Kelly looked thoughtful for a moment. 'Without making them want to get a restraining order? Erm… I don't actually know. How would *you* do it?'

Brooke shook her head. 'I wouldn't. It's all a bit scary, if you ask me. Besides, I've got Morgan now. I don't need anyone else.'

Kelly returned a look that said *I don't believe you.*

She pondered, whilst she filled a container with warm, soapy water, whether someone like Matt, who had already been broken once by loving someone, would ever feel he could fall in love again. Probably not. He had his hands full, too. Both of them had a strenuous full-time job and both of them were single parents. Did either of them have time to fit in the needs and wants of another person who would control their hearts?

Not me. Definitely not me.

But as she headed back to the cubicle and began soaking the clasped hands of the two teenagers, who were still staring into each other's eyes, she couldn't help but think about Matt and how he managed to lift her spirits every moment she spent time with him...

There'd been a frost that morning. The first one of autumn, which was Brooke's favourite time of year. There was nothing she liked better than chilly weather, as long as it wasn't raining. Having to wrap up in woolly scarves, hats and gloves, her nose going red as she watched her own breath freeze in the air around you... And autumn brought Halloween and Bonfire Night, with hot potatoes wrapped in foil and everyone gazing heavenwards at the inky black sky, awaiting the fireworks show.

November the fifth was just a few short days away, and already she'd spent some of her nights listening to the occasional firework or banger going off in the local neighbourhood.

Last year she'd spent the evening with Eric, and as much as there had been fireworks in the sky there'd also been fireworks as he'd walked her home, arguing that she'd spent her entire evening staring at another man. She hadn't. But Eric had insisted that the man hadn't been able to take his eyes off her and Brooke had been encouraging him. One final nail in the coffin of their relationship.

This year she would go to an organised fireworks show with Morgan and delight in her daughter's pleasure at seeing fireworks for the first time. But in the meantime she had this Music Melody class to get through...

That morning she'd lain in bed, listening to Morgan babble away in the next room, wanting to stay under the duvet. It was the weekend, and she'd been looking forward to her customary lie-in of an extra hour. But the class started early, and she *had* promised she would go, and Matt was right. It would be good for her to get out of the house and it would be good for Morgan to socialise, even though she *did* spend the majority of her week in a crèche.

I do need to do something with my daughter other than drop her off and collect her each day.

And who knew? It might even be fun.

She dressed in some old jeans, threw on a tee shirt, a poncho and a beanie hat, slipped into her boots and got Morgan into her car seat.

'Okay. Now, I'm hoping we're going somewhere that will be melodic and harmonious, but as I'm guessing the majority of the orchestra is going to be under the age of one, I'm not holding out much hope for our ears. So if you could at least pretend to enjoy yourself—that would be great.'

Morgan responded by blowing a bubble with her saliva and smiling.

Brooke kissed her button nose and got into the driving seat. Part of her hoped that she would enjoy herself, but would she really find joy amongst a bunch of babies banging away on drums and tambourines? She'd forearmed herself by putting painkillers into her handbag, just in case the place gave her the mother of all headaches.

The GPS directed her through London to the required church hall, and she parked in its small car park, pulling into a space, noticing that Matt was already there, getting Lily's buggy out of the boot of his own vehicle.

'You made it.'

She got out of her car. 'You doubted me?'

He smiled. 'Not for one moment. Are you ready for this?'

'I've got earplugs, if that's what you mean?'

Matt laughed as he strapped Lily into her buggy.

Brooke scooped Morgan out of her own car seat and decided not to get the buggy out—she would carry her daughter inside.

She hefted her onto her left hip. 'What do you think? Are we about to discover this country's next great virtuoso?'

'You never know.'

Matt led the way into the hall and Brooke could feel nerves building in her stomach. She'd never wanted to come to one of these places. What if the other mothers wanted to talk? What if they asked questions? She'd have to tell them she was a single parent. That Eric had never seen his daughter and didn't care. What did *that* say about her, to have got involved with a man like that? It wasn't good, was it? It was hardly a letter of commendation regarding her assessment skills. Perhaps it would just be best to say she'd used a sperm donor?

But, then again, she was here to stop Matt getting *the looks*. Were they to pretend that they were going out? Were married? She'd noticed he still wore his wedding band. That would make Lily and Morgan twins, wouldn't it?

The church hall was warm and in the centre was a large carpet. Around the edges sat various parents holding their babies on their laps, or letting them crawl around on the floor. Everyone chatted happily, waiting for the class to begin.

Brooke sucked in a breath. *Here goes.* She stepped forward with Matt and they found a spot together on the edge of the circle and let Lily and Morgan say hello to each other in their own cute baby way. Mainly patting each other in the face with their hands.

A young woman wearing a bright yellow tee shirt with the words *Music Melody Maestro* on it clapped her hands together to get everyone's attention.

'Welcome, everyone! It's lovely to see so many of you here, today. My name is Melanie and I'm going to lead our group!'

Like Daisy at the crèche, Melanie appeared to be one of those people with a permanently sunny disposition. Brooke wondered if that was a requirement to work with children. Must always look as if you're having the *best* fun!

She smiled and sat Morgan up against her, holding onto her chubby little hands.

'Now, here at Music Melody classes we want children to grow up loving the language of music! And to do that we're going to start off with simple rhymes and songs that we can all do the actions to, so that our babies learn about rhyme and rhythm and melody. Music can touch the soul and bring happiness to all if we all just take the time to find the right song! So let's start with the simplest: *"Pat-a-cake, Pat-a-cake"*.'

Brooke glanced worriedly at Matt. This wasn't an *instruments* class! This was *singing*! Why hadn't he warned her? Brooke was tone deaf and couldn't carry a note! Singing here, like this, out loud, where other people could *hear* her was not a very good idea at all!

But before she could say anything Melanie launched into the song, and so did everyone else around her.

Brooke opened her mouth and pretended to sing.

Matt seemed to be finding her discomfort terribly amusing. They'd gone from *'Pat-a-Cake, Pat-a-Cake'* to *'Twinkle, Twinkle Little Star'* and had just finished a rousing rendition of *'Old McDonald Had a Farm'*.

But that hadn't been the worst thing. Melanie, the alliterative Music Maestro, had said that each parent would have to suggest an animal, starting the verse off *by themselves*.

Brooke had felt horror creep into her bones, her skin crawling, and wished she could be anywhere but there. And as they'd gone round the circle, getting closer and closer to her, her mind had fixated on a goose, of all things, so she'd started her verse: *'And on that farm there was a goose, e-i-e-i-o. With a honk-honk here and a honk-honk there...'*

Her voice had sounded like a teenage boy's—squeaky one minute, deep the next—and the tune had been mangled beyond all recognition, but she'd got through it without her face melting from the shame, and when she'd glanced at Matt she'd been encouraged by his smile and the way he'd clapped Lily's hands together, as if in small applause.

He'd suggested Old McDonald had a turkey, and after he'd got all the other mothers laughing and singing along with him about gobbling the singing circle finally made it back to Melanie and the torture stopped for them all to get a cup of tea.

Brooke got to her feet thankfully, and headed over to the kitchen to stand in line.

'Enjoying yourself?' Matt caught up with her, his face full of humour and bonhomie.

'I'd rather be doing surgery on myself with a blunt spoon, but apart from that it's a thrill a minute.'

He laughed. 'I thought it was your kind of thing.

Great singing, by the way, Dr Bailey. I've not heard notes achieved like that before.'

She pursed her lips. 'And you'll never hear them again! I think it's safe to say that I will never, *ever* come back here.'

'Why not?'

She turned to face him. 'Because this is not a class for babies. This is a class to humiliate parents and make them think that just because there are other adults in the room they're actually getting decent conversation.'

'You're not having a good time?' He tilted his head to one side and looked curiously at her.

'Sorry. I'm being a killjoy about your bright idea. Forget me. Go and talk to all the other mummies. They all seem very keen to try and get your attention.'

'How do you mean?'

She raised an eyebrow. 'You've not noticed? It's flirtation central here! I don't think I've seen more women flicking and playing with their hair whilst ogling the only person in the room whose testes have descended.'

He laughed. 'I hadn't noticed.'

But she could tell that he had. It had been a concern of his before he'd even got here, and he'd asked *her* along to ward off that sort of thing.

The queue moved forward and Brooke passed him a cup of tea, adding sugar to hers and grabbing a biscuit that felt slightly soft because it was so old. But it would do.

Had he really not noticed how all the other women had reacted when he'd walked in? Brooke had instantly seen them eye him, straightening their clothes, and a few less subtle mothers had even got out a compact mirror and checked they looked okay before beaming a smile in his direction.

Okay, perhaps they weren't being so obvious that a *guy* would notice, but she had. And she could see why they would be noticing. Major Galloway was a handsome guy with come-to-bed eyes and a rugged demeanour that oozed the fact that he worked hard and knew how to *use his hands*. Probably other body parts, too. Quite...erm...effectively.

But Brooke was immune to his charms. She felt sure of it. Besides, they were colleagues—that was all. They just happened to have two kids the same age.

Not being able to find a chair, she settled herself down on the carpet and lay Morgan on her back next to Lily.

'Jen would have found this place hilarious,' she said.

She noticed him stiffen at the mention of his wife's name. 'Probably.'

She dunked her biscuit in her tea and quickly pulled it out before it could break off in the drink, popping the whole thing into her mouth. As she munched on it she noticed that he was staring at her with a smile on his face.

'What?' she asked through a mouthful of crumbs.

'Nothing.' He looked away.

'No, go on. What did I do?'

He glanced back at her, finally capitulating. 'Jen used to do that. Eat the whole biscuit in one go, I mean.'

'Oh.' She hadn't realised. 'I'm sorry.'

He shook his head, smiling. 'You don't have to apologise. It's just a biscuit.'

'I just don't want to...'

'What?'

'Remind you. Make you sad.'

'A million things remind me every day. Especially

Lily. It's good, though. Because why would I want to forget?'

She nodded slowly. 'Has it got a little easier? Since she passed? I know it's only five months since it happened…'

And now she felt awkward for having asked. For her, Jen was the first big loss that she'd ever had to face, since her mother's death. The grief was still difficult some days, but it was getting easier to bear. Sometimes something would happen at work, or with Morgan, and the first thing she'd think would be, *I must tell Jen.* And then she would realise, with a great thud in her heart and stomach, that Jen wasn't here any more. There was a gaping hole in her life and she didn't know how to fill it.

'I've accepted it. When I got back to England I was numb, and then I got angry. Wanted to rage against the world for taking her. But then I'd hold Lily in my arms and I could see Jen looking out at me, through her eyes, and I just knew that if Jen were there still she'd be telling me to stop being such a macho idiot, get a grip and move on.' He smiled. 'Did she ever say that to you?'

Brooke nodded. 'That I'm a macho idiot? Oh, absolutely.' She allowed a smile to play at her lips. 'She hated people being sad. She was always telling me to snap out of it whenever I was feeling low about my situation.'

'Did that ever work?'

'Sometimes. Every day is different, isn't it? Each dawn a new page on which your story can either have a high or a low.'

He nodded, as if he knew what she was saying exactly. 'Jen would want us both to have highs.'

'Not pharmaceutically!' She laughed, the sound escaping her almost like a cry, sudden and short.

She had to look away. Had to blink a few times to

rid herself of the tears that were suddenly threatening. If Jen were here she'd be having a laugh a minute and Brooke knew it. Jen *should* be here. Singing with her baby. But she wasn't. And all because of a cruel twist in fate. Brooke was here instead, with Jen's husband, and suddenly it felt wrong. Very wrong, indeed. This was all just too cosy, too soon.

She put down her tea, scooped up Morgan and stood up. 'I think I need to go.'

Matt got to his feet. 'Go? It's not finished.'

'I just need to—'

He laid a hand on her arm. 'Dr Bailey.' He made her look at him. 'Take a breath. That's it. In for three and out for three. Nice and steady.'

He waited until he saw the panic leave her features.

'She would have wanted you here. With us. With Lily. She's not, but she would have wanted you here. To…' he smiled '…*endure* this. Come on…maybe in part two we can make a request. I think we ought to ask for *"Incy Wincy Spider"*. What do you think?'

She was trying not to be taken in by those eyes of his. Perfectly blue, thickly lashed with dark hair. 'I hate spiders.' She could imagine him leaping to her rescue to rid her of an eight-legged arachnid.

'Then what would *you* ask for?'

She thought for a second. '*"Jack and Jill went up the hill"*?'

He seemed amused. 'Why that one?'

'Jack breaks his crown. I always liked the idea of fixing him afterwards.'

'And Jill? She came tumbling after.'

'Why not? In my version she breaks a bone or two.'

Matt settled her back on the carpet and handed her

the cup of tea. 'We can get through anything together. You and I are strong.'

'You think so? I don't *feel* particularly strong sometimes.'

'Like Jack, it doesn't matter how many times we fall. As long as we always get up again. *Do* you keep getting up again, Dr Bailey?'

'I think I do.'

A smile lifted the corners of his mouth. 'I'm glad.'

Brooke made it through the next thirty minutes of singing. At first she just mouthed along, not feeling any of it, but as Morgan began to smile and squeal at all the actions, jiggling along, she soon got into her rhythm and started singing out loud, not giving one jot that she couldn't hold a note.

Who cared? Were the babies going to criticise her? Hardly. And the other mothers? Well, she was never going to see these people again. She could sound like a gurgling gutter and it wouldn't matter.

She was pleased she had come. And she was pleased to have come with Matt and seen him out of their work environment. He was a completely different person dressed in a long sleeved tee shirt and jeans. So strange, having only ever seen him in scrubs or a shirt and tie.

She was fastening Morgan into her car seat, clipping the buckles together and then closing the car door, when she became aware that Matt was waiting for her. She smiled at him and thanked him for asking her there.

'It was my pleasure.'

'Well, I guess I'll see you next week. Have a good weekend, Major.'

'You too, Dr Bailey.'

'Drive safely.'

'Always.' He began to walk away, but as he did so something inside her made her call out. 'Major Galloway…? There's a fireworks display in a couple of weeks in Hammersmith. It's meant to be really good… I've been looking forward to taking Morgan and I wondered if—you can say no… I won't mind…'

Spend more time with the lovely Matt Galloway? Was that wise? Was she being ridiculous to invite him? To offer to spend more of her free time with him?

How is that ridiculous? You're just being a friend.

'Er…'

'If *I* can get through the singing then it's only fair that you get through a few sparklers.'

She could see he was agonising over it. Had she pushed too hard? Was she reading too much into this friendship that he had promised to honour?

'Okay.'

She nodded. 'Great.'

'I'll see you on Monday, Dr Bailey.'

'Goodbye, Major.' And with a small wave she got into her car and started the engine.

Friendship was a strange thing indeed. It could develop at a lightning pace, go places you'd never imagined and hopefully tie you to someone you would trust your life to.

Whilst Jen had been alive Brooke had never really asked her too much about Matt, and Jen had hardly mentioned him. Acting the single parent to be in solidarity with Brooke's lonesome status? It had never occurred to her to ask more about the man that her best friend had loved.

But now she had the chance to know him.

And she was glad that she did.

CHAPTER FIVE

LILY WAS IN bed fast asleep and Matt was sitting on the couch, holding a cup of coffee and staring at the picture on the mantelpiece.

It was a picture that he and Jen had had taken on his last leave. He in his army uniform, Jen with her back to him, leaning against him as his hands embraced the gentle swell of her pregnant abdomen.

They were both smiling. Both of them imagining the brilliant future before them. His career in the army had been going strong, they'd been about to become parents for the first time and were at the start of their parenthood journey.

It was a trip that he had expected to take with his wife, yet now he was walking alone.

It was hard sometimes to look at that picture. Because how could they have known that everything was about to change for the worse? He hadn't known that that was one of the last times he would ever hold her. Hold them both. The only thing he could hold now was memories. And they were fleeting. Like trying to hold a cloud.

But he *could* hold Lily, and she was the burning image of her mother. Cute blonde hair, twinkling cheeky eyes. And that chuckle of hers… It didn't ever fail to make him laugh, too. It was such pure delight.

Jen would have loved to hear it. To be there for her daughter. Neither of them had suspected that she would succumb to eclampsia. Her pregnancy had been problem-free up to that point. Jen had been an extremely healthy person. She'd run half-marathons for charity every year. Had played in the hospital netball team when she could. The news from his General that Jen had been put on a life support machine had been like a tragic joke. Unbelievable. Surely they'd meant someone else?

Yet it had been horribly true, and each night when Lily was in bed Matt would sit in the heavy silence of the house and be thankful for having got through another day. It was all he requested from life now. Making it from sun-up to sunset. He had no more aspirations than that apart from ensuring that Lily was happy. She was his life now. His number one reason for putting one step in front of another.

It had been difficult in the early days. Caring for a newborn whilst in the grip of grief. People—family, friends—had helped as much as they could. But after a time their own lives, naturally, had pulled them away. And he'd emerged from the dark mire of his pain determined to provide the best life he could for his daughter. Not to flit from one posting to another but to take root, to stay in his new job at London Grace and be the best father he could for his little girl.

Meeting Dr Brooke Bailey had been a surprising bonus. When he'd been accepted by the hospital trust to take on his wife's post he'd known that at some point he would meet the woman who had recently been his wife's confidante. And she was every bit the wonderful person Jen had told him about.

And, though he'd only known her for such a short time—just a few weeks—he did feel as if they had a bond. Their mutual love of Jen, their work, and the fact that they were both single-handedly raising little girls. Since meeting Brooke he'd wondered if she sat in her own home at night, nursing a cup of cocoa, wondering what might have been if fate hadn't designated her to raise a child alone? How her life might be different with someone in it to help her?

Not that she needed someone. He wasn't implying that she couldn't do it alone. But Matt knew what having someone to love and lean on felt like, and he hoped for her that one day she would find that happiness.

The paramedics had wheeled in a little old lady, swaddled in a blanket, strapped to a chair. Ambling along behind them, struggling to keep pace, was an elderly gent whom Matt presumed was the husband.

Tina, the paramedic, handed over the details. 'This is Patricia Hodgson. She's ninety-one years young and a resident at Castle House. Normally fit and well, Patricia was found this morning by her husband, Arthur, with a droop to the left side of her face and aphasia. A FAST test was positive. BP was ninety over sixty and pulse eighty-four. SATS were normal at ninety-five per cent, but oxygen therapy was given anyway. Patricia was diagnosed with Alzheimer's two years ago and has a previous history of breast cancer during her seventieth year.'

Matt thanked the paramedics and organised his team, including Brooke, to transfer Patricia from the chair to a bed so the ambulance crew could leave and get to their next job.

Patricia looked tiny and frail upon the bed, and he

noticed how gentle Brooke was with her as she covered the old lady's legs with a blanket and spoke gently to her, explaining what she was doing.

Patricia's husband, Arthur, stood off to one side, looking frightened and lost. 'Is she all right?' he asked in a frightened, gravelly voice.

Matt introduced himself to the husband. 'I'm Major Galloway and I'm going to be in charge of your wife's care, Mr Hodgson.'

'Arthur.'

'Arthur. It appears your wife has had a stroke and that the event has damaged the side of your wife's brain that deals with speech. I'm going to get her assessed quickly and then we'll get her off for a scan to see just what type of stroke she's had.'

'I just want her to be all right. She's frightened by strange places.'

Matt understood. For Alzheimer's patients, strange places that they did not know could cause undue stress. It was imperative that they keep everything as calm as they could.

'Perhaps you'd like to come and hold your wife's hand?' Brooke suggested.

'Won't I be getting in the way?'

'Not at all.'

Matt issued instructions to his team and watched as they all busied themselves around Mrs Hodgson, taking readings, assessments, and doing so in such a way that they did not upset their patient any more than she already was. The world was a confusing place for anyone with Alzheimer's, and not being able to communicate properly had to be an added upset. Not being able to find your memories was one thing. Not being able to find the right words for things must be torture.

When she was stable they took her to be scanned, to see if she'd had a bleed or whether there was a thrombus, or clot, that might need dissolving. A thrombolytic drug would do that, though there were dangers associated with its use.

'Is your wife on any medication that we should know about?' asked Brooke.

'Erm… I think she's on a statin, and something else, but she's not very good at taking them regularly. The nurses have a hard time getting her to swallow her medication. It's in this bag here.'

Arthur handed over to Brooke a small white paper bag that had various boxes in it. She passed it to Matt.

There weren't any drugs there to treat the Alzheimer's. There was no cure for the condition, although some drugs had been developed to try and slow down the progression of the disease. Matt noted the drugs that Arthur had brought in and wrote down his team's observations on Patricia's condition. It was all done within ten minutes of her arriving.

'Let's move her to Scanning, please,' Matt instructed.

They all walked together to the scanning room and watched as the images came down on the screens. A clot was noted in one of Patricia's smaller vessels and when they took her back to Majors department Matt discussed with Arthur the pros and cons of the thrombolytic.

'You do what you have to do, Doc.'

'Thank you. As your wife is unable to give me verbal consent, it's important that I get your permission. We'll give her the medication and then observe her closely.'

'And then she'll be able to talk to me again?'

Matt could hear the distress in the husband's voice. 'Hopefully.'

'She's all I've got. Me and her…we're the only ones

left. She doesn't always remember me, but when she does she likes to talk. Words are all we have. And music. Funny how she can remember song lyrics from the nineteen-forties yet not remember me.'

'Alzheimer's is a difficult condition. It chips away at people. From one day to the next you don't know which piece has been taken until suddenly it's not there any more.'

Arthur nodded, his face grim. 'When memories are all she has, it's heartbreaking when she loses them. Not for her, so much. But for me. I need her to still be *with* me, you know?'

Matt did know, and nodded solemnly. He administered the drug that Patricia needed and went to update his notes. When he came back to check on her Arthur was sitting next to her, holding her hand as she dozed.

'Are you married, Doctor?' Arthur asked.

How was he to answer that? Yes? No?

'I was. Once.'

Arthur turned to look at him through rheumy eyes, hidden behind thick glasses. 'Was it happy?'

Now, *that* was easier to answer. 'It was.'

'I've had sixty-three years with my Patty. Sixty-three glorious years. There were moments, I'm sure, when she would've liked to have had me done in, but mostly we got on. She was a wonderful wife.'

'She still is.'

The old man nodded and looked back to his beloved in the bed. 'Yes. She is, but...' He shook his head, rubbing at his brow with his free hand. 'I feel selfish sometimes. And cruel.'

Matt tried to work out what he meant. 'Why cruel?'

'Since she was diagnosed with the Alzheimer's I've had to say goodbye to my wife. For the last two years

I've watched her slowly vanish. There were times I wanted to shake her, to tell her it was *me*, her husband, to beg her for a moment when she might recognise me again. Then a few months back there came a day when she was lucid. She knew who she was, where she was, who I was—but the most horrible thing of all was that she knew what was wrong with her. What had happened to her and that soon she would be lost again. I've never seen my wife so terrified, Doctor. She grabbed my hands, begged me to stay with her until the end. Then, when the disease claimed her again, I was grateful. *Grateful!* And now all I want is for it to be over for her. So that it'll be over for me.'

Matt listened intently, understanding the man's pain. 'That's not selfishness. It's self-preservation. It's love. You don't want to see her suffer any more.'

Arthur met his gaze and nodded. 'I don't. I really don't. I've said goodbye so many times, thinking it was the end. Now, with the stroke, I wonder if it really is. Because I'm not sure I'm ready.'

'None of us are ever ready to say goodbye.'

He laid a reassuring hand on Arthur's shoulder and stood for a moment, watching Patricia's breathing. As he watched she opened her eyes a little and looked around the small bay in which she was situated, her gaze eventually falling on her husband.

'Arthur?'

Her husband grasped her hand. 'Oh! Patty!'

'Is it time for bed, yet, Arthur?'

'Oh, yes, my love! Yes, it is.'

Matt left them to have a moment alone and went to complete his notes. He sat at the desk, deep in thought.

Arthur had been saying goodbye for two years and it still wasn't enough time. And even though his situation was stressful Matt still felt that the man was lucky. He'd got to say goodbye. To hold his wife's hand. And no doubt when the time eventually came he would have the chance to be with her at the end.

Was he envious of Arthur?

As he considered this Brooke came into Majors with the results of Patty's blood tests.

'How is she?'

'Talking.'

'That's good. That's progress.'

'Yeah…'

He could feel her looking at him.

'Why so blue?'

'Because he gets to be with his wife as she nears the end. I never got that, and sometimes it just makes me feel like…'

'Like what?'

He laughed. 'Do you know what my wife's last words were?'

Brooke shook her head. 'I don't.'

'She was with her mum. Her mum had driven Jen to the hospital because of how unwell she was feeling. She was trying to be bright and optimistic, as she always was, and apparently the last conversation they had was about whether Jen should get her nose pierced.'

He looked at Brooke to see her reaction.

She smiled. 'That's good.'

'Good?'

'Yeah. Because she was talking about normal stuff. Everyday stuff. She didn't spend her last few minutes of consciousness terrified and crying. She was being herself. So…that's good.'

He looked back at the old couple, clutching each other's hands and staring into each other's eyes. 'I never thought about it like that before.'

Brooke glanced over at Arthur and Patty too. 'They seem very dedicated to each other.'

'He said they've been together for sixty-three years. I can't even imagine what that might feel like.'

'Sixty-three years of marriage?' Brooke sighed, supporting her chin on the back of her hand as she leant against the desk. 'I think that would be comfortable. Warm and snug, like a nest. All those years, all that *history*, surrounding you both like a safety net.'

'You're a romantic, Dr Bailey!'

She smiled at him, before her gaze returned to the couple in front of them. 'And a dreamer. But don't we all hope and dream for happiness in some way?'

Matt didn't answer. He stared at her profile—at the way her nose turned up slightly at the end, the fullness of her smiling lips, the gentle way one brown tress of her hair had escaped its messy bun and rested upon her shoulder. It looked soft and silky, and it seemed wrong to him that someone as sweet and lovely as her should be alone when clearly she had so much love to give.

He concentrated for a moment on his notes. *Blood pressure. Respirations. Pulse. Patient.* But his mind wouldn't stay focused. It was as if there was a small cyclone of thoughts whizzing around in there, picking up the leaves of his thoughts and tossing them into the mix—Jen, Brooke, Jen, Brooke.

Lily.

Yes. His daughter had to be his priority. Worrying about Brooke's love-life was not his responsibility. Nothing to do with him. She was his friend, but that was all she would ever be. He couldn't allow himself to think any more of her than that.

But if that was the case then why was the thought of her the only thing he could concentrate on?

Patricia recovered well, and after a few days spent in the hospital was returned to Castle House residential care, with Arthur still at her side.

Matt had watched them go, envious and yet also happy for Arthur and his wife. They still had precious days together, despite the Alzheimer's. Patricia was still there. Arthur could hear her voice. See her. Touch her.

It was a gift. And having met the two of them was giving him a new outlook on life. Yes, he still missed Jen. He always would—no doubt about it. But he had to be thankful for the short time they'd had together, and more than anything he had to be thankful for Lily and his friends and colleagues.

They were still here. They were here to talk to and spend time with. There was no point in locking himself away just because he felt alone. He had a duty to enjoy life. He'd promised Jen that he would. He'd promised to honour Jen's wish to help Brooke and Morgan. He was *still living*.

His wife, who had embraced life and fun and happiness, would not have wanted to think of him pining away for her. She would have wanted him to be out and about, showing their daughter the wonders of the world. Proving to her that the world was a beautiful place and that she was loved and cherished. Lily was the centre of his universe and he owed her that.

So he tried not to feel guilty each time he smiled, or laughed, or forgot about his grief. He tried not to dwell on it. Sometimes that was difficult. Especially late at night when he was alone and it would make him feel bad.

Keeping busy helped. When Lily was in bed, he'd

start on his DIY projects. He'd finally got around to fixing that wonky kitchen cupboard, finally shaved a few millimetres off the bottom of the lounge door, replaced the broken tiles in the bathroom and repainted the main bedroom. He'd taught himself how to cook some recipes he'd never tried before, and given himself permission to relax and read all those books he'd never got around to.

At work he was trying to be more available for those people around him. He sat with them in the staffroom more, rather than returning to his office alone, he joined in with staff sweepstakes and signed up to do quiz nights and charity runs. He knew that everyone had noticed the change in him and it had made him smile inside.

After much thought, he'd finally removed his wedding ring. It now sat on his bedside table, where he could look at it each night and remember the day it had first been put on his finger.

And yet throughout it all he still sometimes felt a little lonely. Despite being surrounded by smiling faces, by people who knew him and cared for him. He still felt alone.

Brooke in particular, kept asking him if he was all right.

'I'm fine.'

'Really?'

'Absolutely.'

'Because usually when *I* say *I'm fine*, it means something else. Like, *Please leave me alone. I'm pretending to be okay.*'

He smiled at her. 'I really am okay. I'm…embracing all that life has to offer.'

'Are you?' She looked at him, assessing him, and he grew hot under her gaze.

'Yes.'

'You're still coming to the fireworks night this weekend?'

A pause. Then, 'Yes.'

'You don't sound that thrilled about it.'

'Dr Bailey, I am most definitely looking forward to coming with you and the lovely Morgan to the fireworks display. Lily will love it.'

She narrowed her eyes at him, her eyebrows wiggling, and it made him laugh.

Brooke smiled. 'That's better.'

'What is?'

'You laughing. You look better that way.'

'How do I look when I'm *not* laughing?'

She paused to consider her answer. 'Thoughtful. Brooding...'

He noticed her blush, which she quickly tried to cover up by taking a sip of tea from an oversized mug. What else had she been about to say?

It was probably best to spare her blushes and change the subject. 'How's Morgan getting on? Still teething?'

She nodded quickly, grateful for the change of topic. 'Yes, but she's not as grouchy about it now. The teething gel has been helping.'

'Lily got a tooth through just last night. She was so much happier when it was over. I got some sleep, anyway.'

Brooke smiled, but he realised it wasn't one of her usual smiles. It didn't light up her eyes the way it usually did. In fact she still looked a little perturbed by whatever she'd been thinking about when she'd mentioned how he was looking.

Odd...

Was she looking *guilty*? It was kind of reassuring to

know he wasn't the only one who succumbed to guilt occasionally. But why would she feel guilty about *him*?

Unless…

Oh…

Eager to make her feel more comfortable, he got up. 'Well, I must get a move on. There are plenty of patients in the waiting room.'

She downed the rest of her tea and stood up, too. Just as eager, it seemed, to get past this little awkward moment as he was. 'Yes. My patient should be back from X-ray by now.'

'Anything interesting?'

'Just a query fracture of a metatarsal. He accidentally kicked a metal post.'

'Right. Okay. Well, I'll see you later, Dr Bailey.'

'Yes.'

She looked at him a little uncertainly and the only thing he could think of to do was give her a brief nod before he walked away. His heart was pounding, though, and his mouth was dry. But now he was away from her he could breathe.

Just what was that all about?

A simple conversation. Completely innocent. And then…*something.*

Determined to ignore it—perhaps he'd imagined something that hadn't actually been there?—he scooped up the next triage file and went to call his patient. Patients were good. Patients were intriguing. You could get lost in their problems as you diagnosed them.

And they'll damn well help stop me obsessing about Brooke!

Brooke stared at the X-ray on her computer screen, absently biting at her thumbnail. Her patient was lucky.

There was no fracture anywhere to be seen. The kick had obviously just caused a soft tissue injury and that was responsible for the bruising and swelling. He'd just need rest, painkillers, and to put his foot up when he could.

If only she could diagnose herself as easily.

Something weird had just happened with Matt. Something odd. They'd been talking about whether they really felt fine, and she'd mentioned that he usually looked thoughtful, and brooding. And then...

She grimaced. *Sexy.* She thought he looked *sexy*! And as she'd realised that thought her body had leapt into overdrive. Her heart had begun to pound, she'd blushed like a teenager talking to her crush and her body had begun to tingle in all sorts of places! The kind of places that she hadn't used since giving birth to Morgan. And realising that, becoming aware of all that, had made her feel incredibly...what? Mad? Guilty? *Aroused?*

How could she be aroused by him? He was Jen's husband! He was totally off the market and not available, and quite frankly ought to have *Do Not Touch* signs draped around his neck, but...

Brooke groaned out loud.

'Something wrong?' Kelly peered at her from across the desktop.

Yes. She was wrong. She couldn't feel that way about him. Not *him*! What kind of friend did that make her?

'Everything,' she said.

'Oh, dear. Come on, spill—tell me all the grisly details.'

She looked at Kelly. She was another good friend.

Married. Happily. Was Brooke going to end up fancy-ing *her* husband, too?

'I hate myself.'

Kelly laughed. 'Oh, right. It's one of *those* days. I've got chocolate, if you need it. Whatever it is shall pass, don't you worry.'

'You promise?'

'Absolutely. Whatever it is will go away. Just like magic.'

Brooke wasn't too sure if that was true. Because now she'd admitted her thoughts to herself it was as if her mind was scrolling through all her previous interactions with Matt and she could see the subtle flirting that had been going on the whole time. Well, maybe not *flirting,* but she could sense in herself all those moments that she'd really *looked* at him and felt *something.*

So would it pass? Or was it something that had been inside her ever since she and Matt had met in the hospi-tal crèche? Had it been bubbling away inside of her im-perceptibly, the pressure slowly rising, until now she'd become aware of the heat?

Because it certainly felt as if she had a furnace in-side her right now, and it was making her feel dreadful. Because what about Jen? Her memory? Lily? Morgan? She and Matt were *parents.* They both had their priori-ties, they both had excellent reasons for staying away from each other, and yet...

I've invited him out. To a fireworks night. I should never have done that! And he doesn't want to go. I can tell that he doesn't. He's just trying to be nice and...

Brooke knew what she had to do. Standing up abruptly, making her chair skid away from her slightly, she turned to Kelly. 'Where's Major Galloway?'

'Minors, I think.'

'Right.'

She went off to find him. Her chin jutting out with determination, her mind set on what she had to do to put this right. To end this nonsense here and now so that she and Matt could go back to being just colleagues.

As she passed the curtained cubicles she could hear his voice talking to a patient about what caused gout, and his dulcet tones, dark and soft, sent shivers down her spine. Good shivers. The kind that—

She opened the curtain slightly and popped her head in. 'Sorry to interrupt you, Major, but might I have a quick word with you when you're finished here?'

He turned to her, smiling. A smile that lit up her heart and confused her all the more.

'Sure.'

'Thanks.'

She closed the curtain and stood there, her eyes closed tightly, as she concentrated on her breathing. This was getting ridiculous. He was just a friend. *Just. A. Friend.*

She set off to see her patient with the damaged foot to give him the good news. He seemed mightily relieved not to have broken anything, but she sent him home with some crutches and instructions to stay off the foot for about a week. As she typed her patient notes into the computer she sensed rather than saw Matt arrive beside her.

'What's up?'

Her fingers froze over the keyboard as she sucked up a rallying breath. 'Bonfire Night.'

'Yes?'

'You don't want to go. I know you don't. So I'm let-

ting you off the hook. You don't have to go with me. I'll
be perfectly all right on my own with Morgan.'

He looked at her askance. 'Are you okay?'

She nodded quickly, smiling. 'I'm fine!'

Matt raised an eyebrow. 'Ah, yes—the *I'm fine* response.'

Then he laid a hand on her shoulder—supposedly
in a friendly gesture, but to her it was something else.
Something that was doing weird and wonderful tricks
with her insides.

'I *want* to go with you. It'll be…good for me. Honestly. And I want Lily to enjoy it. Is that okay?'

*He's touching me. His hand is just millimetres away
from my skin…*

She couldn't tear her eyes away from her paperwork.
Afraid that if she looked into his eyes right now she'd
be at risk of losing any last crumb of self-control she
had. There were fireworks going off inside *her*, never
mind at any display. Her skin felt as if it was sizzling.
Sizzling! How had that happened? *Why* was it happening? And how the hell could she get herself out of this
predicament?

*I'm just going to have to keep my distance. Go with
him to the display and make sure I keep a buggy's distance between us at all times. Oh, and not look at him.
Because if he smiles at me then I'm done for.*

'Okay,' she croaked.

He let go of her and returned to his patient, and she
was finally able to breathe once more.

CHAPTER SIX

HE SHOULD NEVER have touched her like that. He'd suspected that maybe she was feeling a little attracted to him and he to her, but then it had gone out of his mind as he'd talked to his patient about uric acid and crystals and—

He'd reached for her to show her that it meant a lot to him that she should ask him to come to the fireworks display. Not just him, but Lily too. And yet the second he'd laid his hand on her he'd realised—too late—just what touching her was doing to him!

He'd let go as quickly as he could. Had turned away so he could gather himself and get his racing heart under control.

Bonfire Night for him wasn't just about sharing an evening with her. About watching a firework display in the sky. He was trying to get over something. To face up to his fears. To expose himself to something that he just knew was going to be difficult.

He didn't want to be afraid any more.

Bonfire Night was harmless. He kept trying to reason with himself. Nothing dangerous in it at all. Harmless rockets and cheap thrills, that was all. A few loud noises. Surely he could cope with that?

But now there was the other danger. Spending time

with Brooke. Standing by her side, huddled close to her in the cold night, both of them staring up at the sky. She would be smiling and pointing things out to Morgan and he would be...

Matt sighed. He'd promised Jen's memory that he would show Lily the world. That he would not hide her from it. That they would continue to survive without her. That they would not pine, would not spend their life grieving. That they would join in, partake, engage. That he would be there for Brooke and Morgan the way Jen could not.

But there had to be a line. A line he would not cross no matter how she made him feel.

Lily was his world. He could not confuse her like that. Not that she understood, at this age, that she didn't have a mother.

But *he* did. He knew. And he wasn't looking for a replacement. He never would. It was just going to be Lily and him. And friends. Brooke would be a good friend, but nothing more.

He didn't want to admit that he felt disappointment at the thought. That he even felt a little sad. Brooke made his heart race. Her smile lit up his world and he felt good spending time with her. She made him feel safe and warm. She was easy to be with and he loved the way she laughed. It was infectious.

But it was scary how she made him question himself. His principles. His moral duty to uphold the memory of his wife and be respectful of how recently he'd lost her. Not even a year had passed yet!

Here he was, spending time with a wonderful woman, enjoying her company, feeling his heart racing madly, unable to pull his gaze away from her. And it was making him disturbed and afraid and guilty in equal measures.

Was it wrong? To be this close to her?

Whatever the answer was, it would have to wait. The fireworks display was tonight and he would be meeting Brooke there at six. The show started at six-thirty, which was perfect, because by the time it was over they wouldn't be too late putting the babies down for their bedtimes.

Lily's schedule was very important to him. She didn't have too many certainties in this world, but she did have a bedtime, and set naptimes and set feeds. Imposing a solid structure on her had helped him in those painful early days when he'd still been struggling with the loss of his wife. The hours of the day all checked off in a reassuring routine.

For now he was sitting on the floor with her, watching her play with soft, squishy bricks, babbling away as streams of saliva fell down her chin onto the bib that seemed permanently attached recently.

'We're going to see some fireworks tonight, Lily. Big, pretty lights and things that go bang. You'll like that. Yes, you will. Daddy won't, but you will. And you'll keep me strong, won't you? You always have.'

Lily looked up at him and smiled, a bubble forming at the corner of her mouth as she threw one block down on the floor. It bounced and rolled to him.

He picked it up and rolled it back, causing Lily to squeal with joy.

Such simple things. It didn't take much to make her happy. She was such an easy-going baby. Jen would have been so proud of her, their sweet little girl.

'I think I might put earplugs in—what do you think? Will that help?'

Lily offered him another brick.

'Too big, honey.' He smiled at her and took the brick and, delighted, tried to clap her hands together, slightly missing.

He envied the easy joy of babies. They didn't seem to need much. They didn't seem to have cares or worries. They didn't know great pain or suffering. It was a pity that they all couldn't live in such simple terms.

He briefly wondered what Brooke was doing now. Was she sitting at home too, waiting for tonight? She was probably excited about it. She loved fireworks. He wished he had her enthusiasm.

It would seem that I am not content with my lot.

That bothered him. The fact that he felt something was missing but couldn't pinpoint it. He was healthy, he had a good job, a secure home, a beautiful baby girl. He should be happy. Satisfied.

But it was loneliness that impaired his wellbeing. He'd never been solitary before. He'd never imagined he would have to be. And yet here he was, counting down the hours until he could be with someone again. Someone who lifted his spirits and made him feel good.

Was that so wrong?

Or was he terrified in case it was right?

Brooke was counting down the hours. She'd been looking forward to this for a long time. Bonfire Night—one of the best nights of the year! It never lasted long, but there was nothing quite like forgetting all your worries and standing in the crisp, chilly evening, watching the amazing show up above.

It was carefree. There weren't many moments in life during which you could be carefree, but the night of November the fifth was one of them. And she had one particular fond memory of that night from childhood, when her dad had actually been sober enough to enjoy it with her.

She'd stood there, aged maybe seven or eight, and as the first fireworks had zoomed up into the sky, to explode in a mass of blue and green sparkles, she'd felt her dad slip his hand into hers and squeeze her fingers through her woollen mitten. Such a simple thing, but coming from a man who had been using alcohol to escape the grief he felt it had been an uplifting moment. Brooke had squeezed back and laid her head against his arm, her face turned up to the sky as she'd revelled in that singular moment in which her dad had seemed to say, *I'm here, sweetheart.*

They'd stood together holding hands for about half an hour, and then, when the display had been over, he'd walked her home, settled her into bed and then gone in search of his next drink. The loneliness of being at home without his wife's voice, his wife's presence, had been too much for him to bear.

She'd lived for those brief moments in which he reached out to her. But more often than not he hadn't. He'd told her once in a drunken rage that she looked too much like her mother and it was painful for him to look at her. That had broken her heart. But what could she do? She couldn't change her face, and though she'd tried dyeing her hair different colours she'd never liked the way she looked as a blonde, or a redhead, and had always reverted back to her long brown hair.

When she'd had Morgan she'd vowed to herself that no matter how much her daughter reminded her of Eric she would never blame her daughter for it. Even if every one of her features matched her father's and looked little to do with her mother she would love her child.

She would treasure her always. She would never let her daughter feel that type of rejection from anyone.

But she did hope that her daughter would enjoy fireworks as much as she did. For a child they were magical and special, as long as they weren't afraid of the loud noises. She'd heard that tonight's display was going to be extra-special—the fireworks were going to be set in time to music. How amazing was *that* going to be?

Once again she checked she had everything ready. Warm clothes, tights and ear muffs for Morgan, fleece-lined boots, a thick cardigan and woolly hat, mittens for her. Perfect. She didn't want Morgan getting cold. There would probably be hot drinks available for adults, but not for babies!

And Matt would be coming.

Brooke let out a long, slow breath. She'd tried her hardest to let him off the hook, to tell him he didn't have to come with her, but he'd seemed determined. She liked it that he was sure he wanted to go, because at first she'd thought he wasn't. But now that she was experiencing these weird feelings about him she wasn't sure how she'd cope spending all that time with him. Away from work. Where people were relaxed and uninhibited.

She hoped and prayed she wouldn't do something stupid. Like gaze into his eyes for too long, or accidentally brush his hand, or—worse—*kiss him!* Because, heck, even though the *thought* of kissing Matt did spectacular, exciting things to her insides, she knew in the long run that it would be a mistake.

He was a widower. Still grieving. He was *off-limits*. It ought to be the law of the land that handsome, charming widowers should not be hit on for at least one year after their partner's passing, surely!

And she was going to be spending this special night

with him. Perhaps it wasn't all that special to him, though. Perhaps it was just her? Remembering the night that her father had finally seen her, reliving her childish excitement? Whereas for Matt perhaps it was just another night—a few bangs, a few lights, a waste of money going up in smoke. No doubt pretty, but he'd be happy for it to be over, so they could look forward to the *real* best night of the year—Christmas Eve.

Who knew? What she *did* know was that she couldn't let giddy excitement get the better of her. Carry her away on a frivolous impulse to do something stupid. Because—and she must make no mistake—doing *something stupid* with Matt would be appallingly embarrassing. They would have to work together afterwards, and she highly doubted that Matt would be receptive to her lips touching his.

No.

She would need to concentrate and keep her wits about her.

No forgetting his boundaries.

And no kissing Major Galloway!

The place was heaving with people waiting for the display to start. At first Brooke couldn't see Matt at all. Too many bodies…too many people bundled up in unfamiliar thick coats. She thought maybe he'd had a change of heart. Hadn't come after all. The disappointment that shot through her almost winded her. Until finally—suddenly—she spotted him. It was almost as if the crowd parted just for them.

Their eyes met and she sucked in a breath.

He's here.

The breath allowed her a moment to steady herself, get her heartbeat under control again. Back to its normal pace—or as near as she could make it. But his proximity, his singular presence, was having an effect on her. He looked particularly dark and dangerous in that black jacket, and his cobalt scarf brought out the sparkling blue of his eyes. Both his and Lily's cheeks already looked a little rosy in what was for her the perfect November evening. Crisp. Cold. With the promise of a frost tomorrow morning. He hadn't shaved either. She'd never seen him with stubble before and it added a certain delicious note to his appearance.

'You made it,' she said as he made his way through the throng towards her, using Lily's buggy like a plough.

Brooke saw various women notice him, just as they had at that awful Music Melody class, their eyes glinting in the darkness, hoping that he might notice them.

Only he didn't. He kept his gaze upon her, his face breaking into a smile as he got close. 'Just. I've been looking all over for you. I even considered putting up a flare.'

She smiled. 'No need for that.'

'No.'

She bent to say hello to Lily, who was sitting in her buggy kicking and swinging her feet as she batted hopelessly at the string of toys across the front of it. Like Morgan, she was wearing ear muffs. 'Hello, little one. Are you ready for all the pretty fireworks?'

'Bah-bah... Mmm... Pfft!'

Brooke smiled at her and looked up at Matt.

'I feel the same,' he added.

'Oh, really?' she stood up again and fought the urge to nudge his arm playfully. What was happening? One minute with the man and she was already feeling flirty.

Stop it, Brooke.

'How...erm...close do you want to get?' She meant

to the fireworks, but as soon as the words were out of her mouth she cringed.

'Er...not too close. You know—just in case the babies don't like it.'

He seemed apprehensive. Had he picked up on her feelings? Was he already at this minute regretting his decision to come out with her because she was starting to act like some crazy woman?

Because, looking at him right now, she saw he looked as if he wanted to run out of there. His gaze was flitting here, there and everywhere, as if checking for exit strategies. Only occasionally did his gaze fall upon her, as if to reassure her that, yes, of *course* he wanted to be here.

Everything about him—his face, his twitching jaw muscle, his body language—screamed that he wanted out. That this was the last place he wanted to be.

Brooke felt as if she was torturing the man by making him stay. Keen for him not to walk away and leave her standing there like an idiot, though, she sought to reassure him. 'It should start soon. Not long now.'

'That's great.' He stooped to pick Lily up out of her buggy and, thinking that was a good idea, she did the same thing with Morgan. At least holding her child she would have no spare hand to snuggle into his.

Both babies greeted each other by squealing and vaguely waving their arms in some approximation of saying hello, causing both parents to beam.

'I think they recognise each other!'

'I should think so. After all the time they spend together in the crèche. Daisy tells me they're quite the terrible twosome.'

Daisy was right. Brooke had seen them when she'd gone to the crèche to pick up her daughter after a long day. She'd often found Lily and Morgan playing side by side, or squealing with joy in the ball pit together. It was almost as if they were sisters.

'Should we get a drink or anything? Are you thirsty? I think they're selling hot chocolate somewhere.'

Matt shook his head. 'No spare hands for a hot drink. I'll survive, thanks.'

She nodded. He was right. They could hardly hold the girls *and* a steaming hot beverage. That would be a disaster.

All around them couples huddled together, and there was the aroma of hot chocolate, tea, coffee, and from somewhere jacket potatoes with beans was being served. It all reminded Brooke of Bonfire Nights from long ago, when her neighbours had cooked jacket potatoes in tin foil and served polystyrene cups filled with hot mushy peas and vinegar. There was something amazing about those familiar smells under the cloudless night sky.

From somewhere a PA system squealed into life and a man's voice welcomed them to the show. There was a little bit of housekeeping—they were told to stay behind the barrier at all times, given fire escape plans in case something dreadful happened, that kind of thing—and then his voice fell silent and a musical symphony began.

Brooke felt her heart accelerate. This was it! The moment they'd all been waiting for. She turned to look at Matt, to smile at him, and frowned slightly, noticing he looked rather hesitant and apprehensive.

But before she could say anything the fireworks began, screaming up into the night sky and pulling her attention away from Matt.

The colours lit up the night sky—pinks, purples, reds, greens, blues. There was a cacophony of explosions from rockets and sparkling glitter balls, whistling comets scattering light like flowers in bursts that split into smaller blasts—all of it to a background of music, the fireworks and the noise perfectly in time with the beat and rhythm.

Morgan was squealing with joy, clapping her little hands together, and Brooke was over the moon that her daughter loved it as much as she did! Her little face was lit up by the display above her.

'You love it! You *love it!*'

She turned to see if Lily loved it too, and was jolted from her bliss when she saw Matt standing there, frozen like a statue, his eyes tightly closed, his face screwed up as if he was in some sort of agony...

'Major? *Matt?* Are you all right?'

She grabbed at his arm to make him look at her, but he didn't open his eyes. He was muttering something to himself. Over and over. But she couldn't catch it. Couldn't make out what he was saying.

Hesitantly she reached up to lay a hand on his face. Standing close to him, almost face to face, she said loudly, '*Matt!* Open your eyes. Look at me. It's okay. Just look at me.'

She was scared. What was going on? Why did he look so terrified? He was an army doctor! He should be used to this kind of thing. He should—

And then realisation came to the fore and she knew what was wrong.

How could I have been so stupid?

Quickly she turned and put Morgan back into her buggy, strapping her in. She could still see the fireworks, but right now she needed to bring Matt back into the present. Because his mind was elsewhere. Stuck in a terrifying past event. She had to centre him. Ground him in reality.

Concerned for Lily, she raised her voice so he could hear her. 'Matt? It's Brooke. Give me Lily. Let go of her. I've got her. That's it...'

She took the little girl and placed her in her own buggy. Strapped her in.

Then she turned back to Matt, placing a hand on either side of his face. 'Matt?' She waited a moment, torn with anguish at the look of pain on his face. *'Matt...'*

He opened his eyes, his gaze frantic until he tuned in to her voice and then it settled upon her.

As the fireworks continued above them, the bangs and cracks and whistling sound of gunpowder crackling all around them, people whooping and oohing at the sight, Brooke stood in front of Matt, her hands on his face, and made him look at her.

'Keep your eyes on me. You're okay. I've got you. They're just fireworks. They're not what you think they are. You're safe, Matt. Do you hear me? You're *safe.*'

His frightened gaze settled on her own and fixed upon her. 'I... I hear you. I'm s-s-safe.'

'Put your hands on Lily's buggy. That's it. Now, just listen to my voice and follow me. We're going to move away from here. But slowly! No need for us to rush. We're safe.'

She saw his hands were trembling, but he followed her orders.

Feeling sick, and guilty at what she'd put him through, she led the way out through the crowd, away from the field and onto the pathway, and then the road, over to where she had parked her car and beyond.

There was a small café lighting up the street, still decorated with spider's webs and pumpkins from Halloween a few nights earlier. They went in and settled down at a table.

Brooke ordered a couple of teas from the waitress and gave Morgan a sippy cup of juice from her bag. Then she sat opposite Matt and took his freezing cold hands in her own and waited. Waited for him to be able to speak.

He looked a little worn out, but not embarrassed, which was good. For there was no shame in what had happened.

When the drinks arrived she added plenty of sugar to his and pushed the cup in front of him. 'Drink,' she ordered.

He reached for the cup and took a small sip, wincing at the sweetness. 'Thanks.'

'Is it okay if I give Lily a rusk?'

He nodded and took another sip before he looked up at her face and grimaced. 'I'm sorry I spoilt your night.'

Brooke shook her head. 'No. You didn't spoil it. It was *my* fault. I should have thought that you might have... I didn't know. I don't know where you were stationed, or what happened, but I should have considered the possibility.'

'The PTSD...it's...mild, actually. I hardly notice it until nights like these.' He glanced out of the window at the display that was still thrilling all the onlookers. 'I should have said something when you asked me to the fireworks, but I thought I could tough it out. For Lily.' He laughed ruefully. 'They're just fireworks, right?'

Post-traumatic stress disorder could be a crippling condition. It was an anxiety disorder brought on by a previous stressful, frightening or distressing event. Someone suffering from the condition would often re-live that event through flashbacks brought on by triggers in the present day.

'Do you want to talk about it?'

She couldn't get his face out of her mind. The way he had looked as she had held his face in her hands. The way he had felt frozen, chilled by the night air and paralysed by fear. She didn't ever want to see him go through that again. And *she'd* caused it. By bringing him here.

If there was one thing her father had taught her it was that you avoided pain as much as you could. You evaded it, you did what you had to not to face it. The fact that Matt had chosen to come here anyway, knowing how the fireworks might affect him, made her feel proud of him. This wasn't a man who ran away from things that hurt. He was brave, and she wanted to be there for him because of that.

'I was pinned down by enemy fire in Afghanistan. We'd been ambushed. I was part of a medevac team. We weren't heavily armed—we'd been treating the locals, offering vaccinations and first aid, and then we were asked to relocate to help re-staff a field hospital. Twelve men and women were killed when the first trucks blew. Men and women I knew. Had worked alongside. People who just wanted to help, no matter who they were— English, American, locals. It didn't matter. People were people, you know?'

She nodded, listening.

'I dragged a soldier out of the road. He'd been hit in the leg and was bleeding heavily. He was screaming. We found shelter and we had to sit there. Waiting for hours. All around us there was the sound of gunfire and explosions. It just never stopped. I sat there, shivering in the freezing cold, not knowing whether I would live to see the sun rise. And all that time the shooting never stopped. I could hear bullets hitting the walls next to my head. Could hear people shouting. Yelling. Calling for help. But I was pinned down. I couldn't do anything to help them.'

She reached across the table to lay her hand upon his. 'I'm so sorry.'

'It was combat. It happened. It's just hard for me being outside at night, and then the sounds of all those fireworks going off... I...'

He didn't have to say any more. Didn't have to explain. She understood. Could see why tonight had affected him so. But still he had come to spend time with her. Honouring his wife's promise to her friend to be there for her despite the risk to himself.

That meant a lot to her. More than she could put into words. Because no one had ever been there for her like that. No one had ever put aside their own pain like that to be there for *her*. Not her father. No one.

He pulled his hand out from under hers and took hold of her hand, squeezing her fingers in thanks. 'You called me Matt.'

She blushed, nodded with a smile. 'I did.'

'Thank you.'

Unsure of how to respond, she sipped her own tea. 'I've put you through a lot tonight. I'd hate to think of you going home to your own place and being on your own after all of this. I have a spare bed at mine. And a travel cot that Lily could sleep in. Just so you're not alone tonight. If you want.'

She fully expected him to turn her down, but she really did hate the idea that he would have to go home alone after this. She knew what the nights were like once you'd put the baby to bed. Solitude could hit you like a brick. The house was empty. No sounds save for the ticking of a clock to remind you of your life passing with no one else in it.

Matt might be alone, but he had her as a friend and she wanted him to know that. It was an innocent invitation. One friend to another.

Please don't be alone tonight. I can be there for you like you were for me.

'Oh…that's really kind, but—'

'Please. I'd really like it if you came. Tomorrow is Sunday—neither of us have to work. We could spend the day doing something nice. Replace this memory with a good one. Lily can borrow Morgan's clothes if you don't have enough with you, and I have nappies and bottles and baby food. I even have a spare toothbrush.'

She was smiling, trying to think of all the reasons he might say he couldn't do it. She really wanted to spend this time with him. He'd done so much for her.

'You'd have to turn your underwear inside out, but…' She blushed, laughing. 'Come on—it'll be fun.'

He was smiling back at her. 'You've thought of everything.'

'I'm ambushing you again. But hopefully in a good way.'

Matt nodded. 'Okay. That'll be nice. A sleepover! I haven't done one of those since I was about eight years old.'

Brooke smiled back, pleased that he'd accepted. 'I don't think the concept has changed. You stay up late watching movies and eating popcorn. Or I can provide wine, if you need it.'

'I don't really touch alcohol, but I'll have cocoa if you have any?'

His cuteness broadened the grin on her face. 'Cocoa it is.'

Matt made her happy.

Very happy indeed.

And she was glad that she could make him smile. Especially after tonight. Outside, the fireworks were still raging in the sky, but not for much longer. They would leave when it was all over and the streets were filled with happy families.

For now she was content to sit in the café with him, nursing her tea with him still holding her hand.

It felt good. His touch. And even though earlier she'd been determined to keep her distance from him his contact now made her feel completely different.

They were people. People were tactile. They expressed care and affection through touch, didn't they? A hug to make people feel better. A hand on another to say, *I'm here for you. I care. You matter to me.*

And Major Matt Galloway mattered to her very much indeed.

CHAPTER SEVEN

'So this is home sweet home?' Matt carried Lily into Brooke's house and followed her through to the lounge. He hadn't known what to expect, but now that he was here he could see that it suited her perfectly.

It was just a two-bedroomed flat, in a tall tower of concrete and glass, but inside she had turned it into a perfect little retreat. He'd never had the eye of an interior designer, but he wished that he had. Dr Bailey had clearly known the kind of feeling she had wanted here.

There were comfy sofas covered in scatter cushions with cosy throws draped over the back. A bookcase in the corner was filled with well-thumbed books, and next to it was a lamp draped with a silk scarf, a recliner and a small cherry-red table piled high with more books. There was a small fireplace, filled with candles rather than coal, and protected by a screen so that Morgan couldn't get close. On the walls were soft watercolour paintings of animals, but instead of being portrayed in the normal colours of brown and grey they were pink and blue and rainbow-coloured.

It was a happy room. A cosy room. It oozed warmth and comfort.

'I like what you've done with the place. Love the artwork.'

'Thanks.'

He went over to a painting of a swan, created with brush strokes of green and blue, peering closer at it. Then he turned to look at her in surprise. '*You* painted these?'

'I'm just an amateur, but I like painting.'

'They're brilliant! If ever we run out of patients in A&E you've got another career you can fall back on.'

'Well, as I don't see A&E emptying soon, the art world has a lot to be grateful for.'

She went to put Morgan down, aware that both babies would need to go to bed soon. She opened the storage cupboard by the front door and pulled out the travel cot that she'd been given but never used yet. It would be perfect for Lily to sleep in.

Scrunching up her nose, she undid the straps and worked out how to open it. Thankfully it was easy. and she set it up in no time. 'I'll put this in the spare room. Morgan's cot is in my bedroom, so she shouldn't wake you.'

'I probably need to change Lily. Have you got a place I can do that?'

'There's a changing station in your room, or I've got a mat you can borrow if you don't have one.'

'Thanks. I'll give Lily her last bottle and then get her ready for bed.'

'Same.'

They both busied themselves settling their daughters. Brooke ran a bath, so that the two girls could have a bit of a splash, and once that was done they gave the babies their bottles and settled them to sleep.

Morgan settled quickly, as usual, so Brooke had a bit of a tidy-up whilst she waited for Matt to emerge from what would be his room for the night.

She felt strangely on edge. As if she'd had a shot of adrenaline. She used it to clean the kitchen, being quite thorough, lifting things to wipe underneath, pulling out the toaster, making sure there were no crumbs left behind, wiping down the fridge handles—that kind of thing. It seemed easier to think about what needed doing than to think about how it would be to sit down with Matt in her *home*.

No man had ever made it back here since she'd left Eric. Even *he* had only seen the place a couple of times, preferring to spend time in his own place and make her come to him.

She liked it that it was her sanctuary. Her book nook. A warm, welcoming space that was just for her and Morgan. Their bolthole from the world.

To have Matt here felt…odd. But good.

Brooke rinsed out the sink and then filled the kettle to make them both a hot drink. Just as the kettle came to the boil Matt joined her in the kitchen.

'Finally! Thought she'd never settle.'

'She's in a strange place. Different bedroom, different bed—she was bound to be a little unsettled.'

He nodded. 'Thanks again for offering to put up with us for the entire weekend.'

She smiled at him. 'Not a problem. Kettle's boiled. Still up for that cocoa?'

'If you're having one.'

'Cocoa it is.'

'Thanks. I know I said it earlier, but this really is a great place you have here.'

She spooned cocoa powder into mugs. 'Thanks. It was important to me to get it right. It's the first space I've owned that's truly mine.'

'You've only lived with your father?'

'If *lived* is the right word for it, then, yeah. *Co-existed* might be more precise.' She added sugar and a splash of milk, then poured in the hot water.

'What was he like? Before, I mean…'

Brooke appreciated him not actually saying *before he became an alcoholic* out loud. She sighed, her back to him as she stirred the drinks. 'He was an artist. A good one.'

'Really? Watercolours like yours?'

'No. Acrylics, mostly.'

'What sort of thing did he paint?'

She turned to hand him his drink. 'I'll show you. Come with me.'

She led him through to the lounge area and settled onto one of the couches. She picked up the tablet that she'd left charging by the side of it. She typed the name Phillip Bailey into a search engine and various artwork soon showed up in the results.

A yellow buttercup sprouting through a solitary crack of cement; a rose growing in the middle of a desert; a vibrant tree with thick green foliage living in a wasteland desolated by war.

'He painted hope.'

'Hope?'

'He wanted to show that even in the darkest places life could grow. That beauty and joy could still be found in places you wouldn't expect.'

'They're amazing. Does he still paint?'

'He hasn't touched his palette since my mother died.'

Matt was silent for a moment, staring at the pictures, enlarging one that showed a flowering water lily in an oil slick. 'He lost his belief system?'

Brooke nodded. 'Yes.'

'When devastation struck him he couldn't see the

flowers right before him? He couldn't see the light any more?'

'There wasn't any,' she said.

Matt turned to face her. 'But there was. There was *you*.'

Her? No. Matt was wrong. She'd never been her father's guiding light. His North Star. *Never*.

Her confusion must have shown on her face, because Matt went on.

'I've been where he has. We've both lost our wives and I know how that must have made him feel. Words can't describe it. To lose someone suddenly. Without warning. The one person who brightened your day inexplicably taken away. And suddenly there's this new person. This tiny newborn person who needs you the most, even as your heart is open, bleeding and raw, and you feel you can't dig yourself out of the mire.'

'But *you* did it. You didn't turn to drink.'

'No. But I wanted to turn to *something*. Anything that would take away the pain. In A&E we see all the different ways that people numb themselves. It's the human condition. We're not strong.'

'But you didn't do any of those things.'

'No. I saw Lily. Hours old. Wrinkly and squawky and crying. And I realised that what she needed to take away her pain was me. She'd not been held by her mother, so she needed her father. I was the only one who could help her. So I picked her up and promised her that I would protect her to the end of my days.'

He swallowed.

'I was still lost without my wife, my love. I was still bleeding with the pain of losing her. But Lily was my light. My guide through it all. I would have been nothing without her to keep me here. To keep me sane. Perhaps your father never saw that…that you could have been his rose in the desert.'

Brooke blinked back tears. 'He told me he couldn't look at me. That I reminded him too much of my mother.'

'I see Jen in Lily, too.'

'So why didn't my father hold on to *me*? Why did he not care? Why did he walk away from me when it mattered? If I was his light?'

Matt shook his head. 'I can't answer for him. I don't know.'

'He was weak. You're strong. That's the difference.'

'I'm not strong.'

'Yes, you are. All that you've been through and yet you're here. Lily's father. Dedicated, hard-working. *Sober*. A soldier who went to war and survived. You've got scars, but you've never weakened. Being a father is what drives you and I've never been enough to drive anyone.'

The words were out before she could stop them, and her cheeks coloured.

'Sorry—ignore that. I was just having a pity party. It's over now.' She gave a brief smile and sipped at her cocoa.

'You're entitled to be mad at him. He let you down. But I really don't think there's anything you could say to him that he hasn't already said to himself. He's still in hell, I'd say. The drink puts out some of the flames. For a while. But then when the pain comes back…the regret, the sorrow…'

'He goes back to the booze. To numb himself again.'

Could it be true? That her father hated himself for what he'd done to her? That he berated himself day after day after day for letting all these years pass, letting his baby grow into a woman and still not putting things right?

'Lily's lucky to have you. If my father had been *half* the man you are...' She glanced at him, not intending to hold his gaze, but she did.

The intensity in his eyes was shocking. It was as if he could see deep inside her soul and liked what he saw. As if he saw *her*. Not the public persona—not Dr Bailey, A&E consultant, a single mum—he saw *her*. The frightened, self-doubting version. But even seeing her vulnerable and exposed like that didn't make him turn away.

He was staying. Interested. Intrigued.

It was too much.

Brooke stood up, still holding her mug. 'Well, it's... er...been a long day. I ought to...turn in.' She vaguely waved her arm in the direction of her bedroom. 'Goodnight, Major.'

He stood up, facing her. 'Goodnight, Dr Bailey.'

She had to tear her gaze away. It was hard. As if he was a magnet, pulling her in, and it took every ounce of her nerve and strength to walk in the other direction.

Brooke lay in bed and stared at the ceiling.

Morgan was sleeping soundly in her cot, one little fist tucked up underneath her chin, her other arm cast over her head. She'd be good now, at least. The latest teething episode seemed to be over, which meant Brooke should be getting a full night of sleep.

But sleep remained elusive. Out of arm's reach. Ridiculously, she felt wide awake, and completely physically aware that Matt was just in the next room to hers. Literally feet away. Separated by a wall. A line of bricks. That was it.

He was in the next room!

She'd bet that he was asleep. He'd had a stressful evening, what with the panic attack at the display. The adrenaline of that must have made him tired. He was probably snoozing away in dreamland, completely unaware of where he was. Where *she* was.

Through a small slit in her curtains she could see the stars in the night sky. Twinkling points of light in the darkness.

Could it be true what Matt had said about her father? She'd always been angry with him for not being there for her, at the fact that he never wanted to talk about her mother or even spend any time with his daughter. She'd thought it was because she was worthless. Why else would he ignore her?

It had never occurred to her that it was too painful for him. That he'd loved her mother so much that the pain of her loss was too much. Because human beings didn't deal with pain very well. Self-medicating with whatever worked to take the pain away—pills, drugs, alcohol, cigarettes, food. When a child cried and wouldn't stop what did most parents do? They offered a biscuit or another indulgent treat, teaching children that to make the pain go away you filled yourself with something else instead.

Was her father still trying to make himself feel better? Could that be it? Perhaps it wasn't that *she* was worthless, not worth loving. It was just that he couldn't cope and had found the thing that worked for him, no matter how bad it was. He might once have made a living painting hope, but what if she who *should* have been his hope, his light in the darkness of his grief, had been too bright for him to look at?

Who wouldn't give anything to be numb when pain struck?

Yet Matt had pushed through *his* pain. Had been able to put his pain to one side so he could be there for his baby. He was solid. Dependable.

Attractive, gorgeous, a gentleman...

She let out a heavy breath and turned to her bedside table for her glass of water.

Damn! I didn't bring one in, did I? I was in such a hurry to escape that look in his eyes.

She needed a drink. She felt parched. And now she was aware of it she'd focus on it so much she'd never get any sleep!

Matt was bound to be asleep, right? If she crept out there, past his room, he'd never hear her go into the kitchen for a glass of water. It wasn't as if she was going to put the kettle on, or anything. She would be safe, right?

Perhaps I don't need a drink of water that badly?

Only she really did. And her legs felt restless. She needed to get up and walk, and he was in another room. It wasn't as if he was sleeping on the couch or anything.

Having persuaded herself that it would be safe to go and get her drink, Brooke threw back the covers and swung her legs out of bed. She wrapped her robe around her waist and carefully opened the door, aware that the bedroom door might make a sound at its widest point. She slipped through the gap and padded down the hallway, past his bedroom door and into the kitchen.

She breathed a sigh of relief and switched on the light. Blinking rapidly, she quietly opened the kitchen cupboard and grabbed a glass, filling it with water from the tap. Taking a long swallow of the refreshing fluid, she turned to go—and saw Matt standing in the doorway.

Instantly her heart began to pound. He was wearing only a tee shirt and boxers, and she couldn't help but notice his fine arms and long, muscled legs.

'I hope I didn't scare you—I needed a drink. I usually have one beside my bed, but being in a strange place I forgot all about it,' he explained.

'Same. About needing the drink, that is.' She gestured with her glass and smiled, noticing his hair looked a little ruffled, as if he'd been tossing and turning. 'Lily still asleep?'

'Out like a light.'

'Good.'

It was as if she couldn't take her eyes off him. He filled her vision.

'I'd best be getting back, then.' She went to move past him, through the doorway, and he did step to one side so that she could pass. But she made the mistake of looking up at him and smiling her thanks as she did so. Pausing. Ever so briefly.

His gaze locked with hers and she could read desire in his eyes—apprehension, fear, but most of all yearning.

She wanted to kiss him so badly, but she didn't want to overstep the mark in case he—

Matt stepped forward, his gaze going to her lips, then to her eyes, then her lips again.

Brooke's breathing changed and she stared back, taking in all the features of this beautiful man up close.

They weren't touching. Neither of them was overstepping their boundary, but both were fighting the urge to reach out and take what they wanted.

'Brooke, I...'

She looked directly into his soul. He'd said her name. 'You called me Brooke.'

'Yes.'

'Not Dr Bailey.'

'No.'

And he came ever closer, watching her intently, as if he expected her to place her hand on his chest at any moment to stop him. But she didn't stop him. She wanted him close to her—wanted to see what it would feel like. She wanted him to kiss her.

Brooke closed her eyes as his head dipped and his lips touched hers—feather-light, brief. She stood there, her entire nervous system lit up like the national grid, waiting, anticipating more.

And he gave her what she wanted.

His hands came up to cradle each side of her face as he drew her to him and deepened the kiss.

Her whole body ached, desiring more of him as she kissed him back. He was all she could think of, and his lips, his kiss, fuelled a fire inside her that had long lain dormant.

All thoughts of caution, of whether this was right or wrong, went straight out of her head. All that seemed to matter to her at that moment was that he continued to kiss her.

Hesitantly, her arms embraced him, feeling the raw, hard muscles beneath his skin.

This man desired her. Wanted her. She had not expected this. She'd known—felt—that she was developing feelings of attraction for him, but she had told herself it was one-sided. That he would not feel the same. And yet here they were...

What did this mean? Was it just one kiss, or would it

be more? She wanted more. Wanted to give in to what she was feeling right now and take all of him. Have everything he could offer right now and the future be damned!

But...they had to work together. They had their children to consider. They had to be responsible.

'Matt.' She broke the kiss and, breathing heavily, stared deeply into his eyes. 'We need to think about this.'

He stared back, then nodded, releasing her. And as he did so disappointment entered every cell in her body. She'd felt on fire, and instead of allowing herself to blaze she had doused the flames. She hated herself for doing so.

'You're right.' He stepped back, leaning his body against the doorframe.

She mirrored his movements opposite. 'We're work colleagues...we...' She couldn't think of what else to say. Her body, her mind was screaming at her to forget the doubts, just kiss him again!

'Have to be sensible?' He finished for her.

'Yes.'

No!

They stared at each other for a moment more, and then suddenly they were back in each other's arms, their lips pressed against each other's, the long lengths of their bodies pressed tight as his tongue found hers and she groaned.

She *needed* him. More than she had ever allowed herself to need a man. She didn't care about the consequences now. *Need* trumped everything else, and she cast her hesitations aside as quickly as he cast aside her robe.

She could feel him against her, his desire pressing

into her, and then she was reaching for his tee shirt to pull it free over his head.

They staggered into the lounge and Matt reached under her long tee. She felt the wondrous heat of his hands upon her bare flesh, her breasts, and it was *everything*. His touch, his taste, his heat. It fed her. It was life.

How was it possible that he could make her feel this way? It had never felt this *urgent* with Eric and he was the father of her child. It hadn't felt this way *ever*. With any man. Not this intensity. Not this much.

Was it because there was already so much history between them? Even before they'd met they'd shared a history. A love for the same person. And that bond, that strength they shared, had pulled them together.

They were the same, Matt and her. Both traumatised, both alone, both single parents facing the same struggles in the same work environment. Both of them hurt by previous encounters. There was a saying that misery liked company... Did hurt people naturally seek each other out?

No. It had to be more than that for them. They shared the same wound. They were two halves of the same scar. Perhaps that was why it felt so right to be in his arms. Because only together could they heal.

Brooke breathed his name as he moved into her. Felt the force of his need within her and sighed delightfully. This felt *right*. That was what counted. Even though she had tried to fight it, tried to keep her distance. Perhaps the reason they had failed at that was because they were meant to be?

No. She wouldn't allow herself to think that far ahead. Experience had taught her that people generally let her down. People she had thought she could rely on.

What mattered was the here and now. She would deal with today and not worry about tomorrow.

Not yet.

And it helped that the today—the *now*—felt so damned good!

He woke in Brooke's bed. It was still dark and the sun had not yet risen. He was used to waking early. A habit from his early army days, when he'd tried to cheat the agony of the drill sergeant crashing into his dorm, shouting and yelling.

He still liked to wake early. To lie there for a moment and mentally prepare himself for the day. It was a habit that had come in handy after Jen had died. He'd lie there for a few minutes, thinking of all he had to do to get through the day. Things that Lily would need. Things he would need to get done in the house. Whether they would need to go food shopping. The five-mile walk he would try to fit in, with Lily in her buggy, because it was important to get out of the house and not pine away in grief.

Grief, guilt, sorrow—they were all time-stealers and he could never allow them a place in his life. Not until he had control back. Not until the intensity of that grief had been absorbed and wasn't as sharp as it had been.

It took a moment or two for him to remind himself of where he was. Not his own home…not his own bed.

Brooke's bed. And she was in his arms as he spooned her. He inhaled her scent, her perfume, as she lay there and felt a pang in his heart.

She looked so beautiful. Her long dark hair over the pillow. Her naked shoulders so smooth and feminine. The feel of the length of her against his body.

His own body stirred in response and he closed his eyes to regain control of himself.

Last night had been...*amazing*. A gift that he hadn't expected at all. He'd been lying there, staring at the ceiling, unable to get his pillows right, tossing and turning, berating himself for his forbidden feelings for this woman who wasn't his wife.

His attraction for her had been growing steadily. He'd known that for a long time. But he'd told himself over and over that he would control it and do nothing about it—because it wasn't right.

But at the fireworks display he'd lost the present, had been thrown right back into the horror of Khost Province in Afghanistan. And as he'd heard the cracks and whistles of the fireworks he'd seen in his head the two trucks ahead of him being blown off their axles and thrown to one side. Felt the rush of adrenaline as he'd taken cover, aware that a bullet might rip through his heart at any second, but still going back for a fallen comrade.

He had no longer been standing in a field, watching fireworks with delight, he'd been back there, cowering under a hail of bullets, and she—Brooke—had brought him out of that.

He would not have thought it possible. But her touch, her voice, her insistence that he listen to her, had cut through the hell in his mind and pulled him out of his terror.

Her eyes... That look in her eyes had held him in the present and made him breathe, made him take root in reality again, and he'd been so thankful for that. When she'd said that she didn't want him to be alone he'd been grateful. The idea of returning home with Lily to put her to bed and be alone again with his torturous thoughts had been enough to make him accept.

He'd not said yes to get her into bed. He'd not said yes to see what would happen. He'd said yes because he'd genuinely wanted to be with her. To be wrapped in her protection and soothed by her presence, knowing she was just in the next room. Not to be alone again. Not again. Just for one night.

He'd got up for a drink not knowing that she was already up, and when he'd walked out of his room and seen that the kitchen light was on he'd almost faltered. Had almost gone back to his room. Only he hadn't. He'd wanted to see her. To say goodnight properly.

And then he'd kissed her.

Again, *she* had been the strong one—had tried to make them pause for a moment. Take a breather. Think things through. And he'd tried… But he'd still had the taste of her on his lips and he'd stamped down on all the doubt, on all the voices in his head telling him it was a bad idea, because his body, his being, had been screaming that it needed her. That she was the other half of himself. The one who could save him.

And like a drowning man grabbing at a buoy, he'd reached out and pulled her towards him, felt his soul drowning in the pleasure of her touch, her kiss, her heat—so much so that all logical thought had gone out of his head.

But now the cold light of day was approaching. He could feel it. Inching closer over the horizon accompanied by his old friends guilt and doubt.

I buried my wife just months ago and already I'm in another woman's bed.

Brooke thought he was strong. But he wasn't. He was weak. And he'd proved that. Sleeping with Brooke, staying the night with her, had been everything he might have dreamed of—but now he felt as if he was in a nightmare. Racked by the intrusive thoughts in his head that told him he'd taken things a step too far.

She'd asked him to stay over. To spend Sunday with her too. And though he could imagine it would be delightful, and the babies would have fun, he knew he had to think practically. Right now they were in a bubble. A lovely bubble. One he would struggle to leave. But it was the right thing to do.

He couldn't live in a bubble. He had to return to reality. Strong people, the people to admire, were the ones who survived in harsh reality.

He couldn't stay here, warm and cosy, pressed up against her body. Because already he was wanting more of her, could feel his body awakened by its need to have her again, But it would be wrong. He'd be taking advantage. Brooke had tried to put the brakes on last night and she'd been right to do so. He ought to be the strong man she kept telling him he was and do something about it.

Gently he rolled away from her and slipped out of bed. He stood there for a moment to see if she would wake, and already he could feel his reluctance to leave. But, no.

I have to do this.

He padded softly away, wincing slightly as the door creaked, and crept into the lounge, where their clothes had been discarded the night before. He got dressed and hung her robe and long tee shirt over the back of the couch, neatly folded. Then he went into the other bedroom and grabbed the rest of his clothes and checked on Lily. She was starting to stir. Snuffling and rubbing at her face with her hands.

Matt checked the time. Six-thirty a.m. Lily was right

on cue. He had no idea what time Brooke and Morgan would wake, but if he had the nerve to wait and let Lily wake on her own then he would be able to get her out of here without her crying.

Back in the lounge, he found a notepad and pen by the phone and scribbled Brooke a note. He tried to make it sound friendly, and not as if he were rejecting her. Saying that he just needed to pop home, and as he'd woken early he'd decided to leave her to rest and sleep in on her day off before work tomorrow.

He read the note over and over, wondering if he'd pitched it right. It seemed okay to him, but he was very aware of the fact that Brooke felt men always rejected her, and he didn't want her to think the same of him.

They would be sensible. Sort this out. Work through it. Like adults.

They'd be able to do that, right?

He had to believe that they would.

CHAPTER EIGHT

HE'D SPENT SUNDAY trying to put the night he and Brooke had spent together out of his mind—but it had been impossible. All he'd been able to think of was the way she had felt, the way she had tasted, those little sounds she had made in the back of her throat as he had made love to her and how good it had made him feel to be wrapped in her arms.

It had been one hot night, and he knew it was a night that he would never forget.

He'd left his mobile phone at home and taken Lily out for their usual five-mile walk. He'd gone all touristy and caught the bus to Trafalgar Square. He and Lily had fed the pigeons, walked through Covent Garden and along the Embankment. They'd eaten out at a small family-friendly cafeteria, and then he'd taken her to a small park where there were baby swings and small slides for her to play on.

And all the time he had been looking at Lily, talking to her, laughing with her, he'd seen his wife looking at him out of her eyes and he'd felt terrible for moving on. Felt as if he was horribly leaving his wife behind.

They'd had so many dreams, he and Jen, for their future. And what had he done? Taken *her* old job, in *her* old department, in some kind of sad effort to be in the place where his wife had lived and worked so that somehow he could still stay connected to her. So that he could touch the things that she had touched, chat with the people who had become her work family, and so that he could meet the famous Dr Brooke Bailey, whom he'd heard so much about and who was owed a promise.

I think I might have taken that promise too far.

And now he was at work early, waiting for his shift to start and fanning through the pages of the most recent medical journal.

There were some cutting edge developments happening in the world of medicine. On every page was evidence of people moving forward. Doctors and professors looking to see how they could improve things for the future. They weren't sitting still, being static. They knew that to improve you had to change with the times. Take risks.

And when he came to the back of the journal, where all the job vacancies were, his eyes were drawn to one in particular.

Auckland City Hospital.

Auckland, New Zealand. The place where he and Jen had planned to go in the future. The city that had been their ultimate goal—a place to raise their daughter. A place where Jen had spent time during her gap year and had loved.

But would considering something like that now be a move forward or a move backwards? It was an old dream. A dream that he'd shared with his wife.

She wasn't here any more and he was. And although they'd spent many a time talking about how wonderful it would be for their daughter, would doing it now, applying for the post, be the best thing for Lily? Jen had promised Brooke that she would be there to help her raise Morgan, but she'd also wanted to emigrate. To do what was best for *their* little family. Shouldn't that be his priority?

He'd taken this job to put down roots. He wanted the future to be stable for Lily. She'd already lost her mother—did she need to be moved from pillar to post? Never quite sure where her home was? It wasn't a simple case of packing up your things and jumping on a plane. It meant leaving people behind. Leaving behind a life he'd already started to create and never planning for the future.

He'd had that sort of childhood, following his father in his postings abroad. Sometimes he'd liked it—other times he'd hated it. But he had grown to love it. Had matured and chosen the same life for himself. Had enrolled as a doctor in the army and flitted around the globe whilst Jen had stayed rooted in one spot.

Was it the right thing to do?

'Looking for another job?' asked Kelly as she glanced over his shoulder, walking to her locker and removing her coat and scarf. 'Have we driven you crazy so soon?'

He stared at the advertisement and grimaced. 'Not sure...'

Kelly hung up her things and then grabbed her stethoscope, draping it around her neck, then her ID card to pin to the waistband of her skirt. She came over and sat beside him, glancing at the advert. 'New Zealand? Beautiful place.'

'You've been there?'

'No. But I've always wanted to.' She took the magazine from him and smiled. 'Perhaps I ought to apply? Give you some competition.'

He laughed. 'I don't know what to do. Jen and I always said that that's where we'd end up working. We wanted to give Lily an amazing life in a brand-new beautiful country.'

Kelly nodded. 'And it would be. Do it now—whilst she's a baby—and she'll probably never even remember the UK.'

Hmm… He'd not thought about that part. She *wouldn't* remember, would she? But *he* would. And he'd never forget all the wonderful people he had met here. His friends and his family were all here. And he'd be leaving behind Brooke.

That would be hard. Reneging on a promise.

He tossed the journal onto the table. 'It was just a thought. Anyway, are you trying to get rid of me, Kelly?' he asked with a smile.

'Gawd, no! You're the only decent thing to look at around here. If you left I don't know what I'd do!' She got up to make herself a quick cup of tea, and as she stood by the kettle raised an empty mug. 'Want one?'

'Sure.'

At that moment Brooke walked in, her face stony, and headed straight to her locker.

Matt got up and went over to her. 'Hi.'

She didn't look at him. She yanked open her locker and shrugged off her coat, then got out all the accoutrements she'd need for the day. She closed her locker and walked out again, without saying a word.

He watched her go, feeling awful inside. Perhaps he hadn't pitched his note as well as he'd thought? And perhaps leaving his phone behind all day on Sunday had not been a good idea either, because when he'd got back he'd seen missed calls and texts from Brooke, clearly wanting to talk to him.

Which he'd never answered.

'What did you *do*?' asked Kelly. 'If looks could've killed you'd be lying on a mortuary slab right now.'

'Looks like I need to apologise.' He put his hands in his pockets as he thought about how best to do that.

Kelly handed him his mug of tea. 'Well, I sure as hell hope you're good at grovelling, because that girl looked like she meant business.'

He sipped his tea and was thoughtful.

There was a hell of a lot he needed to think through today.

Brooke couldn't believe it! That he'd just said *hi* to her as if everything was okay between them! As if he hadn't walked out on her like that and left a stupid note.

He'd said that he would spend the day with them on Sunday. She'd made plans in her head—a walk in the park, maybe a meal out, a good chat over some good comfort food, maybe taking some pictures of the babies together—something like that. Nothing special. Just things they could do together.

But then they'd made love—unexpectedly—and it had been the single most amazing thing that had ever happened to her. No man had ever made her feel that way. It had been as if...as if...

As if he loved me...

That *had* to be wrong, right?

But the way he'd made love to her... That couldn't have been just sex. It hadn't been just a quickie—wham, bam, thank you, ma'am. It had been *special*. Tender. Loving. She'd felt as if she'd found the lost part of herself, one she'd never known was missing.

Falling asleep in his arms, in her bed, had felt *so good*. To know that he was wrapped around her, the length of his strong body against hers, had made her feel safe and secure for the first time since *for ever*.

The scent of him, the feel of his hard body moulded around hers…

She'd woken with a smile upon her face. A silly, dreamy smile as she'd yawned and stretched—and suddenly realised that there was no one next to her.

Brooke had sat up, alert, feeling the sheets to see if they were warm, to see if maybe she had dreamed it all. The sheets had been cold and she'd been naked, and she never slept naked, and her body had felt pleasantly used. As if she were glowing.

She'd thought that maybe he was in the kitchen. Or perhaps he'd had to get up to check on Lily in the next room?

So she'd lain back in bed against the pillows, still with a smile upon her face, thinking that at any minute he would come through the door and say good morning, and maybe—just maybe—if the babies weren't yet awake, have a repeat of what had happened last night?

She'd felt glad that they had come together. She'd had no regrets. Not then. Because she'd felt sure that of all the men in the world Matt was not one of those who would walk away from her and leave her behind. And they'd moved forward in their relationship, hadn't they? You didn't have a night like that with someone and walk away.

But she'd waited, and she'd waited, and when she'd started to get that funny feeling in her stomach she'd got up and slipped on a tee shirt and knickers to go and look for him.

And discovered that the only thing left of Matt and Lily was a note.

Brooke,
I'm sorry, but I had to go. We crossed a line last night, and I should never have allowed it to happen.
I didn't want to wake you. I know you offered for us to spend the day with you and Morgan, but I really think we should respect each other's boundaries, so I'll see you at work on Monday.
Many thanks once again,
Matt x

Many thanks? That was the response she got after what they had shared? *Many thanks?*

It was insulting. She'd tried to call him on his mobile, but it had just kept going to voicemail. She'd messaged him. Once. Then a second time. Then she'd worried that she might seem like some sort of obsessive stalker, so she'd stopped.

He would ring *her*, right? Surely it had *meant something* to him? Yes, they had crossed a line, but they had both wanted to. Hadn't they...?

But perhaps to him it hadn't meant anything at all? Perhaps she'd misread what was happening between them. And maybe she, so desperate for love and attention had mistaken his kindness for something more? To be left again like this was just so...painful.

When his silence had continued she'd got angrier and angrier that he'd apparently just dropped her like a hot potato after getting her into bed.

She was horrified that he could do that to her. Appalled. Aggrieved. Upset.

I've been used. He needed physical comfort and used me. Like I've always been used.

She wasn't sure she had anything to say to him. How

could he treat her like that after she'd told him how her dad had been with her? How Eric had been with her.

Brooke wasn't sure whether she wanted to rage at him, slap him across the face, or just never speak to him again. And his guilt had made her think of her own. Sleeping with Jen's husband, of all things! What had she been *thinking*?

But they had to work together. They had to be a team if the department was to run smoothly. So she'd thought the best way to be would be to say nothing at all. Not until the right moment presented itself. *Then* she would have something to say.

So she'd gone straight to work. Determined to fill her day with patient after patient after patient. With no more need to check in with Major Galloway she could get through her day without having to interact with him at all.

'Sarah Greenwood?' Brooke called for her first patient of the day.

A middle-aged woman stood up and followed her through to a cubicle.

'Hello, Miss Greenwood, my name's Dr Bailey. What can I do for you today?'

'I've been having these really bad abdominal pains. Like there's something trying to burst out of me. I feel... *full*. Bloated. It's horrible.'

'And how long have you been feeling like this?'

'A couple of weeks... I tried to call my GP to get an appointment, but I can't get in till near Christmas! I'm sorry, but I just had to come here—just to put my mind at rest if nothing else.'

'Okay. What type of pain is it? Is it a dull pain or a sharp one?'

Sarah shrugged. 'Both. It depends, sometimes, on what I'm doing.'

'And when was your last period?'

'Middle of October.'

'And is the pain all over, or just in one particular area?'

'It seems to be more on the left side.'

Knowing it could be any number of things, Brooke took Sarah's blood pressure, her temperature and her pulse. All seemed normal. 'Is there a chance that you could be pregnant?'

Sarah shook her head. 'No. I'm not with anybody right now.'

'No casual partners?'

'No.'

'When was the last time you had sex?'

Her patient blushed. 'Over a year ago.'

'Can I have a feel of your tummy?'

Sarah lay down on the bed and Brooke gave her a thorough examination of the abdomen. She thought she could feel a swelling on her patient's left side, possibly on her ovary, but she'd need an ultrasound to be sure.

'You can sit up now. Okay, Miss Greenwood, I'm not sure what this is, so I'll need to run a few more tests. Maybe get an ultrasound done—have you had one of those before?'

'No, but I know what they are. What do you think it is?'

'It could be several things at this stage. Let's do the ultrasound and see what happens. But don't worry—you're here now. I'll look after you.'

'I'm just worried that it's something serious. My mum had ovarian cancer, you see, and she started off the same way. I want to have children. I'm still young enough. And if it's something serious…'

The patient's family history was important, and it did not bode well. But that did not mean Sarah had ovarian cancer. It might be an ovarian cyst, which was often something simple to sort out.

'Do you have children, Doctor?'

Brooke nodded. 'I have a daughter.'

'You're lucky. I haven't found anyone yet who wants to stick around long enough to have children with me.'

Technically, neither had Brooke. Eric had been useless, and Matt… Well, she'd begun to think that he was the solid, dependable type, but she'd been wrong. Perhaps her radar was off? How had she managed to find men like that time after time? Did she have a big sign pointing at her head that read *'Needy and naïve'*?

'I worry I've left it too late, and now this…'

Brooke laid a reassuring hand on her patient's. 'Let's see what the tests say. It's way too early for you to be worrying before the results are in. I'm going to take a blood sample, too. Just to check and make sure there are no STDs.'

'Oh, I don't think I've got anything like that—'

'You'd be surprised, sometimes. Did you always use protection the last time you had a sexual partner?'

'Not every time, no.'

'And were you exclusive?'

She grimaced. '*I* was.'

Brooke smiled in sympathy. 'I'm sorry. So let's check that out anyway. I'll be back in a tick.'

'Thank you, Doctor.'

Brooke headed off to get a kit that would allow her to take blood, and also to ask one of the healthcare

assistants to bring the portable ultrasound to her cubicle
when it was next free.

'Dr Bailey?'

Hearing Matt's voice, she closed her eyes, telling
herself silently to remain calm. She opened them again
and turned around. 'Yes?'

'Could I have a moment of your time to talk to you?'

'I'm busy with a patient right now.'

'It's important.'

'My patient is important, Major Galloway. Now, if
you'll excuse me?'

And she headed back, proud of herself for staying calm and polite and for not having looked at him.
Because if she had she might have faltered. And she
wanted to remain angry right now. It helped. Somehow...

She took Sarah's blood and then performed the ultrasound, moving the Doppler over her patient's abdomen and soon noting a large cyst on the left ovary. It
looked benign, filled with fluid, but due to the patient's
history it needed to be checked and tested to be on the
safe side. It might burst on its own in time, or be reab-
sorbed, but it might have been there for a while. Sarah
would need to see a specialist for further tests they just
couldn't do in A&E at this time.

Brooke explained the situation and promised to write
to her GP to arrange the referral. 'Try not to worry,
Miss Greenwood.'

'Thank you, I'll try. But I can't promise. Not until I
know for sure.'

'I understand. Take care.' And she waved her patient goodbye.

She went back to write up her notes. As she did so

Matt came striding out of Majors, with Kelly following behind him.

'Dr Bailey, I need you to come with us for a major incident. There's been a large traffic collision just down the road and there are people trapped in vehicles. The paramedic on scene has requested doctors.'

'There are none on scene?'

'All mobile doctors and the HEMS crew are busy on other cases, and the advanced paramedics have been called to another incident ten miles away. We're the closest, and you and Kelly are the most experienced on my team.'

'Okay.' She'd been called out on a field team twice before. Once to the London bus bombings some years before, and a second time to a train crash. Both times had been horrendous.

She hurried to grab the jacket that would identify her as a doctor at the scene, grabbed the kit bags that were always ready and prepped for occasions such as this, and quickly hurried after Matt and Kelly.

They were taken to the RRV—rapid response vehicle—that would drive them to the scene.

Her thoughts were whizzing like mad as they negotiated their way through the thick traffic that had built up. It was agonising to sit there, inching forward like a snail. She almost felt as if it would be faster to get out and run, but then suddenly the cars parted and they could get through, and they arrived to find a refuse collection lorry had crashed through a car, up a pathway and into a café.

There was smashed glass everywhere, alarms were going off, and people were crying, looking horrified. Sickeningly, she spotted one or two people with their mobile phones out, filming it all or taking pictures.

But she had no time to worry about them. That was for the police to take care of. *She* was here for the casualties.

A fire engine was already there, and a fireman in a white helmet, indicating his high rank, was letting them in on who their casualties were.

'The driver of the lorry had a heart attack at the wheel. My guys have been giving CPR, but there's been no sign of life now for over twenty minutes. There were two other men in the truck, both have cuts and lacerations. The driver of the car that was smashed up is trapped within the vehicle and we're working to free her. There are also numerous casualties in the café, including a pregnant woman who has taken a blow to the abdomen. Multiple lacerations throughout, and we have victims in shock. One customer of the café was knocked down by the truck as it entered the building and appears to have broken his leg.'

Matt nodded. 'I'll take the guy in the truck. Dr Bailey, if you could handle the driver of the car and, Kelly, you check out the café customers. Triage only. Understood? I'll join you as soon as I can.'

They all nodded and headed off to deal with their patients.

Brooke made her way to the smashed up car, its bonnet crumpled and steaming, watching whilst firefighters tried to remove the roof. A fireman sat in the back seat, holding the driver's head still.

'What's the patient's name?'

'Vijaya.'

'Okay.' She removed a cervical collar from her kit, ready to attach it to the patient's neck. 'Vijaya? My name's Brooke and I'm a doctor from the London Grace. Are you in any pain?'

'My neck hurts—and my leg.'

'Okay... Well, you've got a handsome fireman holding your spine nice and straight for me, and I'm just going to have a quick feel of your neck before I put this collar on. I want you to tell me if anything hurts.'

With her fingers she probed Vijaya's neck, feeling along the vertebrae. 'Anything?'

'I don't know. It just hurts.'

'Were you stationary when the lorry hit you?'

'Yes. I'd just got in...was about to pull away. I'd just released the handbrake when the lorry hit me.'

'I'm going to check out the rest of you, if I can.' Brooke made a primary survey—checking for breaks, bleeds, anything obvious. 'Does your chest hurt?'

'A little.'

'Did you have your seatbelt on?'

'Yes.'

'And how does your breathing feel? Does it hurt to breathe in?'

'No.'

'Take a deep breath for me.'

Vijaya did so. 'It doesn't hurt.'

That was good. Brooke peered in as far as she could and saw that the engine block had been pushed in somewhat, and was pinning Vijaya's left leg. There was some bleeding.

'Can you wiggle your toes for me?'

'Yes.'

'You can feel both feet?'

'Yes. My leg hurts, though.'

'Your leg seems trapped, Vijaya. I don't know how badly you're injured—we won't know until we get you free. It shouldn't be long. Do you have any medical problems I need to know about?'

'I'm a Type Two diabetic.'

'Okay, anything else?'

'No. Well, I'm claustrophobic…'

Brooke could see the frantic look in Vijaya's eyes as the firemen put up a sheet to protect her from glass as they cut away the car's roof. Being trapped in the car with all these firemen about, and now the tarpaulin, must be very scary indeed.

She reached in and took Vijaya's hand in hers. 'I've got you. Just a moment or two more. Do you have any family I can call?'

'My husband is probably wondering where I am.'

'What's his name?'

'Rav.'

'And his number?' With her free hand she pulled out her mobile and as Vijaya told them to her punched in the digits and listened to the phone ringing at the other end. 'He's not answering. I'll try again in a minute.'

The firemen suddenly lifted off the roof of the car and Brooke went round to the other side of the vehicle to try and get a better look at Vijaya's leg. She couldn't be sure, but she didn't think there was too much damage. It looked like a simple entrapment. The wound would need cleaning, an X-ray to check for any bone damage and possibly a few stitches. It was her patient's neck she was more worried about.

As the firemen worked to free her patient's leg, Brooke became aware of Matt at her side. 'Can you give me an update?'

Brooke gave details of her patient to Matt, being as robotic as she could, because right now, her anger and her upset had to wait. Matt nodded and then ran to check on Kelly. She watched him go, registering a look in his eyes that she had never seen before. But she guessed he must be used to scenes of such carnage. This sort of thing didn't faze him. He had a place in his head he could go to that allowed him to keep a professional distance and look past the screams, the yells, and see what needed to be done in the most efficient manner he could.

In moments he'd left Kelly and nipped into the café's interior, where she lost sight of him.

He was a good doctor. He really was. And she'd thought he was a good man. One whom she could finally lean upon.

I should have known better.

The firemen freed Vijaya's leg quickly, and as a team they managed to get her onto a back board and lift her free of the vehicle. Brooke attended to the wound on her patient's leg, applying a dressing quickly to prevent further blood loss, knowing that she would get full treatment soon in an A&E.

She clutched Vijaya's hand one more time. 'You're going in an ambulance now. I've got to stay here to help more patients, but I'll come and check on you when I get back.'

'Which hospital am I going to?'

'The London Grace.'

'Oh. Right.'

'I'll see you there.'

She picked up her kit bag, disposed of her gloves and put on fresh ones, and then ran into the café to assist Matt.

She was like a bee. Flitting from patient to patient, assessing, dressing wounds, giving reassuring smiles and holding the hands of those who were wounded or frightened.

Matt watched her, glad that he had picked her for

his field team, still hoping that she would give him the chance to explain himself.

He'd hurt her. He knew that. And that did not sit well with him. He was not the kind of guy to walk over someone else's feelings and it unsettled him.

He finished applying a splint to the patient with a broken leg and got him onto a spinal board for transport to an ambulance. He held the patient's hand as he walked alongside the trolley to the vehicle and he was smiling when he heard an almighty rumble and turned to see what the noise was.

The front of the café was obscured by a thick dust cloud and rubble lay all around. *Had the front of the café collapsed?* He saw, to his left, Kelly clambering out of the back of an ambulance. Was Brooke still inside?

He ran over to the front of the café, but a fireman held him back. 'You can't go in—it's not stable.'

'I've got a doctor inside!'

'We need to stabilise the area. Stand back.'

The firemen pushed him back, away from the frontage of the building. All he could think about were the people inside. The patients. *Brooke!* How close had she been to the front of the café? Was she under the rubble? Was she hurt?

Was he ever going to see her again and get the chance to say he was sorry?

I need to get in!

He made to dart forward, but the firemen had been watching him and placed a solid hand upon his chest. 'Stay right where you are.'

It took far too long for the firemen to put up joists and clear the rubble but finally, when the moment came and they allowed him in, he rushed forward, desperate to make sure that Brooke was okay.

He was met by a stream of walking wounded who were all clambering out into the light. He helped them all, his mind going crazy, before he was able to clamber over the debris to find Brooke—packing up her kit bag and hauling it over her shoulder.

The relief he felt was palpable. 'You're okay. Thank God.'

She looked at him, seemed slightly shocked, but nodded. 'I'm fine.'

'When the front of the café fell in I…' He swallowed. 'But you're okay. That's what matters.'

'I'm all right.'

'When we get back you and me are going to have that talk.'

'I'm tired, Matt, and I need a drink. Maybe a shower. I'm covered in dust.'

'Okay. But afterwards?'

She nodded. 'Afterwards.'

He pulled her kit bag from her shoulder and slung it over his, then took her hand, to her surprise, and led her safely out over the rubble.

Blinking again at the brightness, Brooke pulled her hand free of his and headed back to the RRV. Kelly got in beside her and he saw them exchange looks.

He got into the front and sat beside the driver. 'You did a great job—both of you.'

'Thanks.'

'There was just the one fatality. The lorry driver. I think he had a massive MI.'

The driver's myocardial infarction—heart attack—must have been instantaneous, and unfortunately, he'd been driving a large, powerful vehicle that had spun out of control.

You never knew when your time would come. Matt had once thought *his* time had come in Khost Province. Had been sure that at any moment he would be struck down. But he'd survived. Survived to become a father. To know his daughter. To know Brooke. And she was special. And he didn't want to waste all the good opportunities he had in life and make people miserable.

He'd lost his wife unexpectedly.

Did he really want to lose Brooke, too?

CHAPTER NINE

His mind was in turmoil. Now that the adrenaline had gone—now that he was thinking rationally as he waited for Brooke to get out of the hospital's showers—he began seriously to analyse just how he'd felt when the frontage of that café had collapsed.

How had it come to be that he had allowed himself to develop feelings for another woman? And so deeply? Okay, so he'd never told himself that he wouldn't get involved again after Jen. He'd never said that. He'd known there might be the possibility at *some point* that someone might come along. He'd just never expected it this soon. And he'd certainly never expected it to be his wife's best friend.

He'd assumed it would be someone a long time in the future—when Lily was a teenager, maybe.

But for it to have happened this fast... That was what he was having trouble with.

Because when the front of that café had collapsed his heart had almost stopped. The horror, the dread that had filled him at the idea that Brooke was trapped, or hurt, or even dead under that rubble, had almost killed *him*, too. That another woman he cared for could be cruelly taken from him without warning... *Again*...

Matt looked down at the table and saw the journal

he'd been looking at earlier. It was still open at the page he'd left it. The tantalising possibility of a job at Auckland City Hospital.

It was an amazing opportunity. Fortuitous. Something he'd once dreamed of going for. Moving Lily to New Zealand would give her an amazing life, but no matter what he decided he would always put the welfare of his little girl first.

So what *was* best for her? The new life he and Jen had always wanted? Or staying here, where life was getting complicated? Could he have Brooke enter his life so deeply and be so integrated into it that Lily might call her *Mama?*

The thought of that made him feel terrible. Not because Brooke would be a bad role model as a mother. She was an excellent mum to her own daughter. But he wasn't sure he could cope with having his daughter call Brooke *Mum*. It felt treacherous.

He'd imagined raising his little girl and sitting her on his knee, getting out the photo albums and showing her pictures of her mummy and telling her all about Jen. About how like Jen she was. About how much they looked alike and how much her mother had loved her. He needed Lily to know that. And if Brooke was in their lives would that make things more complicated?

He picked up the journal and looked at it once again. Read through the job description, the requirements, the contact details...

Perhaps I need to keep my options open? I could just ring them for a quick chat. I could just see what it would all be about.

Yes, if he went to New Zealand he'd be leaving Brooke and everyone here behind, but perhaps that was what they needed? A fresh start. By staying he had enveloped himself in *Jen's* past, not his own. He had come here in an effort to know her better, to meet those who had loved her, in an attempt to keep her alive in his head. Getting involved with Brooke had been wrong. He'd lost his focus in a moment of lust and his feelings for his wife's best friend were strong now. He wasn't sure he should be feeling that way.

It was entirely possible that going to New Zealand would also be the wrong thing to do. He couldn't live Jen's life. He had to live his own. But his own life had also included the aspiration to move to New Zealand. To emigrate. To give his daughter a bright future in an amazing country. It was all so confusing.

Matt headed to his office and closed the door. He picked up the phone and called the number. He wasn't sure of the time difference, or even if anyone would answer, but he figured he could leave his details and ask them to email him.

But someone answered.

An actual person.

And so he began his enquiries about the vacancy.

The shower felt great. To just stand there motionless, letting the hot spray hit her body, her head, her shoulders, her back, feeling it washing away the dust and debris…pounding sore muscles that were still recovering from the adrenaline rush that had smothered her when the front wall of the café had collapsed.

For a moment she had thought she would die.

She'd been helping a patient, wrapping gauze around a penetrative leg injury, when she'd heard a strange creak and a groan. As if the world itself was about to crumble. And then it had felt as if the sky had fallen as the front of the café had come crashing down, filling her lungs with dust and grit as everything went dark.

She'd leaned over her patient, protecting her, covering her own head and hoping that somehow she would survive.

The only thought in her head had been *Morgan!*

Her little girl. In the hospital crèche, probably playing happily with something, or sitting in a puddle of paint, smiling, laughing. She could lose her mother at any minute. Morgan might have to grow without a mother as well as without a father.

Who would care for her?

Not her dad. Social services would never give a baby to a drunk. So that just left Eric, Morgan's father, and there was no way she would want that. And there was no way *he'd* want the intrusion of his child turning up in his sad little life.

And then she'd thought of poor Lily, who actually had no mother but did have a loving, kind father, and she'd begun to wonder, as she coughed dirt and dust from her lungs and wiped the grime from her face, whether she had misjudged Matt?

He wasn't a bad guy. She knew that. Deep down. He was a brilliant doctor. Kind and caring. Professional. He ran the A&E department beautifully. It had never been as efficient as it was now, under his leadership. And as a father, he was top notch. She saw it in his face whenever he collected his daughter at the end of the day. Just how much he'd missed her was in his eyes. In the way he would pull her towards him and breathe in the scent of her hair and kiss her. He was determined to be everything his little girl needed now that she was motherless.

And that night they'd spent together... Cads and users didn't make love to a woman like that. It had been more than sex, she was sure of it, so why had he walked away? And if he *was* a user of women—which she now doubted—he would never have left a note, would he? He would have just walked out. And, okay, he hadn't answered her text messages or phone calls, but she had no idea what had happened to him after he'd left her flat.

She owed him the opportunity—his chance to explain. Because life was too short to waste it on petty grievances. Matt was not her father. He wasn't Eric. And he deserved his chance to speak.

Switching off the shower, she got dressed and dried her hair, sweeping it up into a ponytail and then went to find him.

He was in his office, on the phone. His gaze met hers as she stood in the doorway and he held up his hand as if to say *two minutes*.

She nodded, happy to wait, and sat in the chair opposite, trying not to listen in but hearing words like *New Zealand* and *emigrating* and wondering who on earth he could be talking to.

Eventually he put down the phone and looked her over. Then he smiled, as if he was happy to see she had no cuts, no bruises, no injuries.

'You're okay?' he asked.

She nodded. 'I am. A little weary, but good.'

'I'm glad to hear it. When I saw what had happened I didn't know what to think.'

She gave him a polite smile, acknowledging his worry about her wellbeing. 'What happened, Matt?'

'The front of the café collap—'

'No. After our night together. You just left. You never answered my calls.'

He had the decency to look appalled with himself. 'I'm sorry. Did you see my note?'

Unfortunately. 'Yes.'

'I did want to stay with you. Spend the day with you, like we'd planned, but...'

'But?'

'I've not been with a woman since Jen died. I hadn't expected to be with a woman like that for a long time. And yet somehow there I was, in your bed, with you in my arms, and it felt *so right*... But I felt guilty. Terribly guilty. I don't know...it was a knee-jerk reaction, and I justified it to myself by thinking that I needed a shower and a change of clothes, and that I didn't want to monopolise your whole weekend... I'm sorry. It's not a good enough excuse. It was an instinctual thing. I just left. It was wrong of me.'

'And you didn't answer my messages.'

'I left my phone behind and went out for the whole day. I felt like I owed it to Lily—as if I'd betrayed her mother's memory and I owed it to her. It was no slight on you. What we had was...'

She waited to hear how he'd describe their night together. Hoping that he would confirm to her that he had felt the same way. That they'd discovered a deep connection between them...that it had been more than just sex. More than just a cheap night—something passionate and intimate and loving.

'Just magical.'

She allowed herself a small smile. So he *had* felt it too. That was good. She hadn't been imagining things. 'It meant something. Didn't it?'

'More than I suspected it would.'

Her smile broadened. 'What happened today at the café, when the roof came in. I thought that... I thought

I might die. I'm not trying to be dramatic, but it made me think about life and how short it is. We've both lost Jen. I thought Morgan might lose me as well.'

'*I* would have lost you, too.'

She nodded. *Yes.* They'd both been hit by the events of today. 'I didn't want to waste any more time on being angry with you. That night showed me that we could have something special.'

'Brooke—'

'Let me finish. Please.' She leaned forward. 'You *mean* something to me. I never expected it. I never thought for a moment that I would feel this way about you. But I do, and I think if we're offered the chance of happiness in our lives we should take it.' She smiled. 'I don't often put myself out on the line like this. I don't declare my feelings. But I'd like to think that if you feel the same way about me as I do about you then we should embrace that.'

Her stomach was rolling as she spoke. Butterflies in their thousands were flitting around in her insides as she waited for his response. She hoped he would smile. Hoped he would come out from behind the desk and take her in his arms and hold her tight. Press her up against his body and whisper into her hair that he loved her.

But he remained seated behind his desk. His face was a mass of conflicting emotions. 'We *should* take chances—you're right. It's too easy to stay in our comfort zones, wrapping ourselves up in the familiar. We *should* take chances.'

She might be wrong, but she felt as if he was saying that to himself, rather than to her. Perhaps he was trying to persuade himself? He'd admitted to feeling guilty about what they'd shared, and she could understand that. It wasn't that long ago that his wife had died, and perhaps he was struggling with that more than she knew? Perhaps he needed a little extra time to get used to this change? To accept the fact that she had feelings for him and wanted to pursue a relationship with him.

Because she absolutely did. She might have been burned by men in the past, but the way she felt about Matt... She absolutely felt sure that he was worth it. That by putting her cards on the table she was making herself vulnerable, yes, but she was also being brave. She wasn't going to let her past dictate her future. She was going to take a chance on love *despite* that.

She'd thought she might die today. And she would have died without letting Matt know how she really felt. He needed to know. Anybody who loved needed to let the person they cherished understand just how they felt. It was an important thing to hear. Words had power. Magic. It wasn't just actions that proved how you felt.

Brooke decided to give him some time to digest what she'd said. 'I'm just going to go check on Morgan before I return to work, if that's okay?'

He looked up at her as if he'd been lost in his own thoughts. 'What? Oh, right. Yes. Sure...'

She headed to the door, and then a thought occurred to her. 'Earlier, when I first came in, you were talking on the phone about emigration... New Zealand. What was that about? Have we got a new doctor joining us?'

His face coloured. 'No. I... I was just chatting to a colleague who's thinking of going. Making a new life out there.'

'Oh. Sounds wonderful. I've heard it's beautiful out there. I think Jen mentioned it once.'

He nodded, his face stern.

'Well, I'll see you later, then?'

'Yes.'

She smiled a goodbye and left his office. He was clearly stunned by what she'd said. Surprised at the depth of her feelings for him. But it was important to her to be honest with him. Then there'd be no surprises, no disappointments. If he didn't feel the same way then she would hurt for a while, but she would get over it. In time. And she would know that she had been honest and open, and that was what was important. Honesty. Truth.

Because if you didn't have that then there was no point in having anything at all.

Morgan's face lit up at the sight of her mummy's unexpected visit. She raised her arms, asking to be picked up, and Brooke scooped her up and held her tight, kissing her cheeks and just breathing her in.

She stayed with her for a while, watching her play with pasta shapes, squealing and burbling, making all her happy sounds, picking up a particular piece she wanted to show her mummy and beaming when Brooke made a happy face.

Moments like these were precious. Watching her daughter made Brooke realise just how much she was missing out on. Morgan had long days here in the crèche. Ten hours every day. Monday to Friday. That was fifty hours a week that she didn't get to spend with her child. Morgan was growing quickly, developing at a breakneck pace, and she was missing it.

When she'd left Morgan at the crèche that morning it had been no big deal. She'd dropped her off, given her one last kiss and then walked away, sure that in ten hours she would see her again. No biggie.

Only she might have died today and she'd been so *nonchalant* about leaving her child. Had taken no time to breathe in her scent, to give her one last hug, to tell her that she loved her.

These early days were important and she was missing them—crossing off the days of her calendar at work instead of by her daughter's side.

Matt wasn't the only one who suffered from guilt. She did, too. It was something she would have to think about.

So she kissed her daughter goodbye, breathed in the scent of her daughter's hair and gave her one last hug before she returned to work. Maybe she could claim a week's holiday? Spend it at home with Morgan. Some of it with Matt, perhaps. Take some time out together to just *be*.

Entering A&E, she saw Kelly give her a wave, and as Kelly had been at the accident site this morning with her and Matt she went to give her friend a hug.

'Hey, what's that for?' Kelly asked, surprised.

'Just a hug to say I appreciate you. That I love you.'

'Aw, thanks. I love you, too.'

Brooke smiled. 'Crazy start to the day, huh?'

'You're telling me. But it was thrilling to get out into the field. We don't often get that opportunity. It was good to see the paramedics' side of it.'

Brooke nodded. That was true. The guys in green brought in the majority of their patients, and she was so used to them just turning up with people on stretchers or backboards it didn't occur to her to think about the sights they saw during the course of their working day.

'True.'

'I think it's good to have change, don't you? Keeps you fresh. Keeps you on your toes.'

'I think you're right.'

'I believe our Major is looking for change, too.'

Brooke frowned. 'What do you mean?'

'He was looking at a new job opportunity this morning. In New Zealand, of all places! You can't get more of a change than that.'

She felt her blood run cold as she began to understand. '*He* wants to go to New Zealand?'

'That's what he said. We'll miss him here, but I wouldn't blame him for going and giving it a try.'

Brooke's heart pounded fast and heavy in her chest as all sound around her seemed to grow fuzzy and indistinct. She became incredibly aware of each breath, her gaze dropping to the floor as she fought just to stay upright.

He lied to me!

She'd asked him outright! After all that had happened that morning—the collapse of the café, how close she had come to losing her life—the first thing he'd done was enquire about a job on the other side of the world?

Perhaps I don't mean anything to him at all!

'Brooke? You okay? You've gone very pale.'

'I… I don't feel very well.'

'Sit down for a minute.' Kelly pulled out a chair.

'No. I think I need to go home. It's nearly the end of my shift anyway. I'm going to go pick up Morgan. I need to be with her. Spend time with her. With the people who love me back.'

And she hurriedly began to walk away.

As each step took her further and further away from A&E her anger and despair rose inside her, and she fought back tears as she smacked the button to call for the lift. *Why?* Why had he outright *lied*? She'd laid herself bare before him and he'd lied. That he could do that to her, when she'd exposed herself like that…made herself open and vulnerable…

At the crèche, Daisy looked surprised to see her again so quickly. 'Dr Bailey! Everything okay?'

'I've come to collect Morgan. I… We need to go home.'

'Oh, okay. I've just put her down for a nap. Should I wake her?'

'Yes. Please. Hurry.'

'Of course.' Daisy scurried away.

Brooke stood there waiting, feeling humiliated beyond belief.

How many times would a man stamp all over her heart?

How many times would she allow that to happen?

Not any more.

Never, ever again!

Matt hammered on Brooke's front door. 'Brooke? Brooke, it's me. Please, would you just open the door and let me in? We need to talk.' He banged on the door again.

Behind him a door opened and the occupant came out. It was a young man wearing very loose jogging bottoms and a black vest, showing his perfectly honed gym body to perfection. 'Dude? What's with the noise? I'm trying to sleep in here.'

Matt looked at him, irritated. 'It's four o'clock in the afternoon.'

'You never heard of night shifts? Brooke's at work. She works every day.'

'She came home. I know she's in there.'

'Well, she's not the type to ignore people, so you must have upset her big-time, dude.'

'Thank you for that observation.' Exasperated, Matt closed his eyes and turned back to hammer on Brooke's door.

Behind him, the man closed his door. Matt knelt down and opened Brooke's letterbox. 'Brooke? Please let me in! I'm disturbing the neighbours and I know you don't want me to—'

The door was yanked open and he almost fell forward. But he instantly got to his feet and stared at the woman he had too many feelings for.

'I'm sorry.'

'You say that a lot to me just recently. I'm not sure it means anything any more.'

'Can I please come in? Would you just give me a moment to explain?'

Brooke shook her head, tears glazing her eyes. 'No. You can't. I told you *everything*. Everything I felt. I laid myself bare to you. I gave you the opportunity to be truthful to me. But you lied. You want to go to New Zealand? Then you go, Matt. Don't you worry about me. I'll be fine.'

She went to close the door, but he blocked it with his foot.

'I wanted to tell you! I *did*! But I couldn't. Because if I had told you exactly how I feel then that would've made it real. If I'd told you that I love you then that would have been me closing the door on everything I had with Jen, and I couldn't do that. New Zealand was a dream. An escapist fantasy that I indulged in because I was afraid of what was happening between us! Don't you *see*?'

She stared down at his foot in disdain, then looked back up at him. 'No. You don't get to have the monopoly on being afraid! You think you're the only one?

That because you've already lost one love you have the most to lose?'

She banged at his foot with the door.

'I lost her too! My best friend in the whole world! But you know what? I started to find another. I started to believe that this new friend was going to mean just as much. And I gave my heart willingly, only for it to be crushed—once again—by an unfeeling, inconsiderate coward who's afraid to admit how he feels! Now, you'd better remove that foot right now, or I'm going to go into my kitchen, find the sharpest knife I have and surgically remove it!'

She glared at him, tears and fury blurring her eyes, and he could do nothing but remove his foot and allow the door to be slammed in his face.

He stood there, momentarily stunned. Unsure of what to do. He didn't hear the door behind him open once again. Wasn't aware of the guy standing watching him, an amused smirk on his face, until he heard, 'Dude, you messed up.'

He closed his eyes, felt tears sting behind closed lids, and felt his heart break.

Brooke called in sick that first week. Then Personnel informed him that Brooke had taken some annual leave owed to her.

Matt sat in his office in between patients, feeling numb and broken. He'd made a big mess of everything. He had disrupted not only the department—because everyone wanted to know what was wrong with Brooke—but also his own life.

He was lost without her here. Not seeing her every day was torture, plain and simple.

He'd had fights with Jen, but nothing like this. Life

seemed so bleak. He found it hard to smile. Found it hard to concentrate on what anyone was saying. Found himself drifting off into thoughts of that last argument as he sat in departmental meetings. He tried his hardest to find joy and smile and laugh when he was with Lily, but even she seemed subdued by his mood and cried a lot, constantly needing his hugs.

Hugging his daughter was the only thing that brought relief. He'd just sit and watch Lily playing on the carpet. He *didn't* want to uproot them and take them to New Zealand. He'd panicked. Brooke was right on that score. He'd been scared. Scared of what his feelings for her meant. He'd lost control, just for a moment, and rung about that stupid job.

He should have told her about it from the beginning, but as he hadn't been definite about going he hadn't thought it was worth mentioning. It had been a blip. A small error in judgement as he'd frantically fought to regain control over his feelings. Because he'd felt as if they were running away from him. Like wild horses, their glorious manes flowing behind them as they ran across a grassy plain.

He'd tried to rein his feelings in, and he could see now that it had been the wrong thing to do. Because you couldn't rein in love. It was a wild thing. An uncontrollable animal that defied attempts to tame it. It would always be free. It demanded to be free. And accepting his feelings as truth was a big step for him.

He'd loved Jen. He would always love her. Every single day. But that love was not lessened by his love for Brooke. They were two separate things.

The fact that he still had the capacity to fall deeply in love had, at first been startling. But now it was painful. Because he'd screwed it up. He'd hurt the woman he loved and he didn't know how to fix it.

He'd tried apologising. He'd sent flowers. Had texted. Called. But she hadn't responded and he wasn't sure he could face the hurt of having her slam the door in his face yet again.

So he was giving her time. Because if he'd learned anything from Jen's death it was that time lessened the hurt. It didn't take it away. It didn't get rid of it completely. But you absorbed it better. It wasn't so raw and painful as it could be in the early days.

Time allowed you to take a deep breath and just *breathe*.

He was biding his time and hoping that maybe—just maybe—when she was ready to return to work she would let him tell her everything.

She had to return to work. Even if it was just to work out her notice.

So much had changed for her recently, and there'd been some startling revelations, but she knew she had to do what was right for her. And for Morgan. And...

Brooke closed her eyes and took a deep breath as she handed Morgan over to Daisy in the crèche. She wouldn't have to do this much longer. Not here, anyway.

Brooke had decided that what she and Morgan needed was a change and some rest. So she was taking a leaf out of Matt's book. She'd been rash before, hurrying back to work after her maternity leave, when she wasn't fully ready. And that rashness had caused her to do something silly. To fall in love with a man who was wholeheartedly unavailable.

She should have seen that—acknowledged that—but

she'd been silly and allowed him into her heart. And, as in all the times before, in every single relationship she had ever had with a man, her feelings had been crushed.

But things were different now. She was taking back control. No longer a passive observer in her own life, letting things happen to her. *She* was going to be the one who made the changes. If Matt could consider going to New Zealand and leaving, then she could make huge changes too.

That meant putting in her notice, working it out, and then she and Morgan were going to head to the south west coast for a while. Maybe Cornwall. She'd heard it was beautiful there. She was going to hire a mobile home and they'd pootle around the area for a few weeks whilst she waited to start the job that she'd accepted just yesterday.

She would be working at another A&E—far, far away from London and its great impersonal greyness. Its hustle and bustle. Its demand for you to hurry. For you to pay, pay, pay. It was a city in which you could lose yourself, and Brooke didn't want that. She wanted to relax more. To enjoy nature.

Her new job was in a town, yes, but the cottage that she'd seen was by the coast. It would be perfect to raise her children there. To live. To lie in bed and hear waves crashing against the beach. To hear the gulls. To take long walks along the coast, squeezing sand between her toes, watching her daughter and whoever was next to come sitting in the sand, making sandcastles...

Discovering she was carrying Matt's baby had come as a shock. They'd used protection, but she'd found herself one morning, peeing onto a stick and then watching the blue lines appear, bright as day.

How *could* she have got herself in the same mess

she'd been in when she got pregnant with Morgan? Was she so naïve regarding her own feelings that she'd be one of those women with a brood of children, each of them with a different father?

She had no expectations of him. She could imagine his hurt, his pain at the prospect of a child who would become just another piece of evidence that he had somehow betrayed his wife.

I can't compete with a ghost.

She'd loved Jen so much! And she felt guilty to think that she was carrying her best friend's husband's child. Even if a small part of her thought that Jen might be smiling at the development, up there in heaven. That Jen might even have plotted this herself!

Thrown you another curve ball, honey!

So Matt would receive two big pieces of news this morning.

She hoped he would be a big enough man to let her go. But another part of her hoped that somehow he might tell her everything she wanted to hear.

Miracles happened, didn't they? Wasn't she deserving of a turn at happiness? Hadn't she paid her dues? Finding out she was pregnant with Morgan had been a huge turning point in her life, and it was going to be the same with Matt's baby.

Now or never.

A new life was on its way. A new baby. Brooke had always wanted a family—a few kids, a husband. The perfect little unit.

So, okay, maybe life wanted to challenge her with this. Make her fight for what she needed. She'd never backed down from a fight. Had always stood her ground. Maybe she would get what she wanted some day, even if it wasn't now.

But she *would* get it.

She was determined.

CHAPTER TEN

MATT WAS IN his office. For a moment she watched him through the small window, saw the hunching of his shoulders, the lifeless look in his eyes as he stared numbly at a staffing rota.

She didn't normally like to see anyone hurting like that. But a tiny part of her was *glad* that it wasn't easy for him. Because she'd been feeling as if she was the only one suffering.

She rapped her knuckles on the door and he looked up, standing instantly, becoming alert when he saw who was standing there.

Brooke opened the door and went in. The envelope in her hand contained her notice. 'I've come to give you this.'

She passed it over and he took it from her with confusion, turning it over to see if the envelope gave any clue to its contents.

'What is it?'

'My notice.'

His face fell. 'Brooke, no…there's no need for that.'

'There's every need. I'll work my notice. I won't drop you in it by leaving you down a doctor.'

'Brooke—'

'I'm late. I need to get on.'

And she hurried out, her nerve failing her in delivering the extra bit of news that she knew would change everything. Handing in her notice and walking away was one thing. It showed courage and determination. Telling a man she was pregnant and having him want nothing to do with her turned the tables and would make her feel pathetic and alone. And she wasn't ready to face that just yet.

Maybe she could hold the news until her last day at work? She was in no hurry for him to reject her. She'd been there once before with Eric. She was in no rush to hear it a second time.

Even though she suspected Matt would probably want to do the right thing, him being the kind of person she knew him to be, a small part of her was worried that he would not. Lily was the most important thing in his world, and another baby, with another woman, was not ever going to be part of his life plan. It would throw him completely. And he would tear himself apart trying to do the honourable thing and yet also bear the weight of his betrayal to his wife.

She would wait. She still had time before there were any signs of her pregnancy.

Shoulders back, chin up, she grabbed the first patient's chart and headed back to work.

The letter was stark and to the point. She was leaving. Brooke was going to leave the London Grace!

Just the idea of that was…

He had no words for how it made him feel. His heart had jumped when he'd seen her at his office door. He'd been hoping that she had reconsidered. Was now willing to listen to his explanation. But she'd been brusque and kept their conversation short.

But she was here now. He had a month to get her to listen to him. And he didn't have to send her letter of notice up to Personnel just yet. He would hold on to it for a while.

Maybe he wouldn't be able to stop her from leaving, but he was determined that somehow he would get her to listen to him. Even if it changed nothing between them, he needed to tell her how he felt. How their relationship had blossomed into something that he'd never expected. How his feelings for her had grown into something he couldn't control and how that had made him feel.

Another knock on his door interrupted his thoughts and he stood up abruptly, hoping it might be Brooke. Only it wasn't. An old man stood there. A man who looked familiar.

'Arthur?'

It was Patricia's husband. The man who had brought in his wife after a stroke.

'You remember me?'

The old man shuffled in and Matt indicated that he should take a seat.

'Of course. How are you?'

Still reeling from Brooke's news, Matt forced himself to focus as he sank back into his chair.

'I wanted to come here to thank you, Doctor. You and your team.'

'Oh, well, there's no need—we were just doing our jobs. How is your wife?'

Arthur's eyes darkened slightly. 'She passed away a day or two after we returned her to the care home. It was peaceful. Her funeral was yesterday.'

'Oh. I'm so sorry for your loss.' He knew how Arthur must feel right now. He'd lost his wife. Had had to bury her. But *he'd* only had a few years with his wife. Arthur had had sixty-three years of marriage. He couldn't possibly imagine the level of loneliness the old man must be feeling.

'It was expected. The stroke took a lot out of her, I think.' Arthur cleared his throat and wiped his nose with the proper handkerchief he'd drawn from his jacket pocket. 'But I just wanted to say thank you for giving me a few extra days with her. They were important, all those minutes and hours we had, because she was sometimes lucid.'

'She was?'

Arthur nodded, smiling. 'Not for the entire time, but here and there—over the two days… You gave me back my wife. The stroke should have done her in, but you doctors—all your medicine, all your technology—gave her back to me. Just for a little while. I'd been afraid of her being lucid again. She'd been so upset the last time, discovering what was happening to her, but after the stroke it was like she came back to say goodbye. And that was precious to me, Dr Galloway.'

Matt gave a smile, but it was tinged with a resolute sadness.

'You never know how long you'll get with your loved ones on this planet, but when it comes to the end it's never enough, don't you think? We spend so much of life worrying about what other people think, what other people say, but when it comes to your final days is that what you worry about? Is that the most important thing? No, it's not. It's being with those you love. And if you're lucky enough to love, you embrace it. That's what Patty and I had in those final days. Love. And I needed to come here today to thank you for that.'

Arthur's words sank deep into Matt's soul.

He was right. The old guy was *right!* All the petty day-to-day worries that he'd allowed to fester away in his skull meant nothing when he thought about it. If he was on his deathbed right now would he be worrying about what everyone thought of his feelings for Brooke? *No!* He'd want to be lying there holding her hand. Telling her how much he loved her! And knowing that she loved him!

Who were other people to judge when he should love again? Why was he allowing guilt to determine his feelings for her? Because, looking at himself right now, he saw that guilt was making him feel damned miserable! And who wanted to be miserable? When he was with Brooke he felt joy and contentment and happiness. Why couldn't he have that? Why couldn't *they?*

It didn't diminish the love he'd had for Jen. Not by one iota. And if other people thought that it did, then that was *their* issue.

Love—true love—was rare and beautiful, and if you were lucky enough to discover it you should embrace it, as Arthur had said. Not hide from it, nor feel guilty for having it. And there wasn't a clock or a timer on love. It could spring from anywhere. Unexpected and surprising. And didn't that make it all the more special?

'Thank you, Arthur. For coming here today. I really appreciate it.'

'Well, we appreciated *you*, Doc. That's it, really. I don't want to keep you. I know you're busy. Saving lives.'

Arthur was right. He had to save his *own* life. Because for the last few days he'd been drowning in guilt and grief and dying inside. *No more!*

He shook Arthur's outstretched hand and watched him go, and then he hurried off to find Brooke. He had to tell her everything. And if he hadn't messed it up too much he could be about to change both their lives.

It was hard to concentrate. Handing in her notice, knowing she was pregnant a second time and still not in a solid relationship, weighed heavily. But Brooke did her best. No matter what was going on in her personal life, she still had to put her patients first.

She was good at that. Putting other people before herself. It was something she'd had to do as a child and she'd chosen it as a profession. But though it usually brought her joy and satisfaction she felt no happiness today.

For her, contentment was a long way away, and she knew she would have to travel many a mile—both mentally and geographically—before she found her happy place.

Her current patient should not even be in A&E. He had only come here because he couldn't get an appointment at his GP for another three weeks and he was concerned about a pain that he kept getting in his knee.

She did her best. She examined the knee. Couldn't see or feel anything wrong with it. Her patient could put weight on it, and he had a full range of movement, but he kept getting 'a painful twinge' that would make him gasp out loud when it struck.

Brooke suspected he might possibly be developing arthritis. The man had it in his family history. So she wrote him a prescription for some painkillers and told him to see his GP if it got worse. There was nothing else she could do for him now.

Her patient left, grumbling under his breath about shoddy patient care, and though normally that would have angered her today she had no energy for it. She had no energy for anything. Since she'd fallen out with Matt it was as if the life had gone out of her. All her vim, all her pep, was gone.

'Brooke? I must speak with you!' Matt came barrelling down the small corridor like a man on a mission.

She turned away. 'I'm not retracting my notice, so please don't ask.'

It hurt that he wouldn't just let it be. Couldn't he accept the fact that she was walking away to save her heart? Her soul? It was painful to be here with him and not be able to wrap her arms around him freely and share his kisses. It hurt that he'd shown her what love between them could be like and then cruelly torn it away.

She tried to pick up her stride. To get back to the doctors' desk, write up her notes, and then see her next patient. Anything that would make him go away—because it hurt too much to have him here and not be allowed to love him.

'I'm not here about your notice. I'm here about you. And me.'

Brooke turned to look at him, despair written across her features. 'I really don't think there's anything left to say. You've made it clear how you feel about us.'

'*No!* I haven't!'

She almost flinched at his raised voice, and she looked about them and noticed that some people were listening in—Kelly from the cubicle she was in, applying a splint; Michael the senior nurse, who was restocking a trolley, and further away the healthcare assistant, Michelle, who was bringing in a pile of blankets.

Feeling her cheeks colour, and not used to being the centre of everyone's attention, she glared at him. 'Keep your voice down.'

He lifted his chin. 'I will not. I don't care who hears. In fact, they all need to hear it.'

'Hear what?'

'That I love you, Dr Brooke Bailey. I'm in love with you and I will *always* be in love with you.'

Brooke swallowed. 'What?'

'I made a mistake. I'm human. I'm fallible. I panicked when I realised just how much you were coming to mean to me.'

'Matt—'

'I know I hurt you. It was never my intention.' He made her lock eyes with his. 'That New Zealand job… It was a dream that Jen and I once had. For Lily. Since Jen died I've tried to do everything in my power to make sure that Lily will know who her mother was. I put her in the crèche that Jen would have taken her to. I took her to the classes she signed her up for, and I took her job, so that Lily would know the place and the people who shared her mother's life. I rock her to sleep at night, telling her stories about her mother. And then I met you.'

Brooke could see there were tears in his eyes, and it made her feel like crying too.

'You were like a cyclone in my ordered world. You were at the crèche. You were here at work, and even at home. When I was alone my thoughts were of you. And after that night we spent together—'

Brooke blushed.

'I didn't know what to think. I felt guilty, yes. Not for what we did. What we had was beautiful and magical and perfect, and I've never felt that way with anyone. But I felt guilty for the fact that I wanted to stay with you. Stay in your flat and never leave. Take every part of you that you might offer. I forgot Jen for a few hours. And that made me feel so...'

He couldn't find the word he wanted.

'I had to soak up my old life. Remind myself of what I thought was important. What other people would expect of me. To be the grieving widower. To show respect—to take years, not months, before I fell in love with another woman. But feeling like I've lost you has almost killed me. I've been miserable. Ask anyone— they'll tell you. Lily's kept me going, as she did before, but she shouldn't have to be my crutch. Like you were for your father. I want her to feel loved and celebrated and valued and cherished—the way that I... I feel for you. You kept telling me I was honourable and brave but I didn't believe it. I've only just begun to believe that I am, and I feel that way, because of *you*. I love you, Brooke, and I want us to be together. You and me. For ever.'

Tears trickled down her cheeks as she heard his words. They were *real*. Heartfelt. Honest. And all around them the staff were smiling. Waiting for her reaction. She looked down, saw his hands. His wedding band was gone.

'You let me down, Matt.'

'I know. But if you just let me love you I promise, on my life, that it will never happen again.'

'I want to believe you. I *do*.'

'Then take a chance on us.'

She took in a breath. Then another. Tried to steady her frazzled nerves. 'I want to, but I'm scared.'

He stepped forward and took her hands in his. 'So am I. But that's okay, because I think we're *meant* to be scared. Nothing worth having is ever risk-free, but

I think if we're scared *together* then we can face anything that life throws at us.'

She looked down at their hands, stroked the pale stripe on his finger where his wedding band had used to sit. 'Life has thrown a lot at us, hasn't it?'

He squeezed her fingers in response. 'It has.'

She looked up into his eyes. Those beautiful blue eyes that she knew so well and saw in her dreams. Wasn't this what she wanted? His love? And he'd announced it to everyone! No hiding. No shame. He had admitted his feelings for her in front of them all. All she had to do was be brave enough to accept it.

He was speaking again. 'A wise man told me recently that all that matters in this world is love. That if you have it you should embrace it, tell the person who's your everything that you love them. Because at the end of the day—at the end of life—that's all any of us ever want to say. I want to tell you I love you every day, Brooke Bailey. Every *single* day.'

A hesitant smile lifted the corners of her mouth. Reached her eyes. It was as if lights were slowly being turned on inside her, and she could feel warmth filling her once again as she opened herself up to the possibility that everything was about to turn out all right.

'I love you, Major Matthew Galloway.'

He smiled, joy lighting his eyes. 'You do?'

She nodded.

'Then let's be together. For ever.'

He lifted her hands to his lips and kissed the backs of her fingers, one after the other, and then pulled her close and kissed her properly.

Brooke sank into his embrace, feeling as if all the missing pieces of her puzzle were found. She was complete. Whole. It was terrifying, yes, but they would face the fear of this journey together.

Being back in his arms felt wonderful. It was soothing to her frazzled and exhausted body, and just by pressing up against him she could feel her energy returning. As if he was recharging her spent batteries with the depth of his emotion. His embrace, his touch, was everything. And she would never have to be without it again.

'There's one more thing,' she said.

He pulled back, looked at her. 'What is it?'

She lowered her voice so that only he could hear it. 'I'm pregnant.'

His eyes widened in surprise and then, barely milliseconds later, he lifted her off her feet and began swinging her around in happiness.

Brooke squealed and laughed and begged him to put her down—which he did.

'You're pregnant? That's amazing!'

'It's still early days. Anything could happen.'

He nodded. 'But we'll face it together.' He linked his hand into hers. 'Have I told you today that I love you?'

She smiled. 'Once or twice.'

'Well, I do. I do, I do, I *do*.'

'Well, Major, that's a good thing. Because I love you, too.'

They fell back into each other's arms, and all around everyone who knew them smiled with happiness.

There was no judgement.

Just joy.

For them.

As there always would be.

* * * * *

SAVING BABY AMY

BY
ANNIE CLAYDON

MILLS & BOON®

Published in Great Britain 2017
By Mills & Boon, an imprint of HarperCollins*Publishers*
1 London Bridge Street, London, SE1 9GF

© 2017 Annie Claydon

ISBN: 978-0-263-92658-3

Printed and bound in Spain
by CPI, Barcelona

Dear Reader,

There are times when I dream of perfection. But in reality I know that it *is* just a dream. Because, to me, a world without any flaws would hold no challenge—nothing to strive for. And perhaps it's the way we deal with situations which are less than perfect that is the truest measure of our spirit and humanity.

So a hero who wants perfection isn't someone I'd normally see eye to eye with. Perhaps that's why I gave Dr Jon Lambert a particularly hard time in this book, throwing him together with a heroine who resists taking the help he offers and facing them both with a situation that tests Jon to the limit. But, like any true hero, Jon has it in him to rise to the challenge—even if it does mean that he's forced to re-examine his perspective on life.

When Chloe Delancourt's niece, baby Amy, is in danger of being abandoned by her mother, Chloe must fight to reunite her family and secure Amy's future. Jon isn't her first choice of ally, but she has no choice but to admit she needs his help. And in working together to save baby Amy both Jon and Chloe discover that perfection isn't something either of them needs in order to find true happiness and fulfilment.

Thank you for reading Jon and Chloe's story. I'm always thrilled to hear from readers, and you can contact me via my website at annieclaydon.com.

Annie x

To Rosie, with love.

Books by Annie Claydon

Mills & Boon Medical Romance

Stranded in His Arms

Rescued by Dr Rafe
Saved by the Single Dad

The Doctor She'd Never Forget
Discovering Dr Riley
The Doctor's Diamond Proposal
English Rose for the Sicilian Doc

Visit the Author Profile page
at millsandboon.co.uk for more titles.

CHAPTER ONE

HOSPITAL GOSSIP WAS a bit like the wind: unpredictable
and prone to sudden gusts in one direction or another.
Information could easily end up at the furthest corner
of the hospital before it came to the notice of the people involved. So it was no particular surprise to Chloe
Delancourt that she'd walked all the way over to the
canteen before hearing a piece of news that quite obviously pertained to her.

'So what's all this about your boyfriend and a baby?'
One of the other junior doctors joined her at the end of
the queue.

'*My* boyfriend?' Jake was long gone, and if he did
have a baby it was nothing to do with her.

Petra grinned. 'All right, so he's not your boyfriend.
Since he's good looking, single and living with you, that
might be classed as an omission on your part.'

'You mean Jon?' Chloe had only seen Dr Jonathan
Lambert for a total of about ten minutes since he'd
moved in two weeks ago.

'How many good-looking men are you living with
currently?'

'Just the one…' The ten minutes had been more than
enough to notice that he *was* good looking. And that he
had a delicious smile. But apart from that all she really

knew about him was that he was a good friend of her brother's and he kept the bathroom tidy. He'd started his new job at the hospital six weeks earlier than anticipated and had needed a place to stay because the renovations on his own house weren't finished yet.

'Glad to hear it. If there was more than one of them, I'd be looking for an invitation to come over for dinner at the weekend.'

Chloe shrugged. 'Come over anyway, I'm not doing anything tomorrow. It'll be just the two of us, though, he's not exactly made his presence felt.'

'If he's working nights then I suppose you wouldn't see much of him during the week…' Petra was obviously turning the idea over in her head.

'Or the weekend. He spends every waking hour over at his place. I've hardly seen him.' Maybe Jon *was* avoiding her. Or maybe he just took the promise that she'd hardly know he was there very seriously. Whatever. It suited Chloe not to get too involved with a face as handsome as his.

'Well, he's here now. With a baby.'

'What kind of baby?'

Petra rolled her eyes. 'Two arms, two legs…the usual. A little girl, he was calling her Amy…'

'What?' Chloe almost dropped her tray and instead thrust it into Petra's hands. 'Where is he?'

'He was in A and E about five minutes ago. Someone said he'd asked for directions up to Orthopaedics—.' Petra broke off as Chloe turned, running for the doors of the canteen.

Chloe had sprinted across the courtyard and up three flights of stairs, back to her own department. Jon had been up to Orthopaedics and left a message that he was going back downstairs to A and E. By the time she got down to the Paediatric A and E department she could hardly breathe so it was just as well that the receptionist knew what she wanted without Chloe having to say so.

'That was quick, I've only just paged you. They've just gone through. Consulting Room Three.'

The pager in Chloe's pocket buzzed suddenly and she jumped, switching it off. Taking a deep breath, in an effort to slow her racing heart, she thanked the receptionist and walked slowly towards the consulting rooms.

If Amy was here, then where was Hannah? And if Hannah had left her child with Jon that posed a whole slew of other questions that Chloe really didn't want to think about until she was sure of the situation. She knocked and turned the handle of the consulting-room door before whoever was inside had a chance to answer.

Jon was lifting Amy out of her car seat. He'd obviously dressed quickly, because his shirt was buttoned up wrong, leaving one red checked tail slightly longer than the other at the front. Amy fretted a little, and then seemed to decide that the strong cradle of Jon's arms was a safe place.

'What…?'

She hadn't noticed how blue his eyes were before, or how tender. Or that his light brown hair, falling across his brow, gave him a slightly boyish look. Or that his hands seemed so large and capable next to Amy's tiny fingers.

'Sit down.' Amy stirred slightly at Jon's words, and then snuggled back against his chest. For a moment it seemed the best place in the world to be. Held in his arms without a care in the world.

But if Amy didn't seem concerned about the whereabouts of her mother, Chloe was. 'Where's my sister?'

'Hannah's at your place.' The tenderness in his eyes seemed reserved just for Amy, and he gave Chloe a more dispassionate look. 'Sit…'

Clearly something was up, and he wasn't going to tell her until she was sitting down. She bit back the temptation to tell him that she was a doctor too, and that she'd been working at this hospital a good deal longer than he had. Even if she did feel far more like a slightly panicky aunt than a doctor at the moment.

The dark blue windcheater on the chair next to him had been hanging in her hallway for the past two weeks, and was probably the most familiar thing about him. Chloe moved it, draping it over the backrest. When she sat down, an elusive hint of his scent halted the clamour of her senses for a moment, as if they'd paused to appreciate it. This wasn't the time, or the place…

His eyes and the slight curve of his lips invited calm. No… Actually, they invited surrender, and that wasn't something that Chloe was prepared to give. 'Tell me what's happened.'

'Hannah was worried about Amy and she took her to her own doctor this morning. He told her that Amy just had a virus, but Hannah thought it was something more so she brought her to you.'

'And…?' Chloe reached across to feel Amy's forehead. She was a little feverish, and her cheeks were flushed.

'I agreed with Hannah. So I brought Amy here, where she could be examined and treated properly.'

'But where's Hannah?' Chloe couldn't keep the frustration from her voice.

'She's at your place. She was…a little distressed.'

'A little distressed?' Chloe frowned at him. Jon didn't need to play the situation down for her benefit.

'She was crying her eyes out, and she insisted on staying behind while I brought Amy here.' Chloe's eyebrows shot up and he flashed her a cool smile. 'It's okay. I got to know Hannah quite well when she was staying with James. She wasn't entrusting Amy to a stranger.'

So, however distressed Hannah was, she was still thinking straight. That was something. James had mentioned that a friend of his had helped out a lot with Hannah, spending time with her and letting her talk, but Chloe hadn't realised it was Jon.

But if Hannah had found someone to talk to in Jon, then Chloe couldn't see how. He seemed somehow distant, as if Amy was the only person in the room he could trust with an unreserved smile.

'Then you'll know that Hannah's...vulnerable.' Chloe twisted her lips. Vulnerable wasn't quite the right word. Hannah could be surprisingly strong and very determined. But she was young. Troubled sometimes.

'I know that she's almost ten years younger than you, and that she was only nine when you lost both your parents. That you and James have done your best to look after her, but it hasn't always been easy.'

'No, it hasn't.' Chloe hadn't made it any easier. Hannah had always wanted to live with her, and Chloe had worked hard, saving every penny she could and adding to her third of the money from the sale of their parents' house so that she could afford a home for the two of them. She'd bought the house, and then two months after they'd moved in Chloe had fallen ill. Hannah had gone to live with James instead, but had never really settled.

'Look, Hannah's okay for the moment.'

Okay for the moment. Most people had learned to

settle for that where Hannah was concerned, but Chloe wanted more for her sister.

'You do know that Hannah's still only eighteen? And that Amy's father isn't on the scene?' Hannah had run away two weeks before her sixteenth birthday. Chloe had been too ill to do anything but worry, while James had moved heaven and earth to find their sister. When he had, she'd been living with a boy of nineteen, who had been more than eager to give her up when James had wondered aloud whether Hannah's queasy spells might be morning sickness.

'Yes, I know. She's all right.' It seemed that Chloe was going to have to take his word for it, because Jon's face showed no evidence that he really understood the gravity of the situation. His whole attention was focussed on Amy.

'I'd just feel a bit better if she were here and I could see for myself.' Her words sounded rather more accusing than Chloe had meant them to.

'I felt that Amy needed to be looked at sooner rather than later, and that was my first priority. Hannah calmed down when she saw I was taking her concerns seriously and promised to stay put while I was gone.'

'Yes... I'm sorry. Thanks.' None of this was Jon's fault. Hannah had put him in a difficult position and he'd taken the only decision he could. Chloe stretched her arms out towards Amy. 'I'll take her now.'

He didn't move. 'Why don't you let me examine her? I can do it now—my shift won't be starting for another three hours.'

'And you're better qualified than me?' There was something he wasn't saying, and Chloe guessed it might be that. It was true, after all. Jon's speciality was paediatric emergencies, and even though he'd only been here a couple of weeks he was already gaining something of a reputation as an excellent doctor.

'Yes, I am. And I'm not Amy's aunt.' He said the words dispassionately. 'I dare say you're a lot better at dealing with Hannah than I am. Why don't you give her a call, while I fetch my stethoscope from my locker?'

Maybe he was just giving her something to do to keep her quiet, because it seemed that he had already come to some kind of agreement with Hannah. But he was right. Chloe nodded and Jon delivered Amy into her arms.

'She's two years old. All of her immunisations are up to date and she's on no medication.' If she was going to take up the role of concerned aunt then she may as well give Jon all the relevant information. And ask the relevant questions. 'What do you think?'

'I don't know anything for sure yet.' He got to his feet and walked out of the room, without looking back.

Jon had woken to the sound of the front door banging closed, and had got out of bed, groggily thinking that he must have overslept if Chloe was home already. And then he'd heard Amy crying and had gone downstairs to find that it was Hannah.

He shouldn't really have been there at all. But the hospital had asked him to fill in for someone who was sick, six weeks before he was due to start his new job there, and he'd had to find a place to stay in the area. Chloe's place wasn't ideal as it reminded him too much of the family that he'd never again be a part of. But the renovations on the new house he'd bought had been the perfect excuse to stay out of her way and only return to her place to get some sleep while she was at work.

Although he'd seen little of Chloe herself, the slightly

shabby, eclectic warmth of her home surrounded him.
He slept between her sheets, saw her bottles in the bathroom when he went to take a shower and her food in
the fridge when he went downstairs to make coffee.
And if love had been something he ever wanted to do
again, he would already have been a little in love with
Chloe's scent.

But that wasn't an option. He walked back into the
consulting room, armed to the teeth with all the reasons why he shouldn't get involved with Chloe. She was
cuddling Amy in her lap, her phone tucked against her
shoulder, her brow creased in concentration.

'Yes, don't worry, we'll make absolutely sure she's
all right. What about you?'

A pause, and then her lips twitched into a smile. It
seemed that whatever was being said at the other end
of the line was a reassurance.

'Okay. You'll stay there until I get back. Promise?
Yeah, love you too.' Chloe caught her phone as it slid
from her ear and ended the call.

'Hannah?'

'Yes. She sounds all right, but she won't come to
the hospital. She says…' Chloe shook her head. 'She's
so terrified that she's not doing well enough, and that
people will think she's a bad mother.'

Jon nodded. It wasn't the first time he'd heard that
particular sentiment, and it was ironic that it was often
the most loving and capable mothers who voiced it.
But, then, family relationships weren't exactly his forte.

'First things first. I'll take a look at Amy.' That he
could do, and he knew he could do it well.

He was aware that Chloe's gaze was on him, an intrusion that felt so warm and welcome that all he could
do was try to shut it out. Amy was fretting a little, obvi-

ously out of sorts, and he concentrated on soothing her, trying to make the examination into a game.

'I think she may have a urinary tract infection.' Finally he turned and faced Chloe.

'Why?'

A fair enough question. She was a doctor too, and he couldn't completely relegate her to the role of faceless care-giver. 'She has a fever, but there's no sign of a cold. Her blood pressure is slightly high, which is a concern, and...' He shrugged. 'I changed her nappy pants before I brought her here.'

'And?'

This was the part where instinct corroborated medical fact. 'There's a particular smell that can point to a UTI in young children. Not always, but it's an indicator.'

She nodded and Jon thought he saw her lips purse slightly. Maybe it was just his imagination. 'Is that an old wives' tale?'

'It was something that a very experienced health visitor told me when I was starting out. It's been statistically confirmed since.'

'Which means you need a mid-stream urine sample?'

'Yes. I think I can get that the natural way, without having to catheterise her.'

He passed this test every day. Concerned parents, who needed to know whether they could really trust him or not. It was only right that care-givers should question him and weigh everything he did up for themselves, but it was different with Chloe. He wanted very badly to make her smile.

Suddenly she did, and the effect left him momentarily transfixed, taking in all the tiny details that he'd forced himself not to notice before. The way her light auburn hair, scraped back away from her face, escaped in curls around her brow. The tiny freckles across her nose, and her pale skin. Long legs encased in a neat, business-like skirt. She was the kind of woman that a man could spend a lot of time watching.

She reddened slightly—enchantingly—and Jon looked away quickly. It was nothing. He was human, and it was just an echo from a long-gone past, when wanting to watch every move a woman made had been something that might lead somewhere.

'Did your very experienced health visitor give you any clues about how to get a two-year-old to pee on demand?'

'As it happens, no. But I've picked up a few pointers from their mothers. And I gave her a drink as soon as I got here.'

He bent over Amy, smiling at her, and she rewarded him with a smile in return. That's what he liked so much about children, they were usually a lot less complicated than adults. 'Right, young lady. Let's give this a go.'

CHAPTER TWO

HE WAS SO good with Amy. Confident, gentle and playful. The kind of doctor that every parent wanted to see when their child was sick. Chloe knew that a midstream urine sample, one that wasn't contaminated by any bacteria from the skin, wasn't an easy proposition, and she waited to see what Jon was going to come up with.

He didn't disappoint. Taking Amy's nappy pants off and cleaning her carefully, he made a game out of sitting her on a potty and splashing her hands and feet in a bowl of warm water. Even though she was fretful and drowsy, he somehow managed to make her drink a little more and make her laugh at the faces he pulled. When she did finally give in, he seized the opportunity and deftly caught a mid-stream sample in the small container he had ready.

'Well done, sweetheart.' He hugged Amy and she grabbed at the sample bottle, almost spilling its precious contents. Chloe took it from him, snapping the lid on firmly, and Jon set about dressing Amy.

'The urinalysis test kits are over there.' He nodded towards a cupboard in the corner of the consulting room.

It seemed that, finally, she was going to be allowed

to do something, instead of sitting and watching Jon work. Even if sitting and watching him did have its good points. Chloe carefully divided the small sample into two, one for the lab, if needed, and the other for the test strip from the urinalysis kit.

'You were right.' She showed the coloured test strip to Jon and his brow darkened. There was a clear indication of the presence of white blood cells and bacteria.

'I think it's best if we take her into the children's ward, for tonight at least. The infection's clearly putting her under some stress.'

And Amy's home situation wasn't ideal at the moment. At least he had the delicacy not to mention that. Or maybe he was just ignoring it, since that was Chloe's problem, not his.

'Yes, I agree. Thanks, Jon.'

'Are you finished for the day?'

Chloe nodded. 'Yes, I've seen all the patients on my list. I had some paperwork to catch up on but that can wait.'

'Then what do you say to my staying here with Amy and sorting out a bed for her? I think it's time you went home and had a conversation with Hannah.'

He was absolutely right and wishing that Jon would come with her, in the hope that he might be able to conquer Hannah's fears as effortlessly as he'd conquered Amy's, was just selfish. Amy needed someone with her here, and Hannah needed some support too. This was the obvious solution.

'Are you sure? I don't know how long I'll be.'

'I'm fine here until my shift starts. You'll be back by then?'

'Yes, I'll make sure if it. With or without Hannah.' A thought occurred to her. 'Have you eaten?' He shook his head, as if that didn't really matter. 'I'll get you something. I've got some rosehip teabags if you'd like tea?'

From the look on his face, rosehip teabags didn't quite hit the spot. 'Thanks, but…actually anything with caffeine and a few calories would be great. And a drink for Amy. My wallet's in my jacket pocket.'

He picked Amy up, soothing her gently. Chloe ignored his jacket and made for the door. The least she could do for him was to stand him breakfast, even if it was just a sandwich from the canteen.

Chloe had left a large cup of coffee and a sandwich from the canteen perched on the window sill, well out of Amy's reach. Then she'd hugged Amy, gifted Jon with a smile that had been as delicious as it had been hurried, and had left.

'Just you and me, then, eh?' He rocked Amy in his arms. She was becoming increasingly fretful, and the sooner he started the antibiotic drip the better. He'd sent one of the nurses to get what he needed, and he was alone for a moment.

'Don't you worry, now, sweetheart. Everything's going to be okay, and we'll make you better.' Making Amy better was reasonably straightforward. Making everything okay was a lot more fraught with uncertainty. Hannah hadn't just been distressed when she'd arrived at Chloe's house, there had been a wild look in her eyes that had told Jon she was very close to breaking point. He'd been loath to leave her alone, but Hannah hadn't given him much choice in the matter.

'Mum-eee…' Amy's little face started to scrunch up and tears escaped her eyes. Jon held her close, soothing her.

'All right. Mummy's coming.' Not straight away but soon, he hoped. 'You want to know a secret, Amy?'

'I love secrets...' Jon jumped as someone spoke. He hadn't heard the calm-faced nurse re-enter the room, and when he turned she was standing behind him.

'This one is that I'm gasping for that cup of coffee over there.' Jon gave her a smile and a shrug when her lip curled slightly in disbelief.

'I'll take her. Go and drink your coffee.'

'Thanks.'

He'd leave the real secret until later. It was one thing to tell Amy that her Aunt Chloe was one of the most beautiful women he'd seen in a long while but, then, Amy could be relied on not to syphon that information into the hospital gossip network. Neither would she betray the part about Chloe's special magic. Jon couldn't quite put his finger on what kind of magic it was, but he wasn't so far gone that he couldn't recognise it was there.

He sipped his coffee, watching as the nurse busied herself, trying to tell himself that he shouldn't be shaken by any of this. It was straightforward. A housemate for six weeks while he made his own place habitable. A child who needed his help. It was neat and clean and nothing that he couldn't deal with.

Not like his marriage. Jon had often wondered whether the time bomb that had finally blown everything apart had been primed on his and Helen's wedding day. Ticking away the moments of pure happiness, measuring all the times that attention to two blossoming careers had demanded they spend apart, and tallying up each moment of tired indifference. Then exploding suddenly, sending shards of vitriol that scattered themselves across every aspect of Jon's life, embedding themselves deep into his heart.

A heart that had been hardened by time, but now felt under attack. Chloe's house was a long way away from the perfect, magazine-cover home that he and Helen had shared, but he'd found himself suddenly at ease there, as if he'd just pulled on a favourite shirt. Maybe it was a little frayed in places but it was warm and comfortable, fitting him perfectly. And if her house made him yearn for something he didn't have, then Chloe herself turned an obscure ache into an urgent stab of longing.

'Chloe's gone now?' The nurse interrupted his reverie.

'Yeah.'

'So you're left holding the baby...' The nurse bent down, smoothing Amy's brow in a motion of comfort. 'Pretty little thing, isn't she?'

'Yes, she is.' Jon had always assumed that Amy's light auburn curls and the freckles across her nose must be inherited from her father. But some quirk of genetics had rendered the little girl the image of her aunt, right down to her honey-brown eyes.

The feeling that he was being sucked in by Chloe's eyes wasn't an entirely unpleasant one. But he was in control of his life now. He could decide to ignore whatever part of Chloe he wanted to.

'This is the last thing Chloe needs right now. I hope she doesn't overdo things.' The nurse smoothed the blanket over Amy in one of those entirely unnecessary acts of caring that always made Jon proud to be part of a team.

'I heard she'd been ill.'

'Yes. I don't think that any of the doctors down here

could miss a case of Guillain-Barré syndrome if they tried. Chloe made sure of that.'

The thought made Jon smile. Guillain-Barré was enough to deal with on its own, without undertaking an information awareness exercise. But somehow he expected no less of Chloe.

'She shared her experience?'

'You bet she did. Before she could even walk, she persuaded someone to wheel her down here and told the senior houseman that if any of the juniors hadn't seen Guillain-Barré before, she was ready to be examined. It was pretty painful for her, but she sat through it and slurred her way through all of their questions as well.'

'That's...' Suddenly Jon couldn't find the words.

'Beyond the call of duty, I'd say.'

'Yeah. Way beyond...' If Chloe could do that, then backing off now was suddenly unthinkable. Jon put his cup down, ignoring the film-wrapped sandwich. 'Why don't you get on, now? I've everything I need here, and I'll make sure that Amy's all right.'

Chloe had expected to find that Hannah was upset, but the reality had been much worse. Hannah had been sitting in the lounge, her arms wound around her stomach, her face impassive apart from the tears that had trickled down her cheeks. She'd looked almost as if she was in shock, rocking slightly as if to comfort herself.

Chloe had made a cup of tea and they'd talked for a while. Or rather Chloe had done most of the talking, while Hannah had listened disinterestedly, as if the words had meant nothing to her. But Chloe knew she'd got through to Hannah because when she'd suggested that she come and see Amy, to make sure she was all right, Hannah had stood up and put on her jacket.

Jon had left a message with the paediatric A and E receptionist, and Chloe led Hannah up to the children's ward. She could see him, sitting next to Amy's cot, through the large window that divided the ward from the reception area, and when he caught sight of them, he rose.

'How is she?' Hannah's first question for Jon was the one she'd asked Chloe as soon as she'd walked through the door.

'She's doing well. I wanted her admitted to hospital as a precaution, but the antibiotics will clear the UTI and she'll be fine.' His voice was gentle but very firm, as if just saying it was going to make it happen.

'I'm sorry.' There was nothing but dull despair in Hannah's voice.

'There's nothing to be sorry for. You did exactly the right thing for Amy. I wish that some other mothers were as sensible as you.'

Hannah looked up at him. Jon seemed to be making about as much impression on Hannah as Chloe had, but he was trying. And somewhere, on some level, Hannah must be hearing all of this.

'Why don't you come and see her, eh?' Jon picked up Hannah's hand, tucking it into the crook of his arm. He flashed a smile towards Chloe and she nodded. She'd done her best to convince Hannah that she was a good mother and she'd done nothing wrong, but Hannah had just shrugged. *'You're my sister, you would say that.'* Maybe the words would have greater weight if they came from someone else.

She watched as Jon walked Hannah into the ward, getting her to sit down in the chair that he'd been occupying. He gestured towards the drip, obviously explaining everything that was being done for Amy, and waited as Hannah slowly reached out to touch Amy's hand. Then he turned, walking out of the ward to stand next to Chloe.

'She seems…fragile.' Jon was watching Hannah and Amy intently.

'Yes, she is.' Chloe looked up at him, but he didn't return her gaze. 'She's doing a good job of beating herself up over what's happened.'

Jon frowned. 'What *has* happened? As far as I can see, Hannah thought that there was something wrong with Amy and did everything she could to get the proper medical treatment for her.'

If only he would look at her. Chloe could really do with just a moment in the warmth of his reassurance. But it seemed that was carefully rationed, and that only Amy and Hannah were entitled to it.

'When she went to see the doctor, she said that he looked at Amy and said it was most likely just a virus, and to call him immediately if she was worried. Hannah started to cry and he asked a lot of questions about how she was doing. She thinks that the doctor put all of her worries about Amy down to her own mental state.'

The frown deepened. 'Hannah was crying when I saw her. *And* she had a sick baby…'

'Yes. Well, that was a few hours later and maybe Amy's symptoms were a lot more pronounced.' Or maybe Jon was just a good doctor, who understood people. 'Apparently Hannah's been to her doctor before, about feeling she can't cope.'

'You knew this?'

That was the bitterest part of it. Hannah had been in trouble and she hadn't said anything. 'No. Neither did James.'

'What are you going to do?' He turned suddenly,

and the warmth in his face cut through the feeling that Chloe had failed Hannah yet again. This time, it was all going to be different.

'I've given James a call. He's on holiday in Cornwall, but he's driving back up tonight and he'll stay with Hannah at my place. I'll stay here with Amy, and we can talk in the morning.'

'Sounds like a plan. If there's anything I can do...' He shrugged, as if he couldn't think of what that anything might be. A moment in his arms perhaps. Having him tell her that everything was going to be fine. But that was something that could only be given, not asked for.

'You've done a great deal already. I'm very grateful.' If that sounded a lot like a *thank you and goodbye*, then maybe it was. Relying on other people to help her was only going to lead to disappointment.

'It's nothing. Just paying it forward.' Chloe shot him a querying look. 'James was very good to me when my marriage broke up, he put me up until I found a place of my own. That was when I got to know Hannah.'

'I'm sorry, I didn't realise—'

'It's water under the bridge now.' The downward quirk of his lips told Chloe that even if it was, it was something that still pained him. 'From what James tells me, you were dealing with your own problems at that time. I've only ever come across one case of Guillain-Barré syndrome but I know it's a tough journey to take.'

It *had* been tough, suddenly losing any sensation other than pain in both legs and one arm, contending with the real fear that the accompanying paralysis might keep spreading until it reached her chest and the other side of her face.

'That's water under the bridge, too.'

Suddenly he was looking at her again, his face suffused with all the warmth that he'd offered to Amy and Hannah. 'You're sure about that. Because if you can't cope...'

'I *can* cope.' The words were defensive on her lips. 'Sorry.'

'No... I'm sorry, I didn't mean to snap.' It wasn't Jon's fault that few of the promises that had been made around her hospital bed had come to fruition. That both Jake and her best friend had sworn they'd stand by her through this, and they'd ended up standing by each other.

Chloe took a deep breath, trying to puff out the echoes of the lonely despair she'd felt when she'd realised that her partner and her friend were now an item and that neither of them had the guts to come and tell her. This wasn't the time to be raking over old memories because she had to think about the challenges of the present.

'Look, I... I couldn't give Hannah the support she needed when I was ill. I can now.'

He nodded. 'And that's important to you.'

'Yes, it is. Hannah's not had an easy time, she was so young when our parents died. James and I tried to help her through it, but we were both at university and neither of us were in a position to give her a stable home. My mother's sister fostered her, and... Aunt Sylvie's very kind, very loving, but Hannah always wanted to live with me. When she was fifteen I took her.'

'But you fell ill?'

'Yes, and Hannah went to live with James. I don't think she really understood why I wouldn't keep her. She told me that she'd help look after me, but I didn't want to make her into my carer. She deserved more than that.'

The frank approval in his eyes meant a lot more than it should. Chloe had wanted his understanding, craved his warmth, and now that she had it, it was too much to bear. She looked away, staring at Hannah and Amy.

'Hannah was almost sixteen when she ran away. I couldn't help look for her, I could hardly manage to get out of the house. It was James who found her and brought her back, and he was the one who looked after her when she realised that she was pregnant.'

'And you think you let Hannah down?' His tone suggested that Jon thought quite the opposite, but Chloe begged to differ.

'I think that Hannah and Amy need me right now. And that I'm going to be there for both of them.' It was too late to save Hannah from the turbulence of her teenage years, but she would find a way to put things right now. Because this time it wasn't only a matter of saving Hannah, it was a matter of saving Amy, too.

CHAPTER THREE

IT HAD BEEN a restless night, sleeping in the folding bed next to Amy's cot, and so far the morning hadn't been much easier. Chloe hadn't seen Jon when she'd returned home to talk to Hannah and James, and she'd assumed that he'd escaped over to his place when his shift had ended this morning.

But when she got back to the hospital he was there, sitting in the chair next to Amy's cot with Amy on his lap, talking to her and gently stopping her from grabbing at the bandage on her arm that covered the cannula.

'She's a lot better this morning.' One of the nurses had stopped at Chloe's side, and Chloe dragged her gaze away from Jon. Each time she saw him with Amy it was impossible not to notice that someone so strong could be so gentle.

'Does he usually check up on his patients like this?'

The nurse grinned. 'He's no stranger up here, he often pops in to see how the children he's had admitted are doing. He seems to have taken a bit of a shine to Amy, though.'

It seemed that he had. And Amy had clearly taken a bit of a shine to Jon, looking up at him, her hand reaching to touch his face.

But Chloe was here now. And she could cope. Thanking the nurse, she walked into the ward.

'Good morning.' Jon had been so bound up with Amy that he'd failed to register Chloe's approach until she'd spoken.

He made to deliver Amy into her arms, and the little girl started to cry, clinging on to him. Jon pulled an embarrassed face, which didn't quite conceal his pleasure at Amy being so determined not to let him go, and Chloe motioned for him to stay as he was.

'How are things?' He took a moment out from Amy to ask the question.

'We're getting there. I think…' Chloe took her jacket off and sat down. 'James is taking Hannah back down to Cornwall with him, and I'm going to look after Amy for a while.'

His attention was suddenly all hers. 'She doesn't want to stay here?'

'She's…' Chloe shrugged. 'She's got it into her head that I can look after Amy better than she can. Maybe that's true for the moment. Hannah definitely needs a break so she can think things through.'

'And when she has?' Concern was etched deep into his face.

'When she has, she'll see that she's a great mother and that James and I are both here for her to give her all the support she needs to make a good life for herself and for Amy.'

'Sounds good to me.'

'You don't seem very convinced.' He obviously knew as well as Chloe did that things probably weren't going to be as easy as that.

He shrugged. 'I'm…not really the one to ask about families.'

'You mean the kids are a lot less complicated?'

'Now you mention it…' Amy grabbed at his nose and he gave her a look of exaggerated shock. Then he pinched her nose, putting his thumb between his fingers as he pulled his hand away and showing it to Amy.

'Mine…!' Amy reached for his hand.

'That's your nose, is it?' Jon wiggled his thumb and Amy nodded.

It was almost painful to watch. All the support and love that anyone could want, and which Chloe couldn't bring herself to trust in. But Jon had just said it himself. Something had persuaded him that families weren't his strong point, and for him it was all about the children.

He was busy replacing Amy's nose and threading an imaginary needle to stitch it back on again while Amy held it in place. 'How's that, then? Let Auntie Chloe have a look, see if I've got it straight.'

'It's straight…' Suddenly the game seemed too good to end it here. Chloe clapped her hand theatrically over her mouth. 'Call yourself a doctor? Amy…he's put your nose back on upside down!'

Amy pulled at her nose, inspecting her empty hand, and Jon laughed.

'Look, this is the way you do it… Perhaps Auntie Chloe can do a better job putting it back on again.' A flash of his blue eyes, full of intoxicating fun. 'She's obviously the expert around here.'

The make-believe needle and thread was handed over to Chloe, and she pulled her chair a little closer. Amy held her nose on, giggling, while Chloe pretended to sew it back, her knees almost touching Jon's. When he leaned over to gently untangle the drip attached to Amy's arm, his fingers brushed hers, making her shiver.

'Perfect.' Jon inspected her handiwork, then dropped

a kiss onto his finger, planting it on Amy's nose then lifting the little girl onto Chloe's lap.

'Are you okay here?' He pulled his chair back, as if he knew that suddenly he'd got altogether too close. 'What about Amy's things?'

'James is dealing with that. He's taking Hannah back to her place to pack and then he'll drop Amy's things back at my place and take Hannah on down to Cornwall.'

Jon nodded. 'I guess Cornwall's not so far. If Hannah needs to come back.'

'Yes.' Chloe sighed. 'I hate them being apart but... Hannah seems to need some time at the moment. And some sleep as well.'

'Yeah. I can identify with that.' He rubbed one hand across his face, seeming suddenly drawn.

'Why don't you go home and get some rest? James and Hannah will be gone by now and I'll give them a call and tell them not to wake you up when they get back with Amy's things.'

'You want anything before I go? Something to eat?'

'No, I've eaten. Go.'

Amy seemed to have run out of energy too, and Chloe felt her snuggle against her, refusing to wake up and wave goodbye to Jon. He grinned, brushing Amy's cheek with his finger, and Chloe watched his back as he walked away.

He turned for one final wave through the window from the lobby outside. Even distance, even the glass couldn't dim the bright blue of his tired eyes and Chloe wished that he wasn't leaving her behind.

It was the first step on a long and slippery slope. A look, a shared smile that would catapult her into neediness and leave her in a tangled heap on the floor when

Jon went his own way. However much she liked his smile, it just wasn't worth it.

Amy started to fret in her arms and Chloe leaned down to comfort her. 'It's going to be okay, Amy. Everything's going to be okay, you'll see.'

Jon hadn't thought that a battered teddy bear and a bar of chocolate could possibly be such controversial items. He'd selected the teddy bear from the bag of toys that James had left in the hall while he'd slept, reckoning that the most worn was probably the most loved. And the chocolate was the same seventy per cent cocoa blend that he'd found stashed away at the back of one of the kitchen cabinets.

But when he'd gone to the children's ward that evening, Chloe had looked at them both as if they were poisoned. She propped the teddy bear up in Amy's cot, leaving the chocolate untouched on the locker.

'Isn't your shift about to start?' It was a clear invitation for him to go, even if he'd only just arrived. He probably should go, but something stopped him. Maybe the fact that no one in their right mind refused a visitor when they were in hospital, and that Chloe's attitude betrayed some other worry.

'Not for another hour.' He drew up a chair and sat down. He could probably find somewhere else to be, but sleep had rearranged his muddled thoughts, and on waking the decision had seemed obvious. Chloe needed help, and he was there to give it.

She hesitated. She looked different tonight, softer, dressed in a pair of casual trousers with a top that he reckoned was supposed to slide from one shoulder to reveal the strap of a cotton vest underneath. The warmth in here had touched her cheeks with pink, and her hair curled loosely around her face in what seemed like an invitation to touch.

Clearly that invitation wasn't extended to him. And even if it had been, Jon had no intention of taking it up. The decision on that point had been clear, too. Help out, but don't touch.

'You don't need to do this.' She pressed her lips together, and they too became a little pinker. Jon wondered whether they tasted pink, and dismissed the thought with no more than a moment's regret.

'Do what?'

'You know…' A small, delicious frown indicated that Chloe understood quite well that he was going to make her explain. 'We all really appreciate what you did yesterday, Jon. But you don't have to feel responsible for us, just because… You have other things to be getting on with.'

For a moment he couldn't imagine what those other things might be. Chloe and Amy seemed more important than anything.

'My house, you mean?'

'Yes. And your job.'

'I imagine the builders will be quite pleased to find that I haven't been interfering with things over the weekend. And my job doesn't require twenty-four-hour input.'

'All the same…' She shrugged. 'Amy and I are fine, really. We're not your problem.'

He was beginning to feel that they were—which was a problem in itself. But Jon could handle it.

'I can help, can't I? It's never easy, taking responsibility for a sick child.'

'No, but I can manage. You don't need to keep popping in to see if we're all right.'

Leaning forward, he picked up the chocolate, un-wrapping one end and breaking off a piece. 'Okay. I get it. You're managing.'

The look on her face, when he started to eat, was a classic. Clearly she had reckoned on saving the choco-late and eating it when he was safely out of the way. He hesitated for a moment before he popped a second piece into his mouth and she broke suddenly.

'You're eating my chocolate.'

Jon grinned, as innocently as he could manage. 'Yeah. Since you're managing so well, I thought you wouldn't want it.'

She seemed on the cusp of either smiling or sulk-ing. Chloe went for the smile. 'That's different. Don't you know that some people have a special relationship with chocolate?'

That was exactly what he'd been banking on. Jon handed her the bar and she broke a piece off. 'So I'm allowed to bring you chocolate, then?'

She twisted her mouth, obviously willing to accept that she was beaten. 'Yes. You're allowed to bring me chocolate.'

'And Amy her bear?' He glanced over to where Amy was subjecting the bear to her own version of nursing care, shoving it under the blanket of her cot.

'Yes, that was a kind thought. Papa Bear's her favou-rite.' She smiled at Amy, who ignored her, in favour of banging Papa Bear on the nose, presumably in an at-tempt to make him go to sleep.

'She seems much better.'

'Yes, she is. She's stopped clinging to me and want-ing to be held. They should be letting her go on Mon-day when the tests come back.'

Chloe turned her gaze back onto Jon. 'Look, I'm

sorry if I seemed ungrateful. When I was ill… You get to understand who you can really rely on at times like that.'

'Yourself?' It wasn't a universal experience. Many—most—people were comforted by the support of those around them when they became gravely ill.

'Yes, myself. James did the best he could, but he had Carol and the kids *and* Hannah to worry about.'

'So you told him that you were fine and that you didn't need anything.' Which was exactly what Chloe was telling him now. Jon's determination to take that with a pinch of salt strengthened.

She shrugged. 'I might have intimated something of the sort.'

'And since you're a doctor, and James probably wouldn't have heard of Guillain-Barré syndrome, he'd have just taken your word for it.'

'Well, he looked it up on the internet. But the internet can be wrong sometimes.' Chloe fixed Jon with a glare. 'And you're not telling him any different now.'

'What you choose to tell anyone about your illness is none of my business.' James would be horrified if he knew what Jon suspected, that Chloe had been incapacitated and coping alone for a long time after she'd been released from hospital. But there was no point in telling him that now.

'Thank you.'

It was obvious why Chloe had been reluctant to rely on her brother, but it was rather more of a puzzle why she'd applied the same principle to everyone. And why she seemed so intent on applying it again now. But that wasn't his business either. As long as she accepted that she could at least tell him if she needed something, they'd get along just fine. He took the small lint bandage that he'd found in the kitchen drawer out of his pocket.

'Hey, Amy.' The little girl turned to look at him. 'Is Papa Bear ill?'

'Yes.' Amy nodded gravely.

'Right. Shall we see if we can make him better?' It wasn't unusual for children to transfer what was going on in their heads onto their toys, and making the battered bear better would help Amy too.

Chloe caught onto the idea and grinned. 'Do you think he needs a bandage?' She leaned over, lifting Amy out of the cot and onto her lap, and Jon reached for the bear.

'Poor Papa Bear. Make him better.' Amy turned her trusting eyes on him.

'All right, Nurse Amy. You hold him, and I'll just put this bandage on his arm.' Jon nodded to the dressing on Amy's arm, which protected the cannula. 'Just like yours.'

Amy nodded, and Chloe kissed the top of her niece's head. 'See Amy. Doctor Jon's going to make him better.'

It was a start, at least. If Chloe didn't trust him enough to take anything for herself, she was much more comfortable with taking all she could get for Amy. And Jon was sure of his ground. He'd be in and then out again, a clean operation, carried out with all the precision that his medical training had taught him to apply. It was perfectly possible to help the sister of a good friend out without doing anything stupid like falling in love with her.

CHAPTER FOUR

CHLOE WASN'T ABOUT to admit that she'd overreacted. It might have looked that way to Jon, but he clearly hadn't learned yet that even the best of friends would choose their own agenda when it came to the crunch.

That actually wasn't the problem. The problem was that every time she saw him she wanted to hold onto him, to make him stay. Wanted him to prove that Jake had been mistaken.

Not that she cared all that much about what Jake thought, or did, any more. He'd left her because he'd been unable to see past her illness, and wouldn't believe that she could make a full recovery, and she'd shown that he was wrong on that score. But she was human, and wanting to be touched by a man was natural. Wanting to show herself that her body could be a source of pleasure and not pain…that was natural enough, too.

But Jon wasn't the one to prove that point with. If she touched him, and let him touch her, she wouldn't want to let him go.

What he said made sense, though. Chloe was dreading talking to her supervisor on Monday and telling him that she had a sick baby to look after. He'd been so understanding over the Guillain-Barré, taking her back in her old job and letting her work part time for as long as she'd needed to. Everyone's patience ran out sooner or later, and hopefully this wasn't going to be the last straw. If it turned out that she would have to look after Amy for longer than the next two weeks, she was going to need all the help she could get.

A restless night did little to quell her worries, but a new arrival in the ward early on Sunday morning put them into perspective—a little boy of around three, a breathing mask over his face, who lay surrounded by monitoring equipment.

'What's the matter with him?' she whispered to the nurse who was with him.

'Smoke inhalation.' The nurses all knew that Chloe was a doctor, and were more frank with her than with the other parents on the ward.

'Where are his parents?'

'Dad's on the burns unit. I think Mum's still down in A and E.'

'Shall I go down and see if I can find her? She must be worried sick.'

'I think... Yeah, I think that's her now.' The nurse grinned. 'With Amy's favourite doctor.'

There was no question about who that was. Chloe looked up and saw Jon pushing a woman in a wheel-chair into the lobby. She was wearing a hospital gown and a nasal cannula indicated that there was probably an oxygen cylinder tucked under the blanket over her knees. Chloe left the nurse with the boy and went out-side to meet them.

Jon was looking around, trying to catch the atten-tion of one of the nurses but they were all busy. When he saw Chloe he spoke to the woman.

'Ah. Here's someone who might know...' He turned

his blue eyes up to meet hers. 'There's a little boy, three years old. He's just been admitted.'

'Through here.' Chloe indicated the ward, and Jon nodded a thank-you, wheeling the woman through.

'Nicky…' The woman's voice was hoarse and cracked. She stretched out her hand towards the boy in the bed and tried to get out of the wheelchair but Jon laid his hand on her shoulder, stopping her.

'Stay there, Kathy. He's all right.'

'His hands…' Kathy wouldn't stop reaching, and Chloe saw that one of Nicky's hands was still blackened by smoke.

'It's all right. His hands aren't burned, I cleaned him up and checked. He must have picked that bit of soot up when I took his pyjamas off.' Jon's reassurance calmed Kathy a little.

'He's not burned at all?'

'Nothing. Your husband did a good job, Kathy, he got him out of the house without a scratch on him. It's just the smoke inhalation. We need to watch him carefully for a little while, just the same as we need to watch you.'

'I'm all right.' Kathy didn't take her eyes off her son.

'Well, we need to make sure. I sprang you out of observation on the strict condition that I made sure you stayed in the chair and breathed through your nose. You're not getting the full benefit of the oxygen if you breathe through your mouth.'

Jon gave Kathy a look of gentle reproof and she closed her mouth, her chest moving as she took a deep breath through her nose.

'Better. Thank you.' Jon grinned at her and she managed a smile. Chloe stepped forward, taking Kathy's hand.

'I'm Chloe. That's my niece over there, but I'm a

doctor too. Would you like me to clean Nicky's hand?' It made little difference whether the boy's hand was clean or dirty at the moment, but it was all that Chloe could think of to make Kathy feel better.

Kathy nodded, giving her a tight smile.

Chloe fetched some warm water and carefully wiped and dried Nicky's hand. Jon had stepped away from them and was talking quietly on his phone, and Chloe pushed the wheelchair a little closer to the bed so that Kathy could touch her son.

'Is there anyone we can call for you? A friend or relative?'

'Dr Lambert's calling my sister. He's so kind...' A tear rolled down Kathy's cheek.

'Yes, he is. He's a very good doctor as well, and Nicky's in good hands here.' Chloe put her arm around Kathy's shoulders. 'Don't cry, now. Just breathe.'

Jon was still on the phone, talking intently. He saw Chloe watching him, and before she could avert her eyes he flashed her a smile and ended the call.

'Your sister's coming, she'll be here in an hour. She's going to get the children to school and then come straight here.' He bent down, squatting on his heels in front of Kathy. 'I called down to see how your husband's doing—'

'Is he all right?' Kathy's hand flew to her mouth.

'He's comfortable and in no danger. He needs care, he has smoke inhalation and burns to his arm, but they'll heal.'

'Thank you... Thank you...'

That smile again. The one that would have calmed a charging rhino. Or made a stone feel something. 'I hear your husband was a hero.'

Tears rolled down Kathy's cheeks. 'He told me to

go downstairs. He went to fetch Nicky and rolled him up in a blanket…'

'The doctor said that you could see him for ten minutes. I can take you down, and bring you straight back here to be with Nicky.'

Kathy's gaze moved to her son and then back to Jon, in a dilemma. Nicky was lying quietly at the moment, but he was going to need his mother's comfort when the trauma of the last few hours started to sink in.

'Will you let me watch Nicky for you while you're gone? I'll call you if there's any change or if he becomes distressed.' Chloe spoke up.

'Would you…?' Kathy was still uncertain.

'I'll stay right here, by his bed. I can call Jon, and he'll bring you straight back here.'

Jon nodded, taking his phone from the trouser pocket of his scrubs and putting it in Kathy's hand. 'Here. Hang onto it for me.'

Kathy nodded. 'I'd like to see him. I want to tell him—'

Jon got to his feet, smiling. 'He'll be wanting to hear it. And Chloe will keep a good eye on Nicky. If we all share the load, we can cover everything.'

Chloe had been wondering whether that last comment had been aimed at her. Jon's glance had flipped momentarily towards her when he'd said it, and she'd pretended not to notice.

He took Kathy away, and brought her back again twenty minutes later. Even though his shift had ended almost an hour ago, he waited until Kathy's sister arrived, taking ten minutes to change out of his scrubs and then returning to the ward. This time Chloe couldn't help a little thrill of excitement because he was quite obviously here just for her.

'Breakfast?'

'Shouldn't you be getting home for some sleep?' Her treacherous heart hoped that he wouldn't go.

'I'm not quite tired enough yet.'

They left Amy playing quietly and walked down to the canteen. Jon piled a plate full of all the breakfast items on the menu and Chloe rummaged in her handbag for the small sachet of teabags.

'Hot water? Or can I tempt you to something else?' He gestured towards the pile of flapjacks.

'No, that's okay. I'll watch you eat.'

They found a table in a quiet corner and Jon attacked his food like a man who hadn't eaten in the last week. She waited until he slowed a little, sipping her tea.

'So how's Kathy's husband?'

'Second- and third-degree burns on the top of his arm and shoulder. He could well need skin grafts.'

'But he'll be okay.'

'Yes. Apparently he was pretty lucky to escape with just that.'

'He knew Kathy was there?'

Jon's face broke into a smile. 'He was drowsy from the pain relief but he knew all right. Brave man.'

'Going to fetch Nicky like that.'

'Yes. And the way he told Kathy that it all looked worse than it felt, and that she wasn't to worry about him. He was okay, and she should stay with Nicky.'

He paused for a moment, looking at Chloe, and then started to eat again. She wondered whether *that* comment was aimed at her as well. If it was, she didn't deserve the kind of respect that Kathy's husband did. She'd just done what she'd had to do, when she'd sent Hannah away to live with James.

'I'll go down there later. If he can't have visitors, I can at least take a message from Kathy. Let him know how she and Nicky are doing.'

'That's nice. I'm sure he'd appreciate it.'

He finished the last few mouthfuls from his plate and leaned back in his seat with a satisfied sigh. Then he turned to the toast.

'I've been thinking...'

Chloe asked the question that he was clearly waiting for. 'What about?'

'What are you going to do when Amy comes out of hospital?'

'I'll take some time off work. She should be coming out on Monday but it won't be until the afternoon so I'll speak to my head of department in the morning. When she's fully well, I'll make enquiries about getting her into the hospital crèche.'

He nodded. 'I could look after her next week.'

'You can't work nights and look after a baby all day. You're not *that* superhuman.'

'Ah, so you think I'm just a bit superhuman...' Jon grinned at her. 'But, no, I wasn't thinking of doing that. The guy I'm covering for is back from sick leave next week. I'm working on Monday night, but I'm not needed again until the following Sunday. After that I've got some more time off arranged before I start work permanently, and I can use that to work on the house.'

It was tempting. Very tempting, in more ways than just the practical. Chloe stared at him, trying to frame a polite but firm refusal.

'What?' He didn't wait for her answer. 'Come on,

you know Amy will be safe with me. And a week off
with her might be relaxing.'

'You think so?'

Jon shrugged. 'Well, a change is as good as a rest.
Amy can't frame a sensible sentence about either medicine *or* building materials.'

He seemed so sure. And although it was difficult
to fault his logic, his absolute commitment to the idea
didn't make any sense.

'This is my responsibility, Jon. Why won't you take
no for an answer?'

It was a fair enough question. If he were in Chloe's
shoes, he'd be asking the same thing. Avoiding her like
the plague and then suddenly jumping in with both feet
might not be a very good basis for trust, but he'd just
have to use a bit of persuasion.

'When do you think Hannah's going to be able to
take full-time responsibility for Amy?' He avoided the
question with one of his own.

She sighed. 'I spoke with James last night. We both
agreed to take things slowly.'

'Then you're going to need to pace yourself. Save
your leave for when you really need it.'

'That's true, and it's a very good point. You haven't
answered my question, though.'

So he wasn't getting off the hook that easily. 'Families are important.'

'That's true too.' She was circling the rim of her
empty cup with her finger. Jon could practically hear
the next question forming and he didn't want to answer
that one either.

'Look, James will tell you that I'm not close to my

family. I speak with my sister regularly, once a fort-night. I mark it in my diary to remind me.'

She looked up at him thoughtfully, obviously trying to comprehend an arrangement that was so different from the way she kept in touch with James and Hannah, just picking up the phone whenever she had something to say. Never needing to remember to do it, because her brother and sister were a part of her life.

'Do you say much?'

'Yeah, we say quite a bit. We've learned not to say anything that really matters, because that's likely to get us into trouble. It's a long story. But you and James and Hannah…you have something special. It's worth taking care of.'

'When our parents died, all we had was each other.' She pointed to his empty cup. 'Do you want a refill?'

'There's still another cup in the pot.' Jon picked up the small, stainless-steel coffee pot and poured the rest of its contents into his cup. 'Am I going to need this?'

'I'm not sure. You said it was a long story.'

Suddenly he wanted everything out in the open. He wanted to let Chloe know where he stood, and then they could forget about these games and get on with the practical.

'Right…' Jon wondered where to start, and decided that the very beginning was probably best. 'Well…boy meets girl, I guess…'

Her eyes widened suddenly. For one delicious moment Jon let the misunderstanding hang in the air between them.

'I met my ex-wife at the Freshers' Ball at medical school.'

'Ah. Yes, of course.' She found another teabag from the seemingly endless supply in her bag and put it into her cup, splashing hot water onto it. 'And…then you got married?'

'Yes, we did, after we'd both qualified. Everyone pretty much expected we would, we had the same interests, the same goals in life…our families got on so well that Helen's parents and mine used to go on weekend breaks together.'

Chloe's hand flew to her mouth, stifling the inevitable comment. Jon couldn't help smiling, even though there wasn't a great deal to smile about in all of this.

'Yeah, I know. When the in-laws start planning Christmas together there's a certain amount of expectation involved. But we didn't let them down, we got a nice house together, both of us had good jobs that we loved. We were very happy.'

Chloe didn't look convinced about any of this. Maybe she was smarter than he'd been. He'd thought then that love was something he could catch and keep, but now he knew better.

'I got a promotion, and Helen started working nights. We saw less and less of each other, and when we did there were more and more arguments. We became like strangers living in the same house.'

Even now, the quiet hopelessness, the feeling that if this was all there was to life it had somehow fallen short of what he'd wanted, reverberated through Jon's heart. He'd never smelled Helen's soap, the way he had Chloe's. Never checked the sell-by dates of her food in the fridge. Maybe if he had, things would have been different, but it was too late to think about that now.

'In the end, Helen asked me to leave. When we told our families that we were splitting up, the crash of broken expectations was deafening. Everyone was looking for a reason, why the perfect marriage should no longer be so perfect, and I couldn't give them one. My parents talked to Helen's, and then came to me and demanded to know whether I'd had an affair. I hadn't...'

'And you set them straight?' It was warming to find that Chloe's first reaction was one of belief, and not the disbelief that his parents had voiced.

'I tried to.' Jon shrugged. 'They were always very fond of Helen, though. And she was ready to believe anything that anyone said about me at that point. The whole thing blew up in our faces and became very bitter. Helen's solicitor drew up the divorce papers, and when I got them they cited adultery.'

'But...if that wasn't true...' Chloe's brow was creased with thought. 'I mean, they're legal papers. Wouldn't they be null and void? You'd still be married.'

Maybe it was the odd twist of logic. Or maybe just that Chloe was basing that logic on such an unquestioning belief. Jon couldn't help laughing.

'I've no idea. I wouldn't sign them, I held out for irreconcilable differences. There was no doubt at all about that one. My mother was furious with me, and that was when James came to the rescue and offered me a place to stay. I moved out of my parents' house...'

He shrugged. The softness in Chloe's eyes said all that there was left to say. The stupid, needless conflict, which had broken his family apart and driven him away because he'd been unable to handle all the back-biting.

'So, you see, I know how easily families can break. And I know how hard you and James have fought for yours and that's special. Call it meddling, but if I can help you now...'

He didn't know what he was hoping for. Maybe Chloe did. Jon reached forward, taking her hand, curling his fingers around hers.

'If you can help me now, it won't make anything right for you.'

Jon was used to people taking his help without question. Without even thinking about what it might mean to him. That was okay, it was his job and it was what he'd chosen to do, but Chloe... Chloe was different from anyone he'd ever met, and each time she showed that, it touched him.

'I know. I'm past caring about that now, and I concentrate on what I'm good at, my job and my friendships. I've given up on everything else, but you won't give up on Hannah, and that means something.'

Suddenly she looked up at him, her eyes as soft as honey. 'So...do you really think you're prepared for this? Amy can be quite a handful.'

'I doubt it, but I'll give it a go. What can go wrong?'

She smiled suddenly. 'I don't know. I dare say Amy will come up with something.'

CHAPTER FIVE

IN A WORLD full of imperfect relationships, Jon had bucked the trend and got himself something perfect. And it had broken and then descended into a chaos of hard feelings and lies. No wonder he didn't want to go back there again.

And that suited Chloe. Promises to stay for ever hadn't meant much when her parents had died, and even less when Jake had left. Even Hannah couldn't stay with Amy right now. But Jon had made it clear that there was a limit to what he could promise, and that was oddly reassuring.

But the silence in the house when she opened the front door wasn't. Amy had been released from hospital on Monday, and when Jon had got home from work on Tuesday morning, Chloe had left her niece in his care. She'd resisted the temptation to phone him any more than a couple of times during the day to ask if everything was all right, and left work at five-thirty on the dot.

She closed the front door. Maybe he'd taken Amy out for a while. But the car seat was still in the hall. Chloe walked into the sitting room and found Jon sprawled on the sofa, with Amy lying fast asleep on his chest.

It was odd, but every time she saw him he seemed a

little more deliciously handsome. Perhaps it was Amy's tiny hands, clutching at his shirt as she slept, his own arms providing a safe enclosure for her. Who could resist that?

Amy stirred and he opened his eyes immediately, his hand moving to spread protectively across her back. Then he caught sight of Chloe and she stepped back instinctively, aware that she'd been caught watching him.

'Hi…' She smiled foolishly as he sat up, bringing Amy with him. 'Good day?'

'Yeah.' He surveyed the toys, scattered across the floor. 'I'm afraid I didn't get much time to tidy up, though…'

'Amy's okay?'

'Yes, she's been fine.'

Chloe grinned. 'That's your mission for the day sorted, then.' She picked up a few of the toys, piling them up in the corner of the room, and then sat down next to him.

'How was your day?'

'Good.' She leaned over towards Amy, who was waking up in his arms. 'I missed you, Amy.'

Amy wriggled round, reaching for Chloe. 'Beautiful Auntie Chloe…'

Amy enunciated the words perfectly. Something she'd heard, maybe, and was mimicking…?

No. They were just words. Probably jumbled together without any particular meaning. Amy was beginning to do that, mixing the baby talk with the odd word that sounded as if it had some thought behind it, but generally didn't.

Jon looked as startled as she was. 'I…wonder where she picked that up from.'

'So I'm *not* beautiful?' Teasing him wasn't a bad way to cover her own discomfiture.

Jon narrowed his eyes. 'I'm a little too tired to come up with an answer that's not going to incriminate me.'

So maybe Amy *had* heard it from him. If so, it was probably best not to enquire. She took Amy from him, hugging her. 'So what did you get up to today?'

'We went to the park. There's a great playground…' He grinned. 'Amy enjoyed it too.'

'She didn't give you a chance to sleep?' Jon had reassembled Amy's cot, and it stood next to the sofa.

'She slept. I reckoned I might sleep, but…' He shrugged. 'I ended up watching her.'

'Just to make sure her dreams were good ones.' Chloe had done exactly the same when she'd been with Amy at the hospital. Hours when she could have been sleeping had somehow turned into hours watching Amy sleep.

'Yeah. I'll get an early night tonight. If I drop off before about nine o'clock perhaps you'll give me a good shake and wake me up.'

A good shake or just the flutter of a child, sleeping on his chest. It seemed that either would be equally as effective. 'How does the smell of coffee work?'

Jon nodded. 'Every time.'

She'd brought him coffee and then disappeared upstairs, taking Amy with her. The transformation between work, the plain blouse and skirt, which weren't plain at all when draped around Chloe's curves, and the casual trousers and tops she wore at home took place out of sight, but that didn't mean that Jon was unaware of it. Just thinking about it woke him up more effectively than if she'd flattened him with a steamroller.

He sat for a while, listening to her moving around

in the kitchen. She was singing, and he heard Amy's voice joining in with hers. He collected the rest of the toys off the floor, adding them to the pile, and wondered whether he should get a proper toy box. Perhaps not. Today might have felt like a new venture, but it was too temporary to warrant anything as solid as the wooden toy box he'd seen in the window of the furniture shop by the park gates.

The smell of cooking drew him into the kitchen. Chloe was chopping tomatoes to add to a bowl of salad, and he could see a large dish of lasagne in the oven. Amy held out her arms to him and instead of just smiling at her and getting on with his job, the way he did with the children at the hospital, picking her up seemed suddenly as if it *was* his job.

'Again…'

'Again?' He raised his eyebrows. 'Again what? I haven't done anything yet.'

The logic was lost on Amy. 'Again!'

'Ah. You mean this?' He swung her up above his head and the little girl laughed with delight.

'You've done it now.' Chloe's face was bright as she looked up from the chopping board.

'Yeah. She kept this up for half an hour this morning.'

'And then she was sick on your head?' Chloe shared the joke with the tomato in front of her, slicing it decisively. Jon swung Amy up one more time then sat down with her on his lap before she could stop squirming and laughing long enough to get out the dreaded word.

'No. I managed to avoid that indignity.' Amy hiccupped, and he jiggled her gently and rubbed her stomach.

Chloe turned. 'You want me to take her?'

That was usually the way. A child got hiccups and either their parents or one of the nurses dealt with it. His job was to deal with the rather more serious issues.

Amy hiccupped again, scrunching her face up. At the moment this seemed just as serious, but rather more difficult to deal with than any medical problem. Living with a child was different from treating them. For one thing, he didn't get so many breaks.

'No, that's okay. Amy and I will deal with this.'

Amy had been fed, and they'd eaten. Jon had taken the cot upstairs, and Chloe had bathed Amy and put her down to sleep. He opened his eyes, after dozing on the sofa, to find her standing in the doorway.

'Do you think if I sit down she'll start crying?'

He smiled. 'Maybe. Would you like a cup of tea?' Suddenly it was as if the one thing he'd tried to avoid, becoming a part of the household and living here instead of just sleeping here, had become a reality. It wasn't as bad as he'd thought it might be.

Chloe nodded. 'Yes, thanks.'

She followed him into the kitchen, sitting down at the table while he made the tea. 'Do you mind my asking? About the Guillain-Barré…?'

'You mean am I feeling tired yet?' She grinned, saving him the awkwardness of working his way onto the question that had been bothering Jon for much of the day.

'Yeah. The last few days have been a break in your routine.' She must have been worried about Amy, and Hannah. And she can't have had a great deal of sleep next to Amy's cot at the hospital.

'I'm okay. I still have a few after-effects, but they haven't got any worse.' Jon shot her a querying look and she grinned. 'Don't worry. I'm not keeping quiet about anything.'

'Okay. Just as a matter of interest, what *are* the after-effects?' He put her tea down in front of her and sat down.

'Sometimes my toes tingle a bit, or the bottom of my foot feels a little numb. But I've been pretty lucky on the whole, and I don't get any pain.' She leaned forward towards him. 'Go on. You can ask whatever you like. It's actually a good thing if doctors know a bit more about it.'

He took her at her word. 'So what caused it?'

'I had campylobacter. I'd got over that, and had gone back to work and then…' She shrugged, taking a sip of her tea.

One of the more common triggers for a rare disease. Guillain-Barré Syndrome was a result of the immune system being triggered by a viral infection and attacking the nerves. First a tingling in the hands and feet, which could spread throughout the whole body, causing weakness, paralysis and pain.

'I had a fall at work. Lucky really, because there were a lot of doctors on hand and someone recognised the symptoms and called in a neurologist. He ordered an EMG test and before I know it I was in the neuro ward, with about a thousand medical students hanging around, taking furious notes.'

'I heard you made the best of your audience.'

Her eyebrows shot up. 'You've been talking about me behind my back, have you?'

'No, one of the nurses in A and E mentioned it. I've been listening to other people talking about you behind your back.'

'I suppose I did give them a very full list of my

symptoms, so they'd recognise them if they saw them again. My right arm and my legs were completely paralysed for some weeks, but I could still talk if I put my mind to it.' Jon saw a trace of mischief in her smile and almost choked on his drink. She was indomitable.

'They say doctors make the worst patients.'

'I was a very good patient. I did exactly as I was told, and tried to smile at everyone, which isn't all that easy when one side of your face is paralysed. Dr Malik used to say that he didn't need to explain much to his students, he just sent them to me.' She took another sip of her tea. 'I think he was humouring me.'

Chloe was fingering the gold chain at her neck, absently winding it around her finger. She always seemed to wear it, and what hung on it must be of some special significance to her because it was usually hidden inside her clothes. But he could see now that it was a yellowish crystal.

'Did humouring you work?'

'Lots of things work. Intravenous immunoglobulin for starters. Good food, plenty of sleep. The kindness of strangers...'

'Herbal tea and crystals?' Jon had seen the crystals on the mantelpiece in the sitting room but hadn't realised that Chloe wore one as well. It surprised him that a doctor should put any store in such things.

'Who knows? Not being able to move isn't just something that affects your body.' She shrugged. It seemed that was where Chloe drew the line. She talked about the physical aspects of her illness freely enough, but Jon knew that the emotional ones could be just as devastating and she kept those to herself.

But he'd have to wonder about that later. He was

so tired now that whatever conclusion he came to was bound to be the wrong one.

'I really should turn in…' He looked at his watch. It was almost nine o' clock.

She grinned. 'Will you sleep? After a cup of coffee?'

'I needed the coffee to get me up the stairs. I'll sleep.'

It was odd that Chloe should note that the house had been quiet for the last hour, because generally it *was* quiet. But this was a different kind of quiet, one that seemed to curl around everyone in the house, both sleeping and awake.

She heard a whimpering cry from her bedroom and hurried upstairs. For all Jon's assertions that he could sleep through Armageddon, he'd already proved that a child's crying was enough to wake him, and Chloe picked Amy up from her cot, soothing her.

'All right, sweetie. Mummy can't be here right now, but she'll be back soon. You'll see.' Amy might not fully understand the words, and almost certainly didn't see all of their implications, but they gave Chloe some comfort.

'Papa…' Amy struggled in her arms, and Chloe leaned over, picking up Papa Bear and wiggling him in front of Amy. She quietened for a moment and then pushed him away.

'Okay then…' Chloe decided to try something different and started to hum the tune of the song that she'd heard Jon sing to her to quieten her tears.

It appeared that Amy liked rock 'n' roll a bit better. She settled into Chloe's arms, staring up at her face for a while and then reaching up, catching the dark yellow citrine that had slipped from the neck of her T-shirt and pulling it.

'No, sweetie, you'll break it.' Chloe pulled the chain

over her head, dangling the citrine in front of Amy, who batted it with her hand, seemingly mesmerised by its sparkle in the half-light.

'See how pretty it is? It's magic as well. If you hold it in your hand, it makes all the bad things in your heart go away.'

Chloe had needed something like that when she'd been ill. Something to help her summon her courage at the times she'd felt most alone. The crystal had been like a mascot, something for her to hold onto and remember the promises she'd made to herself.

And now she'd made a promise to Amy. She'd promised that, whatever happened, she would make things right, find a way to support Hannah so that she felt confident about being a good mother to Amy. That was one, inviolable promise that wouldn't be broken. Jon's promises to help might or might not be followed through, and Chloe couldn't bring herself to rely on them, however much the warmth in his eyes tempted her to.

'Mummy's coming back, sweetie. You'll see.' She whispered the words, cuddling Amy tight, and the child's eyelids began to droop.

CHAPTER SIX

HE'D SLEPT DEEPLY and for enough hours to make him feel human again. When the smell of cooking wafted up the stairs, Jon levered himself from his bed and made for the bathroom. But the time he'd emerged, the smell of coffee had been added to the mix.

He hadn't expected her to be cooking for him, and when Jon went downstairs to the kitchen-diner he didn't expect her bright smile either. Both were very welcome.

'What's that?' He craned over her shoulder as she slammed the lid down on a large electric waffle iron.

'Oat waffles. And coffee for you.' She switched off the coffee machine and put the flask of coffee on the table.

'You didn't need to do that.' He sat down anyway at the place that was laid for him. No one had cooked him breakfast since… Jon's mind recoiled at the thought. This was nothing like that, it was probably just a thank-you for taking care of Amy.

'A decent breakfast never did anyone any harm.'

That was obviously a matter of pride with her. Chloe's fridge was always well stocked with good, fresh food, and he didn't need to look in the larder to know that there would be fruit and vegetables there.

He poured the coffee, noticing that her cup stood next

to the kettle, with the tag from a herbal teabag hanging over the side. Chloe struggled momentarily with the waffle maker, and just as he was about to go and help her she got it open and the waffles out onto two plates.

'You like bananas?' She turned to him and Jon nodded. 'Good.'

A liberal helping of sliced banana, along with kiwi fruit and blueberries went on top of the waffles, and she carried the plates across. One waffle for her and three for him.

'You're sure you don't want any more?' Jon could eat three. He could probably eat half a dozen, but he didn't like the idea that she was giving him the lion's share.

'No, one's enough for me.' A glass jar with homemade nut butter clattered onto the table in front of him in a no-nonsense invitation to help himself. Then Chloe fetched her tea and sat down.

'These look really good.' Jon took a mouthful and it tasted even better than it looked. 'Where's Amy?'

'In her playpen, in the sitting room. Let's see whether we can get breakfast eaten before she realises we're not paying enough attention to her.'

Chloe managed it, and was halfway out of the front door before Amy started to grizzle. Jon's fuller plate was only part finished, and he picked it up and walked into the sitting room.

'It's just you and me, then, Amy. Let's see what we can get up to today.'

Despite all Chloe's misgivings, they'd fallen into a routine that worked. Every morning, she ignored Jon's assertions that he'd probably stumble across something that would pass for breakfast later and made a proper breakfast for all of them. And every morning he cleared his plate and said that he might be tempted into getting used to this.

Each evening was different, too. Someone to ask about her day, and give an account of how Amy had fed the ducks in the park, or almost managed to sneak a packet of chocolate buttons out of the supermarket without paying.

Amy was beginning to settle, and wasn't waking up so many times during the night. Jon and Amy had become firm friends. He talked to her all the time, and just the sound of his voice was enough to have her gazing wide-eyed into his face. Chloe sometimes envied her niece the privilege of looking at him so unashamedly when her own glances at Jon were so often stolen. The way Amy had no hesitation about being close to him, steadying herself against his legs as she heaved herself up into his lap, curling up there while he read the paper or a book.

But there was one, magic hour. After Amy was in bed, and when the house was quiet, they sat together in the kitchen, talking about everything and nothing. Jon spent two evenings assembling a moon and stars mobile to hang over Amy's cot that somehow failed to catch Amy's eye but which Chloe gazed at every night before she closed her eyes to go to sleep.

'She doesn't like my cookies, then?' Breakfast at six on a Saturday morning made jumbo sized cookies with elevenses all the more welcome. But Amy had licked the icing off hers and thrown the rest on the floor.

'Maybe she's just saving the world as we know it.' Jon took his second cookie from the plate, and Amy started to make loud explosive noises, clapping her hands together.

'Ah. And who taught her how to do that?'

'If you're going to make Dalek cookies, you can't expect them not to fight a bit before you eat them.' He bit off the Dalek's head, rolling his eyes at Amy, while the little girl crowed with glee. 'Although I've never seen a pink Dalek before.'

'The pink ones are the ones you have to look out for. Much more dangerous. And when I looked in the cupboard for some colouring for the icing, I only had pink.'

'That explains it.' He broke off a piece of his cookie, handing it to Amy, and she put it in her mouth and then spat it back out again. 'Actually, I don't think she does like them. I'll just have to finish them off myself.'

'I'll make some more. That's the last of them.'

He grinned, leaning back in his chair and reaching for the paper. 'I'll get blue food colouring when we go shopping.'

'Aren't you going to your house?' Chloe had expected to be alone with Amy today, but instead Jon had gone out for the paper and seemed ready for a lazy Saturday.

'The builders have it all in hand. But I suppose I should pop in later, just to see what they've been up to…' He paused for a moment and then put the paper down. 'I don't suppose you fancy coming with me? It's a mess at the moment, but I like to think it's got potential.'

'Bit like this place, then.' Chloe stared up at the sitting-room ceiling, wondering how many times she'd lain on the sofa, tracing the cracks with her gaze. Looking at the crystals on the mantelpiece instead had been an exercise in ignoring what she couldn't change and concentrating on something a bit prettier.

He chuckled. 'It's nothing like your place. Mine's *really* a mess. There's absolutely nothing wrong with this house that a bit of filler and a couple of cans of paint wouldn't remedy.'

Chloe quirked her lips downwards. 'That's what I reckoned when I moved in, over three years ago.'

'And instead you gave your sister a home and then battled a debilitating illness. I think you can be forgiven for overlooking a few cracks in the ceiling.'

And Jon knew how to forgive. He seemed to do it with everyone, apart perhaps from himself. 'Okay, then, I'll come. Maybe it'll give me a few ideas on what to do when I get a chance to get started here.'

Jon's house was the only one in a street of neat, sub-urban houses that looked ramshackle, the paint flak-ing off the downstairs window frames. The garden in the front looked as if it had been recently cleared, a few tree stumps sticking out of the sun-baked clay soil and an uneven pile of stones that must have once been crazy paving.

'Watch out. Don't step into any holes.' He grinned at her, taking Amy from her car seat and hoisting her up into his arms, where she couldn't get into any mischief.

Only the newly painted front door gave some clue that the house could be a lot more than it was now. Jon opened it, and when Chloe walked into the hall it was dark and dingy, no wallpaper, no carpets. But it had possibilities. The decorative newel post and the stair bannisters had been stripped down, and once a coat of paint was applied it would bring out the rippling shape of the turned wood.

'This is wonderful.' She turned, running her hand across the sitting-room door. It was caked with so many layers of paint that the mouldings had practically disap-peared, but it still had an original stained-glass panel, along with what looked like a decorative cast-iron back-plate for the door handle.

Jon chuckled. 'Not many people say that. But when it's all done, I think it'll look okay.'

It would look great. It all needed a bit of care and attention, and about a gallon of paint stripper, but Chloe could imagine the house, rising phoenix-like from the dust and the years of neglect. 'You have most of the original features still.' She looked up at the ceiling and saw moulded cornices and plasterwork.

'Yeah. The place belonged to an old guy who'd lived here all his life. He was a hoarder, and it was in a pretty bad state but relatively untouched. You couldn't get past the piles of newspaper to decorate.'

'But you saw something in it.'

'It looked like a challenge. As we cleared everything, we came across some lovely old features. And a few nightmares. All the kitchen floorboards had been soaked through and were rotten. It's a miracle someone didn't fall through them. And the wiring was completely shot—the electrician took one look at it and condemned it as unsafe.'

Despite his less-than-enthusiastic comments, Jon obviously loved this house. Who wouldn't? A chance to give an undiscovered gem a new lease of life.

'It'll be lovely when it's finished, though.'

He grinned. 'That's what I'm hoping. Careful through here, the floorboards have been taken up to run the cabling.'

Jon led the way through to the kitchen, which had obviously taken priority over the decoration of the hallway. Almost finished, it was bright and gleaming, with honey-coloured wooden cabinets and black quartz-effect worktops, which sparkled subtly when the light hit them.

Spotlights were sunk flush with the ceiling. Bright chrome taps and a built-in hob and oven with chrome trimmings. Grey slate on the floor. Chloe gasped.

'Jon... This is gorgeous.'

'Like it?'

'I'd kill for a kitchen like this.' The kitchen units ran along two sides of the large room, and cardboard boxes were stacked neatly along the third. 'What's going in here?'

'I was going to carry the units and worktop on round, but now I've seen it I'm thinking that that's more cupboards than I could possibly use. I quite like the idea of having a table and chairs here instead, the way you have in your kitchen. I think it would make the room warmer.'

Chloe nodded. 'It is handy having the table, and the room's plenty big enough. And it could do with a break to all those clean lines.'

Jon chuckled. 'All I need is Dalek biscuits and a few crystals. That'll take the gleam off it.'

'I'll send Amy round with the biscuits. You need to get your own crystals.'

She walked to the back door, looking out on the weeds and overgrown shrubs. Then they picked their way past the lifted floorboards in the hall and up the stairs to the front bedroom.

Another one of those breath-catching, I-wish-I-lived-here moments. Jon had obviously decided to decorate one room at a time, and this room had fresh paint on the walls and woodwork. There was a cast-iron fireplace, which had been stripped and polished up so that the pattern of twisting stems and flowers shone. A curved bay window, with stained glass in the lights at the top, looked out onto the quiet street. This would be a lovely place to wake up in the morning, dappled colour shining across the polished oak floor.

'I didn't notice these windows from the outside. They're the originals?'

'Yep. They were in pretty good condition under all the layers of paint. I'm not sure how warm they'll be in the winter, but I don't want to put in secondary glazing if I can help it.'

'Thick curtains? I have some with thermal linings in my bedroom and the room's really cosy in the winter.'

Chloe bit her tongue. She could almost see the kind of thing that would match the red and green in the stained glass and bring those colours out. A cold night, closed curtains and candlelight. And the warmth of Jon's arms.

But this wasn't her house. Amy would never sleep soundly in the next bedroom, surrounded by pretty things, and Chloe would never sleep in this one. Amy should be with her mother, and Jon had determinedly left all thoughts of a family behind.

Jon was nodding, looking at the windows. 'I didn't think of that. It's an idea.'

Amy started to struggle in his arms, wanting to explore, and Jon put her down onto her feet, holding both her hands and letting her lead him over to the fireplace. She traced the pattern in the cast iron with her fingers, sitting down suddenly in the hearth.

'So you have a kitchen and a bedroom...' It seemed like a countdown. How much more did he need to do here before he wouldn't need to stay at her place any more?

'And the bathroom's going in over the next few

weeks. That's all I really need, and then I can move in and do the rest as I go.'

'It's a long job.'

'I've found somewhere that I want to be now. If it takes a while to get everything finished, that's okay.' He looked around the room thoughtfully, and then bent to pick Amy up. 'I guess we should make a move if we're going to get some shopping.'

That was best. Get away from here before it gave Chloe any more ideas. She turned, almost bolting out of the room and down the stairs.

It had been right on the tip of his tongue. Jon had almost asked Chloe to come with him to choose curtains.

Calm down! he reasoned with himself as he walked down the stairs, his boots thudding on the bare wood. *Choosing curtains isn't like asking someone to kiss you.*

In some ways it was worse. A kiss could be explained away as the momentary wish for some warmth. Curtains were a more cool-headed statement. And the thought that Chloe might just talk him into the perfect set of curtains for the room was terrifying.

He was done with perfect. He didn't want domestic bliss because he'd seen it crumble into vitriolic chaos. Jon realised he'd left his car keys in the kitchen and left Chloe hovering by the front gate, walking the length of the hallway with Amy in his arms.

'Bye-bye.' Amy waved happily as he picked up his keys and closed the kitchen door behind him.

'That's right, sweetheart. Bye-bye, house. We're going to the supermarket now.'

Out of the mouth of babes... Amy's instinct had divined the truth before he'd had a chance to formulate it in his head. Helping a friend out was one thing. But he wasn't going to ask Chloe back here, for fear that he might be tempted to ask her to stay.

CHAPTER SEVEN

EVERYTHING HAD FALLEN into place. Jon's week off work was long enough to make sure that Amy had fully recovered, and Chloe had secured a place for her at the hospital crèche for the following week. Jon was working days now and their evening routine of cooking, eating, a bath and bedtime for Amy, followed by the precious 'magic hour', needed no adjustment. Hannah would be back home with James at the weekend, and Chloe was beginning to allow herself to believe that her return might be a step forward.

Jon had been too busy to take a break on Monday, but she'd bumped into him at the crèche on Tuesday, and they'd eaten their sandwiches together, playing with Amy. Chloe wondered whether he'd be there today, a little thrill of excitement pulsing through her fingers as she checked her phone.

Almost as if he knew she'd been thinking about him, Jon chose that moment to send a text.

Are you going to lunch now?

At some point they'd dispensed with the formalities of *Hello* and *What's happening?* Maybe because it felt that even though they were working at different ends of the hospital, they were still together.

Yes. Join me?

Busy with a patient. Do you have ten minutes? I'd like your opinion.

In A and E?

The thought was unexpectedly stirring. Jon's work in A and E was one area that was his alone and which Chloe didn't normally have any part of.

Yes. Won't keep you long.

I'll be right down.

She found him at the doctors' and nurses' station at the end of a row of cubicles, staring at one of the computer screens. He motioned for her to sit down in an empty chair next to him.

'Thanks for coming. I've got some X-rays I'd like your opinion about.' His brow was furrowed, and he was clearly wrestling with a knotty problem. Chloe resisted the impulse to wonder what she could possibly add to Jon's expertise, and hoped he wasn't over-estimating her experience.

'Okay.' She sat down, warily.

'What do you see?'

She looked at the X-ray on the screen in front of him. 'A pretty nasty dislocation of the big toe. Do you have the patient's notes?' She reached for the manila folder in front of him, and Jon put his hand on top of it.

'I just want to know what you see here. This is Patient A, right?'

'Okay. Well, Alan's got a dislocated toe.' She could hardly imagine that Jon hadn't seen that.

'Alan?' He shot her a suspicious look, as if she'd been looking at his notes behind his back.

'His name's on the X-ray, Jon.'

'Oh. Well, anyway, how might that have happened?'

'What is this? Have you asked Patient A?' Chloe rolled her eyes. Diagnosis wasn't a guessing game.

'Of course I have. I just want your professional opinion, without knowing any of the context, because, having seen both the boys, I'm struggling not to jump to conclusions.'

'There's a Patient B?'

'Yes. I'm coming to him.'

Chloe heaved a sigh. 'Okay, I'll play along. An injury like this is most probably caused by the foot coming into contact with something hard. Kicking a wall would do it, or a blow to the end of the toe. Something like that.'

'What about another child stamping on the foot?'

'It's possible, I suppose, but not likely. If that's what happened I'd be on the lookout for some underlying condition or deformity of the bones, which meant that a dislocation was particularly easy.' Chloe frowned at him. 'Jon, you know all this.'

He grinned. 'Yes, I do. I just wanted a second opinion.'

Chloe suppressed a smile. It was nice to think that Jon had chosen her for that. 'Have you relocated the toe?'

'Yes.' Jon punched one of the keys on the computer keyboard and another X-ray flashed up on the screen.

'It's been relocated and dressed. I'll be making an appointment for him up in Orthopaedics for ongoing care.'

Chloe studied the X-ray carefully. 'Nice job. I don't see anything here that concerns me. There's a tiny bone fragment there…' She pointed to the X-ray and Jon bent in to look.

'I didn't see that.'

The fragment was so small that it was almost invisible. But it was gratifying to be able to add even this to Jon's assessment. 'I'd say this is definitely an impact injury. Do you want to tell me what this is all about now?'

'In a minute.' He punched the keyboard again, and another set of X-rays appeared on the screen. 'Patient B.'

'Right.' Chloe scanned the X-rays carefully. Three different angles, showing the front and sides of a knee. 'Well, I don't see any fracture of the patella, although there may be a very small hairline one that won't show up on the X-rays until it starts to heal. There's another very small chip just here, and I'd like to have him back in a couple of weeks, just to check on that.'

'Caused by?'

'Impact on a hard surface most probably. I can't say any more that that, Jon. You're going to have to tell me what…' She glanced at the bottom of the screen. 'What Craig told you.'

'You've told me what I need to know.' He looked at his watch. 'Thanks. I won't take any more of your lunch break.'

'What? Come on, Jon, you can't stop there. What's happening?'

He grinned, as if he'd known all along that she couldn't confine herself to just answering his questions. 'Two boys, both twelve years old. They're in the school changing rooms so they both have bare feet and legs, and there are a lot of hard surfaces around.'

'Which would explain the dislocated toe.'

'Yes. Alan says that Craig stamped on his toe, and dislocated it. He jumped back and Craig stumbled, falling on the tiles.'

Chloe frowned. 'Well, I suppose that's possible. Not very likely though. What does Craig say?'

'He's not saying anything. Not a word. I've got a teacher from the school, and both mothers here, and all three of them want *me* to sort this out and tell them exactly what happened.'

'Well, you can't, not categorically. We can say what might have happened, but they're going to have to sort what actually *did* happen between themselves.' Jon knew that as well as she did. 'What's your interest in this?'

'I just want to know. Because if the cause of Alan's injury doesn't explain its severity, there may be some reason for taking a few more X-rays.'

True. But that was something that would usually be assessed in her own department, not A and E. Jon knew that as well as she did. 'And...?'

'Because we're not busy at the moment. And I'm on my lunch break.'

That wasn't good enough either. 'Yes. And?'

Jon puffed out a breath. 'Okay. If you must know, I think that Craig's been bullied. He has psoriasis, and Alan referred to him as "Flaky Craig" a couple of times when he thought that his mother wasn't listening. He's very obviously playing the victim with his mother and teacher, but he's quite cocky when they're not around.'

The look in Jon's eyes was reason enough. 'Would you like me to talk to him?'

Jon shook his head. 'I don't see...'

'Don't worry. I'm not going to confront him with anything.' This was perhaps one area where her experience was a little more useful than Jon's. 'I get the odd alternative version for how someone's come by an injury. A and E sometimes isn't the environment to tell your doctor that you broke your ankle having sex.'

'I don't know about that. We get our share of unlikely injuries. Goes with the job.' His brow creased. 'Someone broke their ankle having sex?'

'Don't ask. I still can't work out how she managed to get into that position... All I'm saying is that Alan might be a little more forthcoming with a different face. One that hasn't already been kind to him. You *have* been kind to him, haven't you?'

'Of course. It's not my place to judge anyone.'

'So why don't you let me give it a go? If his mother agrees.'

Jon got to his feet. 'Okay. I'll speak to her.'

Jon had spoken with Alan's mother and the teacher who was with the boys, and they'd agreed to sit out of his direct line of sight, while Chloe spoke to him. He wondered what she thought she might say that would convince Alan that the truth was better than the obvious lie he'd told.

Or perhaps she wouldn't need to say anything. She walked into the consulting room, leaving the door open so he could stand in the doorway with Alan's mother, watching and listening. Chloe was immaculate as usual, a dark skirt and shoes under a white coat. When she sat down opposite Alan, her smile was composed but held a touch of the confidante. Jon would have told her pretty much anything.

'Hello, Alan. My name's Dr Delancourt. I'm doing a survey—would you mind if I asked you some questions? About how you hurt yourself today.'

Nicely done. Alan nodded, and Chloe turned the page in the notebook she carried, taking a pen from her pocket.

'Thank you. It looks as if you've been in the wars.' Chloe flashed him a mischievous look. 'Did you win?'

Get the boy to brag a little. Jon felt Alan's mother shift uncertainly from one foot to the other beside him.

'Yeah, I won. I showed him.'

'I'll bet you did.' Chloe leaned forward a little, her elbows on her knees. 'So who did you show?'

'There's this boy at my school. When he takes his shirt off in the changing rooms his back's all flaky and horrible. I told him I didn't wanna see it and he needed to get out of there.'

Chloe nodded, as if that was perfectly understandable. Jon saw Alan's mother put her hand to her mouth, staring at the back of her son's head.

'And you had a fight with him?'

'He didn't wanna go. So I shouted it, right in his ear...' Alan stopped suddenly, perhaps realising that he was saying too much. 'That doctor. I told him.'

'Dr Lambert?' Chloe waved her hand dismissively. 'I don't like him very much. He's a bit starchy.'

Chloe's tone was so believable that Jon almost protested. It seemed that Alan agreed with her, though.

The boy leaned towards her, clearly about to impart a secret. 'I kicked him out. Flaky Boy.'

'Really?'

'Yes, really. I kicked his bottom and he ran away.'

'He must be very strong if that's how you hurt your

toe. I saw your X-rays, and it looked very painful.'
Chloe made the observation casually.

'It didn't hurt.' Alan's bravado belied the way he'd
howled when Jon had relocated his toe. 'And that Flaky
Boy's not strong. I kicked him and then he fell over onto
his knees. My toe bashed against the locker.'

'Oh, I see. Show me.'

Chloe was taking Alan through it all again so there
was no mistake, and tears were running down Alan's
mother's face.

'I didn't... We didn't bring him up to do this...' She
whispered the words so quietly that Jon had to strain
to hear them.

He nodded. 'It's okay. We just need to know, that's
all.'

Chloe seemed to have satisfied herself that Alan had
told the truth this time. 'Okay, Alan. I've got to go now.'

She stood and walked towards the door. Alan turned
his head, saw Jon and his mother and flushed bright red,
realising he'd been duped. 'I didn't do anything. That
bitch made me say it—'

'Alan!' His mother rallied suddenly. 'Don't you dare
use that word.' She turned to Chloe. 'I'm so sorry.'

'It's okay.' Chloe took her arm, guiding her away
from the doorway. 'I've been called worse.'

She glanced at Jon, then nodded in the direction of
the drinks machine. He caught her meaning and advanced towards Alan's mother. 'Why don't you come
with me? The nurse will keep an eye on Alan, and we'll
have a cup of tea.'

'What about Craig?' Alan's mother reddened suddenly. 'What am I going to say to his mother? If Alan's
hurt him...'

'Chloe, would you go and take a look at Craig?' Jon

imagined that her technique might be a little different with him, and that the boy would respond to her warmth and perhaps find the courage to voice what had happened to him.

'Yes, I'll go now.'

They'd managed to snatch ten minutes for a cup of tea together before it was time for Chloe to go back to work. Craig had told his side of the story to Chloe, as Jon had thought he might, and now the whole thing was out in the open and could be dealt with.

'Apparently it's not just Alan. Some of the other kids have been bullying Craig as well, but he was too scared to say anything.'

Jon nodded. 'Well, Alan's mother's determined to put a stop to it. That's a good start.'

'A very good start. Poor Craig. He had quite a bruise where Alan kicked him. And that knee's going to be painful for a while.'

'He'll go on your list for a follow-up?'

Chloe smiled. 'I've fitted him in. His mother's bringing him back on Friday and I'll take a look and see how his knee's doing once the ice has brought the swelling down a bit.'

Jon would have expected nothing less. 'Good. Thanks. And thanks for today, too. Remind me never to lie to you. I don't much fancy being on the other end of your interrogation techniques.'

'You were watching. I didn't do anything to Alan, just encouraged him to talk.' Chloe pointed her finger at his chest. 'You I'd be a bit rougher with.'

The temptation was a great deal more than he could be expected to bear. Jon leaned forward across the table.

'There's this new study, just come out. The moon's really made of green cheese, just as everyone thought.'

She snorted with laughter. 'I'll talk to you later. When we get home.'

It was another brick, cemented firmly into the wall. He and Chloe had joined forces to look after Amy, and it seemed that they were just as effective when they worked together. Her approach might be a little different from his, but their differences were what had borne fruit.

'I'll see you then.' He felt his pager buzz in his pocket, and gulped down the rest of his tea. 'Got to go…'

CHAPTER EIGHT

CHLOE SUSPECTED THAT there would be no talk of the moon and none of green cheese either tonight. When she'd picked Amy up from the crèche that evening she'd heard from one of the nurses from A and E, who had come to collect her son, that there had been a multiple car accident on the motorway.

Jon was late home, missing Amy's bathtime and the kiss goodnight. She was sitting in the kitchen, trying not to wait for him, when she heard his key in the door. The front door closed and she waited for him to appear. But there was just silence.

He was in the hallway, his hands in his pockets, his back leaning against the wall. Jon seemed wearier than she'd ever seen him. She walked up to him, touching the sleeve of his jacket, and he seemed almost surprised to find her there.

'Tough afternoon?'

He nodded. 'Yeah. I lost a patient.'

That was hard for any doctor. For one working in Paediatrics, there was an even keener edge to the blow. 'I heard there was an accident.'

He nodded, not meeting her gaze. 'A little boy. The paramedics had already revived him once in the ambulance, but he was failing fast by the time he got to the hospital. I couldn't do anything.'

'You tried, though.'

'Yeah. I tried.'

There was nothing she could say to him that he didn't already know. No way she could make this any better, because it was what it was. Along with all the young lives he saved, or made better, were the ones that Jon couldn't save. The day that didn't hurt was when any doctor should seriously think about changing their profession.

'Have you eaten? I'll make you something.'

'Thanks, but...' He shook his head. 'I'm just going upstairs.'

He obviously wanted some time alone. Chloe walked back into the kitchen and put the kettle on, more for something to do than because she wanted a drink. Sitting down at the table and ignoring the click as the kettle boiled and then switched off, she waited.

Ten minutes. From the creak in the floorboards, just outside her bedroom door, she knew exactly where Jon was. Perhaps he didn't want to be alone after all. Chloe walked upstairs, pausing at the open door of her bedroom. Sitting on the edge of the bed, one hand stretched so that his fingers were gently touching Amy's, Jon was watching the little girl sleep.

When he saw her he got to his feet, whispering so as not to disturb Amy, 'Sorry. The door was open...'

'That's okay. When I heard about the accident, I held her a little tighter.'

'We have to protect her.' Jon's face was anguished.

'We will.' Now wasn't the moment to point out that he didn't have to do anything at all, it was her job to protect Amy. For the moment, at least, he was a part of that. Chloe moved towards him, her trembling fingers reaching out to hug him, but he drew back.

Jon knew that a lot of his colleagues went home and hugged their kids after a day like this. But the way he'd wanted to see Amy, to check that she was still breathing, and that the world could continue to turn, had taken him by surprise.

He and Helen had made an agreement never to bring their work home. He'd stuck by that as best he could, keeping moments like this away from the quiet, gleaming perfection of their house. But as soon as Chloe had touched his arm, downstairs in the hallway, holding her had stopped being something he just wanted to do and had turned into something that he needed.

He'd settled for want, instead of need, and had gone upstairs to check on Amy. But now that Chloe was here... Jon reminded himself that she had her own issues about being touched, and that the intensity with which he wanted to touch her would probably be unwelcome.

But she touched him. He drew away and she touched him again, taking hold of the front of his shirt and pulling him towards her. And then she was in his arms. Chloe reached out, curling her fingers around his neck.

One breath. One look.

There was no longer any him or her, just one frozen moment in time, which they both owned equally. Chloe seemed to understand everything that was in his heart, every question and every sadness. He buried his face in her hair, hanging onto her as tightly as he could.

He was holding her so tight against his chest that she could hardly breathe. Or maybe it was just that her heart was beating so fast that her lungs couldn't keep up.

'I'm sorry…' She felt his arms loosen around her.

'No… Jon, don't be sorry. You shouldn't be sorry for anything.' She didn't want him to push her away now. It was too soon, and the connection that pulsed between them too strong.

She felt him sigh as he gently wrapped his arms around her again. It wasn't quite as thrilling as being crushed against his body, but it was close.

He held her for a long time, neither needing to say anything. But they couldn't stay like this for ever, even if that didn't seem like such an outrageous idea at the moment.

'Tomorrow's another day, Jon.'

He nodded, letting go of her. The room seemed suddenly freezing cold as he gave Amy one last look and then walked out into the hallway. 'I thought I might—'

'Go for a run?' She smiled at him. Chloe was getting to know Jon's coping strategies. He was often up early, running for the joy of it, before she and Amy had gone downstairs to start their day. In the evenings it was different, something to get the cares of the day out of his system.

'Yeah.' He narrowed his eyes. 'You haven't taken up mind-reading, have you? Those crystals of yours…'

The crystals had become a joke between them. When she'd been ill, it had helped her calm her mind to focus on their sparkling depths, in the same way that running cleared Jon's mind.

'Don't knock it. Each to their own.'

'Whatever gets you through the night, eh?' He grinned and suddenly he was very close. He brushed a kiss on her cheek, and almost before Chloe could feel the scrape of newly grown stubble on his chin he was gone, walking into his own room to change into his running gear. In half an hour he'd be back again, out of breath from pushing himself to the limit on the last mile, that easygoing smile returned to his lips. And everything would be back to what passed for normal these days.

This was hopefully the last time they'd have to do this, because James would be bringing Hannah home the day after tomorrow. Amy was bathed and in her pyjamas and Chloe sat down on the sofa, with Amy next to her, positioning her laptop in front of them.

'Mummy...' As usual the sound of the video conferencing call tone prompted the word. In a little less than two weeks Amy had learned to associate the shrill tone with her mother, as if Hannah were now locked away inside the computer. Chloe tried not to think about it too much, because it was heart-breaking.

James answered, looking tanned and smiling. He turned from the screen, beckoning to someone, and Hannah came to sit next to him.

'Mummy!'

'I love you, Amy.' Hannah blew kisses to her daughter, and Amy wriggled forward towards the edge of the sofa, trying to get closer.

Hannah was smiling, but it seemed as if it was an effort. Her eyes had dark circles under them, and James had his arm protectively across the back of her chair, as if he was ready to give her a hug if needed.

'Say, "Love you, Mummy."' Chloe leaned over towards Amy, whispering in her ear. Amy turned to her, her small hand on her cheek.

'Love you, Mummy.' Amy repeated the words perfectly, but she was looking in the wrong direction. Straight up at Chloe.

'No, sweetie...' Chloe swallowed down her embarrassment, trying not to look at Hannah, and then jumped as the front door slammed. Jon had been working late but he was home now. Amy looked round and, forgetting that her mother was on the screen, started to crawl to the far end of the sofa towards the open door of the sitting room.

'Hello, Amy...' Jon popped his head around the door to greet her, and then saw the laptop on the table. 'Oh. Sorry to interrupt.'

'That's all right. Come and say hello.'

If all three of them were in one place, on the sofa, and she held Amy facing the screen, then there could be no more mistakes. Maybe Jon caught the look of desperation that Chloe gave him because he walked straight over and sat down, retrieving Amy and putting her on Chloe's lap.

'Hi, Hannah. How are things?' Jon leaned in a little so that Hannah and James could see him.

'I'm okay.' Chloe looked up at the screen and into Hannah's face. There was no sign that she'd heard what Amy had said, and maybe the words had been lost somewhere between her laptop and James's.

'We went sailing yesterday,' James broke in.

'Yeah, and you nearly went over the side.' Hannah smiled suddenly, nudging her brother, and Jon laughed.

'I would have liked to have seen that.'

'No, you wouldn't. If I was going to get wet, then I'd have made sure you did too,' James retorted, and Chloe began to breathe again. She hugged Amy, directing her attention towards the screen, as James and Jon traded a few good-natured insults, and Hannah joined in, saying a bit about what they'd been doing on their holiday.

'So what are the arrangements for Saturday?' Fi-

nally James got around to the one day that everyone
was thinking about and not mentioning.

'I thought I might drive up with Amy tomorrow night
and stay at your place, if that's okay. Then we'll be there
when you get back, the following morning.'

James nodded. 'Yeah, that's fine. Sounds good.'

Hannah was biting her lip. 'There's no rush.'

Chloe swallowed down her disappointment. It
seemed that Hannah had mixed feelings about coming
home. 'I'm really looking forward to seeing you. And
Amy's been missing you, of course.'

'I miss her too.' A tear rolled down Hannah's cheek,
and James put his arm around her. 'But she's... She
looks so happy. And you love her, don't you...?'

'Yes, I love her. So do you.' Chloe felt as if she were
walking a tightrope, and there was a very long fall beneath her. Telling Hannah that she'd loved having Amy
here might imply that this was a state of affairs that
could continue. Telling her that she had to take Amy
back now might put her under too much pressure.

'But you and Jon... You can both look after her so
much better.'

Jon leaned forward towards the screen, speaking
gently. 'Hannah, there *is* no me and Chloe. I'm moving out in a few days' time.'

Good. That was right. Hannah seemed to be taking
it for granted that the very temporary family that had
been created here could last. Maybe *she* was at fault for
giving that impression. Maybe Hannah had seen her
body language and had realised how much she'd fallen
into depending on him.

'I just think...' Hannah shook her head, as if what
she thought didn't matter.

'Hannah, there's no pressure for us to do anything

right now. I'm taking the next two weeks off work so we can spend some time together. I'll be right there to support you and Amy in any way I can.'

Hannah nodded, wiping her eyes. 'Yes. Okay.'

This was always the way with Hannah. The less she said, the more overwhelmed she was feeling. It was probably best to let things rest for now.

'So I'll see you all on Saturday.'

'Yes.' James answered for Hannah. 'That'll be great.'

They'd talked for a while longer, and even though James and Chloe were both obviously concerned, they'd stayed positive and smiling for Hannah's sake. Amy was becoming drowsy, but Chloe managed to get her to wave and blow kisses to her mother before they ended the call.

Chloe leaned forward, closing her laptop, as Amy snuggled against her. At a loss for anything to say that might help, Jon went into the kitchen and made her a cup of tea.

'I hope I said the right thing. About my not being around for much longer.' He put her tea down on the coffee table in front of her.

'It was exactly the right thing.' Chloe turned her worried face up towards him. 'All of this is about Hannah wanting the best for Amy. Right now, she's feeling so worthless and scared that she thinks that I can give Amy more than she can. But I can't.'

Jon sat down on the sofa next to Chloe, and took Amy from her so she could drink her tea. The little girl stirred and then went back to sleep. No doubt the moment she was taken upstairs and put into her cot, she'd be wide awake again.

'Have you considered the possibility that it might be

better to keep Amy with you for just a little while longer?' Jon chose his words carefully.

'I'll look after Amy for as long as it takes. But Hannah will never get over it if she gives Amy up, and neither will Amy. I've just got to give Hannah the right support.'

'You and James, you mean.' Jon couldn't help smiling. Chloe was so determined to do this alone, and it was oddly gratifying that her unwillingness to take any help extended to James as well as him.

'Me and James, then. Obviously. Although he has his own family to think of, and he doesn't have as much time as I do.'

They sat in silence for a moment, and Chloe sipped her tea. Despite all the uncertainties, all the loose ends, this seemed somehow right. The three of them against the world.

'Hannah never said anything to me about Amy's father.'

Chloe shook her head. 'He's not on the scene. Very deliberately so. We know who he is, he went to the same school as Hannah. It seems that he and Hannah had something going together, and when he went off to university they split up. When Hannah ran away, that's where James found her. Living with him in his student halls.'

'Didn't anyone notice?'

'Apparently not. He used to smuggle her in at night and back out again in the morning. Hannah spent most of the day in coffee bars. When we realised she was pregnant, James went to see the family, but the boy said it was nothing to do with him and his parents didn't want to know either.'

'That must have been hard on Hannah. Has the boy

ever been in touch?' It would be hard on Amy too, when she was old enough to understand. Jon held the sleeping child a little closer.

'Not once. Hannah decided not to pursue it and I couldn't help agreeing with her. If someone lets you down that badly, you're better off without them.'

'I suppose so. Still hurts, though.'

'Yes, it does still hurt.'

Chloe's face showed no emotion, but Jon suspected that she was talking a little about herself, as well as Hannah. Someone had let her down, and she'd decided that she should deal with everything on her own, now.

'You know I didn't tell the exact truth when I said I'd be gone in a couple of days, that was really just for Hannah's benefit. You're off for the next two weeks, and I've given the hospital the time I promised them. I have the next three weeks off.'

'That's supposed to be for you to finish the renovations on your house. So that you'll have it all done when you start work permanently. You agreed that with them.'

'I told you I'd be around to help, and I will be. The builders are putting the new bathroom in, and I can put anything else off until later.'

He could see the disbelief in her eyes, and all he wanted to do was to show her somehow that he really did mean what he said this time.

'Yes, I know. Thanks.'

Chloe's words offered him little comfort. Because, whatever she said, he knew that she didn't believe him.

CHAPTER NINE

JON MADE SURE that he was home from work early the following evening so he could see Amy and Chloe off. It had just been two weeks but now that he was putting Amy's things into Chloe's car, and about to kiss the little girl goodbye, it seemed impossible that he could have come to care so much about her in so short a time.

'I'll be back on Sunday evening.' Jon thought he saw Chloe's lip tremble.

'Yeah. Give me a call if that changes. You never know, I might cook you dinner.' Jon was banking on having the weekend here alone, and he didn't want Chloe walking in on him unannounced.

'It's not going to change. I've said I'll go in to work on Monday for a few hours to do a handover. But you don't need to cook. I'll have had Sunday lunch with the family.'

Jon congratulated himself silently on clearing the final hurdle before his plan could be put into action. 'Okay. Well… Good luck. You'll give me a call if there are any problems, won't you?'

'Yes, I will. Thanks.'

They stood facing each other in the hall. There was nothing more to say, and they both had things to do, but something kept them both glued to the carpet. Finally Jon put his arms around her shoulders.

The awkwardness of it was melted away by the scent of her hair. Chloe clung to him, and he felt himself let out a breath. This was crazy. It was just a weekend.

'Go…' It seemed altogether wrong to let her go anywhere, now that she was so close, but somehow he managed to take a step back.

Chloe looked up at him and the now-familiar feeling of honey oozing across his senses almost made his knees buckle. Then she reached up, standing on her toes to plant a kiss on his cheek. She drew back, almost before he had a chance to register it, walking into the sitting room to fetch Amy.

'Say bye-bye.' Chloe waved her hand, and Amy followed suit. 'See you again soon.'

Amy repeated the words almost perfectly, and Jon gave her a hug and a kiss. Then he walked them out to the car, standing to watch as they drove away, feeling suddenly as if the bottom had just dropped out of his world.

His cheek still burned where her lips had touched it. But now that Chloe had gone, he had forty-eight hours to put into operation the plan that he'd been fine-tuning for the last week. The challenge got him moving, and he strode into the house to fetch his jacket and car keys.

Everything he needed was piled up in the hallway of his house. A thank-you to Chloe for coming to his rescue and letting him stay here for the last month. Something that was easy for him to do and not so easy for her to achieve. And he hoped she'd love it.

Chloe drew up in the road outside her house, sitting for a moment in the car to gather her thoughts. She'd

almost managed to believe that everything was going
to be all right, that Hannah would find the confidence
to take the first vital steps in taking Amy back to look
after her. But everything had fallen apart.

The aching tiredness made her feel almost physically
sick with instinctive fear. Chloe reminded herself that
this was nothing like what she'd felt when she'd been ill,
and that there was a good reason for it. Getting out of
the car, leaving her bag still on the back seat, she pulled
herself straight and walked to the front door.

Another instinct, this one more recently formed,
made her wonder whether Jon would be there. He'd
said that he would, and Jon hadn't broken a promise
yet, but everything else had gone horribly wrong this
weekend. Why not this?

When she opened the front door, the smell hit her
and for a moment she was too fatigued to even know
what it was. As she twisted the handle of the kitchen
door, she realised. Paint.

Maybe Jon had brought something home to paint
at the kitchen table. When all she really wanted was a
cup of tea…

He *was* sitting at the kitchen table, the look on his
face something like that of an agonised boy who had
hoped to do something right. Chloe looked around. The
kitchen looked suddenly lighter and she couldn't understand why for a moment.

It was the new paint on the ceiling and walls. The
unusual tidiness of her worktop was because the old one
had been cleared and removed and a new one installed.
She realised that it was the same worktop she'd admired
at Jon's house, and the new doors on the kitchen cabinets were the same honeyed wood. Her old cooker had
been cleaned to within an inch of its life and a couple

of new spotlights, placed unobtrusively in the darker corners, made the room seem about twice the size.

She took a step inside, her legs almost failing to hold her. Beneath her feet, the old lino had been taken up and the quarry tiles underneath gleamed.

For a moment she couldn't speak. Chloe walked over to the window and saw that the frame had been sanded down and painted—a proper job, not just a lick of paint to cover whatever flaws were hidden beneath it. It hit her suddenly that this was Jon's thank-you to her. He hadn't needed to give her a leaving present, certainly not something like this, but that was what it was.

And she'd given him everything he needed to work with. Chloe realised that the jokey conversation about colours and styles, what she'd do with the kitchen when she had the time, had all been noted down in his head. She'd even lifted a corner of the lino and shown him the quarry tiles underneath, saying she'd hire something to polish them up one day.

'You…' Jon's voice was uncharacteristically full of doubt. 'You could say something…'

No, she couldn't. This was all too much. She'd lost almost everything this weekend, and now she was losing Jon. Chloe felt herself choke, and a sudden burst of energy took her up the stairs to fling herself onto her bed to sob into her pillow.

Jon ran his hand across the wooden tabletop, which just thirty-six hours earlier had been in the garden, being sanded and polished. Maybe everything she'd said last week, about how the colour scheme he had in his kitchen was the one she wanted in hers, had been just idle talk, and not what she wanted at all. But she'd seemed so sure, as if she'd thought about it, and no one could deny that the kitchen looked great.

Or maybe she'd wanted to do it herself. That was a possibility, but Jon knew that she didn't have the time or the energy at the moment. Maybe she was just over-come with delight... Jon shook his head, burying it in his hands. Unless Chloe's delight looked a lot like dis-may, that wasn't very likely.

He hadn't heard from her over the weekend and he'd assumed that things were going the way she'd hoped. But that could just be wishful thinking on his part. Would she really have given him a call to tell him that there was a problem?

Something was wrong. His decision to stay here, be-cause Chloe obviously wanted to be alone, was dropped and Jon walked slowly up the stairs.

He tapped gently on her bedroom door and received no answer, so he pressed his ear against it. He couldn't hear Chloe moving around, so he knocked again, this time a little louder.

She'd heard him. A rasping breath that sounded as if it was laced with tears came from the other side of the door.

'Chloe... What's wrong?' he called to her, and there was still no answer. He supposed he could just go down-stairs and leave her with whatever it was that was both-ering her, but the thought that his actions might have been the cause of her tears glued him to the spot.

He could wait here, or go in. Waiting was obviously about as much good as going back downstairs, so he twisted the door handle slowly, ready to apologise and bang the door closed in his own face if she was undress-ing. But she wasn't. He knew she wasn't.

Just in case, he called her name again and told her

he was coming in. There was still no answer, and he opened the door. Chloe was sitting on the bed, her face buried in her hands.

'Chloe… I'm sorry. I really thought you'd like what I did…' Suddenly it all seemed like a very bad idea. Why hadn't he left well alone? Or just bought her a bunch of flowers.

'It's lovely…' She gulped the words through her tears.

So that wasn't what she was crying about. Or if it was, they were the oddest tears of joy he'd ever seen. He walked towards her, bending down to disentangle the strap of her handbag, which was still over her shoulder, and laying the bag on the bed.

'Chloe…? What's the matter?' She hadn't told him to go yet, and if that wasn't exactly an invitation to stay, he wasn't too proud to take it as such.

She seemed to be making an effort to pull herself together, and Jon pulled a tissue from the box next to the bed and handed it to her. Chloe blew her nose and he handed her another for her eyes.

'Thank you for the kitchen. It looks fantastic.' She heaved a sigh. 'You really shouldn't have done it.'

'Well, I wouldn't have if I'd known it was going to drive you to this.' He'd been telling himself for the whole of the last week that this was just a thank-you. That it was something one friend could do for another. But now he realised that all he'd really wanted to do was make her smile. Give her something that she loved.

He wanted to hug her and dry her tears, but he made do with sitting cautiously down on the bed next to her. 'What's the matter, Chloe?'

She shook her head, reaching for another tissue to

finish mopping up the tears. 'I'm sorry. It's been a difficult weekend.'

'Want to talk about it?'

She shook her head but didn't move. 'I've put too much on you these last two weeks. And now you've done this...' She turned her honey-brown gaze on him. Now, more than ever, it reminded him of sweet pleasure, dripping over his senses.

'I'm here to listen, Chloe.'

'I know you are. But it doesn't matter...' She gave him a teary smile. 'I'll make some supper. We have to have something nice to christen that gorgeous kitchen with.'

She stood up, obviously bent on going downstairs and pretending that everything was all right. He couldn't bear it. Jon caught her hand, pulling her back down onto his lap.

'Forget the kitchen.' It had been the centre of all his hopes and efforts for the last two days, but now he didn't care about it. 'I'm not letting you go until you tell me.'

He had hardly touched her, and the force that had impelled her into his arms must have come from somewhere inside herself. And although he was hardly holding her at all, she couldn't escape. Maybe because her own fingers were clasped tightly together behind his neck.

He must have spent the whole weekend here, working on her kitchen, when he should have been at his place, working there. Of course he'd wanted her to be delighted with it. It was a wonderful present, and she didn't know how she could ever repay him for it.

One thing she was sure of. Tears were no kind of thanks and sharing what had happened this weekend wasn't either. Because he'd only feel that he had to stay, when what he should really do was go and get on with the things he had to do.

But she so wanted this. His strength and solidity. The feeling that she could face anything if he just held her for a little while.

'The kitchen's beautiful. It's a lovely goodbye present.'

He raised his eyebrows. 'It was more of a thank you than a goodbye. Why, are you throwing me out?'

'No.' She nudged her head against his shoulder. 'I'm telling you that you've done enough. You don't need to hang around here, sorting out my problems.'

'So I can stay as long as I want?'

'Of course you can.'

'Where's Amy? Is she back with Hannah now?'

'No, she's with James and Carol.'

'And Hannah?' Chloe didn't answer and his arms tightened around her, pulling her closer. 'You said I could stay as long as I wanted. I'm taking that as an invitation to pry into your personal business as well. I'm not letting you go until you tell me.'

Chloe sighed. There was no way out of this. She was going to have to tell him and *then* perhaps he'd leave Hannah to her.

'James dropped Hannah off at her place on his way home. She said she wanted to do some things there, and that she'd come round after lunch. We waited until three o'clock, and when she didn't answer her phone, we went round there. Hannah had gone.'

'Gone? Where?'

'I don't know. She left a note saying she needed some more time and that it was better for Amy if she was with us right now.'

'And you haven't heard from her?'

'I texted her, and she replied. She says she's okay but she won't say where she is. She promised to text this morning, and she did.'

'So you left Amy with James and Carol'

'I left her there because I'm going to look for Hannah.' The resolution that had taken hold of her, and strengthened over the last twenty-four hours suddenly hardened into certainty. 'I'm going to find her.'

'Do you know where to even start?'

'I'll call her friends. Maybe I can persuade Hannah to tell me where she is, or to come back here if she's not ready to go home. I don't know. Something's got to work.'

Chloe fell silent for a moment, letting herself feel his body against hers. It was a small indulgence, which would have to last through all of the uncertainty of the days ahead. Then she pulled away from him and stood up.

'We should make waffles.'

He looked up at her. 'Waffles? You're sure about that?'

She shrugged. 'James and I have looked everywhere locally we can think of. There's nothing more I can do tonight. I just have to trust that Hannah's being sensible and that she's all right. And I've got some bananas in the car.'

He grinned. 'Banana waffles. Sounds like a plan.'

She made a show of opening and closing all the new cupboard doors because she could see that it pleased him. 'How did you do all this in a weekend?'

'I got into the swing of it when I did my own kitchen. And it's really just cosmetic. The cupboards were good, and they're a standard size, so I just put new doors on them.'

Chloe ran her hand across the worktops. 'They're lovely. They must have cost a fortune. You must let me—'

He laid one finger across her lips, grinning. 'No, you don't. My builder gets a trade discount on everything. And the length of worktop that I didn't use in my own kitchen turned out to be almost enough.'

'So you're trying to kid me that you got all this for free? I don't believe it.'

'Believe whatever you like.' He grinned at her. 'Is it what you wanted?'

'It's better than that. It's gorgeous, and I can't believe you did it all in two days.'

'I had a bit of help, fitting the worktop.'

'Your builder again? The one who gets everything free?'

'Yeah. He's a great guy.'

Chloe wondered whether she should press the point. Jon had obviously spent something on this, but he was unwilling to tell her how much and she should probably accept the gift gracefully. And the most valuable part of it was the thought and care that had gone into it. He'd listened to what she wanted and had made it all happen.

'It's wonderful. I can't thank you enough.'

He grinned. 'It's my pleasure. Now, get on and make the waffles. I'm getting hungry just thinking about them.'

They ate together, taking their time. By the time they'd done the washing up, exhaustion started to kick in for the second time, this time leaving Chloe with little choice but to recognise it.

'You look tired.' He seemed to be reading her mind.

Or more likely he'd noticed that she could hardly keep her eyes open.

'Yes. Think I'll have an early night.'

'What time are you going into the hospital tomorrow?'

'Uh?' Chloe could hardly think, let alone plan. 'Not early. About ten, probably...'

'Okay. I'll see you in the morning, then.'

CHAPTER TEN

EVEN THOUGH SHE'D been tired, she hadn't slept well, and when Chloe woke early she knew that she had no chance of dozing off to sleep again. Dragging herself out of bed, she stumbled to the bathroom and stood for a long time under the shower.

When she went downstairs, Jon was in the kitchen. His face took on a pained expression when she sat down at the table.

'Did you sleep at all?'

'Not much.' Chloe twisted her mouth downwards, pushing her hair back behind her ears. 'Just tell me I look better than I feel and make some coffee, eh?'

'Right you are. You look gorgeous, by the way.'

'Thank you.' She sank her head into her hands. 'Don't overdo it, I might think you're not being sincere.'

He chuckled and made the coffee. Then he fetched her a bowl of muesli and watched her eat it.

'Are we ready to go, then?' He put the empty bowl in the sink.

'We? Are we going somewhere?' Jon's breeziness was obviously concealing some kind of plan.

'I'm popping up to the hospital. I need to get some forms from the HR department. I'll run you in and then we can go and get some lunch, if you like. Think about your next move.'

'Are you sure?' The HR department sounded a bit like an excuse, but Chloe was too tired to argue.

'Yes. Come on. We'll stop and get some more coffee on the way.'

The second cup of coffee had finally woken her up, and by the time they arrived at the hospital Chloe was feeling ready to face the day. She spent two hours handing over to the colleagues who were filling in for her, and found Jon waiting for her in the reception area, talking to an elderly lady with her arm in a sling.

He got to his feet when he saw Chloe. ''Bye, Mavis. Hope they sort your arm out.'

'I expect they will, dear. Don't forget what I told you.'

'No, I'll keep it in mind.' Jon took Chloe's arm and hurried her through the double doors of the department.

'What are you not forgetting?'

Jon shrugged. 'That turnips are high in calcium. Mavis has osteoporosis so she's dispensing advice to the whole of the waiting room about how to keep your bones healthy.'

'Good woman. But, then, you already know how to keep your bones healthy, you're a doctor. Which gives you no excuse not to eat your turnips.'

'Yeah. I thought I'd skip that piece of information, in case she expected me to comment on her X-rays. Fancy a pizza for lunch? We could leave the car here and walk down to that place in the High Street.'

Despite all of the worry that she must feel for Hannah, Chloe still managed to smile, and Jon couldn't help but respect her for it. They talked over lunch, and there was no trace of resentment for all that Hannah had put her through. Just determination to find her sister and somehow make things right again.

'Do you know many of Hannah's friends?' As they walked out into the afternoon sunshine, turning into one of the backstreets that led back to the hospital, Jon's thoughts turned to the next task.

'Quite a few of them. She has some down in Cornwall, from when she lived there with Aunt Sylvie. A few in London. James and I made a list, and I'm going to work through it this afternoon.'

'What if Hannah hears that you've been phoning round, looking for her? Won't she take exception to that?'

'I sent her a text this morning. I thought it was best to be honest and tell her what I'm doing, and that it's because I love her.'

'I think you're right—' Jon broke off as Chloe stumbled suddenly, his arm shooting out instinctively to grab her around the waist and stop her from falling. 'You okay?'

'Yes... Yes, I'm all right.'

She didn't look all right. She was so pale that she would have made a good addition to any Halloween party. 'Sit down for a moment.'

He looked around, and in the absence of anything more suitable Jon guided her to the low front wall that divided someone's front garden from the street and sat her down on it. If anyone objected, he'd tell them he was a doctor.

She was rubbing her leg, just above the ankle. Jon couldn't see any abrasions or swelling.

'Have you hurt yourself? Let me take a look.' He

knelt down in front of her, reaching out for her ankle, and she moved it away. 'Chloe…?'

'It's all right. I'm okay, just… I expect I tripped on that paving stone.' She nodded towards an uneven bit of pavement just where they'd been walking when she'd fallen.

'I expect you did.' Suddenly he realised. She was *hoping* she'd tripped, instead of her legs just giving way beneath her. 'How much sleep did you get over the weekend?'

'Not much.' She looked at him miserably.

'And you didn't sleep last night either. And you've been under stress for the last couple of weeks.' He asked the question that he didn't want to ask, and Chloe obviously didn't want to answer. 'Any tingling in your legs? Or pain?'

'I…don't think so.' She seemed suddenly unable to make her mind up. 'They feel a bit achy.'

'Your legs do ache when you're overtired.' He reached forward, taking her hand in his. 'Chloe, look at me. Now take a breath.'

The first try was more of a shiver than a breath, but the second was a little better. He nodded her on and the third was a good attempt.

'That's good. Now, you know as well as I do that a complete relapse for Guillain-Barré is so rare that we can discount it. Don't you?' He wanted her to say it, but she just nodded. That would have to do.

'Right. And you also know that some of the symptoms might recur from time to time, but that they'll be minor and we can deal with them.'

This time she said it. 'Yes.'

'Now we've got that out of the way, I want you to tell me truthfully whether you have any pain or tingling in your legs. Or if there's any reason for you to believe that you just didn't trip over that paving stone.'

'My legs ache, that's all. I...don't know.'

'Okay, well, that's good. Because being afraid is okay. I would be if I'd been as ill as you have. But I think you'd know if this really was Guillain-Barré and not just the stress you've been under, both physically and mentally.'

'Yes. I think I would.'

'So do you feel all right to stand now? We'll take it slowly back to the hospital.'

'Yes.' She seemed to suddenly pull herself together, smiling up at him. 'I'm okay.'

'Good. Take my arm.'

'I can walk...' She got carefully to her feet, ignoring his outstretched hand.

Jon grinned at her. 'I know. Just humour me, will you?'

She smiled, the warmth in her eyes trickling over his senses. Every time. He was like a bee, unable to ignore the honey in her smile.

He wouldn't let her fall. Not now, and not in the uncertain days that lay ahead. Jon was sure of that now, and all he had to do was to persuade Chloe to let him stay beside her.

When they got home, he made her sit down in the living room and put her through an examination that was rather more for show than anything else. The touch of his fingers as he slipped off her sandals. The look in his eyes as he carefully massaged her feet, his gaze searching for any reaction in her face.

There was a reaction all right. Probably not quite the one that he'd been aiming for. The warm glow of knowing that she was safe in his hands had been tempered by the spice of arousal.

'I'm diagnosing you as stressed and worn out...' He sat down next to her on the sofa, his arm resting on the cushions behind her head. 'And I'm prescribing some sleep. Do you think you can manage that?'

'Yes, but...' What she really wanted—really *needed*—was for Jon to hug her. Just to hold her and tell her everything was going to be all right, because if he said it she knew she'd believe it.

'But what?' He traced his finger around her jaw, tipping her chin up so that he could look into her face. When she reached out for him he was there, wrapping his arms around her and holding her tight.

'I'm sorry. I know I'm being silly...'

'Stop right there. I don't want to hear anything about you being silly or not being allowed to feel anything.'

'But—'

He drew back a little and put one finger over her lips. 'Not a word. You've been stronger than anyone should be expected to be. If you didn't stumble a little from time to time, I'd be tempted to diagnose you as not human.'

Maybe he was right. Maybe the years of making herself cope alone *had* stripped her of a little of her humanity.

'And what would you prescribe for that?' He was so close, and before she could stop herself Chloe stretched up, brushing a kiss against the side of his mouth.

Jon smiled, slowly. 'That would be a treatment option.' He kissed her back, but so fleetingly that she'd hardly tasted him before he drew away again.

'So you're starting with a low-level approach? Or is

that just the best you can do?' She grinned at him to let him know that she knew full well it wasn't.

'No. But we both have our limits.'

Yes, they did. His was that he couldn't believe that even the perfect relationship could work for him. Hers was that she couldn't bring herself to rely on anyone.

'I don't think I've reached mine yet.'

'Neither have I...' He kissed her again, and this time she could feel it. Sweet electricity, flowing through her and making her toes tingle.

His hand moved up her back to her neck. She could feel his fingers in her hair, his thumb brushing the sensitive spot behind her ear, and Chloe shivered.

Jon's mouth curved into a smile, just a breath away from hers. His thumb increased its pressure, making a small circle around the point that was driving her crazy.

'Not fair...' She whispered the words against his lips.

'I found it.' There was a possessive note to his voice, as if now that he'd discovered what he could do with that square inch of skin, he owned it. Maybe he was right. Chloe let out a gasp, tipping her head back, and he brushed a kiss against her neck.

It was a sweet foretaste of what sex might be like. The thought that he might seek out each one of the sensitive points on her body, before concentrating on the more obvious erogenous zones, almost made her cry out. It might take him a long time to find them all...

She took his head between her hands, kissing him on the mouth. That was what turned *him* on, she could feel it. When she just took whatever she wanted. He was strong enough to find that erotic.

And strong enough to stop when it seemed as if there

was no stopping either of them. Ending the kiss, hugging her tight against his chest.

'It would be nice...' Chloe buried her face in his chest so he couldn't see her disappointment. It was impossible for this to go any further and that had been clear right from the start.

'It *was* nice. But maybe we should leave it at that. And maybe you should try to get some sleep.'

She'd had a glimpse of the Jon who was capable of taking everything, but now his arms were gentle again. And suddenly Chloe felt that she could lay her fears aside and sleep.

'I'm very tired...'

'Good. Lie down, then.' He let her go and Chloe curled up on the sofa. 'I'll go and get something to cover you up.'

'But if Hannah calls...' She'd kept her phone with her night and day, ever since Hannah had gone missing, and even now it was sitting on the coffee table in case it rang. Chloe reached for it, hugging it to her chest, wondering if she'd wake if her sister called.

'I'll take it. Just sleep now.' Chloe felt him prise the phone from her fingers and she closed her eyes, drifting off to sleep.

When she woke she was warm under the quilt that she usually kept folded at the end of her bed and the curtains were closed, sunlight filtering through the cracks on each side of the window. She stretched, rubbing her eyes to focus on the clock on the mantelpiece, and saw a note on the coffee table beside her. Not bothering to get up and open the curtains, she reached for it.

I took your phone.

Yes, she remembered that. She wondered where he'd taken it.

My builder called and I've gone to my place for half an hour. If you wake up before I get back I strongly suggest you go back to sleep immediately.

The loop of the 'J' at the bottom of the note curled around in what might be a kiss or might just be a flourish. Chloe's fingers flew to her lips as they started to burn with the memory of his.

She sat up, smoothing her crumpled T-shirt. Maybe she could forget all about the kiss and just pretend it hadn't happened. She imagined that Jon probably wanted to. A shower and a change of clothes seemed like a good start to make.

She was walking back down the stairs when the front door opened. Jon was back, and suddenly she was wide awake.

'How are you feeling?'

'Much better, thanks.' Seeing him again made her body react immediately and her cheeks started to burn.

He was either pretending not to notice how embarrassed she was or he was blind. 'You've only just woken up?'

'About fifteen minutes ago. Jon…' She was trembling, hanging onto the bannister, hardly trusting herself to walk down the remaining stairs towards him. His gaze met hers, and in the warmth of his gentle blue eyes it was suddenly possible to say the words.

'We're okay, aren't we?'

He smiled. 'I'd very much like us to be.'

'Me too.' Suddenly everything moved into sharp

focus. She didn't want to lose the friendship they had. Not for the dream of something they couldn't have.

She walked downstairs, slipping past him and into the sitting room, opening the curtains and folding the quilt that had covered her. When he appeared at the door, she gave him a bright smile.

'Everything all right at your house?'

'Fine. They just wanted to make sure they had lights positioned right in the bathroom and along the hall. Hannah called.'

Chloe caught her breath, dropping the quilt onto the sofa. 'While I was asleep?'

'Yes, I was on my way back here. I managed to pull over in time to answer it.'

'What did she say?' She searched Jon's face for some clue as to whether this was good news or bad, but there was nothing. It was probably just news, because one call wasn't going to solve everything.

'She told me that I should make you stop looking for her. I asked her how she thought I was going to be able to make you do anything you didn't want to, and she loosened up a bit.'

'Thanks.' Chloe imagined that Jon's warm, easy-going tone was the best way to approach Hannah at the moment. He'd probably done a lot better than she could have.

'I told her that you loved her, and that the two of you should talk. That you had no expectations and you were willing to listen to whatever she said.'

'Thank you. That's good.' Very good. Chloe *was* willing to listen but she might not have thought to say it. A thought struck her. 'So how did you leave it? Is she calling back?'

'No. I'm not having you staring at the phone, waiting for her to call. I told her you'd call her.'

Chloe wouldn't have dared be so assertive with Hannah. 'When?'

'Half past five. That gives you half an hour…' Chloe grabbed her phone from his hand and he caught her wrist before she could call.

'No, Chloe. Not like that. Take your time, get your thoughts together and call her in half an hour. You need to do this on your own terms, as well as Hannah's.'

He was right. There was no point in working herself up into a panic and then saying the wrong thing to Hannah. 'Are you strongly suggesting that's what I do?'

A slow, lazy smile spread across his face. 'Yeah. Right in one.'

CHAPTER ELEVEN

SOMEHOW, IN JON'S COMPANY, the dreaded phone call didn't seem so bad. When the time came to make it, she felt almost relaxed, sitting on the sofa next to him.

'I'll wait in the kitchen.' Jon got to his feet.

'Would you stay? I'd…like you to stay, please.' The words still sounded odd in her mouth. But she wanted Jon to stay with her, the way he'd been right at her side through all of this.

He sat back down again. 'You'll have to tell Hannah that I'm here.'

She nodded and looked at her watch. Still two minutes to go but she couldn't wait. Chloe found Hannah in her contacts list and dialled, putting the phone on loudspeaker.

Hannah answered on the second ring.

'Chloe?'

'Yes… Hannah, I'm so glad to hear your voice. Jon's here with me.'

'Yeah? So I suppose I can't ask what's going on with you and him, then…'

Chloe swallowed hard, feeling herself redden. Even if it had just been her and Hannah, she wouldn't have known the answer to that.

'You can ask.' Jon's voice was good-humoured.

'Only if I asked you what was going on in your love life, you'd tell me to mind my own business...'

'Me? I'm about as single as it gets. It's you two I want to know about.'

Chloe wondered whether Jon had been quick-witted enough to turn the question around and find out whether Hannah was with someone. But he was giving nothing away, smiling into the phone as he replied.

'Nothing going on here either. But Chloe needs to know whether you're okay.'

'I'm fine. Good, actually. And there's no point in looking for me because I haven't gone to stay with any of my friends.'

Chloe felt tears prick at the corners of her eyes and pressed her lips together. Jon had been keeping the conversation light, and that was the way it should stay.

'Hannah, what do you expect her to do? If Chloe went missing, you'd look for her, wouldn't you?'

'She wouldn't...' Hannah's voice was tinged with disbelief, but the silence told Chloe that she was thinking about it.

She plucked up the courage to ask the one question that had been hammering in her brain constantly for the last two days. 'Why did you go, Hannah?'

There was a pause at the other end of the line. 'Look, I'm sorry about that. I heard James and Carol talking. James said some things...'

Chloe's mouth went dry. James could be outspoken at times, and Chloe had no doubt that he would have told Carol what was on his mind. 'James says a lot of things, you know that. But he does love you.'

'I know. And what he said he was right.'

'Right?' Something cold twisted around Chloe's heart. This didn't sound good. 'What did he say?'

'He said that if I was going to just leave Amy with you every time things got difficult, she'd be better off without me.'

'Well, that's wrong and James needs to apologise for saying it. You've always taken care of Amy.'

'You don't know, Chloe. I can barely hang on myself some days, let alone take care of Amy. James is right, she would be better off with someone else. Someone who'd love her the way that you do.'

'Me?' Chloe's mouth went dry. How many times over the last two weeks had she wished that Amy was her child, and that she could look after her for ever? This must be some kind of punishment for wanting things that she had no right to.

'You do love her, don't you?'

'What I want is for Amy to be with you. You're her mother...' Chloe looked around wildly, trying to think of something that would persuade Hannah.

Jon was there. Again. Always. 'I don't think this is a conversation that you can have on the phone. You need to talk face to face. What do you say, Hannah?'

There was a long silence, before Hannah replied quietly, 'Okay.'

'Good. Chloe, what do you think?'

In the warmth of his gaze she could suddenly think clearly again. It was time to draw some boundaries. Hannah had to know that she was loved, but she also had to know that her actions had consequences.

'I think... What do you say we make a deal? I know you need some time to think but I need to see you.' Chloe took a deep breath. 'Next Saturday.'

That was five days away and it seemed like an age. But if Hannah would agree to sit down and talk then Chloe could agree to wait.

'It's a long way...'

'I don't care if you're camped out on the moon. Where are you?'

'Remember when I was fifteen. We were going to go on a trip together but we never did get to go.'

Chloe's hand flew to her mouth. 'I'm so sorry...'

'That doesn't matter. I know you meant to take me, but you were ill. But I finally made it back, Chloe...'

'That sounds great, Hannah.' Chloe almost choked on the words. 'You can show me around.'

'Yeah, I'd like that. Saturday?'

'I'll be there. Saturday.'

'I'll be there too. I've got to go now.'

Hannah sounded as if she was crying, but that was okay, because Chloe was crying too.

'Will you call me? Or when can I call you?'

'I'll call. Every evening at eight, I promise. I do have to go...'

'I know. That's okay. I love you, Hannah.'

'Love you too.'

The line suddenly went dead. Chloe stared at the phone for a moment, trying to take in the enormity of what had just happened.

'Where is she?' Jon's quiet voice broke the silence.

'She's in the village where my father was born and where my parents met. In France.'

Chloe seemed almost in shock. That was understandable after the conversation she'd just had. But she'd stood up for herself, let Hannah know what she needed, and Hannah had responded to that. A trickle of pride ran through his chest, making him shiver.

He picked up the phone, putting it out of Chloe's

reach on the mantelpiece. The crystals could look after it for a few minutes.

'What did Hannah mean? When she said she'd finally made it?' He decided to start with the least emotive question he could think of.

'My father never talked much about his family or the place he was brought up. We went back to France every year on holiday, but never there. I suppose that James and I were less curious, because we had more time with our parents, but Hannah was very young when they died. My father's village took on a special significance for her. I think she thought that somehow she might find them there.'

'And you were going to take her back?'

'Yes, I told her I would. I was saving up so we could go there together, but then I became ill and we never did get around to going.'

'Perhaps it's herself she's looking for. As well as your parents.'

'Maybe so.' She heaved a sigh. 'I guess...well, perhaps that's something we can share. And perhaps I'll find some way of convincing her.'

'I imagine she's thinking pretty much the same at the moment. That she's got to find some way of convincing you.'

She quirked her lips downwards, then stood up and stretched her limbs, as if they ached from being in one position for too long. 'Whose side are you on?'

Hers. He was on Chloe's side, and always would be, irrespective of whether she was right or wrong. 'I'm... not really on anyone's side.'

'But?'

Yes, there was a *but*. One that had been bothering Jon

for a little while now. 'I think that Hannah's doing this because she's trying to force you and James to listen…'

'I know.' Tears welled in Chloe's eyes and Jon made himself look away before he gave in to the temptation to hug her and wipe them away. He'd gone too far once today, and a second time wasn't going to help. 'I know, I should have listened to her more…'

'That's not what I'm saying. You've got one solution to all this in your head and Hannah has another. You're trying to persuade her and she's trying to persuade you, and it's not going to work. You need to go right back to the beginning, and tell her how you feel about things, get her to tell you what she's feeling.'

Chloe was trembling, wiping the tears away. 'I want to listen to how she's feeling. I'm trying…'

'Have you told her how you feel? That you feel you've let her down?'

'No, of course not.' She turned suddenly, walking to the mantelpiece and picking up her phone. As if all of her fears, all her worries were centred around it. Then she put it back down again.

'Maybe you're right.' She twisted her mouth in an expression of regret and then the determined smile broke through. If he hadn't been trying so hard not to touch her, Jon would have seriously considered kissing her. 'So… What do I do next?'

It wasn't just a matter of what Chloe did next. In a moment when all he'd wanted to do was make her know that she was far stronger than she gave herself credit for, he had kissed her. And ever since that moment he'd been afraid to touch her again, knowing for sure now that her intoxicating sweetness had the power to overcome his better judgement.

What *he* had to do next was make a decision. Because the only way that they could regain the easy friendship, which had blossomed as they'd looked after Amy together, was to move past the kiss.

'What do you say to getting something to eat and then going for a walk? Somewhere nice. We have the time, and we can forget about all of this for a few hours and take a deep breath.'

She nodded. 'Yes. I'd like that.'

They'd decided against the local park and had taken a drive instead. Jon parked his car at the foot of the hill at Alexandra Palace, and they'd toiled up the steep incline. The breeze was still warm and the lights of London began to emerge through the gloom as dusk fell.

They picked out landmarks on the horizon, laughingly correcting each other when they got them wrong. It was nice. Companionable, as if they were learning to be together again, without flinching away each time they almost touched. Chloe took his arm in the darkness, giving silent thanks that she hadn't lost him.

As they walked back down to the car, she felt that she could breathe again. Start to plan. And it seemed natural to share those plans with Jon as he drove them home.

'I can sort out my plane tickets tomorrow. Fly down on Friday to meet Hannah on Saturday.' The little details, the ones that she knew she could accomplish, were the ones that she should tackle first.

'You could. Or we could drive down together. Take two or three days, find somewhere off the beaten track to stay.'

'That's...' There was no reason why not. Apart from the feeling that dashing down there somehow fitted the urgency of the situation. 'I should be... I might be needed. Somewhere.'

'You might. In which case you won't be around and everyone's just going to have to cope. I'm sure they'll manage.' He shot her a smile, his face angular, a different kind of handsome in the moving shadows.

'It doesn't seem right. James and Carol are looking after Amy and—'

'They'll cope. They have three kids of their own, and Amy will be fine. It strikes me that, however things turn out, this is going to be a long haul. You've got to pace yourself, give yourself a breather from time to time.'

That was good advice. Maybe she should use what time she had and take things a little slower. But maybe not with Jon.

He parked the car in the street outside her house and she got out, stretching her cramped limbs. Home. The last few hours had seemed as if she'd taken a holiday, and it felt as if there should be shoulder-high weeds growing in the front garden, but it was just the way she'd left it.

'I should go on my own. It's good of you to offer, but you have things to do here.' She followed him up the path, searching for her keys in her bag.

'Nothing that won't wait. I'm pretty sure that my house will still be there when I get back.'

'That's my point. It'll still be there, and still need to be done when you get back.' She walked through to the kitchen, putting her keys on the table. 'You don't have a magic kitchen that transforms itself when you're not there, like I do.'

He chuckled quietly. 'You still like it?'

'No. I still *love* it.' She turned to face him in the shadows. 'This is the dramatic pause before I put the light on and see it all over again.'

Actually, the dramatic pause wasn't so bad in itself. She could get lost in that and forget all about the kitchen, staring up at that easygoing smile, which seemed tempered by steel in the shadows.

'Why don't you trust me?' Suddenly he seemed a little more steel than smiles. 'You trust this.'

He gently pulled the gold chain around her neck, freeing the citrine from under her sweater. Chloe realised that her hand had automatically gone to her chest to feel its shape.

'This was given to me by a friend when I was first ill. It was on a silver chain and it broke, but I loved the colour of the citrine and I put it on another chain. The chain was my mother's.'

'So you kept it by you?'

'Yes. When I was alone it...helped me cope.'

'So these crystals *do* have magical properties.' The look on Jon's face said that he didn't believe that for a second.

'I'm a scientist, like you. I believe in what I can quantify. Would you say that the human mind has no bearing on the body?'

He chuckled. 'I've worked in A and E for far too long to think that.'

'Or that holding onto good memories can't get you through the bad times?' She curled her fingers around the citrine.

'No, I wouldn't say that either.' The corners of his mouth turned down. 'But it's not easy to take second place to a piece of crystal, hung around your neck.'

'You're never second best.' Her answer came a little too quickly, too fluently to be anything other than the absolute truth. 'I just don't want to take advantage of you.'

'So you push me away?' He looped his arms loosely

around her. 'Don't do it, Chloe. I know you've been let down before but I'm not going to repeat history.'

'How would you know that?' She suddenly wanted so badly for him to be different, but couldn't dare to believe he was.

'Because I've made up my mind.'

She felt her fingers curl, bunching his shirt in her hand. 'We all make our minds up about a lot of things.'

'Okay. So someone promised they'd be there and then wasn't. Your parents?'

'No. I know they would have been there if they could. Hannah was the one who felt deserted when they died, not me and James.' She moved away from him, and he let her go. Chloe almost wished he'd put up more of a fight and crush her against him, the way he had before. But that had got them nowhere and had only threatened their friendship.

'I had a boyfriend.'

'Ah. A nice boyfriend?' There was a touch of the competitiveness she'd heard in his voice when he'd been talking about the crystal. Jon really didn't like to be second best.

'Fair to middling. We'd been going out for a couple of years and I really liked him at the time. When I was sick he held my hand...not that I could feel it, mind you, because my right hand was paralysed, but I suppose the thought was the main thing.'

'I imagine so.'

'Anyway, he promised me that he was going to be there for me, through thick and thin, whatever happened. That we were going to do this together. I was so grateful to him, and I loved him more than anyone at that moment.' Chloe could feel tears pricking behind her eyelids, and blinked them away.

'Just that moment?' There was only tenderness in his voice now.

'Well, a bit longer than that. A week or so. When I got to rehab he only visited once a week, and by the time I got home he'd gone.' Chloe gulped in a breath, trying not to feel the awful loneliness she'd felt, stuck at home, unable to do anything but wait and hope. 'I heard that he'd been crying on my best friend's shoulder and telling her he couldn't cope.'

'*He* couldn't cope?'

'Well, apparently she couldn't either. Neither of them came to tell me, but when I asked around I was told they were going out together. They had me in common, you see. Both of them were pretty upset about what had happened...' Chloe couldn't keep the bitterness from her voice. And that wasn't fair.

'I don't blame them. It was a lot to ask, it was obvious that I was going to need a lot of help over a long time. But they might have had the decency to come and tell me, you know?'

'That's the least they could have done.' He caught her hand, clasping it to his chest.

'You feel that?'

'Yes, I do.' His heart was beating under her fingertips, strong and steady. The kind of heart you'd want on your side whenever times were tough.

'I promise that I might be there for you, as a friend. I might not, depending on the circumstances.'

She couldn't help laughing. It was honest, at least. 'That's good. Thank you.'

'And I promise that if I tell you I'm going to do something, I'll do it. No excuses, no half-measures.'

'That's very good.'

'And I'm telling you that I'll come to France with you

and stick around for a while. Not for ever. I have to go back to work in three weeks, and if the builders manage to knock my house down I might have to pop back and survey the wreckage. But I'll be there for as long as I can, and I'll do whatever I can to help.'

'That's perfect. I'd like that very much.'

'So that's settled, then.' He smiled down at her. 'Now, are we going to switch the light on and see whether any of the handles have fallen off the kitchen cabinets while we've not been looking?'

CHAPTER TWELVE

It was a strange feeling, inhabiting the space between what was possible and what he wanted. But they'd drawn the lines carefully, and they both understood the boundaries. Those boundaries allowed them the freedom that the kiss had threatened to take away. That casual give and take, which meant they could just enjoy each other's company, without having to examine every touch, every word for a meaning that shouldn't be there.

And luck seemed to be on their side. Tickets and hotel reservations were obtained without too much trouble, and Hannah kept her promise to call the following evening. On Thursday they were up early and ready to go, in the bright crispness of a late summer's morning.

'You're sure about this?' Jon gave her one last chance to go inside and change her clothes.

'Positive. A hundred miles south of here, it's going to be much warmer.' She had a fleece jacket on over a summer dress. He could almost smell the yellow and blue flowers sprinkled across the light fabric.

'All right. Whatever you say.' The morning was imbued with a kind of excitement that was more akin to a new adventure, not the urgency of an emergency where every second counted. For the next two days he had

Chloe all to himself, and as long as they covered the miles, they could do whatever else they liked.

With one, significant exception. Now that he had nothing else to do but keep his eye on the road, Jon had to remind himself that the boundaries they'd set were all for the best, and that *whatever they liked* didn't include stopping the car and claiming Chloe's lips again.

He hadn't been able to keep up with her rapid French when she'd booked their accommodation, but Jon assumed she'd booked a couple of motorway hotels, and doubted they'd provide the ambience for anything other than a meal and some sleep. Which was just as well because, however much he wanted to kiss her—however tantalising the thought of exploring a little further than just a kiss—that was one avenue that should remain closed to them.

By the time they emerged from the Channel Tunnel the sky was looking a lot more promising, a dark clear blue that seemed to beckon them towards the horizon. Sixty miles of motorway driving and then Chloe suddenly indicated a left turn.

The next twenty miles got them no closer to their destination as she turned the map one way and then another, trying to puzzle out where they were going. Somehow they managed to get back on track and Chloe directed him through a set of large, wrought-iron gates and along a long avenue, edged with trees and dappled by sunlight.

'Wow. Look at that.' The avenue had opened up into a wide, sweeping curve, which grazed the entrance of a magnificent chateau. White painted and gleaming in the afternoon sun, it looked like a fairy-tale castle, complete with turrets at each side.

'This is it.' Chloe pointed to a cluster of cars to one side of the entrance. 'I think we can stop there.'

'We're staying *here*?' Jon had imagined that they might be just passing, to find some more modest accommodation somewhere in the grounds.

'Yes.' She turned to him, her face shining. 'Do you like it?'

'I love it, but…' It hadn't been quite what Jon had had in mind when he'd said they'd find somewhere to stay.

'It's my treat.' Chloe shot him a warning glance as he opened his mouth to protest that she hadn't needed to do this. 'Don't argue. You've done so much for me, and this is just to show you how much I appreciate it. I hope the inside is as nice as the outside.'

That would be difficult. The chateau stood in rolling countryside, dominating the landscape. It looked as if the one and only cloud in the sky had landed here, depositing this elegant, fairy-tale castle just to give ordinary mortals a blueprint for the proportions that they should build in.

But somehow the inside was even better. A soaring hallway that managed to be both grand and welcoming, its relaxed elegance extending to the other rooms they passed as their hostess led them up a sweeping staircase and along a wide corridor.

Right at the end, the woman opened a door, speaking in French to Chloe. 'She says she hopes we don't mind a climb.' Chloe responded in French, shaking her head and smiling.

The stone steps wound around a stairwell. Above him, Jon could see layer after layer, like the swirling, ever smaller spirals of an ancient sea creature. Here, the elegance of the rest of the building had been left behind in favour of white-painted stonework, which seemed older and much more utilitarian.

They were both out of breath by the time their hostess unlocked a door that led off the stairs a couple of turns before they got to the top. She beckoned them inside and Jon caught his breath.

The room was enormous, the square back giving way to a huge curve, which must follow the shape of one of the turrets he'd seen from the outside. High windows gave a spectacular view of the countryside, and on this side of the room a stone fireplace, big enough to roast an ox in, was stacked with logs. The bed was big enough to overpower almost any room, but here it looked almost insignificant, standing to the side of the curved space.

'This is amazing. I feel as if I'm in a castle…' Jon dropped their bags, wondering whether Chloe had booked just the one room. That thought sounded even better than their surroundings.

But their hostess beckoned to them again, leading them up to the top of the spiral staircase outside. 'This is your room.' Chloe grinned at him.

It was much the same as the room below, with an even more spectacular edge. In the centre of the curved space a domed glass ceiling let sunlight flood downwards, right onto the bed that was placed beneath it. Jon imagined that its occupant would be able to see the stars at night.

'This is…' He shrugged, smiling. 'Words fail me.'

Their hostess laughed, dropping the keys into Chloe's hand. An exchange in French and she left them alone.

'It's better than the pictures.' Chloe was smiling broadly. 'Our very own castle for the night. You said it would be good to get away for a couple of days.'

'I'm not sure I was imagining we'd do it in this style.'

He walked to one of the windows, looking out. 'If any of our troubles try to get at us we'll be able to pour boiling oil on their heads as they scale the walls.'

'Or you can plunge a sword through them as they make a rush for the stairs.' Her laugh sounded as if she really had left the world behind, and that nothing could assail her here. 'Madame says that we can get up to the roof from here.'

An alcove by the door gave way on one side to a shining bathroom, the large bath standing right in the middle of the room. On the other side, another set of winding stone steps led up to a door that opened onto a flat roof, the glass dome sitting at the centre of it but leaving more than enough space around the edge for a table and chairs, sheltered by the high stone ramparts.

'We can have dinner up here if we like. Although the dining room looked lovely in the pictures.'

'Here. Definitely here.' They only had one night to enjoy this and they should make the most of it. Chloe had made him a make-believe king of a fairy-tale castle, and she was his queen. Her hair was loose at her back, her dress moulding her legs in the breeze. Her honey-brown eyes were bright with excitement. All he really wanted to do at this point was kiss her.

Maybe that would happen. It seemed as if almost anything could happen here, but for now he was content to stand with her, looking out across the gardens at the back and the sweep of the drive at the front. The road seemed a very long way away at the moment, toy cars buzzing back and forth along it. Tomorrow his would be one of them, but that seemed such a long way away that it wasn't even worth considering.

CHAPTER THIRTEEN

THE CHATEAU HAD exceeded her expectations. But best of all was Jon's reaction. She could see that he loved it, and more than that he seemed to have left behind the urgency of the road, and that was exactly what she'd wanted. He needed a break as much as she did, if only he'd admit it.

They still had the rest of the afternoon, and they'd decided to walk down to the village together. Three kilometres of sunshine and birdsong. The scent of flowers in the hedgerows and the quiet buzz of insects. He took her hand, winding his fingers loosely around hers, and everything in the world seemed right.

Sitting on a bench in the village square, watching the world go by, was the only thing on their to-do list. Until Jon suggested hot chocolate, which posed a whole new set of important questions. They took their time answering them, inspecting each of the three cafés set around the square and finally decided which was best.

'It's a long walk back to the chateau.' His smile was delicious, warm and relaxed. 'Do you think we should force ourselves to have a pastry as well?'

More decisions. Chloe had already been eyeing up the choice on offer, and didn't know which to pick. She pushed the menu card across the table towards him.

'You choose. Something that's rich and sweet and really, really bad for us.'

He grinned, beckoning towards the waitress. 'I see you're coming around to my way of thinking...'

It was a succession of one delight after another. They'd indulged in hot chocolate and wickedly delicious pastries, then walked back to the chateau together. They explored the downstairs rooms and then sat on the terrace at the back for a while. Chloe had asked for dinner on the roof, and they'd chosen what they wanted from the menu, then gone back to their rooms to change.

She chose a summer dress with a matching lace woollen shawl, glad to find that they hadn't creased too much in her bag. A little make-up seemed only right, and she brushed her hair carefully, catching it back in a loose arrangement at the back of her neck. As a compromise between wanting to look her best and wanting it to seem that she hadn't spent too much time on her appearance, it would do.

When she ventured up the spiral staircase she saw that the door to Jon's room was open. He turned from the window, his face breaking into a smile.

'You look beautiful.'

A lump lodged in the back of her throat. He was wearing a simple dark blue shirt, open at the neck, with dark blue trousers. Jon looked even more effortlessly gorgeous than usual, slim-hipped and broad-shouldered, the strong set of his jaw giving a delicious sense of purpose to the softness of his eyes.

'Thank you.' Telling him that he looked beautiful might be misconstrued. But he did.

'What do we do to let them know we're ready for dinner? Or do we just wait and see what happens next?'

'Oh. No, we phone. I have the number.' Chloe pulled her phone from the pocket of her dress and dialled.

He helped her up the steps to the roof. Perhaps he knew that her knees were shaking. The evening was warm enough to leave her shawl on the back of the chair, and when the waitress arrived with their meals and lit the candles on the table, the shelter of the stone ramparts stopped them from blowing out immediately. She wished them a smiling *'Bon appétit!'* and left them alone, flipping a switch at the top of the stairs, which lit a string of fairy lights that ran all the way around the edge of the tower's roof.

It was a shame, really. Jon had ordered a very good wine, and the meal was well worthy of more attention than Chloe could give it. But the spectacular view and the fairy lights, which seemed brighter and more magical as the sun went down, were also entrancing. And Jon…every move he made, every gesture and every smile made her forget about everything apart from him.

'Would you like a dessert?' They'd taken their time over the meal, talking as darkness fell.

'Just coffee for me.' It was a little cooler now, and Chloe wrapped her shawl around her shoulders.

'I think even I can manage that.' He grinned, reaching for her phone and asking for two coffees in halting French.

The waitress appeared again, bringing coffee and clearing the table, leaving their glasses and the bottle of wine behind. Chloe sipped her coffee and then reached for the bottle. Jon hadn't refilled her glass while they ate, and it was still more than half-full.

'Not yet.' He laid his fingers on the back of her hand. 'I want you stone cold sober.'

'What for?'

He smiled. 'A turn around the roof? Don't want you falling over the edge.'

That was hardly likely. She'd have to ask him for a leg up if she was going to climb across the wide stones that protected them. All the same, Chloe left the wine where it was and stood up, taking his arm.

Two steps, three… They got almost halfway round before he kissed her, and when he did she was almost trembling with anticipation. The breeze tugged at her senses, making her shiver as he drew her into the warmth of his body.

She wrapped her arms around his neck, staring up into his eyes. 'I didn't mean…for this to happen…'

'You don't want it to?' His hands were spread possessively across her back, and he made a show of moving them so she could step away if she wanted to. He didn't need to, the kiss had told them both exactly what they wanted.

'No, I…' Chloe thought hard. Now wasn't the time to be at all unclear about what she wanted. 'I love that it's happened. I just didn't plan for it…'

'Ah. So you didn't lure me here to have your way with me? I'm afraid that I didn't lure you either.'

'You didn't? I think the least you can do is pretend you planned it all.' She stretched up, brushing her lips against his mouth.

'You'd be very disappointed in me.' He leaned towards her, whispering in her ear, 'I don't have any condoms but that doesn't mean we can't just…improvise a little.'

His fingers moved on her back and Chloe shivered at the thought. She'd take a bet that Jon improvised very, very well. But he didn't need to.

'Actually, you know that I packed a travel kit to give

to Hannah? Things she might need, that she probably didn't think to take with her when she left.'

He chuckled quietly. 'You thought she'd need condoms?'

'Well, you never know. I thought it wouldn't hurt to cover all the possibilities, particularly after last time...' She didn't want to talk about that now. She wanted to kiss him again.

'You are the most resourceful woman.' Clearly he liked that because his kiss almost lifted her off her feet. 'What next, now that we can do whatever we want? I have no expectations...'

She was stone cold sober and she knew exactly what she wanted. 'I don't have any expectations of you either. Can we take the rest of that bottle of wine downstairs with us now, and find out what happens next?'

'That sounds wonderful.'

He kissed her again and she felt his body hard against hers. One hand on her back pulled her in tight against him, the other caressed her jaw, sending shivers of sensation through her. His fingers brushed the sensitive spot right behind her ear, as if he'd remembered how it turned her on, but he wasn't getting to that quite yet.

Instead, she felt his hand move, trailing across the neckline of her dress and lower to cup her breast. At last. It felt like fire, out of control and spreading through the whole of her body.

He responded to her whimper of pleasure by backing her against the high stone ramparts. Her gaze locked with his, as he rubbed his thumb gently over the material that covered her nipple, and when she caught her breath he smiled.

'You feel so good. I want you so much.' He whispered the words into her ear.

That was just fine with her, as long as he took it slowly. The sudden urge to be taken right now, right here had receded into a hotter, more unrelenting fire and she wanted this to last.

'Not yet. Not for a while…'

'You want to drive me crazy?' Jon's gaze burned its way into her senses.

'Yeah, that's the plan. You want to come downstairs?'

Before he let her go, there were more caresses, leaving her in no doubt that Jon intended to show her exactly who was boss, and for her to tell him so. Which was fine, because when she moved her hips against his, his gasp held all the surrender that her whispered words had.

He held the moment for as long as it lasted, his eyes dark in the moonlight. Then he turned, taking her hand and leading her downstairs, picking up her phone and the bottle of wine on the way.

'Not here…' Chloe took her phone from his hand, calling downstairs to say that the waitress could come and clear the coffee things now and that they wouldn't be wanting anything else. Then she led him downstairs to her room, locking the door behind them.

Jon reached for the box of matches on the high mantelpiece and bent to light the candles that stood in the grate. Soft light danced through the room.

Standing between the fireplace and the four-poster bed, he kissed her again, while she struggled with the buttons on his shirt. When she'd pulled it off, he slowly undid the first of the row of buttons that ran down the front of her dress.

One more, and then another. Jon was obviously

enjoying the suspense as much as she was, and she watched as he deftly undid each one.

'You're better with buttons than I am.' She smiled up at him as he slipped her dress from her shoulders and it fell to the floor.

'I've got a good reason to be. You're very beautiful.' The way he was looking at her made her feel beautiful. Made her feel strong.

He ran his finger along the chain that encircled her neck, and when he got to the citrine, nestled between her breasts, he was suddenly still. 'I'll take care of you tonight, Chloe.'

She believed him. The citrine had been all she'd had once, but Jon was here now. 'Will you take it off for me?'

He turned her round, sweeping her hair to one side. She felt him open the catch and then he put the citrine and its chain into her hand.

'Look at me...' Turning her round again to face him, he tipped her chin up. His face held all the promise of pleasure. 'How does it feel when I touch you?'

'It feels wonderful.' She knew what he wanted her to do. He wanted her to put the citrine aside and rely on him completely. That was what she wanted too, but suddenly in the back of her mind the memory formed, clear and insistent, taking her back to a time when every touch had been potentially painful, every loss of control had had to be fought. She felt her hand instinctively close around the citrine.

The moment of uncertainty must have shown in her face and she felt his fingers curl around hers. 'Chloe, you can hold onto this if you want. It doesn't matter.'

She could see that it did matter to him. And it mattered to her, too.

'You'll be there for me? This is the first time…since I've been ill.' She knew that shouldn't matter, but the softness in Jon's eyes told her that he understood.

'I'll be there with you all the way. I promise.'

She reached behind her, putting the citrine and the chain down on the cabinet beside the bed. When Jon kissed her, she didn't miss it at all.

He finished undressing her, caressing her as he did so. Watching for each response until cause merged into effect and all she could feel was one delicious impulse of pleasure and wanting. She reached for the waistband of his trousers, unfastening it.

'I want to touch *you*, now.'

Jon had known that Chloe might hesitate. Known that he must be gentle and watch for any sign of uncertainty on her part. But he hadn't dreamed that she would speak so openly about how she felt, or that it would change their lovemaking so profoundly.

Because speaking about it had seemed to break every barrier. Every touch was met with a word or a sigh. She didn't leave him to guess what she was feeling, she told him, and that empowered him.

When she touched him, it was like electricity running across his skin. Her finger, her tongue tracked delicate patterns of delight across his body, as slowly they pushed each other further.

'Chloe… Chloe…' If he'd known what to beg for he would have done it. His whole body was shaking, sweat trickling down his spine and adrenaline pumping through his veins. And when he touched her, he knew that she was at the same point of no return, where thought was banished and only feeling made any sense.

The curtains around the bed were closed on two

sides, leaving only the side that faced the fireplace open.
When he laid her down, candlelight glimmered across
her body, and he traced the shadows with his fingers.

There was only one thing in the world that he needed
to do now. He needed to make her come, as hard and
as long as he could. From the way she was trembling
in his arms, that wasn't going to be all that difficult.

She accepted him inside her so generously. Holding him tight, making feel as if he really were a king.
Jon gritted his teeth, loving the sight and sound of her
pleasure and wanting to make it last. Almost afraid of
the moment when she might lose control in his arms,
and whether he could hold her tightly enough to reassure her.

But Chloe wasn't afraid. She wound her legs around
his waist, tilting her hips towards him, taking him
deeper. He saw her eyes darken suddenly as the pupils
dilated even further, and she moved against him. When
he took up her rhythm, her body seemed to almost hum
with pleasure.

The further he pushed her, the more she responded to
him. The more she responded, the stronger he became.
When she came, her body arching under his, it felt as
if he was being dragged down with her in the massive
undertow of her pleasure.

Then suddenly everything changed. He lost his bear-
ings, knowing only that the point of no way back was
some way behind him now. His self-control slipped
away. Everything slipped away, and he didn't even think
to miss it because Chloe was there. When she smiled
at him, her fingers digging into his back, he came so
hard that he almost blacked out.

CHAPTER FOURTEEN

CHLOE WOKE, LUXURIATING in the feel of Jon's body curled around hers. When she opened her eyes she found him propped up on the pillows, cradling her in his arms, his body bathed in candlelight.

'How long have I been asleep?'

'An hour. It's still early.' His eyes held all the promise of a long night that was still ahead of them.

'Were you watching me?' If she'd known, she would have kept her eyes closed for another couple of minutes just to feel herself under his gaze.

He smiled. 'I'm taking my duties seriously.'

'Your *duties*?' She reached up, tracing her finger across his lips. 'What duties?'

'Oh, you know. All-purpose mascot. Lucky charm.' He nodded towards the citrine, her gold chain curled around it on the dresser. 'Are you all right?'

'Better than just all right. My toes are still tingling.'

How quickly things changed. There were nights that she'd lain in bed, agonising about whether her toes were tingling or not. The power of suggestion was enough to set anyone's toes tingling if you thought about it hard enough, but Chloe had been unable to ignore it. But all that had been driven into the past now by the delicious tingle that was the aftermath of his touch.

'And that would be a good tingle?'

'Yes. A very good one.'

He bent to kiss her. 'I was thinking…'

'Yes?' She wanted to hear every last thing he was thinking. The warm curve of his lips told her that right now there wasn't a bad thought in his head.

'Seems a terrible shame to waste that bed upstairs. A glass of wine under the stars…'

'It does, doesn't it?'

The first time they'd make love had been a little uncertain, venturing onto new ground with all the excited tremor of discovery. With the second time came a sudden realisation that the first hadn't been the kind of onetime experience that couldn't be repeated. When they woke early, and Jon made love to her yet again, it was a return to that blissful place where only they existed. Lost in each other but knowing that his smile was the only compass she needed.

They were on the road a little later than they'd anticipated. He'd held her close in the bright glow of dawn. Breakfast in bed, hot chocolate and croissants, couldn't be rushed when it was eaten with Jon, and neither could the steaming bathtub, big enough to take them both.

But the road beckoned. As Jon settled into the driver's seat of his car, he quirked his lips downwards. She felt it too. Last night had been special, but they were leaving now.

'Back to reality, then.' He twisted the key in the ignition. 'You know where we're going?'

Chloe reached forward, taking the folded map from the glove compartment. She knew exactly where they were going.

* * *

The cabin could only be reached by walking through the woods. No roads, no other buildings. Just the sound of their feet on the mud path and a flock of geese, squabbling on the lake.

'How on earth did you find this place?' Chloe hadn't said where they were staying tonight, and Jon hadn't asked, but her air of excited anticipation had told him she had something up her sleeve. When they'd drawn up at the farmhouse he'd thought that this would be an idyllic place to spend the night, but the place they were actually headed to was beyond all his expectations.

'We came to stay here for three weeks one summer when I was a child. Marie-Christine and I were the same age and we made friends. We've kept in touch ever since.' The young woman who'd welcomed them had greeted Chloe with a hug and a kiss, and they'd linked arms, talking together as the three of them walked past the stable block, converted for holiday lets, and across the fields to the edge of the wood.

'They don't advertise the cabin for let. It's just for friends and family.' I gave Marie-Christine a call and she said we could have it for tonight. It was a piece of luck.'

'It's fantastic. I didn't think you could find anywhere quite as special as the chateau, but you proved me wrong.' In truth, anywhere that Chloe allowed him to lie next to her was special.

'I thought about what you said—about pacing myself.'

He put his arm around her shoulders, feeling the soft rhythm of her body against his. 'And this is you pacing yourself? Give me a call when you decide to go into overdrive.'

She chuckled. 'I love this place. Holds a lot of happy memories.'

'Your father brought you here, but he never took you to his home?' They only had another hundred miles to drive tomorrow before they reached the village where Hannah was staying.

'No, he never did. I never really thought about it, growing up. He never spoke all that much about his childhood, and you know how it is when you're a kid. You just accept what you're told and don't think to ask.'

'But Hannah wants to know where he came from?'

'I want to know too. I used to think about it a lot after my parents died but life kind of took over. There was Hannah to look after and my studies and then I became ill. It all became swallowed up.'

'But now Hannah and you have some time to explore.'

'Maybe. I hope so.' She opened the door of the cabin. One large room served as a kitchen, dining room and sitting room. 'It's just this room and two bedrooms. There's no electricity and you have to pump whatever water you need.'

'And you cook outside on the barbeque?' He gestured towards the large double barbeque built under the eaves of the cabin.

'Yes. Or if it's raining, we can go to the farmhouse.'

'Or get some bread and cheese. Fresh fruit and a bottle of wine…' He put their bags down on the floor, folding his arms around her shoulders. 'Just the two of us.'

'That sounds so good.' Her fingers traced fire across his chest, bringing back exquisite memories of last night and the promise of another, just as explosively sweet.

'So...' She glanced at the two doors at the far end of the main room. 'Which bedroom are we going to start with?'

They'd travelled three hundred miles in three days. And Chloe felt as if she'd stepped away from her life, surfacing from all the worries and pain that had submerged her and finally taking a deep breath. Perhaps the first since her parents had died.

If she'd made this journey on her own she would have covered the distance, but she would have brought along most of the old familiar baggage. But with Jon that was impossible. It wasn't just the sex, which left her unable to think about anything other than his touch and the urgent need to keep breathing, just so she could feel it again. It was him. Sitting with him in the car, feeling the miles roll by. Eating with him. Talking with him, when there was nothing much to say but they both wanted to hear the other's voice.

And now, driving through the village that spread lazily across the landscape, as if it were basking in the afternoon sun, she felt like a child, pressing her face against the car window, anxious to see everything. In truth, it was unremarkable, not particularly pretty but not completely ugly either. If it had been any other place she would have let it just slip by, but she gazed at every shop in the main street, each café, everyone who walked along the pavement, because any one of them over about fifty might have known her father.

'That woman...' She indicated a woman with a baby buggy outside the small supermarket, whose mid-brown hair was about the same colour as her own. 'She could be a second or third cousin, for all I know.'

He left her to her speculations. Wondering if her

father had climbed the old chestnut tree in the village square. Whether he'd gone to the café, which looked as if it had been there for ever, with his parents. Her grandparents, the ones who looked like strangers in the photographs.

'Did your father have brothers and sisters?'

'No, he was an only child. His mother died just before my parents married.'

'And his father?'

'Apparently he left her. I don't know why, Dad never used to talk about him. He wasn't from around here.'

'And your parents met here?'

'Yes. My mother was doing a gap year before going to art college. She ended up here for a couple of nights on the way somewhere else, and met my father. She decided to stay a week and then…that was it, really. When she came back to England my dad came with her, and after that they always lived there, although they both loved France and came back here as often as they could. Not here, though. I wish I knew why.'

'There might not be any particular reason. I don't go back to my home town all that much.'

'There's a reason for that, isn't there?' The bitterness of his divorce. The way his family had chosen to support his ex-wife and not him.

'I suppose there is.' His brow creased, and it seemed that Jon didn't want to talk about it. 'Where did Hannah say to go?'

'Through the village.' Hannah had told them that she would be away from the village for a day or so but back on Saturday, and that she'd book two rooms for them at the boarding house where she was staying.

They found the place, a neat, whitewashed house at the older and prettier end of the village. Chloe followed

Jon inside, watching as he used a mixture of signs and broken French to indicate that he wanted one double room, not two singles. Chloe didn't step in. It was nice that he'd just done it, without having to refer to her at all. That there was no longer any question about whether they were together.

Their room was quiet and unremarkable. Pale walls and pale fabrics, with dark wooden furniture that didn't quite match but went well enough together. Jon put their bags down on the bed and Chloe stared at them, sitting together. It was almost as if she'd brought someone home to introduce him to her parents, and she half expected them to burst through the door, her mother taking her to one side to put her father's glowering disapproval over booking just one room into a gentler, more persuasive form.

But she was a grown up now. She'd managed for ten years alone, and her parents would surely have respected whatever decision she made about sleeping arrangements.

'Would you like to go and look around the village?' He planted his hands on the deep window sill, looking out of the window. 'There's a church over there, we could take a stroll in that direction.'

'Could we…? Would you mind if we waited for Hannah? Knowing her, she's likely to have a full itinerary of my father's every move, right from when he was born to when he left here. When she gets a bee in her bonnet she gets very single-minded.'

'And you don't want to take a little look yourself first?' His easygoing smile said that it really didn't matter one way or the other.

'I think I'd like Hannah to show me. You know, I've realised that most of the things she knows about Mum and Dad are from when she was young, or what James and I have told her. She's never had anything that she can tell us.'

He nodded. 'That sounds like a nice idea. And, of course, if Hannah's telling the story, then it might give you more of a clue about what she's really doing here.'

'Yes. I thought that too.' She walked over to the window, laying one hand on his shoulder, and he turned and kissed her. Strong and yet so gentle. There for her, giving her his thoughts on things, without telling her what to do.

'Thank you, Jon.'

'What for?' He chuckled suddenly, hugging her tight. 'On second thoughts, I'll be expecting very full recompense. For all these things you seem to think I've done.'

'And what would that be?' She traced her finger across his lips. She had a good idea, and it would be her pleasure.

'I think… Maybe we take a walk in the garden. Have a cup of tea. Then we can come back here and you can take your dress off. As slowly as you like.'

'And then?' Chloe could dispense with the cup of tea.

'We take a shower. Go out and find some dinner.'

'Aren't you missing something?' She flipped the top button of his shirt open and he kissed her again. This time harder, a first step on the road that would take them into each other's arms.

'Probably.' His smile turned wolfish. No one smiled like that at the thought of a walk in the garden and a cup of tea. 'Want to take me through it? In detail?'

CHAPTER FIFTEEN

JON WASN'T SURE that his body could take much more of this. In the months after his marriage had ended and, if the truth be told, for some while before it had ended he'd been unable to work up any enthusiasm for sex. He'd been going through the motions with Helen, hoping that things would get better, and that she wasn't feeling quite so empty inside as he was, but when they'd split up it had been almost a relief that the physical side of things was now at an end.

Since then, there had been a couple of affairs. Consenting adults, no strings, that kind of thing. Where both parties knew exactly what they were doing, and how it was going to end. But although he and Chloe had both gone into this with their eyes open, and it wasn't such a different arrangement, it felt as if it were spinning wildly out of control.

And the thing was, he couldn't stop it. Couldn't help wanting her, every minute of the day. Not just her touch but her sweetness and her strength. Her unpredictability, the times she was wrong, and the times she was right. The way that they seemed so different in so many ways but that together they somehow managed to fit perfectly.

And that wasn't the worst of it. Frequent sex—he could handle that. The kind of sex that didn't feel that burning heat, or sweat, or ragged, incoherent cries were incongruous and should be avoided—he could most definitely handle that. But lying in her arms in the soft darkness, knowing that he'd been broken, was different. Watching one tear trickle from the corner of Chloe's eye, knowing that it wasn't joy or pain but a sign that she had given herself as completely as he had... That was entirely different.

It would cool. Everything cooled at some point and he and Chloe were so different that the cracks would appear soon enough. When Hannah arrived, they would have something else to think about, rather than just the road and each other.

He sat with her on a bench in the bus station, feeling the warm pressure of her body leaning against his. If this was the beginning of the end, it was partly a relief, wholly regrettable, but it was the way things were and he couldn't fight it.

'She said...' Chloe watched as a bus drew up in one of the bays, the doors opening and people starting to get out. 'There must be another bus coming at this time. That can't be the one.'

Probably not. The people getting out of the bus were chatting and laughing amongst themselves, obviously having made friendships. They looked good company, but no one was under fifty, which wasn't the age group that he would have expected Hannah to naturally gravitate towards.

'Well, I never...' Jon followed Chloe's pointing finger and saw Hannah climb down from the bus. Her rucksack was one of the first bags out of the luggage compartment and she collected it, laughing with the couple who were standing next to her as the man teased her about something.

'What's Hannah doing on a silver surfers' bus trip?' Jon couldn't see anything wrong with the people standing around the bus, but he reckoned that Hannah would dismiss them, labelling them as boring.

'No idea.' Chloe stood up, waving to Hannah, and she bade a cheery goodbye to her companions, walking over to them.

Chloe had obviously thought about this and knew exactly what she was going to do. No running at Hannah, no frantic grabbing at her, no tears. She spread her arms, smiling as Hannah gave her a hug and a kiss, and then let her go.

'How's Amy?' Chloe had told him that when Hannah called, those were always the first words from her mouth.

'I called James this morning and she's fine. It's good to see you. You look so well…' Chloe kept hold of Hannah's hand. She did look well, less pale than when she'd been with James in Cornwall. And she'd dyed her hair a lighter, more natural colour, rather than the black that she usually favoured.

'You too.' Hannah grinned at Chloe, and turned her attention to Jon. 'Thanks for coming.'

This was something new too. Whenever he'd seen Hannah with James she'd always been the kid sister. But from the way she put her arm around Chloe's shoulders, it seemed that Hannah had developed a protective streak for her sister. She'd grown up a little.

'My pleasure. We drove down. Had a few days' holiday.'

'Yeah?' Hannah raised her eyebrows. 'That's good.'

'So did you enjoy the coach trip?' Chloe ventured the question.

'Yeah, actually. It was only two days, and I wanted

to take in a bit of the history of the area, so I booked it. I thought it was going to be dreadful when I saw that lot.' Hannah jerked her thumb over her shoulder at her fellow travellers. 'But it was so interesting. One of the guys on the trip is a history teacher—well, he was before he retired—and he really made it all come alive. And his wife's an absolute darling. So funny.'

'Good.' Chloe kept her thoughts to herself over Hannah's abrupt volte face over whether anyone over twenty-five had anything to offer. 'Shall we go back to the boarding house? Then maybe you can show me around a bit.'

'You haven't checked the village out?'

'No, I wanted you to show me.' Chloe had clearly decided that she was going to leave the more difficult questions for later, and for now just watch and wait. It was an approach that Jon reckoned was wholly right.

'Oh, okay, then.' Hannah seemed pleased at the thought. 'Have you got the car with you, or do we need to grab a bus back to the village?'

Jon had let them talk, strolling beside them, hands in pockets as if he was just there for the scenery. But he was there. It made her feel strong enough to wait, to let Hannah dictate the pace.

They dropped Hannah's rucksack at the boarding house and walked into the centre of the village to get some lunch. Hannah had brought a blue plastic folder with her, and from the way she put it on the table next to her, it held something important. Chloe was dreading the moment when Hannah decided to show her what was inside it.

'When you said you were driving, I thought you might be planning to throw a blanket over my head and tie me up. Take me back home.' One of the things that Chloe liked about Hannah was that she didn't beat about the bush. It was sometimes brutal, but at least it was honest.

Although she wasn't quite sure that she knew the answer to this. *No, I wasn't* sounded as if she didn't care. *Yes, I was* wasn't much of a reassurance that she was here to listen and learn.

'I talked Chloe out of it.' Jon seemed to have woken suddenly from his reverie. 'She might not care about losing her licence to practise after being brought up on kidnapping charges, but I do.'

Chloe shot him a silent *thank you* and Hannah grinned. 'So I'm not going to need the pepper spray to defend myself?'

Maybe Hannah was joking and maybe not. Jon smiled. 'That rather depends on what you're defending yourself from.'

He went back to his meal and the matter was dropped. When the waitress brought coffee, Hannah reached for the folder. 'I want to show you... I found some things out. About Dad.'

Chloe breathed a sigh of relief. The nagging fear that perhaps there had been legal papers in the folder, something that formalised Hannah's intention to leave Amy behind, was unfounded. 'Show me. I'd love to see.'

Hannah opened the folder on the first page. A black and white map of the village, a few of the buildings coloured in by hand. 'This is where Dad lived. In blue. And the mauve is where our grandmother was born.'

Chloe leaned over the map. 'Right here? By the village green?'

'Yes, her parents had a shop.' Hannah's face had the

intent look she got when she had hold of something and wasn't letting go. 'Haberdashery.'

Hannah leaned over, flipping through the pages, finding the right one. The photograph was a copy of an older one, the creases showing up on the print. 'Who's that standing outside?'

'Guess.' Hannah's face was flushed with triumph.

'I don't know. The proprietor…our great-grandfather?' Chloe peered at the figure. She could hardly make any features out, just a man in a white apron standing in the shadow of the doorway. He looked as if he had a moustache.

'Yes.'

'Wow.' Chloe looked at the photograph again. 'Where did you get this? You've done it all in the last week?'

'No, I've been working on it for a while, using the internet, but coming here everything fell into place. The *pasteur* at the church gave me the photo. His predecessor had a thing about the village history and he collected a load of things and catalogued them all. It's all still kept up at the church, along with the parish records.'

'But…' The nagging doubt that there was something wrong with the photograph suddenly resolved into certainty. 'The shopfront. It says *Delancourt*. That wasn't our grandmother's name, was it?'

Hannah laughed. 'Wondered when you'd notice. When Dad's father left, she reverted back to her maiden name. And Dad took her name, because he didn't want anything to do with his father.'

Chloe stole a glance at Jon. Families breaking up, not wanting anything to do with each other. If the subject was a sore spot for him, he wasn't showing it.

'Why did Dad do that?'

'His father beat them.'

'How on earth do you know that?'

'The pastor at the church put me in touch with someone who knew Dad. They were at school together. I went and talked to him.'

Sadness suddenly struck Chloe. This was all fascinating, but Hannah had left her own child to chase people who were long dead. She asked the question as gently as she could.

'This is why you left? To find out about our dad?' Chloe swallowed down the impulse to be cross with Hannah. Surely this was no reason to abandon Amy.

The light died in Hannah's eyes. 'No, I...'

'Sometimes, when you can't make sense of the present, it helps to try and make sense of the past. Because the past is over and done with and can't hurt you.' Jon spoke suddenly, his voice gentle.

Hannah's eyes began to blur with tears. 'I'm sorry, Chloe.'

'It's okay. You did the best you could, Hannah, and you made sure that Amy was safe.' Chloe was beginning to see that maybe Hannah had done the only thing she could do. Something was very wrong, and she'd been trying to protect Amy from that. She reached for her sister's hand, holding it tight.

Hannah was retreating fast, her face taking on that look of dumb watchfulness that Chloe had seen so many times before. They had to stop now. She glanced at Jon and the ghost of a nod told her that he understood.

'May I look at your photos, please, Hannah?' He slid his hand across the table towards the blue folder.

Hannah nodded, and Jon started to leaf through the pages, asking questions and complimenting Hannah on what she'd found out. Slowly Hannah began to emerge from her shell and started to talk fluently. It seemed that this project was her way of making sense of something.

'And all the births and marriages of the Delancourt family are in the church records?' Jon was examining the family tree that Hannah had drawn up.

'Most of them. I'll show you. And we can go to the churchyard as well. Our grandmother's buried there. And guess what her name is.'

Chloe shrugged. 'I don't know. I can't remember Dad ever mentioning it.'

'*Flora* Delancourt.'

Jon looked questioningly at Chloe's smile. 'My middle name's Flora.' The more she thought about it the more she liked having her grandmother's name. 'That's so nice, Hannah. That he called me after her.'

Hannah was grinning too. 'Yeah. I think so too.'

Jon's fingers touched Chloe's arm. She followed his gaze across the road and nodded, turning to Hannah. 'Can we take flowers? There's a florist over there, we could get some.'

'Yeah. I think that would be great.'

It had been a long day. They had gone to the church, and then Hannah had walked them around the village, more than once if the familiarity of some of the landmarks and houses wasn't just *déjà vu*.

After dinner, Jon had gone back to their room, making an excuse to leave them alone to talk. As soon as he was out of earshot Hannah had turned to her.

'Well?'

It was the question that Chloe had been dreading, because she'd been asking it of herself for the last few days and hadn't come up with a satisfactory answer. What on earth *was* she doing?

'Good question.'

Hannah leaned back in her seat in the deserted sitting room. 'Which you're not going to answer. Jon told me that you weren't an item.'

'Well, we weren't at that point. It all just…happened. It's not serious.'

Hannah pulled a face. 'Of course it isn't serious. It's been…what, three days? Nothing's serious after three days.'

It felt like a lot longer. It felt as if somehow she'd known Jon her whole life, without actually knowing him. 'Yes, but this… Neither of us have any intention of making it serious in the future.'

A slow smile spread across Hannah's face. 'So…? Friends with benefits?'

'No!' Actually, Hannah had hit the nail pretty squarely on the head, even if there were some important differences. Surely friends with benefits didn't spend most of the day thinking about each other.

'What, then?'

'Okay. It's probably friends with benefits.' That was the closest she could get to explaining it in a few words, even if it didn't cover the feeling that Jon had broken her and then re-made her into someone who was slightly different.

'Shame. He's nice. He'd be good for you. Jake was a creep, leaving you like that.'

'What?' Chloe had never said anything about Jake to Hannah. She'd tried to protect her from the more awkward facts of life, and there had been a few things she hadn't mentioned.

Hannah pressed her lips together. 'I know what you were doing. I was only a kid and you kept all that to yourself. It was pretty obvious, though. You got ill and he walked out.'

This had to stop. And Chloe had to be the one to stop it because Hannah needed to release some of the secrets that seemed to be eating her up. She leaned forward, taking Hannah's hand.

'There's a lot we haven't said to each other, Hannah. But the trouble with secrets is that you hug them close and they come back and smack you in the face.'

Hannah raised her eyebrows. 'Jake smacked you in the face?'

'Not literally.' A few months—just a few weeks ago Chloe wouldn't have been able to bring herself to talk about this. It was an uncomfortable reminder that Jon really *had* changed her.

'Look, Hannah. I was very ill, and I still worry about ever being that way again, even if I do know that it's not going to happen. And I felt so alone when Jake dumped me. I wanted to protect you from all of that but it was wrong of me not to say anything and I'm really sorry for that.'

'It's okay. I did know.'

'Yes, and if we'd discussed it, I could have told you it was okay. It was hard, and I felt dreadful, but in the end I was determined that I'd get through it. Wouldn't that have made you feel better?'

Hannah nodded silently.

Chloe took a deep breath. Jon had given her the courage to tell her own secrets, and maybe he could give her the courage to ask the same of Hannah.

'Whatever it is that's the matter, it can't hurt me, Hannah. And it can't hurt you either. If you'll tell me, I'll just listen and maybe that will help.'

CHAPTER SIXTEEN

IT WAS LATE when she got back to their room, and Chloe opened the door quietly, sure that Jon must be asleep. But the light by the bed was on and he was propped up on the pillows, reading.

'How's Hannah?' He seemed to be able to read Chloe's distress and confusion on her face.

'Sleeping. We talked quite a bit.'

He nodded. 'Can you tell me about it?'

'Yes.' Chloe sat down on the bed next to him. It seemed that tonight he'd made some kind of decision, because even though the evening had been warm he was wearing an old T-shirt, the bedcovers pulled over his legs. It seemed strange not to find him naked in their bed.

'Do you *want* to tell me about it?'

Yes. More than anything. 'I told her about what happened with me and Jake, and how I felt I'd let her down. She told me some things about Amy's father. I thought that there was no contact between them after she came home, but she texted him and told him she was pregnant.'

'What was his reaction?' The look in Jon's eyes told her that he already had some idea.

'He said that the baby probably wasn't his anyway.

When she told him that she loved him and there hadn't been anyone else, he said that if she really loved him she'd terminate the pregnancy, and let him get on with his life.'

Jon shook his head, cursing quietly under his breath. 'If James had only known that. If *I'd* known it even…'

'Why do you think she kept quiet? James was ready to wring his neck anyway. She sent a photo when Amy was born, but he just messaged back telling her never to contact him again. She said that she felt so worthless. Perhaps that's where some of these bad feelings about herself started.'

'It wouldn't be all that surprising.' The tenderness in Jon's eyes was making her melt. 'So all the time you've been putting a brave face on things, and so has Hannah.'

'I was so quick to accept that she didn't care about him because I was trying not to care about Jake. When I told her that maybe she should just let him go, I thought I was giving her my honest opinion, but maybe it was just what I thought *I* should do.'

'It was good advice. I don't see that Hannah would have benefited by having him in her life.'

'Thanks. But I know what I've done wrong.'

'She really *is* better off without him. And so is Amy.'

He reached for her and Chloe shifted towards him on the bed so that he could fold her in his arms. Chloe wanted to just curl up with him, but the bedclothes were in the way. Surely friends with benefits only wanted to be close for the good times, not the bad.

'Thank you. For being here.'

'I just drove.'

She dug her elbow into his ribs. Or where she reckoned his ribs must be under the T-shirt and the duvet. 'No, you didn't. I don't think I would have had the courage to try and break through with Hannah if you hadn't been here. And I know it must have been hard for you.'

'Me? I don't—' He broke off as Chloe reached up, putting her finger over his lips.

'If you're going to tell me that none of this is hard for you, you can save your breath.'

'Yeah, okay. It's hard. You and Hannah and James are all so close and…to be honest, I don't think any of my family would even notice if I went missing, let alone come and find me.'

'I'll find you.' Chloe started to peel away the layers of bedclothes that were wrapped around him.

'Hey. Don't you want to sleep?' He broke off, groaning as Chloe's hand found its way inside his boxer shorts.

'No. I want to let go of the past. Don't you?'

He levered his body over hers, rolling her backwards on the bed and pinning her down. 'Yes, I do. I want to promise you…whatever you want.'

She knew he was sincere, even if he was struggling with the idea. He *did* want to let go of the past and promise her at least a part of his future. But she couldn't ask him to do it. Asked-for promises didn't work.

'Don't promise me anything, Jon. This is what I want. Exactly this.'

'You're sure?'

She pulled him down for a kiss. His kisses held nothing back and promised her everything. 'I just want you to make love to me.'

He smiled down at her, tenderness in his face. 'Take your clothes off, sweetheart.'

He loved watching Chloe undress, and she knew it. When she came to him, all of Jon's resolve, every last bit of his determination to let her just sleep tonight was shattered into tiny pieces.

This time broke the mould yet again. They'd already spent more time than they might reasonably have been expected to spare over the last three days in learning each other's bodies. And each time they'd found some new way of giving each other pleasure.

But when Chloe came to him, stripping off his T-shirt and boxer shorts, all he wanted to do was hold her. Be close to her in every way. Their lovemaking was tender, a reminder of good things when there were so many difficulties threatening, and it touched Jon more deeply than he'd thought possible.

Afterwards, feeling her curled up in the curve of his body, he held her close.

'Chloe…?'

'Hmm?' She snuggled up against him, winding her hand around his, kissing his fingers. It answered all of the questions he wanted to ask.

'Go to sleep, sweetheart. Tomorrow's another day.'

Over the next few days they did all the things that tourists might. Driving to a local chateau that was open to the public, taking a picnic out into the countryside. Chloe and Hannah spent a lot of time talking, sometimes with Jon there and sometimes on their own, and slowly Hannah was beginning to open up.

'Are we going home?' Jon lay in bed, last night's lovemaking still tingling through his senses, watching Chloe brush her hair in the morning sunlight.

'I think so. If that's all right with you. How did you know?'

'You were muttering in your sleep last night.' Chloe

had come to bed late and fallen asleep almost immediately in his arms.

'Was I?' She turned to face him. 'What did I say?'

'Just a few words. Home was one of them.' His name had been another. He'd loved it that she'd cried out for him, even in her sleep.

'Hannah's agreed to come back with us, whenever we're ready to go. She's going to stay with me for a while, along with Amy.'

'And you'll see how things go?'

Chloe shook her head. 'No, we're not leaving things to chance. I'm going to sort out someone for Hannah to talk to and work things through with. I'll go along too, if there are issues that we need to work out together.'

'That sounds like a good plan. So Hannah will be taking over the spare room.'

'There's always room for you. You'd have to sleep with me, though, if that's not too onerous for you.' She smiled at him.

'I'll put a brave face on it. And when you get tired of me, my own place has a bathroom now. The builder texted me last night.'

There was an uncertainty about all this. They were covering it up well with jokes and smiles, but there was a slight tremor to Chloe's tone, which matched the tremor in his heart. They knew how to make love, but neither was quite sure how they fitted into each other's lives.

A knock sounded on the door, along with Hannah's voice. Jon got out of bed, pulling on a pair of jeans and a T-shirt, and Chloe called for her to come in.

'Have you told him?' Hannah dispensed with the usual 'Good morning'. She was obviously looking forward to going home with Chloe, and that had to be a good thing.

'I hear that you're coming back with us. And you'll be staying with Chloe for a while.' Jon grinned at her.

'Yes.' Hannah's smile was radiant, excited, as if this was a new beginning. For her, it was, and her future seemed more assured than his did right now. 'When can we go?'

'We haven't got round to that yet,' Chloe rebuked her gently. So much had changed between the two sisters. They voiced their own wants and needs more freely, no longer afraid to negotiate something that suited them both.

But it was obvious that they were both looking forward to going home. 'We could go today, if you want.'

'Today?' Hannah grinned. 'That's fine with me.'

'Me too.' Chloe looked at Jon. 'Shall I see if I can book a hotel for us? About halfway?'

Suddenly he wanted this done with. To stop worrying about what would happen between him and Chloe when they got home, and just get there. 'Or if you can book a channel crossing for late this afternoon, we could do it in a day. It's still early, and if we're packed and ready to go in an hour...'

Chloe was biting her lip. Perhaps she was as afraid of this as he was. In which case it was better to do it now, before the uncertainty began to gnaw at them both.

'Yes.' She seemed to come to the same conclusion he had. 'We'll do that, then.'

They shared the driving, eating in the car, and made the channel crossing just in time. Hitting the Friday evening traffic as they approached London slowed them down and it was late when Jon drew up outside Chloe's house. Carrying their bags in, they dropped them in the hall.

Chloe seemed on edge, bustling around, opening windows and doors to air the house and then closing them again when the chill evening breeze made her shiver. She switched the kettle on for tea, even though no one wanted it. And the one question that seemed to be on everyone's mind—who was going to sleep where—needed to be answered soon because they were all tired.

In the end, Hannah made the first move, fetching her sleeping bag from where it was tied securely to the top of her rucksack, and laying it on the sofa. 'I'm ready to turn in.'

'Why don't you take the spare room? It'll only take a minute for me to clear my things out, and I can sleep down here.' Jon saw Chloe raise her eyebrows and his heart jumped suddenly. Maybe she did want him in her bed still.

Hannah looked from Jon to Chloe and then back again. Then she rolled her eyes, grabbing her rucksack and stomping up the stairs. Jon could hear her banging around in the spare room, and when she came back downstairs she had the few clothes that he hadn't packed and taken to France with him bundled in her arms.

'Here.' She dropped them onto the sofa and picked up her sleeping bag. 'Work it out, people. I'm going to bed.'

Jon heard Chloe giggle behind him. Then he felt her wrap her arms around his waist, her body pressing against his back. 'I'm sorry. I think she gets the unsubtle streak from James.'

Jon turned. It was the first time he'd held her today, and he hadn't realised how much he'd missed it. It felt like a long, deep breath after hours of fighting for air. 'Don't knock it. It's one of the things I like about James.'

'Me too.' She looked up at him, her gaze melting through his uncertainty. 'Would you come to mine?'

He kissed her forehead. 'I'd like that very much.'

Coming home was so full of promise. A new start for Hannah, this time based on firmer foundations. And so full of questions where Jon was concerned. They'd made no promises and told no lies. The only plan they had was that there was no plan. But reality demanded that they make one, sooner or later.

Not tonight, though. He led her up the stairs and she closed the door of her bedroom behind them. Jon pulled his sweater and shirt off over his head in one movement, and she remembered how much she loved his body. So strong, bulky in all the right places, and yet his eyes were so tender. His arms so warm.

And he knew just what she needed. Tonight was no exception to that. His nakedness was somehow innocent, rather than sexual, as he slipped between the sheets, waiting for her to undress and come to bed.

'What's going to happen now?' It felt as if everything was changing and the only thing she could cling to was him.

'Go to sleep, sweetheart.' He curled his body around hers, holding her. 'We'll work it out in the morning.'

There was no time to work it out in the morning. A call from Jon's builder took him off to his house to decide on what should be done about a leak in the roof that had become apparent after heavy rain a few days ago, and he didn't return until after lunch. By that time, she and

Hannah were getting ready to go to the supermarket and restock the fridge.

'I'll go.' Hannah took her car keys out of her hand.

'No, it's okay...' Making a big thing of this was only going to make things worse. Chloe had spent the whole morning wondering what Jon was going to do next, and she needed to calm down.

'I'll be back this time. Promise.' Hannah kissed her on the cheek and grinned at Jon, then picked up the shopping bags, slamming the front door behind her.

'How's your roof?'

He shrugged. 'Not great. I spent all morning up in the loft, plugging holes. I think I'll have to get the roofers in to renew the back elevation.'

'You look very clean. Your loft obviously isn't as dusty as mine.'

'After the builder went, I tried out the new shower.'

It seemed like one more hole in a structure that was already rapidly disintegrating. Jon was showering at his place now. Chloe told herself not to be stupid. Of course he wanted to use his new bathroom.

'How was it?'

'Good. Great, actually.'

The time was now. Hannah would be gone for at least an hour and they could talk. Work out what happened next. The thought occurred to her that if neither of them cared, they could have avoided this, just letting things slide and walking away. On the other hand, if they both cared enough, that would have been obvious too, and they would have known what to do next without having to talk about it.

'Let's go and sit down.' He walked into the sitting room and Chloe followed him, sitting down in the chair opposite his.

'Jon, I...' Now that the time had come, she didn't know what she wanted to say.

'Chloe, there's nothing that we have to do. Nothing we can't do.' He'd obviously been thinking about this a little more cogently than she had. 'But you have big changes ahead of you and so do I, for that matter.'

'Does that really matter? Life never just stops.'

'No, but we'll both be busy. Maybe we should take a break and think about things. We don't need to make any decisions or promises, just wait a bit until everything settles.'

A glimmer of what was really going on in Jon's head. Just a few days ago it had seemed that they could both read each other's minds effortlessly, but now it was a guessing game. But she knew that he'd been burned like this before, he and his wife drifting apart because of schedules that never included enough time for each other.

Suddenly, it was all very clear. The last few weeks had left them with no option. They'd been so close, not just physically but emotionally as well. They'd supported each other, worked as a team. Loved each other. There had been no need for promises, the commitment had been made.

'Jon, I think I need to tell you where I stand. We're either in a relationship or we aren't. I want to be in a relationship with you, but if that's not possible then I think we should just call it a day. I don't want an on-off affair.'

He stared at her. 'We said—'

'I don't care what we said. That's what I want. I love you and I think we could make a go of it. But I need you to tell me that you love me too, and that you'll be there for me.'

'I do love you, Chloe, but...' He got to his feet and

started to pace. 'I won't just jump in blindly when neither of us is going to have the time or the energy to really make this work. We need to think about it.'

'I don't. I can't, Jon. I've been let down too many
times.'

He turned suddenly, his face dark. 'Did I ever let
you down?'

'No, that's not what I'm saying. I'm just telling you
how I feel.'

'And what about how *I* feel. Don't I get a say in this?'

'Yes, of course you do. You stay or you go.' Chloe felt
tears pricking at the sides of her eyes and blinked them
back. All the anger and frustration that was battering
them seemed to have come out of nowhere.

'All or nothing, you mean. That's crazy, Chloe, we've
known each other three weeks.'

'No, I mean something or nothing. I don't want
you to just turn up whenever you feel like a one-night
stand and can't be bothered to flip through your address
book.' Chloe bit her tongue. She hadn't meant that…

'I'm going to pretend you didn't say that, Chloe. Because if you think that's all you've been to me you're
wrong.' He didn't give her a chance to tell him that she
was sorry and that the words had come out of nowhere.
Jon marched out of the room, stomping upstairs.

He grabbed his shaving kit from the bathroom, throwing it into the holdall that wasn't fully unpacked yet
from yesterday. Sorting through the washing basket,
separating her things from his, he tried not to notice
that her scent still clung to his clothes, like a bitter-
sweet memory.

The worst thing about it was that she was right.
Chloe had been hurt badly, at a time when she'd most

needed love and care, and it just wasn't fair to expect her to continue a relationship without the security of knowing that he'd be there for her when she needed him.

But Jon couldn't do that. Not yet, and maybe not ever. The thought of building something together and then watching it disintegrate, under the pressure of time and other commitments, was too much for him to bear.

The old feeling, that this was the way of things and that any relationship would cool given enough time, reasserted itself. His and Chloe's may have burned a little hotter, but that just meant that it was more difficult when the flame was extinguished.

He zipped the holdall and straightened up, stopping for a moment to make sure he'd packed everything because he knew he wouldn't be back. Then he walked back downstairs.

Chloe was standing in the kitchen doorway. It looked as if she'd been crying.

'I'm sorry. I didn't mean what I said.'

He stayed at the bottom of the stairs. If he went any closer he might not be able to do this.

'You meant it, Chloe. And you're absolutely right. I meant what I said, too.'

She stood stock still. 'And what you need from a relationship is pretty much the exact opposite of what I need.'

'Yes.' Finally they agreed, but it was the last thing he wanted to agree over. He turned for the front door.

'Jon… Wait.'

When he looked back, he saw that she had her hand over her mouth in disbelief, tears running down her cheeks. And that look in her eyes, the one he knew so well, told him all he needed to know.

'I know. I love you too. That's why I have to go.'

He opened the front door and found Hannah standing right in front of him, searching in her bag for her keys. He gave her a nod, silently thanking the heavens above that she was back so soon, and slid past her, walking down the front path to his car.

'What the blazes…?' Hannah left the shopping on the front doorstep and rushed forward, enveloping Chloe in a hug. 'What did he do?'

'Nothing. He didn't do anything.' Chloe blew her nose on a piece of kitchen roll. 'We… It was never going to work out. We both knew that, and… It's okay. I'm okay.'

'No, you aren't.' Hannah marched back to the door and picked up the shopping. 'But you will be. I've got the very thing.'

She took a tub of chocolate-chip ice cream from the bag, and Chloe smiled, despite herself. 'I don't need that.' At the moment she felt that she didn't need anything, other than Jon, but that would pass.

'Do me a favour, would you, and let me be the big sister for a change.' Hannah opened the cutlery drawer, took two spoons out and then reached up to get two glasses from the top shelf of the cabinet.

'What are they for?'

Hannah produced a bottle of red wine from the shopping bag. 'It's you, me and the sofa for the rest of the afternoon. We'll put the TV on, eat ice cream and drink wine.'

'And then we'll be sick?'

'No, we won't. Moderation's the key with this. Eat the ice cream slowly and sip the wine.'

Chloe hugged Hannah, feeling her limbs tremble as she hung onto her sister. She and Jon had done the right thing, however much it hurt. They were never going to be able to make it work. It had been wrong from the start.

She kissed Hannah's cheek. 'Okay, big sis. Let's do it.'

CHAPTER SEVENTEEN

A LOT HAD happened in the last three months. Hannah and Amy had moved in permanently with Chloe, and they'd run a whole gamut of feelings together. Crises were averted, hugs were exchanged, and new avenues and opportunities were explored. But the one thing that hadn't happened was that she'd bumped into Jon at the hospital.

She'd been almost relieved. She knew she couldn't see Jon again, not yet. The idea that they could be friends, with or without benefits, after all that had happened between them was ludicrous.

And he obviously felt the same. Chloe had kept to her side of the hospital and he'd kept to his. She'd heard a few people talk about him, and supposed he must have heard people talk about her, but she'd resisted the temptation to show any interest. His signature had been on the records for some of her patients, children who'd been referred up through A and E, and she'd even traced her finger around the loop of the *J* once or twice. But that was all.

It hurt, but it had to be done. She'd get over it. It was just a matter of when.

Even so, the early morning call from A and E made her hesitate. But there was a patient there with a displaced ankle fracture. Before he was admitted for surgery it required a recommendation from one of the doctors from Orthopaedics, and Chloe was the one who happened to be at work early this morning.

She walked down to A and E, trembling. In and out. Don't look right or left, don't stop to talk. Just do your job. With any luck Jon wouldn't be on shift this morning.

The doctor who had called beckoned her into an empty cubicle and she sat down next to him at the monitor to look at the X-rays.

'He's had a fall, but there doesn't seem to be a concussion, although we'll be keeping a close eye on that, particularly if he needs surgery. I'm reckoning he might...' Dr Marshall had worked in A and E for long enough that nothing much surprised him, and he could usually anticipate what ongoing care his patients would need.

'I'd say so.' Chloe looked carefully at the X-rays. 'That's a nasty one. I'll wait and take the paperwork upstairs with me. I can have it on Mr Saunders's desk for when he comes in.'

'I'd appreciate it. He's one of ours, he works here.'

'Well, he's not going to be at work for a while...' Chloe's eye drifted to the patient's name in the corner of the screen and her hand flew to her mouth. 'Jon?'

'Yes. He's quite new here, you might not know him...'

Never mind that. Chloe didn't have the time to think up something appropriate to explain that she knew Jon very well. 'What happened to him?'

'Apparently he was up in the loft at his house early this morning. Something gave way and his foot went through the ceiling.'

'He fell through the ceiling…' Chloe must have been showing all the signs of panic because Dr Marshall snapped into reassurance mode.

'No, he fell over. There's the damage to his ankle, and he's going to have quite a shiner tomorrow. Apparently he managed to get down from the loft and then down the stairs, trying to reach his phone. But the builders came in at six and found him in the hallway. Called an ambulance.'

'But he's okay?' Suddenly that was all that mattered. Jon had been hurt and there had been no one there to help him.

'Go and take a look for yourself. I've got to wait for the results on some routine tests and I'll be ten minutes with the paperwork….' Chloe was on her feet already and Dr Marshall called after her. 'Cubicle Six.'

His ankle was uncomfortably numb. His left eye was closing fast, and it was more than likely that he'd be staying here for a couple of days. Jon was sick of staring at the ceiling so he closed his eyes for a few moments, drifting in a sea of analgesia.

He heard the door of the cubicle open and ignored it. Probably someone wanting to take his blood pressure or check his pulse. He'd already told them that he was okay and that it was just the ankle they needed to worry about, but the A and E staff, who normally took his word for everything, had been taking it in turns to remind him that they'd be the judge of that.

'Jon…?' He felt a touch on his forehead, as light as a whisper. He must be dreaming. Jon struggled to open his eyes, since those kinds of dreams could probably get him in trouble with his work colleagues, and saw a pair of honey-brown eyes looking down at him.

'How are you?'

All he could think of was that finally someone was asking him how he felt and not telling him. And that he wanted desperately to hold onto Chloe, but that he dared not reach for her.

'Okay…' Suddenly his mouth felt as if it was full of cotton wool.

'I've taken a look at your X-rays. I think you'll need surgery to fix the bone in your ankle, but I'm putting the papers on Mr Saunders's desk as soon as I get them. He's the best, you'll be in good hands.'

She leaned over him, and he caught the scent of her soap. 'That eye looks nasty. I'll get someone to bring an ice pack. Your heart rate's slightly elevated…'

That was hardly a surprise. It had been perfectly normal before Chloe had arrived.

'Is there anything else? Any pain anywhere?'

Suddenly that didn't matter any more. 'Chloe, I'm sorry.'

She stared at him. 'What for?'

'The way I left…'

She reddened slightly, and then recovered her composure. 'We have more important things to think about—'

'No. No, this is more important.' He reached forward, trying to touch her arm, but pain shot up his leg, immobilising him.

'Hey… Hey, it's all right, Jon.' She took his hand, squeezing it.

'Please…it's not all right…' He hung on tight to her hand, trying to pull her a little closer. Chloe must have seen his anguish because she moved towards him, her free hand moving to his brow.

'What's on your mind, then?' She said the words

quietly. At last he had the opportunity that he'd been waiting for, even if this wasn't the time or the place.

'I treated you badly, Chloe. I'm so sorry.'

The pain in her eyes told him exactly how badly he'd treated her. 'We both said things that we shouldn't have. That doesn't matter any more.'

His head was clear now, as if determination to take this opportunity had overwhelmed both the pain in his leg and the effects of the analgesics in his system. 'What I said...what I *did*... It was nothing to do with you, and everything to do with me. I told you that I'd made a decision about my future after the divorce, but that wasn't entirely true. There was no decision, I was just too afraid to do anything else because I'd been too badly hurt. I've been thinking about that a lot lately.'

'You think I didn't know that?' She pursed her lips in a rueful smile. 'Anyway, I was just as much to blame as you were. I couldn't just accept it and let things alone.'

'There's no reason in the world why you should have, Chloe. I...'

She laid her finger over his lips. 'We *could* argue about who was most to blame, if it makes you feel any better. Or we could just say that neither of us wanted to be hurt, and neither of us meant to hurt. Leave it at that, eh? Let it go, because it's not what we are.'

Relief rushed through him, prompting another agonising jab of pain from his leg. Chloe had found it in that gorgeous, loving heart of hers to forgive him. And if putting the past behind them didn't change the future, it was at least a start. Jon nodded, and Chloe took her finger from his lips.

'All right. Now we've got that dealt with, you can lie still.' That schoolmistress tone that he so loved reasserted itself. 'And tell me where it hurts.'

Nothing hurt any more. Not in the light of her smile. 'They've already examined me. And there's no pain if I keep still. The ambulance paramedic gave me a shot of the good stuff.'

'What did he give you?' She snatched the notes up from the end of the bed and leafed through them. 'Okay. That looks okay.'

'Yeah. It was actually better than okay at the time.' He tried for a grin to reassure her, and must have succeeded in part because she rewarded him with a dazzling smile. All he really wanted her to do right now was to take his hand again.

'I want to take a look at your leg.' She glanced at his right ankle, which was covered over with a dressing pad, laid loosely over the top of it.

'Yes. Please do.' Jon had tried to look at the leg himself, after the paramedic had taken off his boot and cut the leg of his jeans, but gentle hands had pushed him back down, and firm voices had told him to relax. Chloe's judgement was the next best thing to his own.

She removed the dressing, tutting when she saw that it had blood on it and throwing it into surgical waste. Her touch was like the whisper of a butterfly's wing, and she bent over, looking at the ankle from one side and then the other, before tearing open a new dressing and laying it over the wound.

'Can you see the bone?'

'Yes, it's a nasty fracture, but from the X-rays, and seeing it now, it looks like a straightforward piece of surgery. It'll take a while to heal, but I don't see any reason why you can't make a full recovery.'

It was exactly what he wanted—no, needed—to hear. The unvarnished truth from someone who he trusted. *We'll get you back on your feet in no time* didn't ring true when he knew that it was beyond the wit of anyone to mend a displaced fracture that fast.

'Thanks. Chloe…'

The door of the cubicle opened and Ben Marshall leaned in. 'I've got the paperwork.'

Chloe practically tore it out of his hand and then directed a dazzling smile at him. 'Thanks. I'll take it up now.'

The thought that she was going now made Jon want to weep. Before she'd arrived he'd been coping. But now that he'd seen her face he couldn't bear to be left alone again. She walked to his bedside and he steeled himself to say one more goodbye and thank her.

'I'm just going to take these upstairs. I need to get them on Mr Saunders's desk right away. But I'll be back.'

'Thank you.' He wouldn't ask when, because maybe she'd think twice about it and not come back. And in any case, he'd be counting the hours in the hope that she did return.

'Ten minutes. I'll be ten minutes.' She took his hand, giving it a squeeze, and in that moment Jon felt completely happy.

'Don't you have patients to see?'

'My first patient's at half past nine. It's only half eight now. I'll see you in ten.' Jon nodded, and closed his eyes again. If Chloe being here was just a dream, he wanted to hold onto it for as long as he possibly could.

He didn't know how long she'd been, but from the way she was slightly out of breath it seemed that she'd been hurrying. Chloe brought an ice pack, wrapping it carefully before she laid it over his eye, and a bottle of spring water from the machine.

'Would you like something to drink?'

'Yes. Thanks.'

She nodded, opening the bottle and putting a red and white striped drinking straw into it. 'You know the drill. Small sips, okay?'

He nodded, and she held the bottle so that he could drink through the straw. Suddenly he realised he was very thirsty, but he tried to drink slowly.

'That's good. You can have a little more in a minute.' She put the bottle down beside the bed and sat down. 'I can stay for three quarters of an hour and then I have to go. But I'll come and find you again at lunchtime.'

'You don't need…' He saw the reproach in her eyes, and realised that he wanted her to come back more than anything. 'Thanks.'

She nodded. 'Whatever were you doing in the loft at six in the morning?'

Ben had told her, then. 'I heard dripping up there after last night's rain. I reckoned it was another leak and went up there just to see what was going on. One of the boards was rotten.'

She knew. Chloe knew what it was like to be alone and helpless. Far better than he did, and this morning had frightened the hell out of him. She reached forward, taking his hand, and suddenly everything was all right.

'It must have been horrible, having to try and get back downstairs.'

All he'd been able to think of had been getting downstairs to his phone before he passed out from the pain. He'd seen the blood soaking the leg of his jeans and had known he had to get help. But Chloe was here now and he could shrug it off.

'My phone was in the kitchen. I wasn't expecting the builder to come, he'd just popped in with some samples for me to look at. When he knocked, I yelled and he let himself in with his key.'

'It was a bit of luck he decided to come round. Don't you go clambering around when you're on your own in the house again.' Her voice took on the timbre of a very sexy schoolmistress.

'I've learned my lesson. May I have some more water, please?'

She reached for the water bottle and let him drink a little more. Then she sat down again, reaching for his hand. It seemed that everything that had happened between them, and the way they'd both been studiously avoiding each other for the last few months, was temporarily forgotten.

'How's Hannah? I've been thinking about her.'

'She's good. She and Amy are living with me and… well, Amy's a joy. So's Hannah. She's having counselling and starting to build up her confidence. And she's doing an Art A-Level by correspondence course. It's something she's always been interested in, and she's been producing some lovely drawings.

Even in his befuddled state, Jon could see that Chloe had changed. Or rather she'd continued on the road that he'd seen her take those first, uncertain steps on in France. She seemed so much more confident that she was doing the right thing and ready to make a success of it, for herself as well as Hannah and Amy.

'I'm glad everything turned out well, Chloe.'

'Thanks. I think you can take more than some of the credit…' She flushed red and picked up the water bottle. 'You want something more to drink?'

It seemed that she'd talked enough about the thing

that had brought them together and then torn them apart. That was okay. Jon was just glad that Chloe had come and that she'd stayed for a while. He reached for the water bottle, gasping as he moved too far and pain shot up his leg.

'Steady on. Just stay down, will you, and let me do the heavy lifting.' She gave him a smile that reached right to his heart and Jon realised that the idea that had been forming in his head for the last month wasn't just a dream. It was something that he was going to make happen.

She came back again at lunchtime, bringing a large carrier bag full of supplies. Toothpaste and a toothbrush, moist tissues for his hands and face, a few pieces of fruit and some dog-eared paperbacks from the hospital book exchange. Jon was taken down to the operating theatre late that afternoon, and when he woke up from the anaesthetic, his leg throbbing and his mouth feeling as if someone had stuffed it with cotton wool, Chloe was holding his hand.

'You should…go…' He didn't know what time it was or how long he'd been out for, but the curtains on the ward were closed and it was dark outside.

'I can stay until visiting time is over.'

She leaned forward, her fingers brushing his hair back from his brow. All he could feel was her tenderness. 'I spoke to Mr Saunders. He says that everything went well, and your leg's going to be fine. Now close your eyes and rest.'

He wanted to stay awake but the drugs in his system were dragging him back into a state of drowsy half-consciousness. The last thing he remembered was holding her hand in his, pressing it possessively against his chest.

CHAPTER EIGHTEEN

JON WOKE THE next morning to find that his eye was throbbing, his leg was in a cast, and pretty much every bone in his body ached. And there was a note from Chloe on his locker.

Today is Saturday.

Jon smiled. He'd been wondering what day it was, and Chloe had clearly anticipated that.

I'll be coming to see you this afternoon. Hannah picked some clothes up from your house yesterday and they're in your locker. If I find you've not been doing as you're told, I'll fill out the forms to have you restrained.

Jon wondered whether Hannah had broken in when she'd gone to collect his things, and decided he didn't care. Chloe was coming, and she could threaten him with whatever she liked. He needed to get out of bed.

He leaned over, reaching for the controller for the bed, just managing to grasp it between the tips of his fingers. Once he was sitting up he felt a little better, and a cup of tea from the breakfast trolley consolidated the improvement. If he lowered the height of the bed a little, he could reach the locker door, and he found a couple of T-shirts, a hooded top and some sweatpants stacked neatly inside.

'Hey...' One of the nurses, whom he knew by sight, was marching across the ward towards him. 'What are you doing?'

'Mobilising.' He gave her a smile and she ignored it.

'Ah. Not playing with the controls on the bed, then.' She picked up the remote, and hooked it on the end of the bed, out of reach.

'Nah. I wouldn't dare.' He tried the smile again, and this time the nurse grinned back. 'But I would like to get out of bed. Have a wash and get dressed.'

'I don't know. You're not supposed to...'

But he was going to. Jon knew exactly what he wanted to say to Chloe, and he couldn't say it like this. He needed to get back on his feet, and the sooner he started, the sooner he'd get there.

'Please.' He flashed the nurse his most winning smile. 'I promise I won't overdo things.'

'All right. Stay there, I'll go and get a wheelchair.'

Jon couldn't help watching the doors of the ward and as the hands of the clock closed on the number twelve he operated the controls of his bed to put him as close to a sitting position as possible. It was crazy. Chloe wouldn't be here this early. She might not be here at all, in which case he'd go and find her, as soon as he was able. But when the first group of visitors came onto the ward she was one of them, a large bag slung over her shoulder and Amy in her arms.

'You're dressed. And sitting up.' She grinned in approval. Amy was looking at him intently, and Jon wondered whether his swollen and bruised eye was frightening her. He covered it with his hand and smiled at her, his eye throbbing with pain.

'Hurt… Kiss it better.' She looked enquiringly up at Chloe.

'Yes, sweetie. You want to kiss it better?'

Amy nodded, and Jon held out his hands towards her. Chloe delivered her into his arms, and he hugged her tight.

'Careful, now, sweetie.' Chloe caught Amy's reaching hand just before it connected with his face. 'We have to be very gentle with him.'

Amy seemed to understand. Stretching up in his arms, she planted a kiss on his cheek, and Jon struggled to keep his composure.

'Thank you, Amy. That feels much better now.' He stroked the little girl's light auburn curls and she snuggled into his arms.

'Would you like to give Jon his get-well parcel?' Chloe sat down on the moulded plastic chair next to his bed and opened her bag.

The parcel was wrapped in sparkly blue and gold paper, which was obviously designed to appeal to Amy. The little girl sat on the bed next to him and Chloe placed the parcel into her lap. She slid one finger under the wrappings, and slowly started to tear them.

Chloe grinned. 'No, Amy, it's for Jon. Give it to him.'

Amy pretended not to hear and Jon leaned over. 'You're going to unwrap it for me, aren't you?'

He helped her with the sticky tape, holding her tight so she didn't slip off the bed, and hoping that none of the nurses saw them and came to tell him that a child really shouldn't be sitting on his bed. Chloe seemed to have the same thought and turned, pulling the cur-

tains a little so that they weren't immediately visible
from the door.

Inside the parcel was a book and a packet of chocolate buttons. Amy left the book for him and picked up
the chocolate.

'Hey, that's lovely, Amy. Thank you.' He picked up
the book and Amy handed him the chocolate buttons,
clearly wanting him to open them and give them straight
back. He shot Chloe an enquiring glance, wondering if
it was all right for Amy to have the chocolate.

'Just a few.' She pressed her lips together in wry humour. 'The chocolate's from me. Amy chose the book.'

He laughed, ignoring the painful protest from his
eye. 'She likes whodunnits, does she? Thank you,
Chloe.'

Thank you for the book and the chocolate, and for
wrapping them up. For bringing Amy. For yesterday,
and for being here today. Thank you for being so beautiful.

'You're welcome.'

He was sure now. Chloe and he weren't perfect for
each other, they were different in so many ways. But
while perfect was nice, wanting was everything. And
Jon knew beyond any shadow of a doubt that everything
he wanted was here now. He would get out of here, get
himself back together and win her back.

She came again on Sunday, this time alone. Amy and
Hannah had gone to James's for lunch, and it was clear
that Chloe had missed the family gathering to come
and see him.

'So they're letting you out today?'

'Looks like it. I'm waiting for the duty doctor to sign
me off, and then me and my crutches are free to go.'

He indicated the pair of crutches that were propped up behind his chair.

'So—how long?'

Jon grinned. 'Who knows? I offered to sign myself off, but the nurses didn't think much of that suggestion.'

'No. Don't suppose they did. Well, I'll wait and take you home.'

'I can get a taxi.' He didn't want to push things just yet.

'Don't you dare.' She got to her feet. 'I'm going to go and ask where the doctor is. Has the pharmacy sent up your drugs yet?'

'Not yet.'

'Then I'll see what I can do to chase them up, too.'

Chloe's enquiries seemed to bear more fruit than his, possibly because she was able to follow people and buttonhole them, rather than having to wait for them to come to her. It took another hour, but by two o'clock he was being wheeled to the hospital entrance by a porter, his possessions packed into a plastic bag. He waited on a bench beside the automatic doors, which delivered a blast of cold air every time someone walked through them, and when he saw Chloe's car draw up outside he got carefully to his feet.

She got him into the car and was on the main road, driving away from the hospital, before she dropped the bombshell. 'You're coming home with me for a decent meal. And you can stay the night. Hannah and Amy are staying over at James's tonight, so you can take their room.'

In her house. Surrounded by her scent. That wasn't a good idea. He needed to be stronger before he could even think about putting his plan into operation.

'Thanks, but… I'm okay. I'd really like to go home.'

'So you can lie in bed and look at the hole in the ceiling? Hannah told me that your bedroom's a right mess.'

'I've got a sofa-bed downstairs, I'll sleep there.' He grinned at her. 'Save me going up and down the stairs for a few days.'

'You can't camp out in your own house, Jon. It's much more comfortable at my place...'

The discussion rumbled on for the duration of the drive to her house. But Chloe had the last word because she was the one driving, and Jon couldn't do anything about where she chose to take him. It was an unfair advantage but Chloe would take whatever she could get.

She helped him out of the car and he carefully negotiated the front path and the step over the threshold and into the house. It seemed that he'd at least reconciled himself to a meal, if not a bed for the night, but she could work on that.

Leading him into the sitting room, she fetched a footstool and a cushion so he could prop his leg up.

'Would you like some tea? Or coffee?' She was trembling suddenly. Being alone with him was different from the bustle of the hospital, where caring was the normal course of action and not a choice.

'Let me—'

'No, you've only just sat down. Don't be silly.' Chloe was feeling more and more nervous. This wouldn't do.

His eyes softened, as if he saw her anguish, and she felt herself redden. This was no time to be thinking about the emotional, she had to think about the practical.

'Chloe, I've got to be able to do things for myself. Let me try, please.'

She felt her legs begin to shake. Before she could

stop it, a tear ran down her cheek. 'No. No, you can't, Jon. I won't let you.'

'Why not?'

'Because…' *Just because.* That was the best answer she could think of, but the worst one was the one that spilled out before she could stop it. 'Because I know you're trying to be independent and look after yourself, and that's a good thing. But I know how much that hurts, too. I know you were afraid when you were alone up there in the loft with a broken leg because I was afraid when I was alone here, all the times I fell over and couldn't get up.'

'Yeah. I was afraid.'

'So why won't you let me look after you a bit? Just stay here for a few days, until you're a bit stronger.'

A shadow passed across his face. She'd blown it all, but suddenly Chloe didn't care. Doing nothing wasn't an option, not any more.

'It's too soon…'

It was always going to be too soon for Jon. There was never going to be a right time. But she could bear that now. She could bear him walking away from her, but what she couldn't live with was never having tried.

'I don't care. It doesn't matter if you're never going to want me the way I want you, and I don't expect anything from you. I just want to be there for you.'

'Chloe…' He struggled to his feet. He was going to go now, she knew it. Even though she'd steeled herself to it, the idea seemed to suck all of the air from the room, and she couldn't breathe.

All the same, she went to help him. If he wouldn't stay here, it would be just as well if he didn't break the other leg.

'Chloe.' She'd given him his crutch and he'd got his

balance now, but he still didn't let go of her shoulder. 'I meant that I'm not well enough to try to win you back. Not yet. But I will...'

He pulled her against him, holding her tight. She could hear his heart beating. Or was it hers?

'What do you mean, you're not well enough? You think I want you to run up and down the stairs ten times?'

'Just the once would be good...' Suddenly everything had changed, and Chloe gave him a playful dig in the ribs. Jon winced, smiling.

'Sorry... Bruises?'

'It doesn't matter. This isn't how I wanted it to be, I wanted to give you flowers and be able to get down on my knees and beg...'

'You know you don't have to do that. I love you. More than I'm afraid of losing you.'

'I love you too. More than I'm afraid of messing this up.'

He kissed her, puffing out an exasperated breath when he wobbled a little and she had to steady him. Then he smiled down at her and Chloe reached up, gently pulling him down for another kiss. This was exactly how it was meant to be. Not caring about who was supporting who, but just stronger together.

'I wish I could sweep you off your feet. There are so many things...' He kissed her brow, his mind obviously working overtime to catalogue the many things.

'Don't keep it to yourself. Tell me about it.'

'The thing I most want right now?' He smiled down at her. 'I just want to hold you, Chloe, and feel your skin against mine. But I'm not sure I can stand up for very much longer.'

Helping him up the stairs and into her bedroom

wasn't exactly what either of them might have fanta-sised about, but it was perfect. Settling him on the bed, propping his leg on a pillow and stripping off his sweat-shirt felt like the most romantic thing in the world, as did having to stand a little to one side to let him see her pull her top off, because his left eye was pretty much closed.

'You'll take me like this?' His fingers brushed the bruises on his left side. 'They're not very pretty.'

'It's just a few bruises. They make you look ruggedly pretty.' Chloe climbed onto the bed, careful not to touch him, but he chuckled, pulling her close.

As she settled against him he let out a contented sigh. All the missing and the longing had been set free, with only love left to replace it.

When he finally spoke, she could hear the smile in his voice. 'So how long do you reckon we'll be able to hold out for?'

He'd been thinking the same thing she was. Her body was buzzing with warm arousal, but the urgency was slaked by the knowledge that Jon was in no condition for anything other than rest right now. And they had a future. They didn't need to rush things.

'I can hold out for a very long time, Jon.'

'Really?'

'Yes, really. You're recovering from a nasty injury, and you need to rest.' She said the words with as much determination as she could muster. 'We're going to have to take things slowly and gently. A little improvisation maybe…'

He chuckled. 'I'm looking forward to seeing what improvisations you'll come up with.'

She looked up into his face, feeling the love that

she saw there reverberate in her heart. 'Are you going to behave or am I going to have to be strict with you?'

Jon pulled her down for a kiss. 'You're going to have to be *very* strict, my love.'

CHAPTER NINETEEN

One year later...

THE LAST YEAR had been...interesting. Jon had needed another minor operation on his leg, and it had taken a while before he'd been fully fit again. Hannah had studied hard and completed the whole of her correspondence course in time to sit her Art A-Level in June, and had then panicked on the day of the exam. Chloe had marched her into the examination room and sat outside to make sure she didn't escape, and when Hannah received her results, she'd passed with flying colours.

Amy was a bright, secure toddler, who brought joy to both her mother and to her aunt and uncle. They'd all moved into the new house together, and Amy loved the bright room with the animal mural.

And Jon and Chloe had been married in the spring. It had rained all day, but the warmth and love had shone through. Despite everything, they were blissfully happy.

Once every month they'd take turns in booking a surprise destination for a date night. The destination wasn't a surprise this time, though. By the time they'd reached Dover Chloe knew exactly where Jon was taking her. It had been a year, to the day, since the night they'd spent at the chateau in France.

It was just the same as before. They dressed up and sat on the roof for dinner. When the table was cleared and they went back downstairs, a bottle of champagne was waiting for them in an ice bucket.

'One year.' Chloe wound her arms around his neck, standing on her toes to kiss him. 'It's been the happiest of my life.'

'Mine too. But next year's going to be better.'

'I think so too.'

He leaned towards her, whispering in her ear. 'I'll always love you, Chloe. Whatever happens, my life with you is perfect.'

There was just one thing missing. They'd been trying for a baby since their wedding night and Chloe knew how much Jon wanted to be a father. She desperately wanted a child of her own too.

'I have something for you.'

'I don't know what you could possibly give me, sweetheart. I have everything I'll ever want.'

'No, you don't. But we will have…' She took his hand between hers, and placed it over her stomach.

'Chloe? You mean…?'

'A baby. We're going to have a baby.'

He stared at her for a moment, as if he didn't quite comprehend. And then he hugged her tight, his limbs trembling. When he kissed her, she saw tears in his eyes.

'We did it, Jon. It took a little while, but we made a baby.'

He lifted her off her feet, holding her tight against his chest. 'We're going to have such fun. We'll get her a train set. Or him…'

Jon had been thinking about this. So had she, and finally it had happened. 'You've been planning ahead.'

'I might need some time to try it out first. Just to make sure it works.'

'Good idea. I love you so much.'

'I love you too. And over the next week I'm going to show you just how much…'

'The next week?'

'Didn't I mention that? Since you probably knew that we were coming here, I decided that I owed you another surprise. So I spoke to your head of department, and he agreed to give you a week's leave. You can sign the leave slip when you get back.'

'A week! Are we staying here?'

'Wait and see. Anything could happen. But right now…'

She was ready for it all. And the best thing about that was that Jon was here, and he was ready for it too.

'Right now everything's perfect.'

He shook his head, smiling. 'No. Not perfect. It's so much better than perfect.'

* * * * *

*If you enjoyed this story, check out these
other great reads from Annie Claydon*

*ENGLISH ROSE FOR THE SICILIAN DOC
THE DOCTOR'S DIAMOND PROPOSAL
RESCUED BY DR RAFE
SAVED BY THE SINGLE DAD*

All available now!